“I shouldn

you,” he m

“I’m not a good b [illegible] in me, you know? I h[illegible] been such a good man in the years since I moved back home. I’ve been a Crawford through and through, you might say—too proud and too sure I knew every damn thing. You deserve a better man than me.”

She only looked at him, eyes wide, bright with the sheen of unshed tears. He wanted to grab her and start kissing her all over again.

And that couldn’t happen. He made himself clearer. “The last eight years, since I’ve been back in town, I’ve gone out with several women. But it never ends well.”

Callie kept her gaze level. He couldn’t tell what she might be thinking. “I understand,” she said.

He leaned a little closer. “Do you really?”

“I do, Nate. Although I happen to think you’re a much better man than you’re giving yourself credit for.”

“You’re just softhearted.”

She gave a tiny shrug. “Maybe I am.”

AN UNEXPECTED HOME

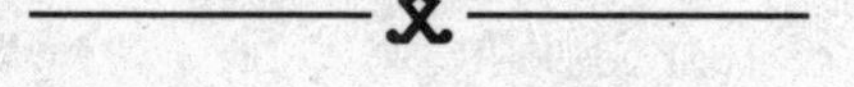

New York Times Bestselling Author

Christine Rimmer

USA TODAY Bestselling Author

Christyne Butler

Previously published as *Million-Dollar Maverick* and *The Last-Chance Maverick*

Special thanks and acknowledgment are given to Christine Rimmer and Christyne Butler for their contributions to the Montana Mavericks: 20 Years in the Saddle! miniseries.

ISBN-13: 978-1-335-46775-1

This edition published by arrangement with Harlequin Books S.A.

For questions and comments about the quality of this book, please contact us at CustomerService@Harlequin.com.

Harlequin Enterprises ULC
22 Adelaide St. West, 40th Floor
Toronto, Ontario M5H 4E3, Canada
www.Harlequin.com

Printed in U.S.A.

CONTENTS

Million-Dollar Maverick 7
by Christine Rimmer

The Last-Chance Maverick 235
by Christyne Butler

Christine Rimmer came to her profession the long way around. She tried everything from acting to teaching to telephone sales. Now she's finally found work that suits her perfectly. She insists she never had a problem keeping a job—she was merely gaining "life experience" for her future as a novelist. Christine lives with her family in Oregon. Visit her at christinerimmer.com.

Books by Christine Rimmer

Harlequin Special Edition

The Bravos of Valentine Bay

The Nanny's Double Trouble
Almost a Bravo
Same Time, Next Christmas
Switched at Birth
A Husband She Couldn't Forget
The Right Reason to Marry

The Bravos of Justice Creek

James Bravo's Shotgun Bride
Ms. Bravo and the Boss
A Bravo for Christmas
The Lawman's Convenient Bride
Garrett Bravo's Runaway Bride
Married Till Christmas

Visit the Author Profile page at Harlequin.com for more titles.

MILLION-DOLLAR MAVERICK

Christine Rimmer

For my mom.

I love you, Mom,

and I'm so grateful

for every moment we had together.

Prologue

January 15

On the ten-year anniversary of the day he lost everything, Nate Crawford got out of bed at 3:15 a.m. He grabbed a quick shower and filled a big thermos with fresh-brewed coffee.

Outside in the yard, his boots crunched on the frozen ground and the predawn air was so cold it seared his lungs when he sucked it in. He had to scrape the rime of ice off his pickup's windshield, but the stars were bright in the wide Montana sky and the cloudless night cheered him a little. Clear weather meant he should make good time this year. He climbed in behind the wheel and cranked the heater up high.

He left the ranch at a quarter of four. With any luck

at all, he would reach his destination before night fell again.

But then, five miles north of Kalispell, he spotted a woman on the far side of the road. She wore a moss-green, quilted coat and skinny jeans tucked into lace-up boots. And she stood by a mud-spattered silver-gray SUV hooked up to a U-Haul trailer. With one hand, she held a red gas can. With the other, she was flagging him down.

Nate grumbled a few discouraging words under his breath. He had a long way to go, and the last thing he needed was to lose time playing Good Samaritan to some woman who couldn't be bothered to check her fuel gauge.

Not that he was even tempted to drive by and leave her there. A man like Nate had no choice when it came to whether or not to help a stranded woman. For him, doing what needed doing was bred in the bone.

He slowed the pickup. There was no one coming either way, so he swung the wheel, crossed the center line and pulled in behind the U-Haul on the far shoulder.

The woman came running. Her bright-striped wool beanie had three pom-poms, one at the crown and one at the end of each tie. They bounced merrily as she ran. He leaned across the seats and shoved open the door for her. A gust of icy air swirled in.

Framed in the open door, she held up the red gas can. Breathlessly, she asked, "Give a girl a lift to the nearest gas station?" It came out slightly muffled by the thick wool scarf she had wrapped around the bottom half of her face.

Nate was known for his smooth-talking ways, but

the cold and his reluctance to stop made him curt. "Get in before all the heat gets out."

Just like a woman, she chose that moment to hesitate. "You're not an ax murderer, are you?"

He let out a humorless chuckle. "If I was, would I tell you so?"

She widened her big dark eyes at him. "Now you've got me worried." She said it jokingly.

He had no time for jokes. "Trust your instincts and do it fast. My teeth are starting to chatter."

She tipped her head to the side, studying him, and then, at last, she shrugged. "All right, cowboy. I'm taking a chance on you." Grabbing the armrest, she hoisted herself up onto the seat. Once there, she set the gas can on the floor of the cab, shut the door and stuck out her hand. "Callie Kennedy. On my way to a fresh start in the beautiful small town of Rust Creek Falls."

"Nate Crawford." He gave her mittened hand a shake. "Shooting Star Ranch. It's a couple of miles outside of Rust Creek—and didn't you just drive through Kalispell five miles back?"

Pom-poms danced as she nodded. "I did, yes."

"I heard they have gas stations in Kalispell. Lots of 'em."

She gave a low laugh. "I should have stopped for gas, I know." She started unwinding the heavy scarf from around her face. He watched with more interest than he wanted to feel, perversely hoping he wouldn't like what he saw. But no. She was as pretty as she was perky. Long wisps of lustrous seal-brown hair escaped the beanie to trail down her flushed cheeks. "I thought I could make it without stopping." Head bent to the task, she snapped the seat belt closed.

"You were wrong."

She turned to look at him again and something sparked in those fine eyes. "Do I hear a lecture coming on, Nate?"

"Ma'am," he said with more of a drawl than was strictly natural to him. "I would not presume."

She gave him a slow once-over. "Oh, I think you would. You look like a man who presumes on a regular basis."

He decided she was annoying. "Have I just been insulted?"

She laughed, a full-out laugh that time. It was such a great laugh he forgot how aggravating he found her. "You came to my rescue." Her eyes were twinkling again. "I would never be so rude as to insult you."

"Well, all right, then," he said, feeling suddenly out of balance somehow. He put the pickup in gear, checked for traffic and then eased back onto the road again. For a minute or two, neither of them spoke. Beyond his headlight beams, there was only the dark, twisting ribbon of road. No other headlights cut the night. Above, the sky was endless, swirling with stars, the rugged, black shadows of the mountains poking up into it. When the silence got too thick, he asked, "So, did you hear about the great flood that took out half of Rust Creek Falls last summer?"

"Oh, yeah." She was nodding. "So scary. So much of Montana was flooded, I heard. It was all over the national news."

The Rust Creek levee had broken on July Fourth, destroying homes and businesses all over the south half of town. Since then, Rust Creek Falls had seen an influx of men and women eager to pitch in with reconstruction. Some in town claimed that a lot of the women had come with more than helping out in mind, that they were hoping to catch themselves a cowboy. Nate couldn't help thinking that if Callie Kennedy wanted a man, she'd have no trouble finding one—even if she was more annoying than most.

Was she hungry? He wouldn't mind a plate of steak and eggs. Maybe he ought to ask her if she wanted to stop for breakfast before they got the gas....

But no. He couldn't do that. It was the fifteenth of January. His job was to get his butt to North Dakota—and to remember all he'd lost. No good-looking, mouthy little brunette with twinkly eyes could be allowed to distract him from his purpose.

He said, "Let me guess. You're here to help with the rebuilding effort. I gotta tell you, it's a bad time of year for it. All the work's pretty much shut down until the weather warms a little." He sent her a quick glance. She just happened to be looking his way.

For a moment, their gazes held—and then they both turned to stare out at the dark road again. "Actually, I have a job waiting for me. I'm a nurse practitioner. I'll be partnering up with Emmet DePaulo. You know Emmet?"

Tall and lean, sixty-plus and bighearted to a fault, Emmet ran the Rust Creek Falls Clinic. "I do. Emmet's a good man."

She made a soft sound of agreement and then asked, "And what about you, Nate? Where are you going before dawn on a cold Wednesday morning?"

He didn't want to say, didn't want to get into it. "I'm on my way to Bismarck," he replied, hoping she'd leave it at that.

No such luck. “I went through there yesterday. It’s a long way from here. What’s in Bismarck?”

He answered her question with one of his own. “Where you from?”

There was a silence from her side of the cab. He prepared to rebuff her if she asked about Bismarck again.

But then she only said, “I’m from Chicago.”

He grunted. “Talk about a long way from here.”

“That is no lie. I’ve been on the road since two in the morning Monday. Sixteen hundred endless miles, stopping only to eat and when I just had to get some sleep....”

“Can’t wait to get started on your new life, huh?”

She flashed him another glowing smile. “I went through Rust Creek Falls with my parents on our way to Glacier National Park when I was eight. Fell in love with the place and always wanted to live there. Now, at last, it’s really happening. And yeah. You’re right. I can’t wait.”

It was none of his business, but he went ahead and asked anyway, “You honestly have *no* doubts about making this move?”

“Not a one.” The woman had a greenhorn’s blind enthusiasm.

“You’ll be surprised, Callie. Montana winters are long and cold.” He slid her another quick glance.

She was smiling wider than ever. “You ever been to Chicago, Nate? Gets pretty cold there, too.”

“It’s not the same,” he insisted.

“Well, I guess I’ll see for myself about that.”

He really was annoyed with her now, annoyed enough that he said scornfully, “You won’t last the winter. You'll be hightailing it back to the Windy City before the snow melts."

"Is that a challenge, Nate?" The woman did not back down. "I never could resist a challenge."

Damn, but he was riled now. Out of proportion and for no reason he could understand. Maybe it was because she was slowing him down from getting where he needed to be. Or maybe because he found her way too easy on the eyes—and then there was her perfume. A little sweet, a little tart. Even mixed with the faint smell of gasoline from the red can between her feet, he liked her perfume.

And it wasn't appropriate for him to like it. It wasn't appropriate for him to be drawn to some strange woman. Not today.

She was watching him, waiting for him to answer her question, to tell him if his mean-spirited prediction had been a challenge or not.

He decided to keep his mouth shut.

Apparently, she thought that was a good idea because she didn't say anything more, either. They rode in tense silence the rest of the way to the gas station. She filled up her can, paid cash for it and got in the pickup again.

He drove her straight back to her waiting SUV.

When he pulled in behind the U-Haul, he suggested grudgingly, "Maybe I'd better just follow you back to town, see that you get there safely."

"No, thanks. I'll be okay."

He felt like a complete jerk—probably because he'd been acting like one. "Come on." He reached for the gas can. "Let me—"

She grabbed the handle before he could take it and

put on a stiff smile. "I can do it. Thank you for your help." And then she leaned on the door, jumped down and hoisted the gas can down, too. "You take care now." In the glow of light from the cab, he watched her breath turn to fog in the icy air.

It was still pitch-dark out. At the edge of the cleared spot behind her, a big, dirty For Sale sign had been nailed on a fence post. Beyond the fence, new-growth ponderosa pines stood black and thick. Farther out in the darkness, perched on a high ridge and silhouetted against the sky, loomed the black outline of a house so enormous it looked like a castle. Built by a very rich man named Nathaniel Bledsoe two decades ago, the house had always been considered a monstrosity by folks in the Rust Creek Falls Valley. From the first, they called the place Bledsoe's Folly. When Bledsoe died, it went up for sale.

But nobody ever bought it. It stood vacant to this day.

Who was to say vagrants hadn't taken up residence? And anyone could be lurking in the close-growing pines.

He didn't like the idea of leaving her there alone. "I mean it, Callie. I'll wait until you're on your way."

Unsmiling now, she gazed at him steadily, her soft chin hitched high. "I *will* last the winter." The words had steel underpinnings. "I'm making myself a new life here. You watch me."

He should say something easy and agreeable. He knew it. But somehow, she'd gotten under his skin. So he just made it worse. "Two hundred dollars says you'll be gone before June first."

She tipped her head to the side then, studying him. "Money doesn't thrill me, Nate."

"If not money, then what?"

One sleek eyebrow lifted and vanished into that bright wool hat. "Let me think it over."

"Think fast," he muttered, perversely driven to continue being a complete ass. "I haven't got all day."

She laughed then, a low, amused sound that seemed to race along his nerve endings. "Nate Crawford, you've got an attitude—and Rust Creek Falls is a small town. I have a feeling I won't have any trouble tracking you down. I'll be in touch." She grabbed the outer handle of the door. "Drive safe now." And then she pushed it shut and turned for her SUV.

He waited as he'd said he would, watching over her until she was back in her vehicle and on her way. In the glare of his headlights, she poured the gas in her tank. It only took a minute and, every second of that time, the good boy his mama had raised ached to get out and do it for her. But he knew she'd refuse him if he tried.

In no time, she had the cap back on the tank, the gas can stowed in the rear of the SUV, and she was getting in behind the wheel. Her headlights flared to life, and the engine started right up.

When she rolled out onto the road again, she tapped the horn once in salute. He waited for the red taillights of the U-Haul to vanish around the next curve before turning his truck around and heading for Bismarck again. As he drove back through Kalispell, he was shaking his head, dead certain that pretty Callie Kennedy would be long gone from Rust Creek come June.

Ten and a half hours later he rolled into a truck stop just west of Dickinson, North Dakota, to gas up. In the diner there, he had a burger with fries and a large Dr Pepper. And then he wandered through the attached convenience store, stretching his legs a little before getting back on the road for the final hour and a half of driving that would take him into Bismarck and his first stop there, a certain florist on Eighth Street.

Turned out he'd made good time after all, even with the delay caused by giving mouthy Nurse Callie a helping hand. This year, he would make it to the florist before they closed. And that meant he wouldn't have to settle for supermarket flowers. The thought pleased him in a grim sort of way.

Before heading out the door, he stopped at the register to buy a PayDay candy bar.

The clerk offered, "Powerball ticket? Jackpot's four hundred and eighty million now."

Nate never played the lottery. He was not a reckless man, not even when it came to something as inexpensive as a lottery ticket. Long shots weren't his style. But then he thought of pretty Callie Kennedy with her pom-pom hat, her gas can and her twinkly eyes.

Money doesn't thrill me, Nate.

Would four hundred and eighty million thrill her?

He chuckled under his breath and nodded. "Sure. Give me ten dollars' worth."

The clerk punched out a ticket with five rows of numbers on it. Nate gave it no more than a cursory glance as she put it in his hand.

He had no idea what he'd just done, felt not so much as a shiver of intuition that one of those rows of numbers was about to change his life forever.

Chapter 1

At seven in the morning on the first day of June, Callie Kennedy knocked on the front door of Nate Crawford's big house on South Pine Street.

Nate hadn't shared two words with her since that cold day last January. But he'd seen her around town. He'd also kept tabs on her, though he would never have admitted that. Word around town was that she was not only a pure pleasure to look at, she was also a fine nurse with a whole lot of heart. Folks had only good things to say about Nurse Callie.

He pulled the door wide. "Well, well. Nurse Callie Kennedy," he drawled. Then he hooked his fingers in the belt loops of his Wranglers. "You're up good and early."

She gave him one of those thousand-watt smiles of hers. "Hello, Nate. Beautiful day, isn't it?"

He knew very well why she'd come. It wasn't to talk about the weather. Still, he leaned on the door frame and played along. "Mighty nice. Not a cloud in the sky."

"Happy June first." She beamed even wider, reminding him of a sunbeam in a yellow cotton dress with a soft yellow sweater thrown across her shoulders and yellow canvas shoes on her slim little feet.

"Let me guess...." He wrinkled his brow as though deep in thought. "Wait. I know. You're here to collect on that bet I made you."

"Nate." Her long lashes swept down. "You remembered." And then she looked up again. "I love your new house."

"Thank you."

"That's some front door."

"Thanks. I had it specially made. Indonesian mahogany." It had leaded glass in the top and sidelights you could open to let in a summer breeze.

"Very nice." She looked at him from under impossibly thick, dark lashes. "And the porch wraps all the way around to the back?"

"That's right, opens out onto a redwood deck." And they might as well get on with it. "Come on in."

"I thought you'd never ask."

He stepped out of the doorway and bowed her in ahead of him. "Coffee?"

"Yes, please." She waited for him to take the lead and then followed him through the central foyer, past the curving staircase, to the kitchen at the back. He gestured at the breakfast area. She took a seat, bracing an elbow on the table and watching him fiddle with his new pod-style coffeemaker.

"I've got about a hundred different flavors for this thing…."

The morning light spilled in the window, making her skin glow and bringing out auburn gleams in her long dark hair. "Got one with hazelnut?"

"Right here." He popped the pod in the top and turned the thing on. Thirty seconds later, he was serving her the steaming cup. "Cream and sugar?"

"I want it all. How many bedrooms?"

He got her the milk and the sugar bowl. "Three to five, depending."

"On what?"

"I have an office down here in the front that could be a bedroom. The master also has a good-sized sitting room with double doors to make a separate space. That sitting room could be a bedroom, too." He got a cup for himself and sat opposite her. "Not a lot of bedrooms, really, but all the rooms are nice and big."

"More than enough for a man living alone, I'd say."

He wasn't sure he liked the way she'd said that. Was she goading him? "What? A single man is only allowed so many rooms?"

She laughed. "Oh, come on, Nate. I'm not here to pick a fight."

He regarded her warily. "Promise?"

"Mmm-hmm." She stirred milk and sugar into her cup. "I heard a rumor you're planning on leaving town."

"Who told you that?"

"You know, I don't recall offhand." She sipped. "This is very good."

"You're welcome," he said gruffly.

She sipped again. "It's odd, really. Three months

ago, you moved from the ranch into town, and now people say that you're leaving altogether."

"What people?" He kept his expression neutral, though his gut twisted. How much did she know?

No more than anyone else, he decided. To account for his new, improved lifestyle, he'd started telling folks that he'd had some luck with his investments. But as for the real source of his sudden wealth, even his family didn't know. Only the Kalispell lawyer he'd hired had the real story—which was exactly how Nate wanted it.

"You know how it is here in town," she said as though she'd been living in Rust Creek Falls all her life. "Everybody's interested in what everyone else is doing."

"No kidding," he muttered wryly.

"Several folks have mentioned to me that you're leaving."

Why not just admit it? "I'm looking for a change, that's all. My brothers can handle things at the ranch, so my bowing out hasn't caused any problems there. At first, I thought moving to town would be change enough."

"But it's not?"

He glanced out the sunny window, where a blue jay flew down and landed on the deck rail and then instantly took flight again. "Maybe I need an even bigger change." He swung his gaze to her again, found her bright eyes waiting. "Who knows? Maybe I'll be heading back the way you came, making myself a whole new start in Chicago. I'm just not sure yet. I don't know what the next step for me should be."

She studied his face with what seemed to be honest

interest. "You, living in Chicago? I don't know, Nate. I'm just not seeing that."

He thought, *You don't know me well enough to tell me where I might want to live.* But he didn't say it. She'd seemed sincere just now. And she was entitled to her opinion.

She wasn't through, either. "I heard you ran for mayor last year—and lost to Collin Traub. They say you're bitter about that because of the generations-long feud between the Traubs and your family, that it really hurt your pride when the town chose bad-boy Collin over an upstanding citizen like you. They say it's personal between you and Collin, that there's always been bad blood between the two of you, that the two of you once got into a knock-down-drag-out over a woman named Cindy Sellers."

"Wow, Callie. You said a mouthful." He actually chuckled.

And she laughed, too. "It's only what I've heard."

"Just because people love to gossip doesn't mean they know what they're talking about."

"So none of it's true, then?"

He admitted, "It's true, for the most part." Strangely, today, he was finding her candor charming—then again, today he wasn't on his way to North Dakota to keep his annual appointment with all that he had lost.

She asked, "What parts did I get wrong?"

He should tell her to mind her own business. But she was so damn pretty and she really did seem interested. "Well, the mayor's race?"

"Yeah?"

"I'm over that. And it's a long story about me and

Collin and Cindy, one I don't have the energy to get into right now—and your cup's already empty."

"It was really good." She smiled at him coaxingly.

He took the hint. "More?"

"Yes, please."

Each pod made six cups. All he had to do was put her mug under the spigot and push the brew button. "You've collected a lot of information about me. Should I be flattered you're so interested?" He gave her back her full cup.

She doctored it up with more sugar and milk. "I think about that day last winter now and then…."

He slid into his seat again. "I'll just bet you do." *Especially today, when it's time to collect.*

Her big eyes were kind of dreamy now. "I wonder about you, Nate. I wonder why you had to get to Bismarck, and I keep thinking there's a lot going on under the surface with you. I love this town more every day that I live here, but sometimes people in a small town can get locked in to their ideas about each other. What I think about you is that you want…more out of life. You just don't know how to get it."

He grunted. "Got me all figured out, don't you?"

"It's just an opinion."

"Yeah, and that and five bucks will get you half a dozen cinnamon buns over at the doughnut shop."

She shrugged, her gaze a little too steady for his peace of mind. Then she asked, "So, what about Bismarck?"

He was never telling her about Bismarck. And, as much as he enjoyed looking at her with all that shiny hair and that beautiful smile, it was time to get down to business. "Excuse me." He rose and turned for the door to the foyer, leaving her sitting there, no doubt staring after him.

In his study at the front of the house, he opened the safe built into his fine wide mahogany desk and took out what she'd come for. Then he locked up the safe again and rejoined her in the kitchen.

"Here you go." He set the two crisp one-hundred-dollar bills on the table in front of her. "I get it. You like it here. You've made some friends. They all say you're an excellent nurse, kind and caring to your patients. You're staying. I was wrong about you."

"Yes, you were." She sat very straight, those soft lips just hinting at a smile now. "I like a man who can admit when he's wrong." She glanced down at the bills and then back up at him. "And I thought I told you way back in January that money doesn't do much for me."

Okay. Now he could start to get annoyed with her again. "Then what *do* you want?"

She turned her coffee mug, slim fingers light and coaxing on the rim. "I've been staying in one of the trailers they brought in for newcomers, over on Sawmill Street."

"I know," he admitted, though he hadn't planned to. Her pupils widened slightly in surprise. It pleased him that he'd succeeded in surprising her. "Maybe I think about you now and then, too."

She gazed at him steadily for a moment. And then there it was, that hint of a smile again. "I'm tired of that trailer."

"I can understand that."

"But as I'm sure you know, housing is still kind of scarce around here." So many homes had been damaged in the flood the year before, and they weren't all rebuilt yet. "I really like the look of the empty house next door to you. And I heard a rumor you might own that one, too."

The woman had nerve, no doubt about it. "You want me to give you a house just for sticking out a Montana winter?"

Her smile got wider. "Not *give* it to me, Nate. Sell it to me."

Sell it to her....

The former owners of both houses had chosen not to rebuild after the flood, so Nate got them cheap. He'd been a long way from rich at the time. His plan then had been to fix the houses up slowly, starting with the smaller one next door. He'd figured he would put money in them when he had it to spare, getting his brothers to lend a hand with the work.

But after his big win, he found he could afford to renovate them both without having to drag it out. With everyone believing his cover story of a windfall on the stock market, he'd told himself it was safe to go for it. He could fix them up and do it right.

He should have been more cautious, probably. Not spent so much on the finishes, not redone both houses. Or at least, if he had to go all out, he should have had his lawyer advise him, maybe put them under the control of the trust he'd established to make sure he would remain an anonymous winner.

Callie kept after him. "Oh, come on, Nate. You can't live in two houses at once, can you? I'm guessing you fixed that other one up with the intention of selling it, anyway."

He thought again that she was one aggravating woman. But she did have a point: he'd bought both houses with the idea that he would eventually turn them around. And really, she didn't seem the least bit suspicious about where his money might have come from. She just wanted to get out of the trailer park. He needed to stop being paranoid when there was absolutely nothing to be worried about. "Finish your coffee."

"And then what?"

"I'll give you a tour of the other house."

Those fine dark eyes gleamed brighter than ever. She pushed back her chair. "I can take my coffee with me. Let's go."

An hour later, after he'd shown her the property and then gone ahead and fed her breakfast, Callie made him an offer. It was a fair offer and he didn't need to quibble over pennies anymore. She stuck out her soft hand and they shook on it. He ignored the thrill that shivered along his skin at the touch of her palm to his.

On the first of July, Callie moved into her new house next door to Nate Crawford. The day before, she'd had a bunch of new furniture delivered, stuff she'd picked out in a couple of Kalispell furniture stores. But she still had to haul all her other things from the trailer park on Sawmill Street.

Emmet DePaulo insisted she take the day off from the clinic and loaned her his pickup. Then, being Emmet, he decided to close the clinic for the morning and give her a hand.

He got a couple of friends of his, Vietnam veterans in their sixties, old guys still in surprisingly good shape, to help load up the pickup for her. Then he drove it to her new house, and he and his pals carried everything inside, after which they returned to the trailer and got the rest of her stuff. With the four of them working, they had the trailer emptied out and everything over at the new house before noon.

In her new kitchen, Callie served them all takeout from the chicken-wing place on North Broomtail Road. Once they'd eaten, Emmet's friends took off. Emmet told her not to work too hard and left to go open the clinic for the afternoon.

She stood out on the porch and waved as he drove away, her gaze wandering to Nate's big house. She hadn't seen him all day. There were no lights shining from inside and no sign of his truck. But then, it was a sunny day, and his house had lots of windows. He could be inside, and his truck could very well be sitting in that roomy three-car garage.

Not that it mattered. She'd bought her house because she liked it, not because of the man next door.

After living in a trailer for six months, her new place felt absolutely palatial. There were two bedrooms and a bath upstairs, for guests or whatever. Downstairs were the kitchen, great room, front hall and master suite. The master suite had two entrances, one across from the great room in the entry hall and the other in the kitchen, through the master bath in back. The master bath was the only bathroom on the first floor. It worked great that you could get to it without going through the bedroom.

Callie got busy putting her new house together, starting with her bedroom. That way, when she got too tired to unpack another box, she'd have a bed to fall into. She put her toiletries in the large downstairs bath and hung up the towels. And then she went out to the kitchen to get going in there.

At a little after three, the doorbell rang.

Nate? Her silly heart beat faster and her cheeks suddenly felt too warm.

Which was flat-out ridiculous.

True, she found Nate intriguing. He was such a big, handsome package of contradictions. He could be a jerk. Paige Traub, her friend and also a patient at the clinic, had once called Nate an "unmitigated douche." There were more than a few people in Rust Creek Falls who agreed with Paige.

But Callie had this feeling about him, a feeling that he wasn't as bad as he could seem sometimes. That deep inside, he was a wounded, lonely soul.

Plus, well, there was the hotness factor. Tall, with muscles. Shoulders for days. Beautiful green eyes and thick brown hair that made a girl want to run her fingers through it.

Callie blinked and shook her head. She reminded herself that after her most recent love disaster, she was swearing off men for at least the next decade. Especially arrogant, know-it-all types like Nate.

The doorbell rang again and her heart beat even faster. Nothing like a visit from a hunky next-door neighbor. Her hands were covered in newsprint from the papers she'd used to wrap the dishes and glassware. She quickly rinsed them in the sink and ran to get the door.

It wasn't Nate.

"Faith!" Like Paige Traub, Faith Harper, Callie's new neighbor on her other side, was a patient at the clinic. Also like Paige, Faith was pregnant. Both women were in their third trimester, but Faith was fast approaching her due date. Faith had big blue eyes and baby-fine blond hair. She and Callie had hit it off from the first.

Faith held out a red casserole dish. "My mom's chicken divan. It's really good. I had to make sure my favorite nurse had something for dinner."

Callie took the dish. "Oh, you are a lifesaver. I was just facing the sad prospect of doing Wings to Go twice in one day."

Beaming, Faith rested both hands on her enormous belly. "Can't have that."

"Come on in…" Callie led the way back to the kitchen, where she put the casserole in the fridge and took out a pitcher of iced herbal tea. "Ta-da! Raspberry leaf." High in calcium and magnesium, raspberry-leaf tea was safe for pregnant women from the second trimester on. It helped to prepare the uterus for labor and to prevent postpartum bleeding. Callie had recommended it to Faith.

Faith laughed. "Did you know I'd be over?"

"Well, I was certainly hoping you would." Callie poured the tea, and they went out on the small back deck to get away from the mess of half-unpacked boxes in the kitchen. The sky had grown cloudy in the past hour or so. Still, it was so nice, sitting in her own backyard with her first visitor. And it was definitely a big step up from the dinky square of back stoop she'd had at the trailer park.

They talked about the home birth Faith planned. Callie would be attending as nurse/midwife. Faith had everything ready for the big day. Her husband, a long-haul trucker, had left five days before on a cross-country trip and was due to return the day after tomorrow.

Faith tenderly stroked her enormous belly. "When Owen gets back from this trip, he's promised he's going nowhere until after this baby is born."

"I love a man who knows when it's time to stay home," Callie agreed.

"Oh, me, too. I— Whoa!" Faith laughed as lightning lit up the underbelly of the thick clouds overhead. Thunder rumbled—and it started to rain.

Callie groaned. Already, in the space of a few seconds, the fat drops were coming down hard and fast. She jumped up. "Come on. Let's go in before we drown."

They cleared a space at the table in the breakfast nook and watched the rain pour down. Faith shivered.

Callie asked, "Are you cold? I can get you a blanket."

"No, I'm fine, really. It's only… Well, it's a little too much like last year." Her soft mouth twisted. "It started coming down just like this, in buckets. That went on for more than twenty-four hours straight. Then the levee broke…."

Callie reached across the table and gave Faith's hand a reassuring squeeze. "There's nothing to worry about." The broken levees had been rebuilt higher and stronger than before. "Emmet told me the new levee will withstand any-and everything Mother Nature can throw at it."

Faith let out a long, slow breath. "You're right. I'm overreacting. Let the rain fall. There'll be no flooding this year."

It rained hard all night.

And on the morning of July second, it was still pouring down. The clinic was just around the block from Callie's new house, and she'd been looking forward to walking to work. But not today. Callie drove her SUV to the clinic.

Overall, it was a typical workday. She performed routine exams, stitched up more than one injury, prescribed painkillers for rheumatoid arthritis and decongestants for summer colds. Emmet was his usual calm, unruffled self. He'd done two tours of duty in Vietnam and Cambodia back in the day. It took a lot more than a little rain to get him worked up.

But everyone else—the patients, Brandy the clinic receptionist and the two pharmaceutical reps who dropped by to fill orders and pass out samples—seemed apprehensive. Probably because the rain just kept coming down so hard, without a break, the same way it had last year before the levee broke. They tried to make jokes about it, agreeing that every time it rained now, people in town got worried. They talked about how the apprehension would fade over time, how eventually a long, hard rainstorm wouldn't scare anyone.

Too bad they weren't there yet.

Then, a half an hour before they closed the doors for the day, something wonderful happened: the rain stopped. Brandy started smiling again. Emmet said, "Great. Now everyone can take a break from predicting disaster."

At five, Callie drove home. She still had plenty of Faith's excellent casserole left for dinner. But she needed milk and bread and eggs for breakfast tomorrow. That meant a quick trip to Crawford's, the general store on North Main run by Nate's parents and sisters, with a little help from Nate and his brothers when needed.

Callie decided she could use a walk after being cooped up in the clinic all day, so she changed her scrubs for jeans and a T-shirt and left her car at home.

It started sprinkling again as she was crossing the Main Street Bridge. She walked faster. Luck was with her. It didn't really start pouring until right after she reached the store and ducked inside.

Callie loved the Crawfords' store. It was just so totally Rust Creek Falls. Your classic country store, Crawford's carried everything from hardware to soft goods to basic foodstuffs. It was all homey pine floors and open rafters. The rafters had baskets and lanterns and buckets hanging from them. There were barrels everywhere, filled with all kinds of things—yard tools, vegetables, bottles of wine. In the corner stood an old-timey woodstove with stools grouped around it. During the winter, the old guys in town would gather there and tell each other stories of the way things used to be.

Even though she knew she was in for a soggy walk home, Callie almost didn't care. Crawford's always made her feel as if everything was right with the world.

"Nurse Callie, what are you doing out in this?" Nate's mother, Laura, called to her from behind the cash register.

"It wasn't raining when I left the house. I thought the walk would do me good."

"How's that new house of yours?" Laura beamed.

"I love it."

"My Nathan has good taste, huh?" Laura's voice was full of pride. Nate was the oldest of her six children. Some claimed he'd always been the favorite.

"He did a wonderful job on it, yes." Callie grabbed a basket. Hoping maybe the rain would stop again before she had to head back home, she collected the items she needed.

Didn't happen. It was coming down harder than ever, drumming the roof of the store good and loud as Laura started ringing up her purchases.

"You stick around," Laura ordered as she handed Callie her receipt. "Have a seat over by the stove. Someone will give you a ride."

Callie didn't argue. "I think I will hang around for a few minutes. Maybe the rain will slow down and…" The sentence wandered off unfinished as Nate emerged through the door that led into the storage areas behind the counter.

He spotted her and nodded. "Callie."

Her heart kind of stuttered in her chest, which was thoroughly silly. For crying out loud, you'd think she had a real thing for Nate Crawford, the way her pulse picked up and her heart skipped a beat just at the sight of him. "Nate. Hey."

For a moment, neither of them said anything else. They just stood there, looking at each other.

And then Laura cleared her throat.

Callie blinked and slid a glance at Nate's mother.

Laura gave her a slow, way-too-knowing smile. Callie hoped her face wasn't as red as it felt.

Nate lurched to life about then. He grabbed a handsome-looking tan cowboy hat from the wall rack behind the counter. "I moved the packaged goods out of the way so they won't get wet and put a bigger bucket under that leak." He put the hat on. It looked great on him. So did his jeans, which hugged his long, hard legs, and that soft chambray shirt that showed off his broad shoulders. "I'll see to getting the roof fixed tomorrow—or as soon as the rain gives us a break."

"Thanks, Nathan." Laura gave him a fond smile. And then she suggested way too offhandedly, "And Callie here needs a ride home...."

Callie automatically opened her mouth to protest—and then shut it without saying a word. It was raining pitchforks and hammer handles out there, and she *did* need a ride home.

Nate said, "Just so happens I'm headed that way. Here, let me help you." He grabbed both of her grocery bags off the counter. "Let's go."

Callie resisted the urge to tell him she could carry her own groceries. What was the point? He already had them. And he wasn't waiting around for instructions from her, anyway. He was headed out the door.

"Um, thanks," she told Laura as she took off after him.

"You are so welcome," beamed Laura with way more enthusiasm than the situation warranted.

Chapter 2

"My mother likes you," Nate said as he drove slowly down Main Street, the wipers on high and the rain coming down so hard it was a miracle he could see anything beyond the streaming windshield.

Callie didn't know how to answer—not so much because of what Nate had said but because of his grim tone. "I like her, too?" she replied so cautiously it came out sounding like a question.

He muttered darkly, "She considers you quality."

Callie didn't get his attitude at all—or understand what he meant. "Quality?"

"Yeah, quality. A quality woman. You're a nurse. A professional. You're not a snob, but you carry yourself with pride. It's a small town and sometimes it takes a while for folks to warm to a newcomer. But not with you. People are drawn to you, and you made friends right away. Plus, it's no hardship to look at you. My mother approves."

She slid him a cautious glance. "But you don't?"

He kept his gaze straight ahead. "Of course I approve of you. What's not to approve of? You've got it all."

She wanted to ask him what on earth he was talking about. Instead, she blew out a breath and said, "Gee, thanks," and let it go at that.

He turned onto Commercial Street a moment later, then onto South Pine and then into her driveway. He switched off the engine and turned to her, frowning. "You okay?"

She gave him a cool look. "I could ask you the same question. Are you mad at your mother or something?"

"What makes you think that?"

She pressed her lips together and drew in a slow breath through her nose. "If you keep answering every question with a question, what's the point of even attempting a conversation?"

He readjusted his cowboy hat and narrowed those gorgeous green eyes at her. "That was another question you just asked me, in case you didn't notice. And *I* asked the first question, which *you* failed to answer."

They glared at each other. She thought how wrong it was for such a hot guy to be such a jerk.

And then he said ruefully, "I'm being an ass, huh?"

And suddenly, she felt a smile trying to pull at the corners of her mouth. "Now, that is a question I can definitely answer. Yes, Nate. You are being an ass."

And then he said, "Sorry."

And she said, "Forgiven."

And they just sat there in the cab of his pickup with

the rain beating hard on the roof overhead, staring at each other the way they had back at the store.

Finally he said, “My parents are good people. Basically. But my mom, well, she kind of thinks of herself as the queen of Rust Creek Falls, if that makes any sense. She married a Crawford, and to her, my dad is king. She gets ideas about people, about who’s okay and who’s not. If she likes you, that’s fine. If she doesn’t like you, you know it. Believe me.”

“You think she’s too hard on people?”

There was a darkness, a deep sadness in his eyes. “Sometimes, yeah.”

“Well, Nate, if your mother’s the queen, that would make you the crown prince.”

He took off his hat and set it on the dashboard—then changed his mind and put it back on again. “You’re right. I was raised to think I should run this town, and for a while in the past seven or eight years, I put most of my energy into doing exactly what I was raised to do.”

“You sound like you’re not so sure about all that now.”

“Lately, there’s a whole lot I’m not sure of—which is one of the reasons I’m planning on leaving town.”

She shook her head. “I don’t believe that. I think you love this town.”

“That doesn’t mean I won’t go.” And then he smiled, a smile that stole the breath right out of her body. “Come on.” He leaned on his door and got out into the pouring rain. He was soaked through in an instant as he opened the backseat door and gathered her groceries into his arms. “Let’s go.” He made a run for the house.

She was hot on his tail and also soaked to the skin as she followed him up her front steps.

Laughing, she opened the door for him and he went right in, racing to the kitchen to get the soggy shopping bags safely onto the counter before they gave way. He made it, barely. And then he took off his dripping hat and set it on the counter next to the split-open bags. “A man could drown out there if he’s not careful.”

It was still daylight out, but the rain and the heavy cloud cover made it gloomy inside. She turned on some lights. “Stay right there,” she instructed. “I’ll get us some towels.”

In the central hall, a box of linens waited for her to carry them upstairs to the extra bath. She dug out two big towels and returned to the kitchen. “Catch.” She tossed him one.

He snatched it from the air. They dried off as much as possible, then she took his towel from him and went to toss them in the hamper. When she got back to him, he was standing in the breakfast nook, studying a group of framed photographs she’d left on the table last night.

She quickly worked her long wet hair into a soggy braid. “I’m going to hang those pictures together on that wall behind you.” And then she gestured at the boxes stacked against that same wall. “As soon as I get all that put away, I mean.”

He picked up one of the pictures. “You were a cute little kid.”

She had no elastic bands handy, so she left the end of the wet braid untied. “You go for braces and knobby knees?”

“Like I said. Cute. Especially the pigtails.” He glanced at her, a warm, speculative glance. “An only child?”

"That's right." She went to the counter and started putting the groceries away. "They divorced when I was ten. My mother died a couple of years ago. My father remarried. He and his second wife live in Vermont."

He set the picture down with the others. "I'm sorry about your mom."

She put the eggs in the fridge. "Thanks. She was great. I miss her a lot."

"Half siblings?"

"Nope. They travel a lot, my dad and my stepmom. They like visiting museums and staying in fine hotels in Europe, going on cruises to exotic locales. He really wasn't into kids, you know? My mom loved camping, packing up the outdoor gear and sleeping under the stars in the national parks. So did I. But my dad? He always acted like he was doing us a favor, that having to deal with sleeping outside and using public restrooms was beneath him. And having a kid cramped his style. I never felt all that close to him, to tell you the truth. And after he and my mom split up, I hardly saw him— Sheesh. Does that sound whiny or what?"

He watched her for a moment. And then he shrugged. "Not whiny. Honest. I like that about you."

She felt ridiculously gratified. "I… Thank you."

He nodded, slowly. They stared at each other too long, the way they had back at the store.

And then she realized that one of them should probably say something. So she piped up with, "On a brighter note, I have a couple of girlfriends in Chicago who are like sisters to me. They'll be coming to visit me here one of these days— Beer?"

He left the pictures and came to stand at the end of the granite counter. "Sure."

She got a longneck from the fridge. "Glass?"

"Just the bottle." He took it, screwed off the top and downed a nice, big gulp. She watched his Adam's apple working, admired the way his wet shirt clung to his deep, hard chest. He set the bottle on the counter and ran those lean, strong fingers through his wet hair. "You leave anyone special behind in Chicago?"

She stopped with the carton of milk held between her two hands. "I told you. My girlfriends."

He picked up the beer, tipped it to his mouth, then changed his mind and didn't drink from it. "I wasn't talking about girlfriends."

She didn't really want to go there. But then, well, why not just get it over with? "There was a doctor, at the hospital where I worked. A surgeon."

"It didn't work out?"

"No, it did not." She glanced toward the bay window that framed the breakfast nook. The rain kept coming down. The wind was up, too. "Listen to that wind."

He nodded. "It's wild out there, all right." Lightning flashed then, and thunder rumbled in the distance. Callie put the milk in the fridge and threw the ruined paper bags away. He held up his beer bottle. "I'll finish this up and get out of your hair."

She had plenty of boxes left to unpack, and the sooner he went home, the sooner she could get going on that. Still, she heard herself offering, "Stick around. Faith Harper brought me a jumbo baking dish full of chicken divan last night. I have plenty left if you want to join me."

He took his hat off the counter and then dropped it back down. "You sure?"

She realized she was. Absolutely. "Yes."

Half an hour later, he'd cleared all the stuff off the table and set it for them with dishes she'd unpacked the night before. She'd cut up a salad and baked a quick batch of packaged drop biscuits. He said yes to a second beer and she poured herself a glass of wine. They sat down to eat.

After a couple bites, he said, "I remember this casserole. Faith's mom always brought it to all the church potlucks. It was a big hit. The water chestnuts make a nice touch."

Callie chuckled and shook her head.

"What?" he demanded.

"I don't know. It's just… Well, that's a small town for you. I love it. I give you chicken divan and you can tell me its history."

He ate another bite. "It's the best." He took a biscuit, buttered it, set down his knife. "So how do you like working with Emmet?"

"What's not to like? He really is the sweetest man, and he's good, you know, with the patients. Everyone loves him, me included." She sipped her wine. "The equipment we're working with, however, is another story altogether."

His brows drew together. "I thought Emmet got some grants after the flood, that everything was back in shape again."

"That's right. He had the building restored. It *is* in good shape now, and he saved most of the equipment by moving it to the upper floor before the levee broke. But was all that stuff even worth saving? It's a long way from state of the art, you know? The diagnostic equipment is practically as old as I am. And the exam table cushions are so worn, they're starting to split."

"You're saying you need funding?" He was looking at her strangely, kind of taking her measure….

"What?" she said sharply. Did she have broccoli between her teeth or something?

"Hey, I'm just asking." That strange expression had vanished—if it had ever been there at all.

She spoke more gently. "Yeah, we could use a serious infusion of cash. So if you know anybody looking to give away their money, send them our way."

"I'll do that," he said. And then he picked up his fork and dug into his food again.

A few minutes later, he helped her clear the table. It was a little after seven. If he left soon, she could still get a couple more hours of unpacking done before calling it a night.

But the longer he stayed, the more she didn't want him to go.

In the back of her mind, a warning voice whispered that she was giving him the wrong signals, that she was supposed to be swearing off men for a while, that she might be really attracted to him, but her friend Paige Traub had called him a douche—and he'd acted like one the first time they met. Plus, well, he kept saying he was moving away, and she never wanted to live anywhere else but Rust Creek Falls.

It couldn't go anywhere. And the last thing she needed was to get herself all tied in knots over a guy who wouldn't be sticking around.

But then, instead of waiting for him to say how he should get going, she opened her big mouth and offered, "Coffee? And if you're lucky, I may even have a bag of Oreos around here somewhere…."

He rinsed his plate in the sink and handed it to her. "Oreos, did you say?"

"Oh, yes, I did."

"And I know you've got milk. I saw you put it away."

She bent to slide the plate into the lower dishwasher rack. "Have I found your weakness?"

He moved in a step closer. "There are just some things a man can't resist…."

She shut the dishwasher door and rose to face him, aware of the warmth of him, so close, of the gold striations in those moss-green eyes, of how she loved the shape of his mouth, with that clear indentation at the bow and the sexy fullness of his lower lip.

He lifted a hand and brushed his fingers along the bare skin of her arm, bringing a lovely little shiver racing across her skin. Outside, the sky lit up and thunder rolled away into the distance. The rain just kept pouring down, making a steady drumming sound on the roof.

She whispered, "Nate…"

And his fingers moved over her shoulder, down her back. He gave a light, teasing tug on her unbound braid. "I keep thinking of those pictures of you, with your braces and your pigtails. I'll bet you had a mouth on you even then."

This close, she could smell his aftershave, and beneath that, the healthy scent of his skin. "What do you mean, a mouth?"

"You know. Sassy. Opinionated."

Her lips felt kind of dry, suddenly. She started to stick out her tongue to moisten them but caught herself just in time and ended up nervously pressing her lips together. "I am not sassy." She meant it to sound firm, strong. But somehow, it came out all breathless and soft.

He chuckled, rough and kind of low. She felt that chuckle down to her toes. It seemed to rub along her nerve endings, setting off sparks. "Yeah," he said. "You are. Sassy as they come."

"Uh-uh."

"Uh-huh."

"No, Nate."

"Yes, Callie." Now his voice was tender.

And she felt warm all over. Warm and tingly and somehow weightless. She'd gone up on her tiptoes and was swaying toward him, like a daisy yearning toward the sun.

His hand was on her shoulder now, rubbing, caressing. And then he said her name again, the word barely a whisper. And then he did what she longed for him to do. He pulled her closer, so she could feel the heat of him all along the front of her body, feel the softness of her own breasts pressed to that broad, hard chest of his.

He made a low questioning sound. And in spite of all her doubts, she didn't even hesitate. She answered with a slow, sure nod, her eyes locked to his as his mouth came down.

And then, in the space of a breath, those lips of his were touching hers, gently. Carefully, too. To the soft, incessant roar of the rain, the constant harsh whistling of the wind, she lifted her arms and wrapped them around his neck, parting her lips for him, letting him in.

The kiss started to change. From something so sweet it made her soul ache to something hotter, deeper. Dangerous.

A low growling sound escaped him. It seemed to

echo all through her, that sound. And then his tongue slid between her lips, grazing her teeth. She shivered in excitement and wrapped her arms tighter around him.

He held her tighter, too, gathering her into him, his big hands now splayed across her back, rubbing, stroking, while she lifted up and into him, fitting her body to his, feeling that weakness and hunger down in the core of her and the growing hardness of him pressed so close against her.

Her mind was spinning and her body was burning and her heart beat in time to the throb of desire within her.

Bad idea, to have kissed him. She knew that, she did—and yet, somehow, at that moment, she didn't even care. She was on fire. Worse, she was right on the verge of dragging the man down the hall to her bedroom, where they could do something even more foolish than kissing.

But before she could take his hand, the whole kitchen lit up in a wash of glaring light so bright she saw it even with her eyes closed. She gasped.

Lightning. It was lightning.

And then thunder exploded, so close and loud it felt as if it was right there in the kitchen with them.

Callie cried out, and her eyes popped wide open. Nate opened his eyes, too. They stared at each other.

He muttered, "What the hell?"

She whispered, "That was way too close," not really sure if she meant the lightning strike—or what had almost happened between the two of them.

He only kept on watching her, his eyes hot and wild.

And right then, the lights went out.

"Terrific," Callie muttered. "What now?"

It wasn't dark out yet—but the rain and the cloud cover made it seem so. He was a tall shadow, filling the space in front of her, as her eyes adjusted to the gloom.

That had been some kiss. Callie needed a moment to collect her shattered senses. Judging by the way Nate braced his hand on the counter and hung his head, she guessed he was having a similar problem.

Finally, he said, "I'll check the breaker box. Got a flashlight?"

She had two, somewhere in the boxes still stacked against the wall. But she knew where another one was. "In my SUV."

So he followed her out to her garage, where she got him the flashlight and then trailed after him over to the breaker box on the side wall. The breakers were perfectly aligned in two even rows.

He turned to her, shining the flashlight onto the concrete floor, so it gave some light but didn't blind her. The rain sounded even louder out here, a steady, unremitting roar on the garage roof. He said what she already knew. "None of the breakers have flipped. I had all the wiring in the house replaced. This box is the best there is. I'm thinking it's not a faulty breaker. A tree must have fallen on a line, or a transformer's blown." The eerie light bouncing off the floor exaggerated the strong planes and angles of his face.

She stared up at him, feeling the pull, resisting the really dumb urge to throw herself into his arms again. Suddenly, she was very close to glad that the power had gone out. If it hadn't, they would probably be in her bedroom by now.

Her throat clutched. She had to cough to clear it. "We can call the power company at least." They trooped back inside. She picked up the phone—and got dead air. "Phone's out, too."

He took a cell from his back pocket and she got hers from her crossbody bag. Neither of them could raise a signal. He tipped his head up toward the ceiling and the incessant drumming of the rain. "I'm not liking this," he muttered, grabbing his hat and sticking it back on his head. "I'll be right back."

"Where are you going?" she demanded. But she was talking to an empty kitchen.

He was already halfway down the central hallway to the front door.

"Nate…" She took off after him, slipping out behind him onto the porch.

No light shone from any of the windows up and down the block. It looked like the power was out all around them. And the rain was still coming down in sheets, the wind carrying it at an angle, so it spattered the porch floor, dampened their jeans and ran in rivulets around their feet. Scarier still, Pine Street was now a minicreek, the water three or four inches deep and churning.

He sent her a flat look. "Go inside. I'm having a look around."

"A look around where?"

But of course, he didn't answer. He took off down the front steps and across her soggy lawn, making for his pickup.

Go inside? No way. She needed to know what was going on as much as he did.

She took off after him at a run and managed to get to the passenger door and yank it open before he could shift into gear and back into the rushing, shallow creek that used to be their street.

"You don't need to be out in this." He glared at her, water dripping from his hat, as she swung herself up to the seat, yanked the door shut and grabbed the seat belt.

She snapped the belt shut and armed water off her forehead. "I'm going. Drive."

He muttered something low, something disparaging to her gender, she was certain, but at least he did what she'd told him to do, shifting the quad cab into gear and backing it into the street. He had a high clearance with those big wheels cowboys liked so much, so at that point the water running in the street posed no threat to the engine. He shifted into Drive, headed toward Commercial Street, which was also under water. He turned left and then right onto Main.

They approached Rust Creek and the Main Street Bridge. In the year since the big flood, the levee had been raised and the bridge rebuilt to cross the racing creek at a higher level.

He drove up the slope that accommodated the raised levee and onto the bridge. The water level was still a long way below them.

"Looks good to me," she said.

With a grudging grunt of agreement, he kept going, down the slope on the other side and past the library and the town hall and the new community center with its Fourth of July Grand Opening banner drooping, rain pouring down it in sheets.

"Um, pardon me," she said gingerly. "But where are we going now?"

He swung the wheel and they went left on Cedar Street. "I'm checking the Commercial Street Bridge, too," he said grimly, narrowed eyes on the streaming road in front of them. "It's the one I'm really worried about. Last year, it was completely washed out."

They went past Strickland's Boarding House and the house where Emmet lived and kept going, turning finally onto a county road just outside town. It was only a couple of minutes from there to Commercial Street. He turned and headed for the bridge.

It wasn't far. And there were county trucks there, parked on either side of the street. A worker in a yellow slicker flagged them to a stop and then slogged over to Nate's side window, which he rolled down, letting in a gust of rain-drenched wind.

Nate knew the man by name. "Angus, what's going on?"

Angus was maybe forty, with a sun-creased face and thick, sandy eyebrows. Water dripped off his prominent nose. "Just keepin' an eye on things, Nate."

"The levee?"

"Holding fine and well above the waterline. It'll have to rain straight through for more than a week before anybody needs to start worryin'."

"Power's out."

"I know, and landlines. And a couple of cell towers took lightning strikes. But crews are already at work on all of that. We're hoping to have services restored in the next few hours." Angus aimed a smile in Callie's direction. "Ma'am." She nodded in response. He said, "With all this water in the streets, it's safer not to go driving around in it. You should go on home and dry out."

"Will do." Nate thanked him, sent the window back up and drove across the bridge and back to South Pine, where he pulled into her driveway again and followed her inside.

As she ran across the lawn, her shoes sinking into the waterlogged ground, she knew she should tell him to go, that she would be fine on her own. But for someone he'd called mouthy, she was suddenly feeling more than a little tongue-tied, not to mention downright reluctant to send him on his way.

Which was beyond foolish. If he stayed, it was going to be far too easy to get cozy together, to take up where they'd left off when the lights went out.

She decided not to even think about that.

Inside, she kicked off her shoes and left them by the door. "I'll bring more towels. And it's pretty chilly. If you'll turn on the fire, we can dry off in front of it." Her new energy-efficient gas fireplace required only the flip of a switch to get it going.

With a low noise of agreement, he turned for the great room off the front hall.

When she came back to him he stood in front of the fire. He'd taken off his boots and set them close by to dry. She gave him a towel and then sat down cross-legged in front of the warm blaze. He dropped down beside her. They got busy with the towels. Once she'd rubbed herself damp-dry, she set her towel on the rectangle of decorative stone that served as a hearth. He tossed his towel on top of hers, bending close to her as he reached across her, bringing the smell of rain on his skin and that nice, clean aftershave he wore.

"Feels good," he said.

And she was oh, so achingly aware of him. "Yep," she agreed. "We'll be dry in no time."

Her makeshift braid was dripping down her back,

so she grabbed her towel again and blotted at it some more, letting her gaze wander to the bare walls he'd painted a warm, inviting butterscotch color and on to her tan sofa, and from there to the box of knickknacks by the coffee table, which she'd yet to unpack....

She looked everywhere but at him.

And then he caught the end of the towel and tugged on it.

Her breath got all tangled up in her chest as she made herself meet his eyes.

And he asked, soft and rough and low, "Do you want me to go?"

She should have said yes or even just nodded. There were so many reasons why she needed *not* to do anything foolish with him tonight.

Or any night, for that matter.

But the problem was, right at the moment, none of those reasons seemed the least bit important to her. None of them could hold a candle to the soft and yearning look in his eyes, the surprisingly tender curve of his sexy mouth, the way he took the towel from her hands and tossed it back over her shoulder in the general direction of the other one.

"Yes or no?" He pressed the question.

And, well, at that moment, by the fire, with him smelling so wonderful and looking at her in that focused, thrilling way, what else could she say but, "No, Nate. I want you to stay."

He smiled then. Such a beautiful, open, true sort of smile. And he laid a hand on the side of her face, making a caress of the touch, fingers sliding back and then down over her hair, curving around her wet braid, bringing it forward over her shoulder.

And then reaching out his other hand, using his fingers so deftly, unbraiding and combing through the damp strands. “There,” he said at last. “Loose. Wet. Curling a little.”

She felt a smile tremble on her mouth. And all she could say was, “Oh, Nate…”

And he said, “That first day, back in January?”

“Yeah?” The single word escaped her lips as barely a whisper, a mere breath of sound.

“You had that heavy scarf covering the bottom of your face. And then you took it off. What’s that old Dwight Yoakum song? ‘Try Not to Look So Pretty.’ That was it—how I felt. I hoped you wouldn’t be so pretty. But you were. And you had that hat on, bright pink and green, with those three pom-poms that bounced every time you shook your head. And your hair, just little bits of it slipping out from under that hat, so soft and shiny, curling a little, making me think about getting my hands in it….”

She said, feeling hesitant, “You seemed so angry at me that day.”

He ran his index finger along the line of her jaw, setting off sparks, in a trail of sensation. “I had somewhere I needed to be.”

“I, um, kind of figured that.”

“I wasn’t prepared for you.” Gruffly, intently.

And then his eyes changed, moss to emerald, and he was leaning into her, cradling the back of her head in his big, warm hand.

And she was leaning his way, too.

And he was pulling her closer, taking her down with him onto the hearth, reaching out and pulling the towels in closer to make a pillow for her head.

She asked his name, “Nate?” And she was asking it against his warm, firm lips.

Because he was kissing her again and she was sighing, reaching her hungry hands up to thread her fingers into his damp hair. She was parting her lips for him, inviting his tongue to come inside.

And he was lifting a little, bracing on his forearms to keep from crushing her against the hard floor, his hands on either side of her face, cradling her, kissing her.

Outside, lightning flashed and thunder rumbled and the rain kept coming down.

She didn’t care. There was only the warmth of the fire and the man in her arms, the man who could be so very aggravating, but also so tender and true and unbelievably sweet.

He lifted his head and he gazed down at her and she thought that his eyes were greener, deeper than ever right then. He opened that wonderful mouth to say something.

But he never got a word out.

Because right about then, they both realized that someone was knocking on the front door.

Chapter 3

Nate stared down at Callie. He wanted to kiss her again, to go on kissing her. Maybe whoever was at the door would just go away.

But the knocking started in again. And then a woman's voice called, "Callie? Callie, are you in there?"

Callie blinked up at him, her mouth swollen from his kisses. "I think that's Faith…."

Bad words scrolled through his mind as he pushed back to his knees and rose, bending to offer a hand. She took it and he helped her up.

Once they were both on their feet, they just stood there, gaping at each other like a couple of sleepwalkers wakened suddenly in some public place. He took a slow breath and willed the bulge at his fly to subside. Just what he needed. Their neighbor knowing exactly what she'd interrupted, spreading the word that he and

Callie had a thing going on. And, okay, yeah. He did have a thing for Callie. But it was a thing he'd never intended to act on....

The knock came again. "Callie?" cried a woman's voice.

Callie called, "I'll be right there!"

Both of them got to work smoothing their hair and straightening their still-damp clothes. Tucking in her snug T-shirt as she went, Callie headed for the door. Since he didn't know what else to do, he trailed in her wake. She disengaged the lock and pulled the door back.

Faith, barefoot in a pale blue cotton maternity dress, stood dripping on the doorstep, holding a battery-powered lantern, a relieved-looking smile on her face. "You're here. I'm so glad...."

Callie stepped back. "Come in, come in...."

Faith spotted Nate. "Hey there, Nathan."

"Ahem. Hi, Faith." He felt like a fool.

But Faith didn't seem especially concerned with what he might be doing in the dark at Callie's house. She said to Callie, "Actually, I came over to get you."

Callie frowned. "Get me?"

Faith's head bobbed up and down. "It's happening. The baby's coming. I've been timing contractions, getting everything ready. They're four minutes apart, about fifty seconds each."

"Active labor," Callie said in a hushed, almost reverent tone.

And Faith chuckled, as if having a baby in the middle of a rainstorm with the phones out and no electricity was something kind of humorous. "I've been waiting for the phones to come on so I could call my mom and call you over. But the phones aren't cooperating. And it feels to me like this baby is going to be born real soon now. I… Uh-oh." She doubled over with a groan, her free hand moving to cradle her giant belly. "Here… comes another one…."

Callie took the lantern from her and shoved it at him. "Here." Blinking, stunned, he took it. This couldn't be happening.

But it was.

Nate stood there, holding the lantern high, gaping at the two of them in complete disbelief.

"Come on," Callie urged. "Just come inside by the fire for a minute…."

Faith made a low, animal sort of sound. "But I… have everything ready, just like we planned…."

"Good. Wonderful. As soon as this one passes, I'll get my equipment and we'll go to your house. Now come on, lean on me." Callie coaxed and coddled, guiding a staggering, moaning Faith into the great room and over to the sofa, not far from the fire.

Still holding the lantern high, Nate watched them go. He stood rooted to the spot, his heart pounding out a swift, ragged rhythm, his worst nightmare unfolding all over again.

They needed to do something. *He* needed to do something. But right at the moment, he found he couldn't move.

Callie had Faith at the sofa by then, near the light and heat of the fire. "Right here, sit down. Easy now, easy…."

Faith panted, groaning some more as she went down to the cushions and Callie went with her.

Right about then, Nate finally made his frozen body

move. The blood rushing so fast in his veins it sounded like a hurricane inside his head, he set down the lantern, dug his cell from his pocket, punched up 9-1-1 and put the phone to his ear.

Nothing.

With a muttered oath, he pulled the phone away from his face and stared at the screen. No bars. So he shoved the useless thing back into his pocket and took off like a shot toward the kitchen, grabbing up the house phone from the counter when he got there and trying it.

It was dead, too.

Dead.

Not a word he wanted in his mind at the moment.

He dropped the phone and raced back to the front of the house. When he got to the foyer, he stopped in the doorway to the great room. By then, Faith seemed to be breathing more normally, and Callie glanced over and saw him standing there.

She gasped at the sight of him. "Nate, what's wrong? You're white as a sheet. Are you all right?"

He made his mouth form words. "I tried my cell and your house phone. Both are still out. We need to get her to my truck, take her to the hospital in Kalispell. We need to do that now."

Faith let out a cry of protest. "No. No, I'm not going to do that." She grabbed Callie's hand again. "Callie, tell him. This is going normally, beautifully. I don't need a hospital. I want the home birth I planned for."

"Home birth." Nate swung his gaze back on Callie and accused, "Are you crazy? Have you both lost your minds?"

Faith said, “You should sit down, Nate. Before you fall down.”

He braced a hand on the door frame and wondered why his knees felt weak. “I’m fine. There’s nothing wrong with me.”

Faith shook her head. “Seriously, now. You don’t look so good.”

Nate clutched the door frame harder. “Like I said. Fine. I’m just fine.” And then he noticed that Callie was on her feet and coming toward him. He demanded, “What is the matter with you two? It’s not safe, not right.” He glared at Callie. “She needs a hospital….”

Callie reached for his hand. “Come on. Over here.”

“What? I don’t…”

“Come on.” She had his hand and she put her other arm around him. And he found he had let go of the door frame and was letting her guide him over to the easy chair close to the fire. “Here,” she said gently, the way you talk to a sick child. “Sit right here.” She pushed him slowly down onto it. “There you go. That’s it….”

He felt light-headed, and he wildly stared up at her as a low, angry sound escaped him.

She kept talking slowly and calmly. “Lower your head, Nate.” She put her hand to his upper back and pushed. At first he resisted, but then he gave in and let her guide him down so his head was between his knees. “Good,” she soothed. “Excellent. Now just stay there for a little while, please. I want you to concentrate on your breathing, make it even, deep and slow….”

“This is crazy,” he insisted to the space on the floor between his stocking feet. “It’s not safe. We have to get Faith to the hospital, where they can take care of her, where she and the baby will be safe.”

Callie kept on in that slow, soothing voice. "It will be okay, Nate. I promise you. Just stay there with your head down. Just breathe slowly and deeply."

He wanted to yell at her, to yell at *both* of them, to get it through to them that they were insane, out of their minds to take a chance like this. He knew what would happen if they did. He knew it from the worst kind of personal experience.

However, he was afraid if he sat up right then and tried to explain to them what idiots they were being, he would throw up. That wouldn't help anyone.

Eventually, Callie asked, "Better?"

He stared at his socks and muttered, "Yeah. Better. I think so."

"Good. Because I need you. I need your help. I need you to pull it together, please. Will you do that for me?"

"Please, Nate," said Faith from over there on the sofa. "Callie's not only a nurse. She's certified as a midwife. We have this handled. It's going to be okay."

He sat up. By some miracle, he didn't throw up and he didn't pass out. He looked from one woman to the other and realized that Callie was right about one thing. He really did need to pull it together. "You're determined to do this?"

"Yes, we are," the women said in unison.

It wasn't the answer he'd hoped for, but it was the answer he got and now he needed to deal with it. "What do you want me to do?"

"Wonderful." Callie let out a long sigh. "Put on your boots and help Faith back to her house. I need to dig my midwife bag out of a packing box upstairs. I'll get it and I'll be right over, I promise."

* * *

Out on the porch, it was still raining as if it was the end of the world. Nate handed Faith the lantern. "I'm just going to carry you."

She bit her lip and nodded. "Okay."

So he scooped her up in his arms and ran with her, down the steps and across the yard, with the rain pelting down on them and his boots sinking into the saturated ground with every step he took.

But at least it wasn't far. He was mounting the steps to the shelter of her porch in seconds. He shoved open the front door as another one of those contractions started.

Faith moaned and almost dropped the lantern. He managed to catch it, keeping one hand on her for support as she slid her feet to the floor, all the while fervently praying that Callie would get over there quick.

The house was warm. Faith had a fire going in the living room heat stove. And she had fat candles lit and more of those electric lanterns set around.

She pointed down the central hallway. "My room," she moaned. "That way…." He waited for the worst of that contraction to pass and then scooped her up again and carried her down there, detouring into the room she indicated.

He set her on the bed, which had been stripped except for a sheet and some kind of plastic cover beneath the sheet, which made faint crinkling sounds as it took her weight. There were candles on the dresser and a lantern by the bed. In the soft glow of light, he saw a basin, stacks of clean towels and diapers and those small cotton blankets that you used on newborns.

Perched on the end of the bed, Faith had started

rocking gently back and forth, kind of humming to herself. He stood over her, feeling like a lump of useless nothing. She actually did seem kind of peaceful and relaxed about the whole thing.

Nothing like Zoe, nothing like that awful day in January so long ago…

He cleared his throat. "Is there anything I can get you?"

Faith looked up at him, big blue eyes so calm. "I didn't know, about you and Callie…." He had no idea what to say to that, so he said nothing. He'd known Faith forever, been five years ahead of her in school. He used to hang out with her older brother Stan. She pinched up her mouth at him and added sternly, "You treat her right, Nate Crawford. She deserves the best."

He gave her a slow nod, figuring that was the easiest way to get off the subject of Callie and him and what might be going on between them.

Faith softened toward him then and granted him a gentle little smile. "What you can do is go to the kitchen and get me some ice chips."

"Ice chips," he repeated.

"That's right. Metal bowl in the high cupboard on the right of the sink, ice pick in the drawer to the left of the stove. Break up some ice into small chips for me. It helps, to suck on the chips, keeps me hydrated."

Relieved to have something constructive to do, he left her.

Callie came in as he was breaking up the ice. She stopped for a moment in the open doorway to the hall. "Ice chips. Good." She gave him a smile. She had a purple rolling canvas bag, like the largest size of carry-on suitcase, with a stylized logo of a mother and child on the front. "Just bring them in when they're nice and small."

"Will do." He kept poking with the ice pick.

She turned and wheeled her midwife suitcase off down the hall.

When he took them the ice chips, Callie met him at the door. "Thanks," she said softly. "We've got it from here."

Did she want him to go back to his house? Well, he wasn't. If something went wrong, at least he would be there to take them wherever they needed to go. "I'll just…wait in the other room, keep the fire going. Anything you need, you give me a holler."

She nodded. "Maybe more ice chips later."

"Whatever you need, you just let me know."

He went back to the kitchen and stood at the sink, gulping down a tall glass of water, and then wandered into the living room to check on the fire in the heat stove. After that, he had no idea what to do with himself.

So he paced for a while. Eventually, Callie came out and asked for a pitcher of water, two cups and more ice chips. He got those things for her.

The time crawled by. He checked his phone frequently and also the landline phone on the side table by the sofa. But the power stayed out and the phones, as well. And the rain just kept on, curtains of water falling out of the sky.

About two hours after Callie joined Faith in the bedroom, he heard a really loud moaning sound coming from in there. He went to the door and put his ear to it.

He heard Callie's soft, soothing voice. And he heard Faith. She was the one moaning, making hard, guttural sounds—loud, harsh grunting noises that reminded him of the way female championship tennis players sounded when they hit the ball.

He wanted to tap on the door and ask if everything was all right, but he figured they wouldn't appreciate him interrupting.

He returned to the living room, stoked the fire, checked the phones. And waited.

And waited some more.

He heard occasional noises from the bedroom but nothing that alarmed him. And he knew that Callie would shout for him if things got out of hand or if she needed him to get her something.

And then, at ten minutes before midnight according to the crystal clock on the spindly little desk in the corner, the lights came on. Nate was pacing the living room floor at that moment, and he stopped in midstride to look up at the ceiling fixture, which had just burst into brightness. He took another step. And then he stopped again, tipping his head to the side, listening.

Silence. He rushed to the front door and pulled it open.

The rain had stopped. Porch lights glowed up and down South Pine. The minicreek of rushing water in the street had drained away. There was only the wet blacktop gleaming in the reflected glow of the street lamps.

"Let there be light," Callie said softly from behind him.

He shut the door and turned to her, his heart suddenly surging into overdrive, a weird coppery taste in his mouth. "Faith? The baby? Are they…" He couldn't quite seem to finish the question.

She put her finger to her lips and whispered, "Come with me."

Terror was messing with him, his heart bouncing around in his chest, his stomach spurting acid. But then her expression got through to him, brought him a degree of calm. If things had gone bad, no way would she be looking up at him with that smug little half smile.

"This way." She turned and started back down the hall. He fell in behind her. When they got to Faith's room, Callie put a finger to her lips again and then gently pushed the door open.

Faith lay propped on a pile of pillows in the now properly made-up bed. She wore a green robe and held a pink bundle in her arms—and she looked up and gave him a tired, happy smile. "Hey, Nathan. Look who's here."

He hardly knew he was moving, but then he found himself standing by the side of the bed.

Faith's hair hung lank around her face and there were dark smudges under her eyes. But still, she looked good, had a kind of glow about her. She seemed so happy, so proud. "We're calling her Tansy," she said.

Nate nodded. He knew her husband's family. "After Owen's grandmother."

"That's right. You want to hold her?"

He wasn't sure about that, but then Callie eased around him and took the pink bundle from Faith—and what could he do?

Callie laid the little girl in his arms. He looked down at her, at Tansy, at her tiny, pink mouth and her button of a nose. She yawned, a giant yawn, and then she gave a big sigh and settled into sleep again without ever opening her eyes.

He dared to hold her for a minute longer, a deep and familiar sadness flowing through him, mingling with his joy for Faith and Owen, with the awe he felt just being in the presence of a person so tiny and perfect and fine.

"She's beautiful," he said and held her out for Callie to take her.

Callie passed her back to Faith, and then she asked him, "How about a cup of coffee?"

He realized he'd been holding his breath and let it out slowly. "Sounds good to me."

In Faith's kitchen, Callie gestured for him to sit at the breakfast bar. He slid onto one of the three high stools, and she got to work, finding coffee and filters in the cupboard, loading up the coffeemaker. He checked the phones again, but they were still out.

Once she had it brewing, she took the stool beside him and braced her cheek on her hand. "You okay?"

He looked into those big brandy-brown eyes and thought about how much he'd liked kissing that sweet, soft mouth of hers, about how he would love to kiss her again.

But he wouldn't. After tonight, he was going to make a concentrated effort to steer clear of pretty Callie Kennedy. Because Faith was right. Callie deserved the best. She deserved a good man to love her and marry her and give her babies, like that angel back in the bedroom in Faith's arms.

He wasn't that man. All that was over for him.

His gaze fell on that purple bag of hers, all packed up and waiting in the corner. "A midwife, a nurse. You kind of do it all, huh?"

She chuckled. "I always wanted a practice like the one at the clinic, but somehow, I ended up in a big Chicago hospital on the administration end. It was better money and I…" She pressed her lips together and he knew there was something she'd decided not to say. "Anyway, I took the midwife training a few years back and got certified. I kept telling myself that maybe someday I would give up the rat race and become a real, hands-on nurse and midwife in some homey small town where everybody knew everybody."

"And just look at you now." He didn't try to hide his admiration.

She beamed. "Living my dream, and that is no lie."

For a moment or two, neither of them spoke. The coffeemaker sputtered away.

Callie spoke again, her voice low now and kind of careful. "You were white around the mouth, back at my house. Faith and I… We both thought you were going to pass out."

He breathed in the reassuring scent of brewing coffee and thought how he was going tell her it was nothing, just a guy thing, that some men were terrified at births.

But instead, he opened his mouth and said, "I was married once."

Softly, she answered, "I didn't know."

He meant to stop there. But then he went and opened his mouth and told her more. "I met my wife in Missoula, when I was in college. At Johnny's Downtown Cafe, where she waited tables. She had red hair and freckles and big hazel eyes. Her name was Zoe Baker and she was the love of my life." He fell silent. He waited for the woman next to him to break the spell, to say something so he could change the subject.

She didn't say a word, only looked at him, her expression tender and gentle and completely accepting.

So he just kept talking. "Me and Zoe, we had two great years together in Missoula while I finished school. When I graduated, I wanted to bring her home to Rust Creek Falls with me. But she'd met my parents, and my mom wasn't warm to her. Zoe didn't feel welcome here. She knew they wanted more than 'just a waitress' for their wonderful firstborn son." He muttered those words. They tasted so bitter in his mouth.

Callie lifted a hand and put it gently on his arm. He felt that touch right down to the center of himself. He knew he ought to shut up.

But he didn't. The old story just kept pushing, demanding to be told.

So he went on with the rest of it, how he and Zoe moved to Bismarck, where Zoe's mom, Anna, lived. How he got a job running a fast-food place, and they were doing all right.

"I loved her," he said. "I loved Zoe so much that I was happy even living away from Rust Creek, away from home. Then Zoe became pregnant." God in heaven. He shut his eyes, breathed in slow through his nose. "The sweetness of that time, I can't begin to tell you about it. I was the happiest man alive. But I did want to move home, and my parents promised to be more welcoming to Zoe. They wanted their grandchild born in Rust Creek Falls. So Zoe agreed to spend Christmas with my family, to see how it went."

Callie didn't say anything. She just kept her hand there, on his forearm, steady and soothing. And she listened, those big brown eyes never shifting, never looking away.

He kept going. "I was so sure of everything, sure it would work out just how I wanted it. Figuring I was coming home for good soon, I quit my job, and we stayed at the Shooting Star, the ranch Grandfather Crawford left to me and my brothers when he passed. At the time, there was only a foreman and a couple of hands living there. I opened up my grandfather's house and Zoe and I stayed there. I hoped she would like that, be impressed with how big and comfortable the house was…."

Callie patted his arm and then left his side to get down the coffee cups. "And was she impressed?"

He shrugged. "Zoe never cared about stuff like that, about money and fancy things." *She was a lot like you that way,* he thought but didn't say.

"How did the visit go?"

"Pretty well. My parents still didn't really warm to Zoe, but they wanted me back home, so they were on good behavior." He watched as she filled two cups and pushed one across the counter at him. He sipped and she put milk and sugar in hers.

She took the stool next to him again.

And he continued, "On Christmas Eve, Zoe had some bleeding. There was cramping, too. I rushed her to the hospital in Kalispell, and the doctor there put her on bed rest. We agreed she would take it easy at the ranch until the baby was born and then we would talk about what to do next. I was glad that we would have to stay in Rust Creek Falls for a while. I was just so sure that the longer Zoe stayed, the more she'd come to love it here. Zoe's mom volunteered to come and help out, but Anna really couldn't afford to take the time off from her job. We told her we were fine, and she stayed in Bismarck…." He stared at Callie, wondering why he was telling her this, wishing he'd never gotten started, knowing he should stop.

And then, not stopping, just going on, telling her the rest of it. "The fourteenth of January, the snow started. By the morning of the fifteenth, it was a blizzard, one for the record books, whiteout conditions. And Zoe was in labor. The phones were out and the roads were closed, with six feet of snow and more coming down. It was just the two of us, and our baby trying to be born, alone in my grandfather's house. There were… How do they always say it?" He sipped his coffee, slowly, set the cup down. "There were complications. They both died, Zoe and our little boy."

Callie didn't say anything. He was grateful for that. And she didn't need to say anything. She understood. He could see that in those big eyes. She touched his arm again, a brief brush of a touch. And then she folded both hands around her coffee cup and waited for him to finish it up.

So he did. "After we buried them I took off. I lived in Wyoming for a while, and Colorado, and Utah, traveling around, picking up odd jobs. I didn't stay in one place for long. I kept moving, kept trying to outrun the pain of what had happened, kept trying to forget. And then, eventually, when I realized there was never going to be any way to forget, I gave up and just came home. I didn't know where else to go."

"I had no idea," Callie said in a whisper.

He shrugged. "Nobody in town remembered Zoe, really. She and I had our life together away from here.

And my parents, they prefer to forget her, not to think about the grandson they never saw. Mostly, everyone's forgotten I was ever married. And I'm good with that. I don't want to talk about it. It hurts too much—and don't even ask me why I'm talking about it now."

Callie shook her head and answered in a gentle voice, "Okay. I won't ask."

He muttered darkly, as a warning, "I shouldn't have been kissing you. I'm not a good bet. There's something…broken in me, you know? I haven't been such a good man in the years since I moved back home. I've been a Crawford through and through, you might say—too proud and too sure I knew every damn thing. You are a quality woman. You deserve a better man than me."

She only looked at him, eyes wide, bright with the sheen of unshed tears. Her mouth was so soft. He wanted to grab her and start kissing her all over again.

And that couldn't happen. He made himself clearer. "The last eight years, since I've been back in town, I've gone out with several women. But it never ends well. They get fed up with waiting for me to get serious. But I never get serious. I've never felt anything like what I had with Zoe. I've pretty much accepted that there's no one else for me."

Callie kept her gaze level. He couldn't tell what she might be thinking. "I understand," she said.

He leaned a little closer. "Do you really?"

"I do, Nate. Although I happen to think you're a much better man than you're giving yourself credit for."

"You're just softhearted."

She gave a tiny shrug. "Maybe I am." Her eyes

seemed so sad. "Just tell me the rest, will you please? Tell me about Bismarck."

Why not? He'd come this far. And he knew she would keep it to herself. She was that kind of woman, the kind a man could depend on to respect his secrets and guard his privacy.

And it seemed only right somehow, to finish the story. "Every year, on January fifteenth, I drive to Bismarck to put flowers on their graves."

Callie made a soft, mournful little sound, but she didn't say a word.

He went on with it. "I used to go and pick up Anna, Zoe's mom, and we would take the flowers together. But then, two years ago, Anna remarried and moved to Florida. I'm glad for her. She's happier than she thought she would ever be, after losing her only child and her grandbaby, too. But she can't make it back to North Dakota every year. So now I make the trip on my own. And then, once I've delivered the flowers, I go straight to a certain roadhouse I know of with a motel out back. I get good and plastered and I remember—all of it, everything that's lost. And I do it a long way from Rust Creek Falls, where no one will see me drunk and disorderly and crying like a fool. Then, when I've finally had enough of the memories and the whiskey, I sleep it off in that motel I mentioned, the one out back behind the bar."

She looked at him for a long time, a patient sort of look. He thought he could stare into her eyes for a century and never want to stop.

He also knew that if he stayed in that kitchen with her much longer, there would be no telling what he might do or say. He could end up telling her everything, including about the lottery ticket he bought the day he met her, about his big win, that not even his family knew about, about how it kind of felt to him that she had brought him good luck, a new start on what, for a decade, had always been the darkest, hardest day of the year.

No. He wasn't going to go there.

"I should leave." He pushed his cup away.

She didn't argue, just went on looking at him as though she could see right down to the core of him.

He got up and headed for the door.

"Good night, Nate," she said softly.

He just kept walking. He knew if he stopped, if he turned back to look at her, he wouldn't be able to go.

Callie heard the front door open and the soft click as he closed it behind him. A minute later, she heard his pickup start up next door—he would be moving it from her driveway to his garage.

Her heart ached for him. And she was way too attracted to him.

And he'd made it more than clear that whatever this thing was between them, it wasn't the kind of thing that could last. Plus, hello, hadn't she promised herself she would steer clear of men in general for a while?

It was all just completely unworkable, and she needed to get over it, get over *him*—which was a ridiculous way to think of it. She didn't know him well enough to need to get over him. Tonight was the first night she'd spent any real time with him, the first night they'd even shared a kiss. She didn't need to get over him. She just needed to forget about him.

The phone on the counter started ringing, the sound startling her, so she let out a sharp, "Oh!"

It was Faith's mom, Brenda. Callie reassured her that there'd been no flooding on South Pine and Faith was fine. Then, before Brenda could ask more questions, Callie told her to hold on and carried the phone down the hall to see if Faith was awake. She was sitting up among the pillows, Tansy in her arms.

Callie held up the phone and mouthed, "Your mom."

"Did you tell her?" Faith whispered back.

Callie shook her head.

Faith gave her a wobbly smile and picked up the extension by the bed. "Mom." A sob escaped her. Fat tears overflowed and trailed down her cheeks. But she was smiling at the same time. "Mom, you won't believe what's happened…."

Callie backed out of the bedroom and shut the door. And then she returned to the kitchen, where she poured a second cup of coffee she really didn't need and tried not to think of Nate, alone in his big, beautiful house with only sad memories to keep him company.

Chapter 4

Nate didn't get a whole lot of sleep that night. He kept thinking of Callie, of how focused and still she'd been when he told her about Zoe, the way she just listened, not needing to fill the air with words or fall all over him with a flood of sympathetic noises.

He kept thinking of the way she'd handled him—and really, there was no other word for it. She had handled him good and proper when he almost lost it over Faith having the baby. Gently and firmly, she had calmed him down and gotten him reluctantly on board with their plan.

And then there were those kisses they'd shared. The woman could get a dead man going.

He wouldn't mind kissing Callie Kennedy again, and frequently.

She was something, all right. Something really special.

And that was why he would keep his distance from here on out. The woman just *did* something to him, made him feel as though she could see inside his head—and his heart, too. He wasn't up for that. After losing Zoe and the baby, he never wanted to care that much again. He had a feeling that with Callie he could get in deep, and it would happen fast. Giving her a wide berth was the best option.

Yeah, that could be a little tricky, given that she lived right next door. But he could be damned determined when he set his mind to it.

The next morning, the third of July, there wasn't a cloud in the sky. Nate had business in Kalispell at nine, so he was up good and early, showered, shaved and dressed and frying himself some eggs when the house phone rang.

It was his mother. "Nathan. Good morning. Everything all right on the south side of town?"

"It's fine here at my house."

"Did you lose power and phone service, too?"

"Yeah." He turned the heat down under the pan and poked at the eggs and had a very strong feeling his mother was leading up to something.

"But everything's back on now?"

"That's right. I woke up this morning, and even my cell was finally showing bars."

"Terrific." A pause and then, way too sweetly, "You and Callie get home all right?"

"Just fine, Mom."

"She's a wonderful person, don't you think?"

He gritted his teeth and kept his voice neutral. "Yep. She's great." He tucked the phone into the crook of his shoulder and slid the eggs onto his plate, then turned to pop the toast from the toaster.

His mother kept on. "She just loves it here in town. Never wants to leave. Did you know that, Nathan?"

"She mentioned that once or twice, yeah." And a change of subject was in order. "Faith Harper had her baby last night." He slathered butter on the toast.

"Now, where did you hear that?" his mother demanded. Laura Crawford never liked it when she wasn't the first to know about a new baby coming or who got engaged or was getting divorced.

"I was there."

"What?"

"Faith had the baby at her house. It was during the storm. She came over to get Callie to help her."

"Over to *your* house?"

"No, Mom. To Callie's house."

"Oh. You were at Callie's house?"

"I drove her home, remember?"

"Do not treat me like I'm senile. Of course I remember."

"Callie's a midwife. Did you know that?"

"Of course I knew. I told you I *like* Callie. She's more than a very pretty face. She has a good head on her shoulders. She's helpful to everyone and a good listener, too. Most times, when she comes in the store, we have a nice chat, Callie and me. Emmet's lucky to have her. More people are going to the clinic when they need a doctor now, because Callie is a top-notch medical professional."

He knocked back a slug of coffee. "So, anyway, Callie delivered Faith's baby."

"I'm so glad she was there when Faith needed her."

"Faith had a little girl and named her Tansy, after Owen's grandma."

"Well, I guess I remember Tansy Harper better than you do."

He stifled a chuckle at how his mom could get all huffy if you dared to think you knew more than her—and then he thought of Zoe, of how his mother had said more nice things about Callie in the space of two minutes than she'd ever said about the woman he'd loved more than life. "Mom, I have to go. My breakfast is getting cold."

"What's the matter? What'd I say now?"

"Not a thing," he lied. There was just no point in plowing that old ground again. "I'll call Delbert Hawser to come fix the roof for you, see if he can get over there today."

"Can't you or one of the other boys do it? I hate to spend good money on a handyman when I've got four strong, capable sons." His mother had plenty of money to pay for the roof repair. But she'd always prided herself on her frugality. She knew how to make a penny beg for mercy.

"I'll tell Delbert to send me the bill. Don't you worry about it."

"I hate for you to waste your money, even though I know you've done well for yourself, investing your inheritance so wisely and all." That was the story he'd given them when he'd fixed up the two houses and then moved off the ranch, that he'd made a killing investing the money that came down to him from Grandpa Crawford.

"It's not a problem," he assured her. "I'm happy to take care of it for you."

"I am proud of you, son." Her voice was soft now, loving. "You know that, don't you?"

"Thanks, Mom."

"I just hope you're rethinking that crazy plan of yours to move away. And you know, if you started seeing someone you really liked here in town, well, you just might come to your senses and realize that you don't even *want* to leave."

"Gotta go. Really. 'Bye, Mom."

She was still talking as he hung up.

He ate his breakfast and called Delbert, who agreed to fix the roof leak at the store that afternoon and send Nate the bill. As he pulled out of the garage for the drive to Kalispell, he couldn't help but glance over at the house next door.

No sign of Callie. No lights on inside that he could see. Would she be at the clinic now or still at Faith's helping out? He really would like to know how Faith and little Tansy were doing....

But he fought the urge to stop the pickup in the driveway and jog across the lawn to see if she might be there. Instead, he backed to the street, shifted into forward gear and hit the gas so hard he laid rubber getting out of there.

Twenty-five minutes later, he was pulling into a parking space behind an office building in downtown Kalispell. He went in the back entrance and took the elevator to the third floor, which housed the offices of Saul Mercury, Attorney-at-Law. The elevator doors opened on a black marble foyer and a middle-aged receptionist behind a wide front desk.

"Hello, Mr. Crawford. Mr. Mercury is expecting you. Go right on back."

He took the hallway on the right, down to the large corner office where Saul was waiting.

"Nate. Always great to see you." The lawyer, tall and broad-shouldered with a thick head of hair so blond Nate was certain it had to be a dye job, met him at the door. They shook hands. "Sit down, sit down," Saul encouraged with a smile that proudly displayed an orthodontist's fantasy of big, straight white teeth. Nate settled into the visitor's chair opposite Saul's giant desk of chrome and glass.

They got down to business.

Saul handed him a folder, and they went over the lawyer's report on what Nate's money was doing under the umbrella of the trust Saul had created for him.

As he did every month during their meeting, Saul suggested that besides all the "good works" Nate kept putting money into, he ought to find—or let Saul find him—some real investment opportunities for his fortune.

Nate said what he always said. "I'll get to that. But for now, I just want to take care of some things that need doing before I leave Rust Creek Falls."

Saul asked what he'd asked every month since Nate had started talking about moving away. "Decided where you're going?"

"I've been thinking Chicago…."

"When will you leave?"

"I haven't firmed anything up yet."

"Ah." Saul's expression said it all. The lawyer found it humorous that Nate kept saying he was leaving and yet he never managed actually to go.

Nate brought them back around to the business at hand. "I have a new project I want you to handle."

Saul's look turned hopeful. "Real estate? The markets? An internet start-up?"

"A donation. Let's say two—no, three—hundred thousand."

"A donation." Saul seemed to stifle a groan—after which he flashed those big white teeth again. "Why am I not surprised?"

"I have plenty of money now," Nate reminded him. "More than I'll ever need."

Saul put up a hand. "Not arguing, Nate. Just advising."

"The point is I've never been what you would call a generous man. It's good for me to give a little."

"And that's admirable. It's only that I think you should let your money *make* money, too."

"I get it, Saul. And I'll start looking for investment opportunities that interest me."

"You could let me help you look." Now the lawyer put up both big hands and patted the air. "Not a big deal, no pressure. But whenever I see an interesting possibility, I'll email you the information. You see one that intrigues you, get back to me. We'll talk."

"I don't want to be rushed into anything."

"Nate. C'mon. I won't send more than a couple of possibilities a week. You're not interested, do nothing."

"Fine. Send them my way. Now, ready for the details on that three hundred K?"

Saul tapped a key on his laptop. "Fire away."

After the meeting with Saul, Nate stopped in at Target to pick up a few things.

And then, on the way home, he turned off the highway at the winding road that led to the Traub family ranch, the Triple T. His sister Nina lived there now. She ran the family store most days, but lately she'd been taking Wednesdays and Thursdays off. Last Christmas, she'd had a daughter, Noelle, and married Dallas Traub, one of Collin's five brothers. Now she and Dallas had a nice ready-made family, with little Noelle and Dallas's three boys.

When Nate pulled into the big yard, there were no Traubs in sight. Not that it would have mattered if there were. The Traubs were civil to him now, as a rule. Yeah, most of them remained leery of him and he didn't blame them. He'd spent way too many years buying into the old family feud between his people and theirs, talking trash about Traubs whenever he got a chance. And then there'd been the long-time, personal animosity between him and Collin and the way he'd played dirty in the mayoral race.

But then he'd lost that race and had to eat an extra-large slice of humble pie. And Nina went and married one of Collin's brothers. And then Nate went to Bismarck in January and ended up a multimillionaire.

Things had changed, as far as he was concerned. True, it was a convoluted relationship between the Crawfords and the Traubs. For generations, they'd hated each other, competed with each other for love and for land, done each other dirty in any number of business deals. But that was then. Nate just couldn't see a reason anymore to keep on with the old feud. Even his parents, who'd clung all their lives to the longtime animosity, couldn't really say specifically what the feud was about in the here and now, let alone why it should continue. There had been rotten behavior on both sides for generations. It needed to stop.

So now he made it a point to speak politely to every Traub he happened to meet on the street. The Traubs weren't exactly wild over him, but they were getting so they kind of put up with him, which meant that when he stopped in to see Nina on the Traub family ranch, no one came out to greet him with a loaded shotgun.

That day, Dallas's boys, Ryder, Jake and Robbie, were off at summer school in town, and Dallas was out in one of the far pastures, tending cattle. It was just Nina and the baby at home. Nate got to hold Noelle, and Nina fussed over him and made him lunch. At Target, he'd bought toys for each of the boys and a few things for Noelle, too.

Nina chided, "You don't always have to bring presents, you know."

"But, Nina, that's what uncles do." In his lap, Noelle giggled and reached for the ring of bright plastic keys he'd brought her. Each one made a different sound when you shook it. He handed them over and she crowed with delight when the blue one made a chiming sound. "See? She loves it."

Nina finished the last of the clothes she was folding and set the hamper aside. She pulled out a chair and sat down across from him. "That was some storm yesterday."

"But it's over now and the levee held."

"Life is good." Nina wore a pleased smile. "Mom called earlier. She said Faith Harper had a little girl during the storm and you were there for the birth."

"Well, I was in the house, but essentially useless. I

brought her ice chips when she needed them and did a lot of pacing in front of the fire."

"Mom also says you're sweet on Nurse Callie Kennedy. She's real happy about that."

"Mom doesn't know what she's talking about."

"Well, now, Nathan," Nina teased. "You did move her in next door to you."

"Move her in? I was selling the house, and she's the one who bought it. That's hardly moving her in."

"Pardon me for saying so, but it seems to me your tone is just a tad defensive."

Noelle leaned back against him and shook the key, which made a rattling sound. He said, "Nope. Not defensive in the least."

"Everyone likes Callie. She's a lovely person. I'm thinking you're a lucky man."

"Callie's great. I like her a lot. But there's nothing going on between her and me." It was the truth, as of now, anyway, he told himself—and tried not to remember the feel of her in his arms or the scent of her hair or the way those big eyes seemed to see down into his soul.

Nina observed, "You seem a little too determined to convince me."

"Not determined. Just telling you how it is, that's all."

She studied him for a count of five. He braced to keep insisting that there was nothing happening with him and Callie.

But then she said, "It's the Fourth tomorrow. Grand opening of the new Grace Traub Community Center."

Nate had donated to the center—anonymously, through the trust. But most of the money had come from a weird old guy named Arthur Swinton, who'd once been mayor down in Thunder Canyon, a town three hundred miles southeast of Rust Creek Falls, where a lot of Traub relatives lived. Swinton had ended up in prison for embezzlement at one point and then managed to get his sentence commuted by the efforts of the Roarke family, led by Shane Roarke, who it turned out was Arthur Swinton and Grace Traub's illegitimate son. Swinton then vowed ever after to do good works. Like…building a community center in Rust Creek Falls and naming it after the woman he'd loved before she'd even been a Traub. It didn't make a whole lot of sense to Nate, but, so what? The community center would be a real plus for Rust Creek Falls.

Nina went on, "And then there'll be the usual street fair on Main and the street dance and fireworks at night."

He gave her a patient look. "I know what goes on for the Fourth of July."

"You're going, right?"

"I haven't decided yet."

"Come on, Nathan. You should be there. Everybody's going. It's a big deal this year, the anniversary of the Great Flood." Nina looked a little misty-eyed. The year before, all the usual events had been canceled due to the incessant rain. And then, in the afternoon, the levee gave way. It had been a dark day for Rust Creek Falls. "We've come back stronger than ever. Mom says she'll run the store so Dallas and I can take the kids to the fair. And then Ellie says she'll help out if we want to try and stay for the dance and the fireworks." Ellie was Dallas's mom, the Traub family matriarch.

Amazing. Laura Crawford, the mother-in-law of a

Traub, and Ellie Traub, with a Crawford for a daughter-in-law. He'd never thought to see such a thing in his life.

In his arms, Noelle started fussing. He surrendered her reluctantly when Nina rose and reached for her.

Nate got up, too. "Thanks for the lunch."

Dark eyes flashing with mischief, Nina rocked from side to side and kissed the fussing baby on her fat, pink cheek. "See you tomorrow. Bring your sweetheart."

"I don't have a sweetheart," he grumbled.

"That's not what Mom says…."

"Knock it off." He headed for the door.

"There is nothing quite as beautiful as young love in bloom," she called after him.

He kept his mouth shut and got out of there, closing the door a little harder than he needed to behind him.

When he got home, Nate saw Owen Harper's red pickup parked in the driveway of the house on the other side of Callie's. So he took over the baby gift he'd bought. Owen invited him in, and Faith's mom came out of the kitchen with a beer for each of them. They toasted the new baby, and he learned that Tansy and Faith were both doing fine.

Faith's mom brought out chips and dip and he hung around some more—longer than he should have, he realized, when Callie showed up at the door.

She wore Hello Kitty nurse's scrubs and hot-pink clogs, and something in his chest ached just at the sight of her, with those unforgettable dark eyes and all that seal-brown hair pinned up haphazardly, making his hands itch to take it down. Faith's mom grabbed her in a hug, and Owen insisted she should have a beer.

But she shook her head. "I would love one, but I have to get back to the clinic. Thought I'd just drop in and have a quick look at Faith and the baby, see how they're doing…." She slid him a glance then. "Hello, Nate." Careful. Contained.

"Hey, Callie." He raised his almost-empty beer to her because he didn't know what else to do, and he felt awkward and empty and kind of forlorn.

Ridiculous, to feel this way. Just because he'd held her in his arms and she'd felt way too right there. Because she was tenderhearted and tough, too. Because she was the kind of woman who made a man want to blather on, pouring out the secrets of his soul that, until her, he'd always had sense enough to keep to himself.

And then, Faith's mom was wrapping an arm around her, turning her toward the back of the house. "They're just resting. Come on…"

He watched her go and wished she would come back, come back and sit with them, have some chips and dip and a cold drink and tell him all about her day.

Really, he could almost start to think that his mom was right. He was gone on Callie Kennedy, mooning around after her like some lovesick teenager.

He finished his beer, shook Owen's hand again and said he really had to go.

Independence Day dawned as bright and sunny as the day before.

Nate got up, thinking he would hang around home for a while and then maybe drive out to the Shooting Star, see how his brothers were doing, ask if they needed a hand with anything on the ranch.

But then his brother Brad called and said that he and

their other brothers, Justin and Jesse, were going to the opening of the community center. "We'll meet you on the town-hall steps." The town hall was directly across from the new center. "We'll make a day of it, the four of us, check out the booths at the street fair, head over to the Ace in the Hole for a beer or two later. And go to the dance tonight."

"I don't know, Brad."

"What do you mean, you don't know? You sound like some crabby old man. Do you know this town is now full of good-lookin' women who have come to help us continue our recovery from the flood of the century?"

"I do know that, yeah."

"And you know they'll all turn out for the Fourth of July, don't you? Nothin' a pretty do-gooder enjoys so much as a quaint small-town celebration and the chance to dance with a cowboy. We need to get friendly with some pretty women, Nate. We need to forget all our troubles." Brad's wife, Janie, had divorced him three years ago. He'd been kind of cynical ever since.

"I think I'll skip it."

"Nathan. I want you to listen and listen good. We're goin'. *You're* goin'. You've been in a funk for months now and you need to snap out of it."

"*I'm* in a funk?"

"You know what I mean, ever since you lost the election to that no-good Collin Traub."

"I'm over the election, Brad." How many times did he have to say it?

"You should look on the bright side. Your investments paid off and now, all of a sudden, you've got money to burn."

"Well, I wouldn't say that." Even if it was true.

"You live in a fancy house and you don't have to spend your days knee-deep in cow crap anymore. You can afford to show a pretty do-gooder a really fine time."

"Damn it, Brad. I mean it. I'm *over* the election, and I don't like the way you're—"

"Be there. In front of the town hall. Ten o'clock."

Before Nate had a chance to say no again, Brad hung up on him.

Nate put the phone down with a sigh of resignation and hit the shower.

On the Fourth of July, Main Street drew the crowds and parking was scarce. So Nate left his pickup at home and walked across the Main Street Bridge to North Main, where most of the festivities would take place.

From the bridge clear to Sawmill Street, people were everywhere. Volunteers had looped patriotic bunting from every available railing and storefront. Old Glory waved wherever you looked—from the flagpole in front of the library to the ones at the town hall and at the new community center, to every possible pillar and post where a flag might be mounted.

The biggest crowd had gathered around the new center, which was all dressed up for the holiday with red, white and blue draped in swags across the facade. A newer, bigger Grand Opening banner replaced the one that had been sagging to the ground during the storm two days before. And a giant blue ribbon with an enormous bow on it had been tied across the big double doors, no doubt to be cut by some beaming official when it was time for everyone to go inside.

They had a band set up on the grass. It was made up of old guys who played for the dances at the Masonic Hall, and several youngsters from the high school. When Nate got there, they were playing a marching song, not very well but really loud and with a lot of enthusiasm.

Brad, Justin and Jesse waited on the town-hall steps, as promised. Brad and Justin were acting like a couple of yahoos, whistling at every pretty girl who walked by. Jesse, the youngest and most sensitive of the four of them, stood a little to the side, looking as if he wished he'd just stayed at the ranch with the horses he loved so much.

Nate was a little embarrassed, too, at the way Brad and Justin were carrying on. But he was also kind of happy to be out in the sunshine on a nice summer day, hanging with his brothers. Even if two of them *were* behaving like fools.

And Brad had been right about the women. There were a lot of new women in town, and most of them were good-looking.

Brad nudged him in the ribs. "See that gorgeous blonde over there? The newcomer? Ponytail?"

The blonde in question turned her head at that moment, and Nate could see her face. She really was a stunner. "I see her."

"Name's Julie Smith. That's all I know, even though I've asked around. Kind of a mystery woman, really. Which is fine. When a girl looks like that, her name's all I *need* to know."

Jesse shook his head. "Brad, you're an embarrassment, you know that?"

"Lighten up, little brother. I'm just having fun."

Nate admired the scenery as the band played on.

Jesse left them temporarily. He wandered down the steps and out to the street and started chatting up Maggie Roarke, an attorney from Los Angeles. Maggie was tall and sleek and blonde. Nate had seen her around town in her classy business suits, looking as if she'd just stepped out of a Calvin Klein ad. She seemed about as wrong for Jesse as a woman could get.

And that got him wondering if maybe sleek, sophisticated Maggie Roarke might be Jesse's problem lately. He'd seemed quieter and more withdrawn than usual. When he came back to join them on the town-hall steps, Nate almost asked him if he had something going on with the lawyer from L.A.

But then the speeches started. Collin got up first. He was a damn fine speaker, Nate had to admit. Collin had a way of connecting with folks when he got up in front of them. He was funny and he gave it to them straight, and people picked up on his sincerity. He spoke of the flood last year and the toad-strangler of a storm two days before, about how the levee had been tested more than once now and come through with flying colors, proving that Rust Creek Falls really was being rebuilt better and stronger than ever. Their town, Collin said, had taken a tragedy and remade it into a triumph of the human spirit.

Though Justin and Brad grumbled under their breaths the whole time about the damn upstart Mayor Traub, Nate only found himself more convinced that Collin was doing a fine job. The thunderous applause rising up from the crowd when Collin finished seemed a seal of approval, not only for his words, but for the man himself and his dedication to the safety, prosperity and betterment of Rust Creek Falls.

Arthur Swinton stepped up next. The old man looked frail, with thinning silver hair and a deeply lined, drawn face. His speech was a rambling one that finally seemed to be wrapping up with: "I dedicate this community center to the beautiful Grace Traub, may she rest in peace. I know I have led a far from exemplary life. But it is my fervent, my true, my lasting hope that, in the end, a man is defined not so much by his past transgressions as by his dedication, now and in the future, to do what's right, to love others more than himself and to…erm, offer all he has in the pursuit and fulfillment of the, uh, greater good." He paused. People began to clap—but then he started in again. "Love each other more, everyone! Give each other all you have! Don't let bitterness or sadness or the failure of your dreams steal away your will to…to…" He seemed to lose his train of thought completely then.

But someone yelled, "Yay! You said it, Arthur! God bless you, old man!" and that got the applause going again. Everyone joined in clapping, and Arthur Swinton blinked and looked around and finally, smiling in a bemused sort of way, sat down—only to pop back up again when the sheriff, Gage Christensen, signaled him over to the center's double doors.

Swinton took the giant pair of scissors from the sheriff's offered hand and cut the ribbon.

And the band started up with a patriotic song, and everyone clapped, hooted and hollered as the doors of the Grace Traub Community Center swung wide.

"Come on," said Justin. "I didn't get breakfast. I heard they got doughnuts and coffee inside."

Nate followed his brothers across the street and joined the crowd pouring through the open doors.

In the auditorium, folding tables had been set up along one wall. There was coffee, juice and sweet rolls for all. Nate got in line for a paper cup full of coffee and a Danish.

He almost spilled the coffee all over himself when he spotted Callie a few feet away, sipping coffee and chatting with a very pregnant Paige Dalton Traub. The Daltons were all fast friends with the Traubs. Last Thanksgiving, Paige had reunited with her high-school boyfriend Sutter Traub, the oldest of Collin's brothers—and also the man who'd run Collin's mayoral campaign and done an excellent job of it.

Nate was not proud of the rotten stunt he'd pulled at the campaign's last debate. He'd known he was losing, that Collin was beating him both on the stump and head-to-head in debate. It had galled him no end at the time that not only was he losing, but the man who would beat him was his lifelong nemesis, the biggest troublemaker of all the Traubs.

So he'd fought dirty, going after Collin's campaign manager, Sutter, exploiting a sensitive subject from the past.

All it had taken was a call to an old friend, a decorated veteran. Master Sergeant Dean Riddell stood up at the end of the final debate and called Sutter on the carpet for having once spoken up against the Iraq war.

In actuality, Sutter had never said a word against the war. He'd simply tried to keep his brother Forrest from re-upping; Sutter had felt that Forrest had given enough for his country already. But folks in town had accused Sutter of speaking out against the war itself.

In Rust Creek Falls, you supported your country. You didn't express doubts about the war. Sutter had left town at the time of the uproar, the anger against him had been so strong. He'd only returned after the flood, to help out with recovery and then to try and get his brother elected mayor. By then, folks were willing to forgive and forget.

Until Nate had his friend the war hero rub the past in all their faces.

But Nate's triumph had lasted only a matter of minutes.

Paige, still a Dalton then, had stood up right there in the town meeting and backed Sutter. She'd called Sutter an honest and ethical man whose sin was to express the doubts he felt in his heart. It had been a strong, impassioned argument, and with it, she'd completely pulled the rug out from under Nate and his candidacy.

Nate had been ready to spit nails at the time. Looking back, though, he just felt ashamed of himself. He knew he'd gotten exactly what he deserved.

His gaze strayed to Callie. God, she looked good. In a snug pair of jeans and a fitted red-and-white-checked shirt, she lit up the room. She hadn't spotted him yet.

But Paige had. And though he'd been making headway at better relations with most of the Traubs, Paige had yet to forgive him for trying to drag Sutter through the mud during that last debate. She gave him a look of icy scorn.

And Callie caught the direction of her gaze and saw him.

They had one of those moments, like the other day at the store. They just stared at each other. He knew he shouldn't do that, shouldn't gape at her like a love-struck fool. But for a long, magic string of seconds, he just couldn't look away.

Apparently, neither could Callie.

Until Paige broke the spell by putting a hand on Callie's shoulder. Callie blinked and turned to Paige and Paige leaned in close to her and started talking fast, shaking her head.

Nate couldn't hear a word of it and he doubted anyone else but Callie could, either. Paige kept her voice down. But he had a pretty good idea she was talking about him and what she was saying was not the least flattering.

Paige and Callie turned together and walked the other way, leaving him standing there by the refreshment tables with his coffee and Danish, feeling about two inches tall, trying to remind himself that it was a good thing if Callie thought less of him. He needed to look on the bright side. If she decided he was a rat bastard, fair enough.

If she wanted nothing to do with him, terrific.

If she hated him, wonderful.

If she couldn't stand the sight of him, then she wouldn't let him near her.

And that would make it a lot easier for him to stay the hell away from her.

Chapter 5

Outside, Callie and Page found an empty bench by the library, in the dappled shade of a cottonwood tree. The spot was tucked back from the street, along the side of the building, far enough from the crowd that they could talk undisturbed.

Paige said, "I know I told you before that I didn't think much of Nate."

Callie blew out a breath. "'An unmitigated douche,' that's what you called him. I guess I kind of understand why you said that now."

Paige winced. "Look. I can see there's… Well, it's obvious you've got a thing for him. And the way he was looking at you… Whoa. That look could burn down a barn. But I just thought you should know what happened last fall, because I don't think he's any kind of bet for a boyfriend."

Callie was still reeling from what Paige had whispered to her back in the auditorium. "I can't believe he pulled a dirty trick like that on poor Sutter, to discredit Collin. Not only because Sutter's a good guy who only wanted to look out for his brother, but also because nothing Sutter ever did has any bearing on whether or not Collin should be mayor. It's so low, so completely unlike the Nate I know."

Paige rested both hands on the ripe bulge of her pregnant belly. "Well, maybe you don't know him all that well."

"Maybe I don't," Callie said regretfully as her heart cried that she *did* know him, that he was a good man, that if he'd once been something less than good, he'd changed and he'd grown.

Paige said, "And he's been out with lots of women over the years, but he seems to have some kind of problem with the concept of getting serious with a girl. Because he never does. From what I've heard, the women get tired of waiting for there to be more with him. Sometimes he breaks it off, sometimes the woman does. But the result is the same. It doesn't last."

Callie longed to ask Paige if she even remembered the wife Nate had loved and lost, if she knew about his baby, who had died being born, if she had any clue how Nate had suffered, how he still hadn't really gotten over losing the family he'd loved so very much.

But she didn't feel right mentioning Zoe and the baby. She didn't think Nate would appreciate that, even if she brought it up in the service of defending him. He'd said that Zoe and the baby weren't common knowledge in town. And he'd told her straight-out that he preferred to keep it that way, that he didn't want his private pain made public.

Plus, even losing a wife and child didn't give a man a right to play dirty, the way he had during the mayor's race. Strangely, she had a feeling Nate would agree with her on that; he wouldn't even want her defending him to Paige. So she kept her peace.

Paige said, "Look. I've still got issues with him, so yeah. Maybe I'm being a little unfair to him. People say he's been…kinder and gentler in the past several months. It seems like losing the mayor's race really took him down a peg, and that was good for him. It's clear he's trying to be a better man. Even I see that. But still, every time I set eyes on him, I want to give him a very large piece of my mind."

"Hey. It's understandable. Really, Paige. I get it."

"Just think about it before you get in too deep with him."

Callie couldn't hold back a rueful chuckle at that. "Get in too deep? Don't worry. Yeah, the attraction is…" She sought the word.

Paige provided it. "Smokin'?"

"Exactly. But we do understand each other, Nate and me. He's leaving town and doesn't want a relationship. And I've sworn off men for the foreseeable future."

"Hold that thought," Paige advised wryly. "At least when it comes to Nate Crawford."

"Hey, Paige! Callie!" Mallory Franklin and her eight-year-old niece, Lily, strode across the grass toward them. Last winter, Mallory had moved with Lily to Rust Creek, seeking the slower pace of small-town life.

Lily, in pink jeans and a yellow shirt, with her shining,

stick-straight black hair tied into two ponytails, seemed to be adapting to the move just fine. She dropped to the grass. “Aunt Mallory, can we *please* go to the street fair now?”

“In a minute.” Mallory took the free space on the bench next to Callie. “Gorgeous day…” Callie and Paige nodded agreement. “Want to check out the street fair with us?”

“Say yes and we can go.” Lily looked up hopefully at them.

Callie was grateful for the interruption. Enough had been said about Nate for now. “Absolutely. Paige?”

“Love to,” Paige agreed. Callie got up and offered her a hand. Paige laughed. “I may look like a beached whale, but I can still get off a bench on my own.” She braced a hand on the bench back, rose and then took a minute to rub the muscles at the base of her spine. “Nine weeks to go. I cannot wait.”

“Let’s go!” Lily bounced to her feet.

So they all strolled up the street and browsed the booths run by local farmers, cooks and craftspeople. Callie bought a dozen cookies from the Community Boosters’ bake sale and a bib apron fringed with rick-rack and printed with cherries from a booth run by the Daughters of the Pioneers.

It was fun, being with her friends and with chatty, gregarious Lily, enjoying the festivities on this sunny holiday. There were other kids running around. Some of them had firecrackers. Lily laughed every time a string of them went off.

Callie tried really hard not to look for Nate. But every time she saw a tall, broad-shouldered cowboy, her heart gave a hopeful little lurch in her chest. Since

Rust Creek was wall-to-wall with tall cowboys, her heart got quite a workout that morning.

Twice when her pulse beat faster, it actually was Nate. She saw him by the Daughters of the Pioneers' booth with his brothers and again near the Forest Service booth. Both times, she looked away before he could catch her watching him. And both times, she couldn't help wishing he might march right up to her and ask her if maybe she'd like to spend the day with him.

In spite of everything—swearing off men, Paige's warnings, the way he'd told her right out that she should stay away from him—in spite of all that, if he'd asked her, she would have boldly laced her fingers with his and strolled from booth to booth with him.

But he didn't ask her. And she just kept telling herself she was glad about that.

She didn't believe it, though. Not for a minute.

Around noon, she decided to take her purchases back to her house and try to get a few more moving boxes unpacked.

Paige said she was done with the fair, too. "I'm heading home to put my feet up."

"You two coming back for the dance and the fireworks tonight?" Mallory wanted to know.

"I'll see how I'm feeling." Paige patted her belly. "Sutter said he'd take me if I'm up for it. So maybe I'll see you."

Yet again, Callie thought of Nate. She couldn't help wishing that he might be there that evening, might ask her to dance. And the fact that she couldn't stop thinking of him deeply annoyed her.

Really, she needed to give all things Nate a rest. "I'll probably be there," she answered at last.

Mallory touched her shoulder. "If I don't see you, remember. First Newcomers' Club meeting. Monday night, seven o'clock, in our new community center."

"Oh, come on," Callie teased. "We've both been in town for more than six months. We're hardly newcomers."

Paige laughed at that. "Six months is nothing in Rust Creek Falls. If you weren't born here, you're a newcomer."

Callie heaved a big pretend sigh. "Well, I guess I better make that meeting, then." She agreed she would be at the center Monday night.

At home, she grabbed a sandwich, then unpacked four more moving boxes and put them away in the hall cabinets.

She still had several boxes to go, but she was getting there. And she felt pretty proud of herself to have the unpacking almost finished in only four short days since she left the Sawmill Street trailer. Her new house was not only beautiful, it was beginning to feel like home.

Inspired by how great everything looked, she unpacked more boxes. By seven that night, she'd done them all. To celebrate, she had a glass of the white wine she'd been saving and finished off the casserole Faith had brought over on moving day.

Then she indulged in a long, lazy bath and took her time with her hair and her makeup. She put on her tightest pair of jeans, a sparkly red top, her fun red straw cowboy hat and her fabulous red Old Gringo cowboy boots. It was a little after nine and she was on her way out the door when the house phone rang. She almost just let it go to voice mail.

But then, what if it was something important? She shut the door and hurried to grab the extension in the great room.

All day long, Nate had been telling himself he was about to go home.

But right after the opening of the community center, Brad had insisted they visit the street fair. Just what a guy needed. Endless booths selling pot holders and afghans and all manner of handcrafts. Women could be damn clever with the stuff they made. But what use did a single man have for a toaster cover or pink towels embroidered along the hems with rows of yellow daisies? Uh-uh.

He saw Callie twice. Both times, she was way too careful not to look his way. He tried to tell himself it was a good thing, that it was what he wanted, for her to avoid him.

But really, it wasn't so good. In fact, it made him feel like crap.

Next, Brad and Justin wanted to head for the Ace in the Hole Saloon, where the beer flowed freely and you could play pool or pick up a card game in the back.

"Just for lunch," he agreed. "Then I've gotta get home."

They had burgers at the Ace—or at least Nate and Jesse did. Justin and Brad were more interested in liquid refreshment. By three or so, Jesse got tired of hanging around the bar and left. Nate would have followed, but his other two brothers were getting pretty plastered. He hung around to provide a little damage control.

He took Brad aside and actually got him to promise to slow down on the alcohol intake. Then Justin started playing pool with a cute little blonde. She was a good player and Justin had his pride. He started concentrating more on the game and the girl than on bending his elbow.

Nate and Brad joined in a game of Texas Hold'em with a couple of carpenters from down in Thunder Canyon, and Delbert Hawser, the handyman. Brad drank Mountain Dew and won steadily, which kept him happy, even without more beer.

It was getting around dinnertime when Nate stood up from the table. Brad was still winning and focused on his cards, so he didn't put up much of a fight when Nate said he was leaving.

By then, the booths on Main Street were starting to close up. Nate got a hot dog and a root beer from one of them. After that, he remembered that the family store was still open and his mom had been working all day. On the Fourth of July, they usually did a landslide business and didn't close until nine. He went to the store instead of home.

His mom stood at the register ringing up a sale when he walked in. She looked tired, he thought. So he hung his hat on the peg by the door to the back rooms and told her he would stay and close up for her.

She gave him one of her warmest smiles. "You're a good boy, Nathan." She said it so fondly, he didn't even take offense or feel the need to remind her that he hadn't been a boy for a very long time. But then she added, "And the street party won't really get going until after nine. You'll have plenty of time for dancing with Callie— Where is she, anyway?"

Nate just shook his head. "I don't even know how to begin to answer that one, Mom."

"She's a prize and I don't want you to let her slip away, that's all."

He reminded himself that she was tired and she meant well. But still, he didn't need her butting in. "Let it go, Mom."

She hitched up her chin. "I hate when you're snippy with me."

"Let it go."

She pursed her lips at him then, but she did keep them shut.

He spotted his father over behind the candy counter. Todd Crawford looked as weary as his wife.

"Take Dad with you. You've both been working long enough today."

Ten minutes later, they left him and his gorgeous blond-haired, blue-eyed baby sister, Natalie, to handle the last two and a half hours. The time flew by. It wasn't too crowded, but customers kept coming in and they had plenty to do.

At eight-thirty, Natalie came up behind him and wrapped her arms around him. She gave a squeeze and wheedled, "Mind if I take off now? I want to go home and put on something sexy for the street dance."

He grumbled, "The last thing a man wants to hear is that his baby sister plans to put on something sexy."

She leaned her head against his back. "Okay, okay. Scratch that. Something pretty."

"Too late. Now I'll have to come to the dance just to beat up any cowboy who makes a wrong move with you."

"Don't you dare. I can handle myself."

The thing was, she could. In a dangerous kind of way. When she was three, she'd figured out how to unlock the front door. Then she climbed into his dad's favorite pickup and actually managed to start it up and roll it several feet into the creek.

He clasped one of her hands and pulled her around in front of him so he could look at her. "Get lost. And have fun."

With a giggle of delight, she bounced on tiptoe to kiss his cheek. "Later, big brother." And she took off.

At nine, he turned the sign around and got busy closing up. There was a list of closing chores, including doing the final count for the day and putting all but a few hundred in change into the safe under the floor in the office.

He had the money in order and put away and was just emerging from the back, pushing through the swinging door into the space behind the main counter, when someone tapped on the double entry doors out front.

Through the etched glass at the top of the door, he saw a red cowboy hat, long, wavy brown hair, a pair of very pretty bare shoulders and arms and a red sequined top. The hat obscured her face.

But he knew it was Callie.

He shouldn't have been so glad. He ought to just turn around and go out through the parking lot in back.

Right. His boots couldn't carry him to her fast enough. He unlocked the door and pulled it open. Out in the street, someone lit up a chain of firecrackers and a cool evening breeze brought him a hint of her tempting scent.

She tipped up her chin and he saw those shining

eyes beneath the brim of her red hat, noted the rather determined set of that plush mouth. "Whatever it is, I'm listening," she said.

He had no idea what she might be talking about. Not that he could bring himself to care. She was right there in front of him, close enough to touch, and the night was falling, the band setting up on the sidewalk in front of the store. He felt like a bottle rocket, about to go off, straight up in the air, shooting off sparks.

"Come on in." He stepped back. She stepped forward. He closed the door behind her.

"Okay," she said, kind of breathless and so damn sweet. "What?" There was a row of pegs by the door. He reached up, lifted the red hat off her head and hung it up. "Hey!" she protested, but those soft lips were smiling and a teasing laugh escaped her. She gazed up at him expectantly.

He leaned an arm on the door frame and stared at that mouth of hers and remembered how fine it had felt to kiss her. "What can I do for you, Callie?" It came out low and a little rough, as though he was trying to seduce her.

And hey. Maybe he was.

She blinked and the tip of her pink tongue came out and touched the beautiful bow of her upper lip. "I…" A frown creased her brow. "I thought you wanted to talk to me."

If he said no straight-out, this moment would be over. He didn't want it to be over, even though he knew he should have never let it get started in the first place. He had so many good intentions when it came to her. But right now, he didn't give two red cents for good intentions.

He wanted only to go on standing here in front of the door in the family store after closing time, standing here with Callie, her perfume on the air and her shining eyes locked with his.

As he tried to decide whether to kiss her or put a little effort into pretending he knew what she was talking about, she spoke again. "Your mother just called me?" she asked hopefully. "She said you were here at the store and you really needed a private word with me…."

"Mom." He shook his head. "Why am I not surprised?"

"So you…didn't ask her to call me?" Her cheeks had turned the most gorgeous shade of pink. And then she groaned and let her head drop back against the door. "Oh, right. Of course you didn't. If you had something to say to me, you would pick up the phone and call me yourself."

"She's shameless, my mother. She doesn't want me to miss my chance with you."

A smile bloomed—and then she seemed to catch herself. The smile dimmed a little. "But what about you, Nate? What do *you* want, really?"

He couldn't resist. He lifted a hand and ran his thumb along the velvet plumpness of her lower lip. Amazing. Touching her. It got to him, got to him real good. She was something special, something real and true. Someone honest to the core, all wrapped up in the prettiest package. Someone he'd tried so hard to be cynical about. Someone the likes of which he'd never thought to find again.

"Nate. Will you please answer me?"

"So beautiful…" He hadn't really meant to say that out loud.

She cleared her throat. “So, um, I should go?”

He touched her chin, traced the soft, firm shape of her jaw with his index finger. “Yeah. You should go. Stay.”

Her tender mouth quivered. “You have to pick one or the other.”

He guided a swatch of glossy hair behind her ear and then, with his index finger, followed the perfect shape of that ear. Up and around and down—and after that, he just kept on going, trailing his finger along the side of her astonishingly silky throat. She shivered a little, and her eyes lowered to half-mast.

“I’m having trouble,” he confessed gruffly. “I can’t seem to get you out of my mind.” He caught her chin and lifted it higher, positioning that unforgettable mouth of hers for a kiss he knew he shouldn’t claim. She let out a slow, shaky breath. He breathed her in, gratefully. “So maybe my mother was right, after all. I did want to talk to you in private. I just couldn’t admit it to myself until you got here. And I have to tell you, I hate it when my mother’s right.”

Those eyes, deepest brown with golden lights, searched his face. “Then…what—”

He could only repeat, “What?”

“—did you want to say to me?”

He went with the first thing that popped into his desire-addled brain. “I saw you talking to Paige today….” Not the best choice of topics, he decided. But it couldn’t be helped. All his conversational filters just stopped working around her.

She drew herself up a little straighter, closed her softly parted lips. And swallowed. “She told me about the war hero you invited to the final debate of the race for mayor."

He still had his hand under her chin. He let it fall. But he didn't step away. He just couldn't bear to put distance between them. Every time he saw her it was like this. And the need to be close to her just kept getting stronger. "It's true," he said in a flat voice. "I went after Sutter to discredit Collin. But I got what I deserved. It backfired on me big-time because Paige stood up and exposed what I'd done for the dirty dealing it was."

She looked at him kind of wonderingly. "You're not going to even try to make excuses for yourself?"

He did step back then. Because if he couldn't stay away from her, she at least had a right to understand—who he was, what he'd done, what kind of man she was dealing with.

"There is no excuse," he said. "I started out on the town council wanting to serve the people of Rust Creek Falls. I really did. But I ended up…losing my perspective, I guess you could say. The day after the flood, for example…."

She stared up at him, waiting. "Yeah?"

Why was he telling her this? Why had he told her half the things he'd already revealed?

"Nate. Please. Go on."

He shook his head. But he did go on. "The mayor had been killed during the storm. I was on the council, and the other members deferred to me. We had nine trained guys on search and rescue. I decided that was enough. That we should get all the volunteers together and put them to work on cleanup. I was more worried about flood damage than the people who might be stranded or injured…or worse. Collin stood up and said we needed everyone on search and rescue first. I tried to back him down. But he knew he was right—and he was. And the whole town got behind him. We did the right thing first, search and rescue.

"Later, when Collin decided to run for mayor, he did it because he wanted to serve, wanted the best for Rust Creek Falls. By then, I only wanted to *win,* to beat him. Serving was an afterthought. I see that now."

"You've changed since then."

"God, I hope so."

"What changed you?"

He shrugged. "I lost. Sometimes a little humbling is good for a man. And then my sister married a Traub. And Collin's turning out to be a better mayor than I ever would have been. And then I…came into a little money. They say money's the root of all evil. I wouldn't say it's been that way for me. I can do what I want now. I've had to do some thinking about that, about what I really want. That's turned out to be good for me. And…" He knew he shouldn't go on.

But she wasn't letting him off the hook. "And what?"

He gave it to her. There was no point in lying about it anymore. "And now there's you. You're…in my mind, Callie Kennedy."

"Oh. Well…" She looked at him as though he'd hung the moon. She shouldn't do that.

He didn't deserve that. "I said I was broken."

"Yeah?"

"Sometimes you make me think I just might be fixable."

She watched him so steadily. And then she reached out her slim hand and wrapped it around the back of his neck. Her fingers were cool. Still, they made him burn. She pulled him into her.

He went without protest—eagerly even—moving back into place with her, up close and personal, bracing his arm against the door frame again.

She said, "Paige doesn't trust you."

"I don't blame her. You probably shouldn't trust me, either."

"She sees the old you. She doesn't know how much you've changed."

"People don't change. Not really."

She tipped her head to the side, considering. "Maybe not. But sometimes they do lose their way. And then some of them manage to find it again. I, um…"

He bent a little closer. He couldn't seem to stop himself. He pressed his rough cheek to her soft one and he whispered in her ear, "You what?"

"I believe you, Nate," she whispered back. "I believe that, wherever you went wrong once, you've found your way again."

He kissed her cheek, heard her soft, sweet sigh. "I don't feel all that confident about where I'm headed. I don't even know where that might be."

"But you're on the right track. I…believe in you. And that's pretty wild, because I'm a girl who wasn't going to believe anything a guy told me ever again, a girl who was supposed to be swearing off men."

He kissed her lips then. They tasted softer, sweeter, better than ever. "You better go ahead and tell me about him."

"Him?"

"Don't play coy. You know what I mean. Tell me about that other guy, the guy in Chicago."

She wrinkled up her nose at him. "It's nothing new, nothing that hasn't happened before. And I feel like such an idiot whenever I think about it."

He stroked a hand down her hair, caught a stray curl and wrapped it around his finger. It made a loose corkscrew when he let it free. "Tell me. I need to know these things about you."

"All the dumb things I've done, you mean?"

"I'm guessing you weren't dumb in the least. You were just your true self, and whoever he was, he let you down."

She shut her eyes and leaned her head back against the door. "All right. Here goes. His name was David. Dr. David Worth."

He nuzzled her neck, pressed a row of kisses along the tender ridge of her collarbone. "A surgeon, you said the other night…."

"Yeah."

"I hate him." He kissed the words onto her skin.

She gave a low chuckle. He drank in that sound. "A plastic surgeon, as a matter of fact."

"I hate him more."

"I guess I was dazzled at first. He had a penthouse apartment downtown, in the Loop, which is arguably the best of the best when it comes to living in Chicago. And…well, you know. Everything money can buy."

"I thought money didn't thrill you."

"And I'm trying to explain to you why it doesn't, how I learned my lesson not to be impressed with some jerk just because he's got money to burn."

"So there's no hope, then?"

"Hope of what?"

"Of changing your mind and thrilling you with the size of my bank account," he teased.

She chuckled. "None."

"I had a feeling you would say that." And then he bent a little closer, close enough to rub noses with her. "Go on."

"I was with him for five years. I kept my own place, but I considered him my guy. I was serious about what I had with him. He took me to the best restaurants. We vacationed all over the world."

"All over the world, huh? The way your dad does with your stepmom?"

She gave him a wry smile. "Yeah. Pretty much."

"The guy was like your dad?"

"Oh, yeah. It was classic, I guess. My father deserts our family—and I grow up and start dating a guy just like him. And David pushed me to stay in administration, where I wasn't happy. He wanted me to be more of a businesswoman than a real nurse. With him, I was someone I didn't want to be."

"So you dumped him." He stroked her cheek with the backs of his fingers and she trembled a little. "Good for you."

"Dumped him?" She sifted her cool hand up into his hair. He wished she would just keep on doing that and never, ever stop. "Not exactly. He wanted me to move in with him. I stalled. I had this feeling that it just wasn't right with him and me. He said he understood, that he would give me time to think it over. And then I decided I was being an idiot, that I loved him and he loved me. I couldn't wait to tell him. I went to his fabulous penthouse apartment to surprise him. And did I ever surprise him. He was there with another woman."

Nate dipped his head to her and breathed a bad word against her neck.

She said, "I decided not to move in with him, after all."

"Good choice."

"I wrote to Emmet instead, and when he said he could make a place for me, I packed up my things in a U-Haul and… Well, you know the rest."

Out on the street, the band had started up. They were playing a great old song by the Man in Black.

Nate framed her face between his hands. "You really loved him?"

She held his eyes. And shook her head. "I look back and, well, I thought I did at the time. But now I just wonder how I got it so wrong. I never really even *wanted* him. It was more that I thought he was what I *should* want, you know? I didn't even see that I was choosing a man way too much like the father who left me until that moment of truth when I found David with that other woman."

"So it was a good thing, that you caught him cheating."

"Well, Nate, it certainly didn't feel that way at the time."

"I'll bet. The bastard."

"But you're right. It was. A good thing in so many ways. I can't begin to tell you. I might never have come here to Rust Creek, never have found the life I always wanted if Dr. David Worth hadn't been such a complete tool."

"And so you swore off men."

"Well, yeah. I did. But then *you* came along. I liked you that first day, when you picked me up by the side of the road. I liked you even though you really pissed me off."

He laughed low at that. "I was a real SOB to you. I wanted you to hate me. I liked you too much."

"And you didn't *want* to like me," she put in softly. "Because that day was Zoe's day, Zoe's and the baby's."

His throat felt tight. "Yeah."

She reached up, laid her slim, smooth hand on the side of his face. He caught her wrist and turned his mouth into the heart of her palm as she whispered, "This thing with us..."

"Yeah?"

She hitched in a ragged breath as he nipped the soft pad at the base of her thumb. "It feels strong to me, Nate. It feels real."

He was through lying about it. He brought her hand against his chest and held it there. "For me, too."

Her fingers moved against his shirt, caressing him, and her gaze didn't waver. "I want to go with it, see where it takes us."

"Me, too."

"Are you still...thinking about leaving?"

"Not when I'm lookin' at you."

"But you are. I can see it in those green, green eyes of yours. You're still thinking about it."

"Yeah."

"I'm not. This is my home now. Rust Creek Falls is the place for me."

With the hand that wasn't holding hers, he guided a soft curl of hair away from her eye. "I know."

"I'm never again making my life over to fit what a man wants."

"And I will never ask you to." Right then, outside,

the band did something downright amazing. They launched into Dwight Yoakum's "Try Not to Look So Pretty." He laughed. "Will you listen to that?"

She looked adorably bewildered. "What?"

He brought her hand to his lips again and kissed her knuckles one by one. "They're playing our song."

She cocked her head, listening. "*That's* our song? I don't think I'd choose *that* one…."

"You're not lookin' at what I'm lookin' at. And come on." He tugged her away from the door and into his waiting arms. "Dance with me."

Her smile lit up the shadowed store. "Nathan Crawford…"

"What?"

"Oh, I don't know. All right. Let's dance."

She tucked her fine, curvy body against him, and they danced across the old pine floor, skirting the pickle barrel, turning in circles around the wine display, stepping up onto the platform that defined the dry-goods section and then dancing right back down to the main floor again.

When the song ended, they stood near the checkout, swaying together. She had both arms twined around his neck, and he had his hands resting nice and snug on the sweet outward curves of her hips.

It was a simple thing, the *only* thing, to pull her closer, to settle his mouth on hers.

She sighed and opened for him. He tasted the slick, hot places beyond her parted lips and wanted the kiss to go on forever. She affected him so strongly.

Too strongly, probably. But he was so gone on her, he didn't even care.

When he lifted his head, she looked up dreamily at

him through those gold-flecked dark eyes and asked, "What now?"

They probably ought to get out of here. If they stayed and he kept kissing her, he wouldn't want to stop with just kisses. And no way their first time was going to happen in the family store.

Their first time...

Until tonight, he'd never really believed there would be a first time for them.

But he did now. And he realized he found that pretty terrific.

She clasped his shoulders. "Nate. Yoo-hoo. You in there?"

"Right here." He dropped a quick kiss on the end of her beautiful nose. "You want to check out the street dance?"

"Sure."

"Get your hat and I'll grab mine."

He locked up and they went out the front door and down to the street, where at least a hundred couples were dancing under the moon, in the added glow of party lights strung from tree to tree and between the street lamps. He was feeling pretty good about everything.

Until he saw Paige Traub dancing with Sutter a few feet away at exactly the same moment that Paige caught sight of him with Callie in his arms.

Chapter 6

Paige gave him a look. It wasn't a good look. It was an unhappy combination of surprise and dismay at the sight of her friend dancing with him.

Nate wanted to sink right through the asphalt beneath his boots and keep going clear to China.

And, apparently, Callie didn't feel so good about the situation, either. She stiffened in his hold, sucked in a sharp breath—and then seemed to collect herself. "Hey, Paige." She waved.

Paige gave a tiny flick of her hand in response. But she didn't manage an actual smile.

A minute later, the song ended. With a hand at the small of her back, Sutter guided his very pregnant, still-unsmiling wife away.

Callie said, "I'll talk to her." He heard the regret in

her voice. "I probably should have talked to her before…" She let the sentence trail off.

He finished for her. "Before being seen in public with me?"

She tried to deny it. "No, I…" The band launched into the next song, a faster number in a two-step rhythm. She leaned in close. "Walk me home?"

Might as well. The good-time feeling had gone from the evening. He took her hand and led her off the street, onto the sidewalk across from the band. People waved and said hi. He and Callie both nodded and smiled, spreading greetings as they went.

But he didn't slow in his brisk stride and she kept up with him.

The crowd thinned out once they passed the library. By the time they crossed the bridge, the music was much fainter behind them. There were no party lights past the bridge. The half-moon glowed brighter above them, suspended in the darkness, surrounded by the thick scatter of the stars.

It wasn't far. In no time, they were turning onto their block. At her place, he led her up the walk and into the shadow of her front porch.

She opened the door and then waited for him to go in ahead of her.

"Beer?" she asked, once they'd hung their hats on the pegs just inside the door.

He shook his head.

She turned on the lights and gestured him into the great room, where he sat in the easy chair and she perched on the sofa. For a minute or two, neither of them knew where to start. He stared at the dark fireplace, trying not to think of the two of them lying there the other night, of kissing her and kissing her and never wanting to stop.

Might as well get down to it. "Look, Callie. I get the picture. You told Paige not to worry about you and me, that you would have nothing to do with me."

The sequins on her top caught and cast back the light, sparkling brightly as she wrapped her arms around herself and launched into denials. "No. I didn't. I mean…" She chewed on her lower lip a little before adding, "Not exactly."

"Then, what exactly *did* you say?"

"That I'd sworn off men and you were leaving town and nothing was going to happen between us." She leaned toward him. "Oh, Nate. At the time I said it, I meant it."

"When was that?"

She winced. "Um. This morning. But then, tonight, your mother tricked me into coming to find you. And then we started talking and…well, I just had to admit to myself that I'm wild for you and I don't care about all the reasons it might not work out. I want us to have a chance together."

"You're wild for me?" The depressing moment took on a hopeful tinge.

She looked exasperated. "Didn't I already tell you that?"

"I think I would have remembered if you had."

"Well, all right." She tipped that cute chin higher. "I'm wild for you—and I should never have said never about you to Paige. I get that now."

He didn't blame her for what she'd said to Paige. It all made sense to him. If anyone had asked him about him and Callie earlier in the day, he would have done what she had—in fact, he *had* done what she had, essentially, when his mother started in on him about not missing out with her.

"Oh, I don't like that look on your face." Callie jumped to her feet, all urgency now. "Really. It's not like that. Not like I know you must be thinking…."

He couldn't bear to see her so torn up, so sure he would lay blame on her. So he rose, too, and he went to her. "You don't know what I'm thinking." He said it gently.

And she let out a cry and slid around the coffee table and into his arms.

He guided her dark head against his shoulder and stroked her shining hair. "Listen. Are you listening?"

"Yeah." Small. Soft. Unhappy.

"I'm not blaming you." He cradled her sweet face between his hands. "If I seem harsh, it's only because I hate that you might lose a friend over me."

"No. That's not going to happen."

"Callie. It's the way things go here."

"Here?"

"Yeah. In Rust Creek Falls, you're with the Crawfords or you side with the Traubs. Most of us are trying to put the old feud behind us, but sometimes it still gets rocky. I don't like you in the middle of it."

Her eyes narrowed mutinously. "Please don't say you're going to stay away from me. Tonight, I've felt that we're finally getting somewhere. And if you turn your back on me now… I mean it, Nate Crawford. Do not do that to me again."

"I won't, I promise you. We're past that now."

"Good."

"It's just that there's something I need to do, something I should have done months ago."

"What?" she demanded.

He bent to press a soft kiss on those upturned lips. "Don't worry. It's nothing that awful."

"But what *is* it?"

"I'll explain, I promise. After I figure out how to go about it, after I…get it done."

"Nathan. Honestly. You are the most aggravating man."

He laughed.

She glared. "This is not funny."

"Yes, it is. Think about it. For so many years, I was the good boy, the fine, upstanding Rust Creek Falls citizen, the one people admired and counted on to take a leadership position. And Collin Traub was the bad one, the troublemaker, the one you couldn't trust with your daughters. And now look what's happened. Our positions have reversed. Collin's happily married to the prim and pretty kindergarten teacher Willa Christensen. Have you met Willa?"

"Yeah. She and Paige are good friends. I really like her."

"Everybody does. She's a great person, and she and Collin are pillars of the community. And I'm the lowlife who used dirty tactics to try and win the mayor's race. I'm the guy Paige is certain is going to do you wrong."

"I *will* talk to her. I'll make her see that you're a much better man than she realizes."

He smoothed a long, thick lock of silky dark hair back over her shoulder. "Thank you. But it's not your mess to straighten out."

She huffed a little. "I don't like where this is going. I don't even *know* where this is going."

He could understand her confusion. He felt it, too. He wanted to soothe her, to promise it would all work out all right. But that would be a promise he might not be able to keep.

She started to say something.

With a muttered oath, he bent his head and kissed her. She made a low, tender noise in her throat, slid her arms up around his neck and kissed him back.

For a few dreamy minutes, he forgot everything but the feel of her mouth under his, the warmth of her sweet body pressed close against him and the hungry thudding of his own yearning heart.

Finally, with aching reluctance, he lifted his head. "I should go…."

She scowled at him. "I don't get it. Here we are, finally working things out…and you want to go."

"I didn't say I *wanted* to go. I just think it's best if I go."

"Well, you're wrong."

"Before we get in any deeper together, I have to do what I can to fix what I've broken." He peeled her arms from around his neck and held her away from him, her hands between his. "Give me a few days to make things right—or at least, as right as I *can* make them."

"What are you planning? Why can't you just tell me?"

"Stop nagging, woman," he commanded, grinning to take the edge off the words. He kissed her again—a hard, quick one—and then he let go of her hands and stepped back from her. "A few days. Please?"

"You always make things so difficult."

"Trust me?"

She braced her fists on her hips. "Actually, I do trust you. Don't make me live to regret it."

"I will be back." He headed for the door.

"And don't just assume I'll be waiting with open arms when you do," she called after him.

He snagged his hat from the peg and pulled open the door. "With you, Callie, I don't assume anything." And he left before he could give himself an excuse to stay.

Callie called Paige the next morning. She got right to the point. "Okay, I'm sure you're probably wondering about what you saw at the street dance last night. I realize I said there was no chance of anything going on between me and Nate. I was wrong. Last night, before the dance, we talked, Nate and me. And, well, yes, now something is definitely going on between us." *Even if he did walk out on me when I told him I wanted him to stay.*

Paige answered carefully, "I just don't want you to get hurt, you know?"

"I know. And *he* knows he did wrong by Sutter. He says he's going to try to make it right."

"How?"

"Well, he didn't exactly explain himself."

"Somehow, I don't feel very reassured by that news." At least there was humor in Paige's tone. "And if he hurts you, he'll be answering to me."

Callie felt equal parts warm-fuzzy and apprehensive. "You're a good friend, Paige. But Nate is a lot better man than you think."

"Just tell him he'd better treat you right or else."

"He's a good man. I believe that."

Paige wasn't buying. "Just…be careful. Please."

What could Callie say to that? Clearly, she *wasn't* being careful. And after all her brave talk about swearing off men, too.

She thought of David. Her brain had kept insisting that David was the right guy when her heart had known all along that he was all wrong.

With Nate, it was the opposite. Her brain warned her that Nate had too many issues, that he might be a good guy deep down, but that didn't mean he was a good bet for love.

Her heart, on the other hand? It kept pushing her toward Nate. With every beat, her heart seemed to whisper his name.

Was she doing it again, falling for the wrong kind of guy and heading for a big, fat heartbreak? Paige certainly seemed to think so.

And Callie understood Paige's doubts. She just didn't share them. Not in her heart, anyway. And with Nate, her heart ruled.

They talked for a few minutes longer. When she hung up, Callie felt better, knowing Paige was still her friend. She also felt thoroughly annoyed at Nate for deciding to "make things right" and then walking out on her without giving her a clue as to how he planned to do that.

Nate spent Saturday checking on what his money had been doing. It soothed him somehow, to witness the results of his financial contributions. It made him feel that he was finally doing something right, that a guy *could* turn his life around—even if he wasn't sure where he was going now he was facing in a whole new direction.

Yeah, all right. Money didn't buy everything. But it sure made life better for folks if they had it when they needed it. He visited three small ranches in the Rust Creek Falls Valley where his lottery winnings had been at work. The money had rebuilt a damaged barn and paid for a new well. It had replaced a house too flood-damaged to salvage and provided college educations for a couple of promising ranchers' daughters who wouldn't have been able to afford to go otherwise.

The ranchers he called on were all good people, people he'd known all his life. They invited him in and offered him coffee and assumed he was just stopping by to be neighborly. They had no idea he was the one behind the mysterious foundation that had helped them to pay for the things they really needed but hadn't known how they would afford.

When he got back to town, he went to the library. Before he checked out a few books, he toured the addition recently built on in back. The new nonfiction wing had increased the library's square footage by 50 percent.

The trust had done that, too. Just as it had paid for the computer room in the new community center, where people who didn't have access to a PC or tablet or smartphone of their own could surf the internet or check their email, where schoolkids could do their homework using state-of-the-art equipment.

By the end of the day, after seeing that he actually had done some good in his town, he felt calmer inside himself. He felt almost able to let go of a little more of his false pride and do what he should have done long before now.

At home alone that night, he sat out on his back deck with a tall, cold one and watched the darkness fall and the stars fill the wide, clear sky. Over the back fence, he could see the top of the window in the side wall of Callie's kitchen. The light was on in there.

He wanted to jump the fence and pound on her back door until she answered. He wanted to grab her close and cover her mouth with his and kiss her until he forgot everything but the wonder of holding her in his arms.

But he did no such thing.

He'd promised himself he wouldn't. Not yet.

Sunday he went out to the Shooting Star and worked alongside Jesse taking care of the horses. In the afternoon, they rode out to check on the other stock, and that night, he went to his parents' house for Sunday dinner. All evening, his mom kept giving him significant looks, waiting for him to say something about the way she'd manipulated Callie into coming to find him at the store.

He praised her pot roast and kissed her cheek as he was leaving. But never once did he give her even a hint of how her matchmaking tricks might have worked out.

Monday morning, he was up well before dawn. It was pitch-dark outside as he backed his pickup from the garage and headed out of town.

Sutter Traub bred and trained horses for a living. He owned a successful stable in Seattle and he'd bought a ranch in Rust Creek Falls Valley when he moved back home. Talk around town was that Sutter and Paige would eventually be renovating the run-down house at the ranch and moving out there to live. But for now, the couple lived in Paige's house at North Pine and Cedar Streets, and Sutter got up good and early most mornings to drive out to the ranch and spend his day with his horses.

Nate was waiting on the steps of the old ranch house when the lights of Sutter's pickup cut through the dark and shone on him sitting there. He rose and stood waiting as Sutter stopped the truck and turned off the engine, dousing the lights. Nate heard the pickup door open and shut as Sutter got out.

"Nate Crawford," Sutter said from the darkness. "I can't say you're welcome here."

"I can't say I blame you," Nate answered slow and clear. "But I would very much appreciate a few minutes of your time."

"Do I need to get my shotgun from the rack?"

Nate didn't know whether to chuckle—or duck. "I'm hoping you won't feel the need to shoot me."

Boots crunched gravel as Sutter approached. He was built broad and brawny and stood an inch or two under Nate's six-three. He kept coming until his dark form was close enough that Nate could have reached out and brushed his sleeve.

For about ten never-ending seconds, the two stood facing each other.

Finally, Sutter broke the thick silence. "Sit." Nate dropped back to the bottom step and Sutter sat down, too. "Okay. What brings you out here before the crack of dawn?"

"I think it's time I made amends to you, Sutter."

There was a silence filled with cricket sounds and

the whinny of one of the horses in a nearby paddock. "Amends for what?" Sutter asked as if he didn't know.

"For coming after you at that last mayoral debate in an attempt to get at Collin. It was a low-down, rotten thing I did that day."

Sutter held his peace for several seconds. Nate braced for a fist in the face. But in the end, Sutter only said mildly, "Yes, it was."

Nate continued with his apology. "I knew the truth, but I twisted it for my own ends. I was willing to do just about anything to win the race for mayor. Even drag you through the mud again to make Collin look bad."

"And how'd that work out for you, Nate?"

Nate's pride jabbed at him. He had to fight the urge to say something hostile. The whole point was to take his licks and convince the man beside him in the dark that he knew he'd done wrong and wanted to make up for it. "It backfired on me, big-time. I got what I deserved."

There was another silence. Nate's nerves stretched taut. Finally, Sutter said, "Well, it all worked out just fine for me. My candidate won. I moved back home where I always wanted to be. And I married the love of my life. I'll be a father soon. I want to teach my son or daughter not to grow up holding grudges. But before I shake your hand, Nathan Crawford, I think you got someone else you need to say sorry to besides me."

Had Nate known that was coming? "Collin," he said so low in his throat it came out like a curse.

Out on the horizon, he saw a sliver of light: dawn on the way.

Sutter got up. Nate rose to stand beside him.

Sutter said, "Tonight. Seven o'clock. The Ace. You can buy me and Collin a beer."

Chapter 7

Collin Traub had thick black hair and eyes to match. Growing up, there wasn't a dare he wouldn't take. He rode the rodeo, broke a lot of hearts and never went to college. Everyone said he would come to no good.

He'd fooled them all. Collin was a talented saddle maker by trade and, as it turned out, a politician by avocation. He'd married Willa Christensen a year ago. They were happy together, Collin and Willa. Everyone remarked on it, even Nate's mother, who'd never in her life until then had a kind thing to say about Collin Traub.

Nate dreaded the meeting with Collin. It was tough enough to try and make amends to Sutter, who had never called him dirty names or punched him in the face hard enough to black both his eyes.

Making amends to Collin Traub? Uh-uh. Never in his life had he planned to do any such thing.

For the rest of the afternoon, Nate considered ways he might back out of apologizing to his lifelong nemesis. But every time he just about convinced himself there was no way he was meeting Collin at the Ace in the Hole, he would think of Callie. He would see her shining eyes looking up at him, see the faith she'd put in him, the trust she had in his supposed deep-down goodness.

And he would know that he had to do it. He had to be…better than he'd ever thought he was capable of being.

He walked into the Ace at six-thirty, figuring he'd do well to get there first, to try and take a little control of a situation in which he found himself at a total disadvantage. He knew of a certain booth in back, in the corner, where he and the Traub brothers could take care of business without the whole town watching.

Unfortunately, the Traub brothers were way ahead of him.

Sutter and Collin were already there, sitting at the bar with Dallas and one of their other brothers, Braden. Collin spotted Nate instantly in the mirror on the back wall.

Their eyes met and locked.

And Nate felt dread and something like fury, all in a lead-weighted ball in the pit of his stomach. He thought of all the names Collin had called him when they were growing up: "Goody-boy" and "Mama's little sweetheart," "butt-wipe" and "Little College Man," among so many others too down and dirty to ever repeat.

And then there were the fights they'd had, the way

they'd go at each other, no holds barred, punching and kicking, each of them determined to finish the other off for good every time.

Never in a hundred million years had he imagined he would come to this moment: to be standing in the Ace, staring eye to eye in the mirror with Collin Traub, planning to humble himself, to tell his enemy that he had gone too far and wanted to apologize.

Collin turned around and faced him. "Nate."

Nate gave him a nod. "Collin."

"You're early," the other man said mildly.

Nate took off his hat. "Not as early as you."

A whisper went through the Ace. And after the whisper, the place went dead silent. You could have heard a toothpick drop to the peanut-shell-strewn floor.

Then Dallas stepped forward. His sister's husband offered his hand. "Hey, Nate."

Nate took it and shook it. "Hey." Gratitude washed through him. He was thankful to his brother-in-law for stepping up like that, for reminding every staring eye in the place that Crawfords and Traubs *could* get along, generations of bitter feuding to the contrary.

And then Sutter said, "How 'bout that corner booth in back?"

Nate knew the one—it was the same one he'd been thinking of. "Sounds good."

Sutter led the way back there, with Collin behind him and Nate taking up the rear. Braden and Dallas remained at the bar. The booth was empty. Collin and Sutter sat on one side, Nate on the other.

One of the waitresses stepped up. They all ordered longnecks.

There was no small talk while they waited for the

beer. Nate put his hat on the seat beside him and reminded himself that he could and would do this, that he would be a better man for it.

Finally, the girl came back with the beers. She put them down quick and hustled away.

Nate lifted his longneck. "To…our town," he said, because it seemed like he ought to say something.

They clinked bottles and drank.

And then, there it was. The moment that was never supposed to happen.

His turn to grovel to a couple of Traubs and be a better man.

He set down his beer, straightened his shoulders and made himself look straight into his lifelong enemy's black eyes. "Okay, it's like this. Collin Traub, I apologize for bringing Sergeant Dean Riddell to that last debate, for coming after Sutter to try and bring you down. It was wrong and it was low and I never should have stooped so far. You have turned out to be a damn fine mayor, so it all worked out as it should, the way I see it now. But I have owed it to you to step up and tell you I know what I did and I know it was wrong and, if it's possible, I would like to find a way to…ahem…" His throat kind of locked up about then. He kept his gaze steady on the man across from him and pushed at the point of lockdown until the words broke through again. "I want to make things right, make it square between us. Or if not square, well, at least I want you to know I regret being such an SOB and I won't be pulling any crap like that again." What else? There was more he should say, wasn't there?

But it was all too unreal. Sitting in a booth across from Collin, trying to make things right.

Could anyone ever make things right after years and years of hatred and bitter battles and continued bad behaviors on both sides?

Collin took another long pull off his beer. He set the bottle down. “Sounds good to me.” He turned to his brother. “What do you say, Sutter?”

Sutter gave a slow nod. “Yeah. I’m good with it. Things are changing in this town. And it’s about time we all got past hating each other just because hating is what we’ve always done.”

Nate stared from one man to the other, not really believing what they were telling him. “So…that’s it, then? You accept my apology?”

Both men answered, “Yeah,” at the same time.

“Well, all right. That’s great. I…” He realized he wanted out of there, right away. Before one of them changed his mind. He reached for his hat. “Guess I’ll be on my way.”

“Wait a minute,” said Sutter.

Dread coiling in his gut again, Nate set his hat back down.

Collin said, “I heard you came into a little extra money….”

Money? He had a moment’s absolute certainty that they knew he’d won the lottery. But then he remembered the cover story, about his supposed investments paying off. Everyone knew about that. “Right. I did the apologizing. Now comes the part where I actually have to make the amends. And that includes money somehow?”

Collin laughed. There didn’t seem to be any malice in the sound. Just humor. And plenty of that. “Well, yeah. But we're not shaking you down or anything. Right, Sutter?"

Sutter grunted. "Not too much, anyway. And it's for a good cause."

Nate eyed them warily. "What cause?"

"People left town after the flood." Collin was suddenly stating the obvious. "But then a whole lot more people came to help us recover. As of now, we've got something of a population boom in Rust Creek Falls."

"Yeah?" Nate encouraged, hoping the other man was getting to the point.

"This town needs jobs," Collin said. "When the rebuilding is over, the new people are going to need work or they're gone. We don't want them to leave. We don't want Rust Creek Falls to turn into one of those towns with a bunch of boarded-up houses and more people getting out every year. We want this town to grow and prosper."

"And we want your help with that," added Sutter.

Nate put in gingerly, "You may have heard that *I'm* planning on leaving town…."

Both men gave him the deadeye. Sutter asked, "Well, *are* you?"

"I haven't decided yet, but it's more than a possibility."

Collin and Sutter shared a speaking glance. Then Sutter said, "Whatever. Your money's good either way, right?"

And Collin went on, "We're thinking a resort, like the one down in Thunder Canyon. The Thunder Canyon Resort has been a real economy booster down there. A successful resort brings in the tourists, which means money for the merchants and jobs for the citizens."

Nate put up both hands. "Look, boys. I know nothing about running a resort—plus, as I said, I'm considering a move."

"We don't want you to run it," said Collin. "We don't expect your participation in the planning or the building, either. We just want you to invest in it, put your money in it."

Nate wondered why he hadn't heard about this resort project before. After all, news traveled fast in Rust Creek Falls. "You have a group of investors together?"

The brothers shared another look, this one kind of rueful. Then Collin said, "We got nothing. It's an idea at this point."

Sutter threw in, "But everything starts with an idea, right?"

Collin added, "*And* with the money."

Nate asked, "You got anything on paper?"

The brothers shook their heads in unison.

And Nate almost laughed. But then he thought about how, if money was needed, he did have that. He thought about what it really meant to make amends. The Traub brothers had been better than civil to him. They'd been downright generous. They'd accepted his apology without making him sweat as much as he probably deserved to.

He wasn't about to laugh in their faces because they brought up some half-baked idea to bring jobs to town. "So it's in the beginning stages, this project," he suggested.

Collin said, "We just want to know, is a resort something you would invest in, given we had a real plan for one, given that we could get a group together?"

Nate thought about all the money he'd given away already. What was a little more in the interest of peace between the Crawfords and the Traubs?

"Yeah," he said finally. "You bring me a plan, and I'm in."

"Welcome to the Rust Creek Falls Newcomers' Club," said Lissa Roarke Christensen. She stood at the portable podium next to the refreshment table in the large meeting room of the Grace Traub Community Center.

Lissa had come to Thunder Canyon early last fall to write about the flood, about the spirit of the little town that could not be broken, even by a disaster of epic proportions. Lissa's blog and articles had raised nationwide awareness and brought a lot of help to Rust Creek Falls. And while she was doing all she could to see that the town recovered, Lissa had found love—and marriage—with the Rust Creek Falls sheriff, Gage Christensen.

"It seems only right," Lissa said, "that we newcomers band together, for the sake of the town we now call home—and for the sake of the friendships we share and hope to build. Tonight, it's a social night only. We'll visit, get to know each other better and maybe start talking about the direction we want to take as a group, the things we want to see accomplished in our new town. There's coffee and soft drinks, cookies and brownies." She gestured at the refreshment table. It was covered with goodies provided by just about everyone present. "All completely calorie free, of course."

Everyone chuckled. "So help yourselves," Lissa said, "and thanks for coming. It's great to be neighbors in our new hometown."

Enthusiastic applause filled the room.

Mallory leaned close to Callie. "Come on. Let's get some coffee."

So Callie helped herself to a cup of decaf and a large, delicious brownie as laughter and conversation filled the air. She and Mallory chatted and she thought how she was glad to be there. It kind of took the edge off waiting around for Nate to show up at her door and tell her he'd done whatever mysterious thing he needed to do before the two of them could continue their relationship.

If they even *had* a relationship. Since he'd left her in her great room Friday night, she'd wondered more than once if the thing between them could even be called a relationship.

She doubted it sometimes.

And sometimes she just wanted to march over to his house and tell him to get over himself. They needed to take this thing between them to…wherever the heck it wanted to go.

Mallory said, "Callie? Did you hear a single word I said?"

Callie shook herself and apologized and said, "I guess you'd better tell me again."

Mallory reshared the latest gossip. Apparently, there was some mysterious benefactor giving out cash around town under cover of a trust called Brighter Horizons.

Lissa Christensen, who was standing with them, nodded. "True. I've been looking into it. I'm sure there's a story there. Brighter Horizons contributed about a third of the money that built this center. And not only that, the trust has put a couple hundred thousand into repairs at the high school and into more upgrades of the elementary school." The elementary school had been badly damaged in the flood and then mostly rebuilt. It had reopened at New Year's. "Not to mention there have been Brighter Horizons' checks going out to several of the local ranchers who are now able to replace equipment, farm buildings and homes destroyed by the flood."

"Wow," said Callie. "We need funds at the clinic. How do I get in touch with Brighter Horizons?"

"I wish I knew," said Lissa. "Nobody seems to know. But whoever's behind all this generosity is deeply familiar with this town and the valley. Whoever it is knows which people and institutions are in need—and has whipped out a very large checkbook to fix a lot of problems. I would love to find out who's behind Brighter Horizons. It would make a great story, an uplifting story. And that's my favorite kind. But so far, Rust Creek Falls's benefactor seems determined to remain anonymous."

The meeting broke up at a little after nine.

It was a beautiful evening and Callie had left her SUV in her garage. She walked home through the gathering darkness thinking about Rust Creek Falls's mysterious benefactor, imagining ways she might let Brighter Horizons know that a needy institution, the clinic, seemed to have slipped under its donation radar.

She stopped on the Main Street Bridge and gazed down at the clear, rushing creek waters and considered maybe putting up notices around town:

Attention Brighter Horizons: The Rust Creek Falls Clinic Needs Your Money, Too!

Chuckling to herself at the idea, she started walking again.

And the thought of Nate kind of drifted into her mind the way such thoughts often did. Her smile faded as she turned onto Commercial Street.

What was he doing tonight? A girl could get discouraged waiting around for him to do whatever it was he just *had* to do and come back around again. A girl could start thinking she'd made another big romantic mistake to get her hopes up over a guy like him.

As she approached her own house she couldn't help but notice that the lights were out at his place.

So, where was he tonight? She told herself to give it up, let it go, don't even wonder.

But then she turned onto her front walk and the man in question materialized from the shadows of her front porch, holding his hat.

Chapter 8

She really did consider playing it cool.

For like maybe a second and a half.

But then she looked in his eyes and she saw so much. Gladness. Hope. Yearning.

All the things she guessed were reflected in her eyes, too.

With a soft cry, she ran to him.

He opened his arms and gathered her in, laughing. And she was laughing with him as he picked her up and swung her around in a circle right there in front of her bottom step.

Her feet touched the ground and she beamed up at him. “Is it done…whatever it is?”

“Yeah,” he said. “Tonight. It’s done. At last.”

And she punched him in the shoulder—not too hard

but hard enough. "Are you ever going to tell me *what* you're talking about?"

He tipped up her chin and brushed the sweetest kiss so lightly across her waiting lips. "Are you ever going to invite me in?"

Fair enough. She took his hand and led him up the steps and into her house. He hooked his hat on the peg by the door as she pulled him into the great room and switched on the lights. "Okay. You're in. And I'm listening."

He took her in his arms again. "You look so good." He ran a hand down her hair. "Really good. But then, that's no surprise. You always do. From the first moment I saw you, standing by the side of the road with your pom-pom hat and your red gas can."

She gazed up at him, thinking that he looked good, too. And not only handsome but…happier inside himself somehow. "Thank you—and I'm waiting."

He cleared his throat. "All right. I'll tell you. Tonight I had a beer with Sutter and Collin at the Ace in the Hole. I apologized for my behavior during the mayor's race. I…took responsibility for being a low-down jackass."

She was more gaping than gazing now. "Seriously?"

"Yeah."

"And?"

"They accepted my apology."

She thought of Paige. Maybe, just maybe, Paige would stop worrying now. "Just like that? You're friends with Collin and Sutter Traub?"

"Well, I wouldn't say we're friends, exactly, but we parted on good terms—after they asked me to contribute to a little project of theirs to get investors together and open a resort."

"I think my head is spinning. Sutter and Collin are opening a resort?"

"It's just in the early stages, something they're trying to get off the ground."

"And you said you'd help them?"

"I said I would invest. And I will, if it goes anywhere."

She pulled him over to the sofa, pushed him down and sat beside him. "Amazing."

He threaded his big fingers between her smaller ones. She rested her head on his shoulder. It felt really good there. "I've been missing you," he said, his voice just a little rough.

"I've been right next door the whole time," she scolded.

"I know. It's been driving me crazy."

"Good. I'm glad."

"You make me think I don't want to move away, after all. You make me think that all I could ever want is right here in my hometown."

"Good," she said again and felt a sharp prick of sadness. "But you still haven't decided, have you, whether to stay or go?"

"No." He said it quietly. But firmly, too.

And she whispered, "Tell you what. Let's not talk about your leaving."

His fingers tightened on hers. "Maybe you'll want to come with me."

"Maybe you don't want to go, not really."

He said her name gently, a little regretfully, "Callie…"

And she put her other hand over their joined ones. "Shh. Let it be."

He made a sound that might have been agreement. And then he turned his head and pressed a kiss into her hair. A shiver moved over her skin. Delicious. Exciting. "I walked back here from the Ace at a little after eight. I didn't even go to my house. Just came here and sat on your porch and waited for you."

She snuggled in closer. He eased his hand from hers, but only so that he could wrap his arm around her and draw her even closer to him.

"I went to the first meeting of the Newcomers' Club," she said. "It's mostly the women who've come to town since the flood." He tugged on a loose lock of her pinned-up hair, then traced a figure eight on her arm with a playful finger. She smiled at the tenderness in his touch. "Lissa Christensen gave a welcome speech and we all ate too many brownies and shared the latest gossip—ever heard of Brighter Horizons?"

His teasing finger stopped in midtrace. "Uh. No, I don't think so...."

Something in his voice—in the stilling of his touch—alerted her. She lifted her head to look at him.

He frowned, asked, "What?" a little too innocently.

She stared at him a moment longer and then shook her head. "I don't know...." And then she settled against him again. "Nothing. Where was I?"

He pressed another kiss into her hair. "Something called Brighter Horizons?"

"Right. Lissa says it's some foundation or something—a trust, I think she said. Nobody knows who's behind it, but the trust has donated a lot of money all over town. Lissa wants to get the inside scoop and write about it."

"I'll bet." He growled the words against her hair.

"Lissa says it has to be someone who knows Rust Creek Falls, because Brighter Horizons seems to be putting money where it's really needed." She chuckled to herself. "While I walked home, I tried to think up ways to get in touch with them, whoever they are, to let them know they forgot about the clinic and we will be glad to make excellent use of any random funds they toss our way."

"How do you know they forgot about you? Maybe they're on it, and you just haven't gotten your big check yet."

"I wish."

"Aw, come on. Have a little faith, will you?"

She lifted away from him and then reached out and clasped the back of his warm, strong neck. "Faith. All right. If you say so...."

He was looking at her as though he never wanted to look away. "I've missed you," he said again. Tonight, his eyes were moss-green, a ring of gold and amber around the dark irises. He smelled so good, of that fresh, outdoorsy aftershave he always wore and something else that was all Nate, all man.

"I'm just glad you're here." She pulled him toward her, wanting his kiss.

He didn't disappoint her. His lips touched hers. She sighed and opened, inviting him in. He kissed her for a long time, sitting there on her sofa with her as night fell outside.

And when he finally pulled back from her, they both

opened their eyes at the same time. She thought that he looked at her trustingly, and longingly, too.

She understood that look. She felt the same way. For months she had tried to deny this thing between them, not even letting herself speak to him until the first of June when she came to collect on that bet she'd won. She'd seen him a lot around town in the months between January and June, and every time she saw him, she yearned to walk right up to him and get him talking, maybe even to ask him if he'd go to dinner with her sometime.

But she hadn't done it. She'd told herself to stay away, that her friend Paige said he was trouble and she was taking a break from the male of the species, anyway.

In the end, though, the attraction she felt for him would not be denied. And now, at last, she'd come to the place within herself where she didn't want to deny it.

He wasn't like David. She knew it to her bones. He'd done wrong things, but he had owned that wrongness, wrestled with it, come to grips with the need to make things right and then taken steps to do just that.

No, not like David, though she knew that, like David, he would probably hurt her. But when he did, it wouldn't be out of cruelty and thoughtlessness and a lying heart. He wouldn't betray her the way that David had, the way her father had when she was only a child. He would hurt her because of that need in him to go, to leave the home she'd come to love. Because of that broken place in him that maybe wasn't quite so broken anymore.

But wasn't completely healed, either.

He wouldn't be happy if he went. She knew that, down in the deepest, truest part of her. But she couldn't make him see that. He had to figure it out for himself.

He touched her face the way he liked to do, his fingers light and cherishing on her cheek. "What now, Callie Kennedy?"

She caught his hand again and stood.

He held on to her fingers, but didn't rise. Instead, he looked up at her from under his brows, a lazy look, more than a little bit hungry, a look that excited her, a look that made that lovely weakness down in the womanly core of her.

"Come on," she whispered and gave a tug.

Still, he didn't rise. "Are you sure?"

"I am, yes." That time, when she pulled on his hand, he rose and stood with her, guiding their joined hands around her and pulling her sharply into him. She gasped at the feel of him, pressed against her, hard and wanting. Their twined hands held her tight at the base of her spine. "Nate…"

"Shh." He lowered his mouth and kissed her again, a hard, hot kiss that time, a kiss that plundered the secrets beyond her parted lips, a kiss that made his intentions clear.

She kissed him back, eagerly. And that time, when he lifted his head, she didn't say anything. She just unwound her body from the circle of his arm and led him out of the great room, across the front hall, past the stairs to the upper floor and into her bedroom.

At the side of the bed, she switched on the lamp and turned back the covers, smoothing open the sheets. And then she went into his arms. He drew her close again.

There were more kisses, lingering and sweet.

Until she pulled away a second time to open the drawer in the nightstand. She took out a box of condoms and removed one, setting it within easy reach of the bed.

He chuckled.

She slid him a look. "Yeah, well, I bought them Saturday in Kalispell, when I went for groceries. Because a girl never knows when the right cowboy will come calling."

He reached into his back pocket and pulled out three more. "Makes perfect sense to me." He set them with hers on the nightstand.

She put the box back in the drawer and pushed it shut. "Call us prepared."

He snaked out a hand and hauled her into him again, cradling her chin with his other hand, his eyes dark green now and intense in their focus, his body hard and ready, calling to hers. "I never thought…" He said it low and a little bit ragged.

"Never thought what?"

He searched her face with those green, green eyes. "This. You. Me. How it is with us. It's really good."

She only nodded. It was the best she could do. Her throat had clutched. And the words wouldn't come.

He didn't seem to mind. "I want to see you. All of you."

Again she nodded.

And he reached up with one hand and pulled out the pins that held up her hair, setting them next to the condoms on the nightstand. He took his time about it, spreading her hair on her shoulders, smoothing it down her back, combing it with his fingers, pausing to wrap it around his hand, only to unwind it carefully once again.

"Silky, warm," he whispered, taking another thick lock of it, bringing the strands to his mouth, rubbing them there. "Smells like flowers and cinnamon."

He began to undress her, his tanned fingers nimble on the buttons of her shirt, easing them out of the buttonholes one by one, carefully spreading the shirt open once he had them all undone. "So pretty..." He bent his head and pressed a kiss on the slope of her right breast, just above the lace of her shell-pink bra. "Callie..." He breathed her name against her flesh, and she relished the hot shiver that skated along the surface of her skin. "Callie." He kissed the top of her other breast.

And then he got back to the business at hand.

He unwrapped her like a much-anticipated present, taking her by the waist and sitting her down on the bed so he could kneel at her feet and pull off her boots and her socks. And after that, rising, taking her hand, urging her to stand again. He took down her snug jeans. When she had just her panties and bra left to cover her, he gathered her close, bent his head and captured her lips for more of those long, slow kisses.

She tried to reciprocate, to get him out of his shirt, at least. Or maybe his big-buckled belt. But every time she got to work on some article of his clothing, he gently took her hands away and kissed her again, and she forgot everything but the hot, wet perfection of his mouth on hers, the hardness of his body pressing along hers, the touch of his hands on her willing flesh, the need to clutch him closer, hold him tighter, never, ever let him go.

He took off her bra, eased away her little panties.

She was naked and it was glorious. "Soft." He whispered the word against her throat. "So smooth…" He nipped her collarbone, making her moan.

And then he bent his head to her breast. She speared her fingers into his hair, pulling him closer, urging him to kiss her, to draw her nipple into his mouth, to flick his tongue around it, swirling.

She made noises, shameless sounds—hungry, yearning, encouraging sounds. His hands caressed her, cradling her breasts, his touch both thrillingly rough and heartbreakingly tender, those clever, knowing fingers moving lower, gliding between her thighs, where she was waiting and wet and longing for him.

He touched her there, where she wanted him most, and she gasped and cried his name and whispered, "Yes, oh, yes. Please, just…there." And he gave her what she begged for, his fingers moving right to the spot that brought her a swift, shining bolt of pure pleasure.

He stroked and he teased. And then he touched her more deeply, opening her. And she was gone, lost, over the moon with the feel of him, the way he knew just where to touch her, how to make her burn and lift her hips to him and beg him not to stop, to give her more.

When he guided her down to the bed again, she went happily, stretching out across the white sheets, her knees at the edge and her feet dangling to the floor.

He knelt. Moaning, she opened her heavy eyes and lifted her head to look down at him. He smiled at her.

"Nate, I…"

"What?"

But already she had forgotten whatever it was she

had meant to say. So she only moaned again and let her head drop back to the mattress.

She felt his warm, rough-tender hands on her thighs, rubbing. Slowly. Clasping, too, spreading her legs wider, revealing every last secret her body might have kept from him. She had no secrets, not now.

And it didn't matter in the least. Except that it was good and right and she didn't care to keep secrets from him, anyway. She rolled her head from side to side against her soft, white sheets and felt those hands of his moving.

Down and inward, finding the burning womanly core of her again. Stroking, teasing. She moaned some more. And then he moved in closer. There was the sweet friction of his shirt against her inner thighs, the warmth of him beneath the crisp fabric…

And then he kissed her.

There.

Just there.

He kissed her and he went on kissing her, using his lips and his tongue and his knowing fingers in the most lovely and exciting ways. She rocked her hips up to him and called his name and clutched at the sheets.

And then it happened. The heat and the wonder spiraled down to that one most sensitive spot—and then opened up wide, coursing in sparks and a swift flow of heat all through her, opening her up and tossing her over the edge, sending her spiraling, spinning, setting her free as she whispered his name.

He stayed with her, easing her down from the peak with gentle kisses at first and then, after, rising up enough to rest his head on her belly. She stroked her fingers through his thick gold-streaked brown hair and thought how right and good it felt to be there with him.

Eventually, he turned his head and placed a long, soft kiss on her belly. Then he levered back on his heels.

"Oh, don't go…." She reached for him. But he was already rising to stand above her. "Come back here," she commanded lazily, her arms still outstretched to him.

"I will," he said, and his eyes said he meant that. "Count on it." He looked at her and she was fine with that, with lying there completely naked under his admiring gaze, her hair all wild and tangled, spread across the sheets.

With a hard sigh, she let her arms drop back to the mattress. "Hurry up." She pouted.

So he got to work undressing. He did it quickly, with a sort of ruthless efficiency that she found almost as exciting as his kiss, as the brush of his strong hands on her skin.

He was a beautiful man, broad and strong, with big shoulders and a deep chest tapering down to a tight waist and narrow hips. A beautiful man who wanted her. The proof of his desire rose up from the dark nest of hair between his heavily muscled thighs. She looked at it and then up into his waiting eyes.

And then she reached out her arms once more.

That time, he didn't hesitate. He came down to the sheets with her, gathering her up into his big arms and rearranging her, until she lay with her head on the pillows and her feet toward the headboard.

"At last." She sighed, pulling him close to her, taking the weight of him and glorying in it, widening her thighs so he could slip between them.

"Callie." He said her name as though it was an answer to some question. A good answer. The right answer. He lifted up on his big arms and gazed down at her and she stared back up at him....

A great moment. One of the best. A moment with nothing of regret in it. Only anticipation and the promise of more pleasure. Only this man who had seemed so impossible, so difficult.

This man who was turning out to be more than she'd understood at first. Tough and tenderhearted, he really got to her. Whatever happened in the end, she would not regret her time with him.

He whispered her name again. "Callie..." Her hair was everywhere, spread out in coils and snarls around them. He buried his fingers in it, bent to rub his cheek against it where it fell along his arm.

And then he was kissing his way over her shoulder, up the side of her throat, scraping his teeth there, sucking a little, hard enough that she knew it would probably leave a mark, a mark that would fade quickly, unlike the one he was making on her heart.

Nipping, nuzzling, he kissed his way into the cove just below her chin, and higher, until his wonderful, warm mouth closed over hers.

They shared another kiss, better than the last one, his tongue sweeping the inner surfaces beyond her parted lips, beckoning hers to follow. And she did follow, tasting him deeply, sharing breath with him, sighing her desire into his mouth. As they kissed, he touched her, his hand straying down to find her wet and open and eager for him.

When he lifted his lips from hers, she moaned and blinked up at him, drowning in the feel of him, lost in his touch.

"Now?" he asked in a rumble so low it came out like a growl.

And she nodded. "Now."

And somehow he already had the condom in his hand. He fumbled with it.

She giggled, a silly, happy sound, and got her hands up between them to take it from him. The top tore off easily.

He pushed back, away from her. She missed the hard, hot weight of him. But, oh, he did look fine, looming above her on his knees, looking down at her with an expression that stole the breath right out of her body.

She took the condom from the wrapper and tossed the wrapper away, reaching for him. He moaned when she touched him and she couldn't resist a few slow, testing strokes. He was silk over steel and she wanted to taste him.

But he shook his head. "I want you, *you,* Callie. Now."

"But I—"

"Now."

She looked into his eyes again, saw heat and hunger and couldn't bear to deny him. So she rolled the protection down over his hard length, carefully so as not to tear it, easing it in nice and close at the base.

And then he was reaching for her, lifting her up and over.

With a cry of surprise, she found herself straddling him, staring down into those beautiful eyes. "What...?"

"Ride me," he commanded in a rough growl.

That sounded like a wonderful idea to her. So she went up on her knees and he positioned himself beneath her and then, with slow, thrilling care, she lowered herself onto him. They both groaned at the feel of that. Her body gave to him, welcoming him, taking him in.

And then he was clasping her hips in his big, strong hands, pulling her down, seating himself in deeper, all the way.

She gasped again and braced her hands on his broad, hard chest.

"Move for me, Callie."

She obeyed. It was only exactly what she wanted to do. She rocked her hips and he lifted his to meet her, keeping rhythm with her, the two of them in matching time. She tipped her head back as she rocked on him and he brought his hands up, caressing, over the outward swells of her hips, inward at her waist and around to her back, which she arched for him. His fingers caught in her tangled hair and he played with it, wrapping it around his hands, tugging on it hard enough to hurt just a little, spiking her pleasure even higher.

And then he was taking her by the waist, rolling her back under him, claiming the dominant position once more, moving on her and in her, filling her so completely. Her mind spun and her body caught fire. She lifted her legs and wrapped them tight around his narrow hips as her climax expanded up from the feminine core of her, rocking through her, rolling over her in waves. When she cried out, he only lowered his mouth and took that cry into himself as he kept on moving within her, filling her so completely, burning her up with pleasure, turning the world inside out.

And then he went still, pressing into her so close and deep that she felt him pulsing, felt his completion as it took form from hers. He broke the endless kiss they shared, his head straining back, the tendons of his powerful neck drawing hard and tight. A low, wordless sound escaped him.

And she reached up, wrapped her fingers around the back of his neck and pulled him close to her again, guiding his head to rest in the curve of her throat.

"Callie…" He groaned her name, his breath hot against her skin.

She held on, sighing, cradling him close to her heart as they eased down from the peak together and slowly settled into afterglow.

In time, he lifted up onto his forearms again. He looked down at her, frowning. "I'm crushing you…."

"Yes, you are." She brushed at his hair where it fell across his forehead. "But I don't mind at all."

"Don't want to crush you," he grumbled. And then he rolled them again. That time they ended up on their sides, still joined. He wrapped his leg across her hip, smoothed her hair back from her face so it flowed out behind her across the pillows. "It's good. To be here, like this, with you…."

"Mmm." She smiled at him and cuddled closer, letting her eyes drift shut.

He brushed his fingers across her cheek. "Are you conking out on me?"

"No way," she muttered lazily. "That would be rude."

"You *are* conking out on me."

"Haven't been sleeping much," she confessed on a sigh. "Man problems."

"That bad?" he asked in a teasing whisper.

"Bad enough."

He drew her closer, kissed her cheek and stroked her hair in the gentlest, sweetest way.

She sighed again. "Just need to close my eyes... Only a minute..."

She woke suddenly in the dark, absolutely certain that making love with him had been a dream.

He wasn't in the bed with her. She sat up and turned on the bedside lamp. The clock by the lamp said it was after midnight. And there were three condoms waiting in front of the clock, next to the pins he'd taken from her hair.

So, then. It had happened. It was real. "Nate?"

"Right here." He emerged from the darkness of the bathroom, wearing nothing but one of those killer smiles of his.

"Come back here."

"Yes, ma'am."

She admired the view as he approached. When he reached her, she flipped back the covers and he rejoined her in the bed.

With a happy sigh, she pulled the covers over them, rested her head on his broad chest and relished the way his strong arms closed around her. "I thought you had left—or maybe you were never here in the first place, that you were just a dream I had."

"Wrong on both counts." He tipped her chin up, kissed the tip of her nose. "Sleep well?"

"I did, actually." She reached up, stroked the manly stubble on his jaw. "Sorry. Were you bored to death?"

"Hell, no. I went to sleep, too. I needed it. Haven't

been sleeping all that much, either. See, there's a certain woman I can't stop thinking about…."

She chuckled. Then she asked if he was hungry. He shook his head, reached over and turned off the light.

They should go back to sleep and she knew it. She had to be at the clinic by nine in the morning.

But she started thinking about what he'd told her earlier, that he'd met Collin and Sutter at the Ace in the Hole and apologized to them. And that made her wonder about all the years that he and Collin were at each other's throats. "Nate…?"

"Go to sleep," he told her.

"In a minute," she said. He rubbed his hand down her arm. It felt wonderful, to be lying there in the dark with him. It felt like something she could so very easily get used to. "I was thinking about you and Collin…."

"What can I tell you? We hated each other for years. Now it's getting better. That's about the size of it."

"I've heard the stories."

He grunted. "Hey, it's Rust Creek Falls. Of course you've heard the stories."

"But they're always vague, the stories. I mean, I don't really understand what went on between you two."

He made a low, ironic sort of sound. "Neither do I, really. He was a wild kid who never did what he was told, and I played by the rules, I guess you could say. We disapproved of each other and we always managed to get on each other's last nerve."

"I would like to hear what really went on with Cindy Sellers."

He tipped up her chin and brushed a quick kiss on her lips. "Why?"

She snuggled against his heart again. "Well, the day you agreed to sell me this house, you wouldn't tell me. I'm still wondering about it, that's all."

"It happened years ago. Cindy moved away shortly after the whole mess went down. She never came back. It doesn't matter now."

"It matters to me, Nate. I want to know everything about you."

He was fooling with her hair, combing his fingers through it. "I'm just not that fascinating."

"Yes, you are. Tell me."

He said nothing for several seconds. She was sure he would never tell her the story. But in the end, he relented. "Cindy and I started going out about seven years ago. She wanted to get married, settle down, have a family. I didn't. I was never getting married again and I told her that. She didn't believe me. She kept waiting for me to see the light and propose. In the two years we were together, whenever she would bring up marriage, I would either tell her it wasn't happening or change the subject. She should have dumped me, but instead, she kept seeing me, pressuring me. I should have stopped seeing her."

"Why didn't you?"

"I liked her, or I did until the end. I'd been back home for about a year when I got together with her. It was three years since Zoe's death, and I was lonely. I was ready for a girlfriend, to be with someone in a steady way. But marriage? Uh-uh. I knew it wasn't working with her, that we wanted different things…."

"But you held on."

"Yeah. Looking back, I think she just got madder and madder at me. Finally, one night, she went looking for Collin at the Ace in the Hole. She told Collin that she and I were through."

"How do you know that?"

"A lot of people saw her at the Ace that night. A lot of people heard her say that it was over with her and me."

"So, you'd broken up with her?"

"No. In fact, the night before she went after Collin, we were together out at the ranch. She spent the night. In the morning when she left, she kissed me goodbye, and we agreed that I would take her out to dinner the following Friday night."

"I want to call her a really bad name about now."

"Yeah, well, she wasn't that way at first. Like I said, I just think she got so mad at me for not being the man she wanted me to be. By the end, she only wanted to hurt me."

"Did she succeed?"

"I remember being furious that she had made a damn fool of me. And somewhere underneath the blind rage, yeah, she did hurt me. Because I cared about her. I couldn't be who she wanted me to be and I didn't have sense enough to just break it off. And Collin was still a wild one back then, not one to turn down a good-looking, eager woman."

"So Collin spent the night with Cindy, and when it got back to you, you blamed him."

"Hey. He's a Traub and I'm a Crawford, so blaming him was always the easiest thing for me to do. Back then, he was the wildest, most troublemaking of all the Traubs, and he and I had gotten into it over and over throughout our lives. I was mad because my girlfriend had climbed in bed with another man. Who better to blame than the other man—especially since that man was Collin Traub? I found him at the Ace and I punched him in the face. He couldn't let that stand, so he punched me back. We ended up pretty much beating the crap out of each other."

"Didn't he tell you that Cindy had told *him* that you two were through?"

"That would have involved discussion. There was no discussion. I went in swinging, and Collin swung back. It was only later I found out that he'd thought Cindy and me were over because Cindy had told him so."

"Who won the fight?"

He gave a low chuckle. "Crawfords will tell you I won. Ask a Traub, he'll swear that Collin wiped up the floor with me."

"Well, whoever won, neither you nor Collin comes off looking like a hero in that story."

"Because we're not heroes. We're just men doing what men do, solving problems with our fists."

"You wouldn't behave that way now."

"I hope not. I like to think I've grown up a little."

She lifted up enough to meet his eyes through the darkness. "You're a good man, Nate."

He shook his head slowly on the white pillow. "Not so sure about that, not so sure about anything anymore, really. Which is pretty damn funny because I used to be certain that I knew everything." He pulled her back down to him again, guiding her head to rest against his shoulder. "Go to sleep."

It sounded like a pretty good idea to her. She closed her eyes.

When she opened them again, daylight was peeking through the blinds.

And someone was ringing the doorbell.

"Huh?" She reached for the clock. "Forgot to set the alarm…"

Beside her Nate came groggily awake. "Doorbell…" He looked wonderful, all rumpled and sexy, with his hair sticking up on one side and a sleep crease bisecting his beard-stubbled cheek.

She tossed back the covers. "I'll get it."

He grabbed her arm. "Close the bedroom door. I'll wait here until you can get rid of whoever it is."

She gave a low, scoffing laugh and pulled her arm free. "Oh, come on."

"Seriously." His lips were a thin line, his expression set. "It could be anyone, including someone with a big mouth, who'll be spreading our business all over town."

The doorbell rang again.

She swung her feet over the edge of the bed and grabbed her robe from the bedside chair. "Nate. Get real." She stuck her arms in the sleeves and swiftly tied the belt. "I'm not sneaking around to be with you. We spent the night together and I don't care who knows it." She headed for the door.

"Spoken like a girl from the big city. Just close the bedroom door," he called after her. "Please."

She did close the bedroom door because he didn't have a stitch on—*not* because she cared who knew that he was in her bed. And then she went straight to the front door and pulled it wide.

Nate's mother was waiting on the other side.

Chapter 9

Laura Crawford let out a sigh of obvious relief. "Callie. I'm so glad you're home. Sorry to wake you."

Callie reached up to guide a tangled lock of hair behind her ear. "No problem. Uh…come on in."

"Oh, no. Really. I don't want to bother you…."

"You're not." She stepped back. "I'll get the coffee going."

Laura shook her head and stayed on the porch side of the threshold. "It's just that I've been trying to reach Nathan. He's not picking up either of his phones, so I came on over hoping to catch him at home and, well, he's not there. So I was wondering if you knew where he…" Laura let the sentence die unfinished. She blinked. Callie followed the direction of her gaze to Nate's hat hanging on the peg by the door. "Oh!" she said. "Well." And then she smiled. A big, happy smile. After which, she leaned close and whispered, "He's going to be furious with me for showing up here."

"Come in," Callie tried again, hoping she wasn't blushing like some teenaged virgin caught necking out at Lover's Lane in a '50s romantic comedy.

Laura said, still whispering gleefully, "I didn't realize things were moving so fast." And then, a little louder, "I need to talk to him about what I've heard, that's all."

"Uh, what you've heard?"

"That he had a meeting with Collin and Sutter Traub last night." Now she was scowling. "Can that really be true? And— Never mind, never mind." Laura reached out and patted Callie's arm. "Just tell him to call me, that I need to talk to him."

"Sure. But if you come in, you can tell him your—"

Laura put up a hand. "No. Bad idea. Tell him to call me." She turned for the steps that led down to the front walk.

"But, I—"

Laura kept going, calling over her shoulder, "Have a lovely morning, hon."

Callie just stood there, feeling more than a little foolish, her arms wrapped around herself, watching as Nate's mom got into her shiny red quad cab and drove away.

"Close the door," Nate said from behind her.

It seemed like a reasonable suggestion, so she shut it and turned around to find him standing in the doorway to her bedroom, wearing only his jeans and looking like every girl's fantasy of a hot cowboy lover. She coughed to clear her suddenly tight throat. "Ahem. That was your mother."

"I know. I heard."

"Somehow, she's already learned that you met with Collin last night."

He leaned in the doorway, big arms crossed over that fine, broad golden-skinned chest. "Of course she already knows."

"She…saw your hat." Callie flicked out a hand in the direction of the hat in question.

"Great. Now we can be certain that our private business will be all over town within twenty-four hours. Was she grinning ear to ear about it?"

"About you and me, yeah. About your meeting with the Traubs, not so much. She wants you to call her."

"I'll bet she does."

"You know, you always seem kind of annoyed with your mother."

He still lounged in the doorway, watching her. "Come here."

"She's a very sweet woman, really."

"I grew up with her. I know exactly how sweet she is. Come here." He said it softly but roughly, too. And there was no mistaking the sexy gleam in his eyes.

Callie felt a hot shiver run up the backs of her bare calves and a sluice of heat low in her belly. "I don't have time to fool around. I have to go to work." She adjusted the front of her robe and gave him a slow smile. "However, *after* work is another story altogether…."

He reached out his hand to her. "Come on over here to me…."

"Oh, all right." She went to him and when she got there, she couldn't resist going on tiptoe and lifting her mouth.

Nate took what she offered in a lazy kiss that started

out smoldering and quickly burned hot. When he lifted his head, she had a hard time not grabbing him and pulling him down to her again. "What time do you have to be at the clinic?"

"Nine."

"You have eggs?"

She nodded. "There's even bacon. And bread for toast. I'll fix us some breakfast. If I hurry, there's time." She turned from the warm circle of his arms.

But he caught her and pulled her back. "I'll do it. You go ahead and get ready."

She sighed and leaned into him again, burying her nose against his chest and breathing in the wonderful scent of him. "A hot cowboy lover who makes breakfast? Is this a dream?"

He took her by the shoulders and turned her toward the bathroom. "Go. Now. Otherwise, I'm going to get you out of this robe and get to work showing you all the reasons you need to call in sick."

Callie took a quick shower and put on her scrubs. When she joined Nate in the kitchen, he had the table set and the food ready. The bacon was crisp, the scrambled eggs light and fluffy. She thanked him for the meal.

He warned, "Expect advice. A boatload of it."

She sipped her coffee. "What kind of advice?"

"Advice about how you need to watch out with me, that I'm not a good bet for a long-term relationship."

Callie laughed. "I've heard that exact advice from *you* already."

"Be ready to hear it again from just about everyone in town—except my mother, of course. She'll tell you the opposite. That I'm just the man for you and we should get married right away and you should make me promise never, ever to leave Rust Creek Falls."

She put down her fork. "Nate."

"What?"

"Stop being glum. Put on your happy face."

"I have a happy face?"

"Seriously. We're in this now, right? You and me, together. We're a thing."

He scowled, thinking about it. And then he said, "Hell, yeah."

That made her smile. "Good, then. Let's enjoy every minute and not borrow trouble."

He broke a piece of bacon in half and stared down at the two halves as if he didn't know what to do with them. "You're right. You're absolutely right." He looked up at her and commanded, "Dinner. Tonight. My place."

"You're cooking?"

"Well, you'll be working all day. Seems like the least I can do is pamper you a little when you get home."

"I do like the way you think. Most of the time, anyway."

Gruffly, he demanded, "Is that a yes on dinner?"

"Absolutely. I'll be there. I get off at five."

When Callie left for the clinic, Nate went back to his house. He'd barely gotten in the door before the phone started ringing.

He knew who it would be and he was right. "Hello, Mom." Just for the heck of it, he checked his cell, which he'd left on silent page. She had called him on it, too. "What's up?"

She answered stiffly, "I would like to speak with you."

"Fine. Speak."

"Face-to-face, Nathan. In private."

Might as well get it over with. "Where?"

"I'll come there," she said. "Ten minutes."

Nine and a half minutes later, she was knocking on his door. He ushered her in, led her to the kitchen and made her a cup of café mocha.

She took the coffee, sipped and then shook her head at him. "I don't know where to start, Nathan."

"Then, don't," he suggested hopefully and sipped from the mug he'd filled for himself.

She failed to take his advice. "I'm happy for you and Callie."

"Great."

"Come to Sunday dinner. Bring Callie. Please."

"I'll invite her."

"Wonderful. As for your visit with the Traub brothers..."

He realized he didn't want to hear her running down the Traubs. "Look. Don't start, okay?"

"You don't even know what I'm going to say."

"Yeah, but I'll bet I can guess."

She blew out a sharp, annoyed little breath and went right on. "I didn't get any details. All I heard was that you met with them and you all ended up shaking hands."

He figured she might as well hear it from him than wait around for the rumor mill to provide all kinds of outlandish stories about what had gone down at the Ace last night. "I apologized to Sutter and Collin for playing dirty during the mayor's race."

She huffed a little. “I wouldn’t say you played dirty.”

“Well, I would. I apologized, the Traubs accepted and they asked me to invest in a little project they’ve got going.”

“What kind of project?”

He really didn’t feel like talking about the resort idea with her. She would only try and warn him off it. “It’s an investment they offered me, that’s all.”

“But what kind of investment?”

“It’s in the very early stages and I don’t want to go into it right now.”

“It’s only that I don’t want you to throw your money away.”

“Let it go, Mom.”

Surprisingly, she did. “All right.” She gave a heavy sigh. “Enough said about the Traubs’ mysterious investment opportunity.”

“Wonderful.”

“And, well, I know that to you, I may seem set in my ways. But even your father and I understand that things change. And we do have a daughter who’s married a Traub.”

He couldn’t help razzing her a little. “You noticed?”

“Nathan, there is no need for you to be sarcastic with me.” She said it in her best injured-mother voice. “Yes, I *have* noticed who my daughter married. And Nina and Dallas seem to be very happy together. They’ve made a lovely family, with his boys and baby Noelle. I want us all to get along.”

“Well, good. So do I.”

“And I want *you* to be happy. I truly do. I know how much you loved Zoe and I am sorry you lost her and the child. So very sorry…”

He stared across the table at her, vaguely stunned. It had been years since she'd said Zoe's name or referred to her in any way. "What are you up to here, Mom?" She gazed steadily back at him, looking sad and… older. The lines around her mouth and at the corners of her eyes seemed suddenly deeper somehow. "You never talk about Zoe. Why start now?"

She drank from her mug, set it down with care. "Because we have to start somewhere, don't we, to try and make a change, make things right?"

"It's too late for you to make things right with Zoe." He said it softly, even gently. But he meant the words to wound her all the same.

And she knew it. A film of tears made her eyes shine. But she was tough, always had been. She blinked the tears away and squared her shoulders. "I should have been kinder to her. I know it. She was a lovely person. And still, I judged her as not right for you—and not because she waited tables for a living, as I know you've always thought. But because she was from out of town and reluctant to move to Rust Creek Falls."

He couldn't let that go. "She was reluctant because you weren't welcoming to her."

His mother pressed her lips together and seemed to be taking slow, careful breaths. "All right," she said at last. "Yes. I behaved distantly to her when I should have opened my arms. My behavior made her feel unwelcome here. But think back. She loved her mama in North Dakota. She wanted to live there, near Anna. Deep down, you know that." He ached to argue just for the sake of disagreeing with her, but he didn't. She was right, after all. His mother's behavior aside, Zoe *had* wanted to live in Bismarck. "I wanted you to find a nice local girl who would ground you here, keep you at home with us. But you found Zoe. And instead of being happy that you had someone to love who loved you in return, I was bitter because you never came home. I blamed *her.* I was wrong."

Was this really happening? Laura Crawford sitting across from him, drinking a café mocha and admitting she'd been wrong?

Never in his life had he expected to have this conversation with her, for her to come right out and admit that she should have behaved differently. He didn't know quite what to make of it. It didn't feel all that good, not really, to hear Zoe's name from his mother's mouth after so many years of silence, of her acting as though his wife had never existed. There was a raw feeling within him, as if someone had taken a cheese grater to his heart.

Finally, he said flatly, "Yeah. You were wrong. And what brings this on?"

She sipped at her café mocha and answered thoughtfully, "I don't know exactly. Maybe I'm old enough to start being a little bit wiser. Or maybe it's this thing with the Traubs. First Nina and Dallas. Now you, going to Collin and making peace. Something that can never change is changing. That gets a person thinking. It truly does. Or maybe it's Callie."

He didn't understand—and he wasn't sure he wanted to. But then he heard himself asking, "Why Callie?"

"*You* and Callie."

"Still not following."

"Oh, come on—the way you looked at each other in the store last week, on the day of the storm?"

"Yeah, so…?"

"You'll never know how happy that look made me."

"You're happy because I finally have strong feelings for a woman who loves Rust Creek Falls?"

She didn't smile, exactly, but somehow she did look less sad. "Believe it or not, the simple fact that you have strong feelings for Callie matters more to me than that she might keep you here in town. All these years…" She stared into the middle distance, a faraway sort of look. "A decade since your Zoe passed away, and there's never been any woman who could reach you. I'd slowly come to accept that Zoe was it for you, that no other woman ever would touch you the way that she did, that I had blown my chance to cherish her for showing you what real love from a good woman can be. And then I saw you look at Callie in that special, deep way, and I realized that anything is possible, Nathan. I saw that you are finally moving on from a terrible heartbreak."

Again, he wanted to take issue with that, just on principal somehow. But what would that prove? That he knew how to be a douche to his mom? He was thirty-three years old, for pity's sake. Grown up enough to sit there and listen while she had her say.

She spoke again, leaning toward him, intent and sincere, "I see things differently now. I see that even the most hidebound of us really can change—if we want it bad enough, if we're willing to do what we have to do to make up for the things that we've done wrong." She fell silent and watched him expectantly.

He knew it was his turn to say something profound. Too bad he had nothing.

She gave him a funny, quirky little smile then and waved a hand at him. "It's okay." She pushed back her chair and carried her empty mug around the peninsula of counter to the sink. "You don't have to say anything. I just came to apologize for what I didn't do for Zoe. And I came to tell you that I am proud of you. And if you want to invest your money in some Traub brothers' project, well, I can't say I'll keep my mouth shut, but I will respect your choice and support you in every way I can." She came back around the jut of counter to stand a few feet from the table and suggested, wincing, "I know this is a lot to ask, but could I maybe have a hug before I go?"

He went to her and put his arms around her. She sighed and hugged him back.

Then she clapped her hands on his shoulders and met his eyes. "You're a good man, Nathan."

He remembered Callie last night, telling him the same thing, and he almost laughed. "Let's say I'm working on it."

"It wasn't your fault that Zoe and the baby died. It was just the way it happened, that you got trapped at the ranch that day. It was tragic and wrong. But not in any way your fault."

He gave her a crooked smile. "I could have made other choices, that's all. Better choices..."

The sad look came back into her eyes again. "Oh, honey. Couldn't we all?"

At a little after ten that morning, Callie was in her office cubicle writing a couple of prescriptions and continuing-care instructions for a patient she'd just seen when her phone chimed.

It was a text from Paige: Lunch? My house. 1:00?

Paige knew her schedule. Emmet took lunch early, at eleven-thirty. She went at one.

Callie bit her lower lip and tried not to feel apprehensive that Paige might be gearing up for more dire warnings about Nate. But then she shook it off. She and Paige were friends, and friends were supposed to tell you what they really thought—even if what they really thought was that they didn't much care for your boyfriend.

She texted back: Gr8. I'll b there.

Emmet was back by quarter of one. "Go on, go ahead," he said when she told him she wanted to walk over to Paige's for lunch.

Paige invited Callie in with a hug and a smile and led her to the kitchen, where Paige served pasta salad, warm rolls and raspberry-leaf iced tea. Callie's apprehensions faded a little as they ate. They chatted about everyday things—like how much Paige, who taught at the elementary school, enjoyed teaching summer school.

"I miss it this year," she said. With the baby coming, she'd decided to take the summer off. "The kids are so much fun."

They discussed Brighter Horizons. Paige thought the town's mystery benefactor was probably some rich out-of-towner who'd read Lissa's blog and gotten swept up in the story of the little town coming back against all odds from the flood of the century. "I know Lissa thinks whoever it is has to be local, but I don't agree, necessarily. It could just be some rich old guy with a generous spirit, someone who wants to help."

Callie was more of Lissa Roarke's opinion, that it was someone local.

While they talked, she kept thinking about what Nate had said that morning, that in no time everyone in town would know that the two of them were together. And the more she thought about that, the more she wanted to be the one to tell Paige that Nate had spent the night at her house. Even if your friend didn't like your boyfriend, she shouldn't be getting hot news about your love life from somebody else.

So when Paige brought out the fruit tarts for dessert, Callie said, "There's something I've been wanting to tell you…."

Paige didn't miss a beat. "Is this about Nate?"

"It is, yes." And Callie went ahead and told her that Nate had slept at her house last night, that she didn't really know where it was going, but it was serious. "I care for him, Paige. I truly do. And tonight he's cooking me dinner at his house."

Paige ate a glazed strawberry. "I appreciate your telling me."

"I wanted you to hear it from me first."

Paige nodded. "Thanks. And I really can't say I'm surprised."

Callie peered at her more closely. "I thought you were going to be upset. But you don't seem all that bothered, really."

Paige ate a slice of kiwi fruit. "Did he tell you that he apologized to Sutter and Collin?" At Callie's nod, she went on, "He's never been my favorite person, but that took guts, to find Sutter at the ranch and say sorry, and then, when Sutter challenged him to say the same to Collin, to meet them at the Ace, bold as brass, right in front of everybody, and offer his apologies all over again. I do admire a man with guts, even when his name happens to be Nathan Crawford. And now he's admitted what a horse's ass he was, well, it wouldn't be right to hold the past against him, would it?"

Callie scooped up a bite of flaky crust, sweet custard and summer berries. "So…you're okay with this, with me and Nate?"

Paige arched a brow at her. "Would you break up with him if I wasn't?"

Callie didn't even stop to think about it. "Sorry. Not a chance." She popped the sweet treat into her mouth.

"I didn't think so."

"I really, really like him, Paige."

"What about how you were swearing off men?"

"You're absolutely right. I was. But the man just… gets to me. There's something so sweet and steadfast in him. And he can be so funny and perceptive. Plus, well, he's just plain hot. What can I say? I'm crazy about him."

"I know, I know. It's written all over your face whenever you talk about him or even when someone just mentions his name."

"I'm that obvious, huh?"

"Well, at least to me, you are. And it's kind of humorous, actually…."

"Terrific. I'm so lovesick, it's funny."

"Come on now." Paige reached across and patted her arm. "That's not what I meant."

"Right."

"No, really. What's humorous is that last year about this time, I was warning Willa Christensen off of Collin, predicting dire consequences if she didn't stay away from him, reminding her that he'd always been a wild one and she didn't need that kind of trouble in her life. Willa wouldn't listen to me. And as it turned out, she had it right. Here they are, happily married, and wild man Collin is the mayor of this town. Life is full of surprises, don't you think?"

Callie agreed that it was. And she couldn't help imagining what it might be like, if she and Nate ended up a couple in a permanent way. The hopeless romantic within her just loved that idea.

But her more realistic, modern-woman self wasn't so sure. Nate was…special to her. Important. And she worried that she'd already let him become *too* important.

Deep inside she feared that his heart would always and forever belong to the woman he'd lost ten years ago.

She got back to the clinic at two, right on time.

There were three patients in the waiting room. One of them was hers, eight-year-old Teddy Trimmer, who'd fallen out of his tree house three weeks ago and ended up with a simple fracture of his left wrist. He was there with his mom, Georgia, to get his removable splint off for good.

Callie gave the boy and his mom a smile, and Teddy held up his splinted wrist and called, "All better, Nurse Callie."

She laughed. "Excellent, Teddy. This could be the big day."

And then Brandy, behind the check-in desk, said, "Callie. At last." She got up from her computer, came around to Callie's side, took her by the arm and pulled her halfway down the hall and into a storage closet, where she shut the door and flicked on the light.

"Brandy, what in the…"

"It's Emmet."

"Is he all right?"

Brandy rolled her eyes. "He's getting so eccentric."

"Hey. Come on. It's part of his charm."

"He took the mail into his office forty-five minutes ago. He said he'd be just a minute, but he's still in there and he's got patients waiting. I can't just stall them forever, you know."

"Did you buzz him?"

"I did. Twice. The first time, he picked up, growled 'Just a minute' at me and then disconnected the line. The second time he didn't even answer."

"Did you knock?"

"I tried that next. He said I should leave him alone, that he just needed a minute—and, Callie, he didn't sound right. Kind of choked up, you know? That was fifteen minutes ago. I'm starting to wonder if somebody died or something."

Well, that was alarming. "Somebody like…?"

"Oh, how would I know? One of his Vietnam war buddies? It's just a guess."

"You want me to try?"

Brandy sighed heavily and smoothed a few loose tendrils of hair back up into the strawberry-blond knot on the top of her head. "Well, I'm all out of new approaches, and that's the truth."

"I'll take care of it. You go on back to the desk."

Emmet's office was the one at the end of the hall. Callie went down there and gave the door a gentle tap.

Nothing.

Quelling her rising apprehension, she tapped again.

"In a *minute,* Brandy," came the weary-sounding reply from within.

"Emmet, it's me..." She had no clue what to say next, so she just let the words trail away.

"Callie?" He sounded more alert.

"Yes. I'm here."

"Come in here, will you?"

Ridiculously anxious as to what she was going to find on the other side of the door, Callie turned the knob. She pushed the door inward, and there was Emmet, looking perfectly fine, sitting at his desk, a sheet of paper in one hand and what looked like a check in the other.

He waved the sheet of paper at her. "Shut the door. Sit down."

She slid into one of the two guest chairs and asked gingerly, "Are you all right?"

"Yeah. I'm fine. I'm better than fine. I'm so fine, I've been sitting here for forty-five minutes asking myself if this is really happening."

"Um, something is happening?"

He handed her the paper. "Take a look at that."

It was a letter. And as soon as she read the letterhead she knew. She blinked and glanced up at him, dazed. "Brighter Horizons. Emmet. It's from Brighter Horizons!"

Emmet's angular face broke into a wide grin. "You've heard of Brighter Horizons?"

She went back to the letter again and started reading. "Everybody in town has heard of them...." And then she gasped. "Omigod. *Three hundred thousand?*"

By way of an answer, he passed her the check.

She gaped at it. "Will you look at all those zeroes?" And then she glanced up at him again and couldn't stop herself from letting out a loud, "Wahoo!"

At which he fisted both hands and brought his elbows sharply down to his sides. "Booyah!"

And then they both started laughing like a couple of crazy people, shouting out "Wahoo!" and "Booyah!" and giving each other a series of high fives across the desk.

The door swung inward. It was Brandy, scowling. "Have you two lost it completely? Are you out of your minds?"

They both turned to stare at her and then looked back at each other, after which Emmet put on his most severe expression and said, "Brandy, you will be getting that raise you're always bugging me for."

"Right." She made a snorting sound. "Heard that one before." And then she accused, "Your patients are beyond tired of hearing me promise that you'll be right with them."

"Brandy." Still straight-faced, Emmet gestured at the other guest chair. "Come in. Sit down. We have something to show you...."

The rest of that afternoon went by in a happy haze of good feelings. Brandy carried the check to the bank and when she got back, she never stopped smiling.

The three of them took a meeting after the last patient of the day had been sent on his way. Each of them kept a long list of priority purchases, including equipment and other improvements to the clinic, improvements that they'd all three constantly doubted they would ever be able to afford. They could afford them now. It was agreed that the priority lists would be taken care of.

And then they would start on their optional lists.

Callie walked on air all the way home. She couldn't wait to tell Nate that Brighter Horizons had come through for the clinic.

But he was cooking for her and she hoped that maybe she'd end up spending the night at his place. She wanted to freshen up a little before knocking on his door.

She went to her house first and called him.

"You're late," he grumbled.

"Sorry. Really. It's been quite a day. I want to hop in the shower, and then I'll be right over."

"Want company?"

"Don't tempt me. We'll never have dinner."

"Dinner can wait."

"Just let me get a shower."

"I think I missed you…." His voice was velvety soft.

A lovely, warm shiver went through her and she teased, "What? You're not sure?"

"I'm sure enough. Hurry."

"Don't worry, I will. I promise. I will."

Twenty minutes later, she was running up his front steps. The door swung open before she reached it, and he was there, in jeans and a soft blue Western shirt, the sleeves rolled to expose his muscular forearms. His feet were bare. They were beautiful, strong, tanned feet.

Her heart did a quick little stutter inside her chest. "Hey," she said. It came out all breathless and dreamy.

He reached out, grabbed her hand, pulled her inside and shoved the door shut. "Kiss me."

"Absolutely."

His mouth swooped down and covered hers.

It was a great kiss, a kiss that made her forget everything, even the giant check that had arrived at the clinic, even that she was holding the bottle of wine she'd brought as her contribution to dinner. She almost dropped the wine.

But he must have felt it slipping. He caught it. "Whoa," he said against her lips. He put the wine on the entry table.

And then he pulled her close again. She went eagerly, lifting her arms to twine them around his neck, kissing him back with fervor, laughing in happy excitement as he lifted her off the floor and she wrapped her legs around him, hooking her sandaled feet at the base of his spine.

Oh, she could feel him, right there at the womanly heart of her, feel the ridge of his arousal beneath the fly of his jeans. She pressed herself closer, wrapped herself tighter, kissed him even more deeply than before.

He carried her that way, with her all over him like a hot coat of paint, their mouths fused together, up the wide staircase, through a sitting area and into his bedroom.

The room was big and luxurious, with a triple-coffered ceiling, beautiful dark furniture and a turned-back bed about half the size of Kansas. He set her down beside the bed, and she blinked and looked around. "This is beautiful, Nate."

He made a low sound in his throat and got to work undressing her. After a few dazed seconds of gaping at the gorgeous room, she helped. Laughing, pausing to share quick, hungry kisses, they undressed each other. He was quicker. She barely got his shirt off, and there she was, in only her panties and little red sandals.

She kicked off the sandals, took down the panties and tossed them away. And then she grabbed his arm and pulled him to her again and kissed him while she undid his belt, whipped it off and then ripped his fly wide.

He didn't wait around for her to do the rest but just shoved down his jeans and stepped out of them. Yanking open the bedside drawer, he produced a condom, which he had out of the wrapper and rolled down over himself so fast it made her head spin.

"Callie. At last..." And he put his hand on her, splaying his fingers on her naked belly, making her groan at the wonderful heat of his touch. He moved lower, fingers seeking, through the short, dark curls at the top of her thighs and then lower still. She groaned again as those warm fingers found her. She lifted her body to him, needful of him, very wet and so ready.

He clasped her waist again. "Callie..."

"Oh, Nate..." She twined her arms and her legs around him once more as he lifted her high.

A hungry moan escaped her as he brought her carefully down onto him, filling her in the most complete and satisfying way. And then they were reeling, turning in circles, endlessly kissing, as he carried her to the other side of the room. By the door to the sitting room, he braced her gently, using the wall for extra support.

After that, it all flew away, everything but him and the pulse of their pleasure. She was free and soaring, rocking with him. And his hands were all over her, stroking, caressing. He bent his head and captured her breast and she cried out and let her head fall back against the wall.

Oh, it was so good, like nothing she'd ever known before.

Nothing careful or wary in it, no sense of otherness, not a hint of self-consciousness. They were in this together, and it was exactly, overwhelmingly right.

It went on for a glorious, fulfilling eternity. Until she hit the peak, crying out as her body contracted around him. He drank that cry right into himself as the finish took him, too.

In the end, they sagged together against the wall, his forehead to hers, both of them breathing hard and heavy as they came back to themselves. He stroked her hair, guiding it out of her eyes, tucking it behind her ear. She buried her face against his throat, breathed in the musky, hot scent of him, couldn't resist sticking out her tongue to lick the sweat off his golden skin.

He kissed her, a tender, so-sweet caress of his lips across her cheek.

And then he was gathering her even closer. She tightened her legs and arms around him as he carried her back across the room to the wide bed. He lowered her onto it with such tender care, coming down with her, gently shifting her until her head rested on the pillows. She curled into him. Content in a way she couldn't remember being before, she closed her eyes and listened as his heartbeat slowed.

After a time, he kissed her temple. "You asleep?"

"Mmf."

"Is that a yes?"

She smiled to herself. "I'm awake."

He lifted her chin and kissed the tip of her nose. "Be right back."

"No, no, please don't go...." She pretended to cling.

But of course, he only rolled away and off the bed. She lifted her head enough to watch him walk away. He did look so fine from behind—as good as he looked from the front.

And then he disappeared through the door into the master bathroom. When he came back, he gathered her nice and cozy against him again.

"Hungry?" He kissed the word into her tangled hair.

"Soon..." She braced up on an elbow, her head on her hand. "But first I have news."

His eyes were very soft, green as new grass. "Good news, I hope."

"Oh, yes. Lots of it, too. Some rather nice news. And also some exciting, fabulous news." She beamed at him.

He caught a thick lock of her hair and wrapped it around his hand the way he liked to do. "I'm waiting."

She pretended to think it over. "I think I'll tell you the rather nice news first. I had lunch with Paige today. She knows that you apologized to Sutter and Collin, and she's pretty much decided you're not so bad, after all."

"I'm happy to hear that," he said sincerely.

"I thought you would be—and now for the fabulous, unbelievably wonderful news."

"Hit me with it."

"You were right." She traced a heart onto his chest. "I should have had faith."

Now he was frowning, unwinding her hair from around his fingers. "Faith about...?"

And then she couldn't tease him any longer.

"Brighter Horizons has given the clinic three hundred thousand dollars," she announced with a laugh of pure glee.

"Wow," he said. And then he grinned. "Congratulations."

She flopped back against the pillows. "Every time I think about it, I just want to dance around the room."

"Be my guest."

She giggled at the coffered ceiling. "Yeah. A naked-lady dance. That would be something."

He canted up to bend over her. "Sounds pretty good to me—especially if you're the one dancing."

"Oh, Nate." She hooked her arm around his neck, pulled him down and gave him a big, smacking kiss. When he lifted up so he could meet her eyes again, she told him, "You should've seen Emmet and me today, high-fiving each other, laughing like a couple of moonstruck fools. Even Brandy, who's always annoyed about something, couldn't stop smiling once we told her the news. That money is needed, Nate. It's going to make a huge difference in the quality of the care we're able to provide."

"Good," he said—and only that. He said it firmly and seriously, his gaze determined. "Good."

Serious. Determined. Why should that seem strange to her?

As she asked herself that question, a weird, prickly shiver went through her. Time spun to a stop in a real, honest-to-goodness déjà vu moment, the kind that people never believed in until it happened to them.

The night of the storm, she thought.

The night of the storm, when she'd told him for the first time how much the clinic needed funds. He'd looked at her kind of strangely then, too, hadn't he? As though he was mulling over what she'd told him, coming to some kind of decision about it.

And right now, the way he'd said *Good*—approvingly, with satisfaction. As though he'd been involved somehow with the clinic getting all that money. As though this moment, this conversation, was a natural conclusion to that other one the night Faith had Tansy.

She was staring at him too sharply.

And he noticed. Suddenly, he was all smiles, faking lightheartedness for all he was worth. "It's terrific, Callie. I can hardly believe it. This is really great news."

She only kept staring at him, convinced beyond any reasonable doubt by then, absolutely positive that the money had come from him—and not knowing exactly why she was so sure.

A certain look, a tone of voice. Was that any kind of proof, really?

Maybe not.

But still. She *knew.*

"What?" he demanded, openly uneasy now.

And she couldn't think of anything else to do but just go ahead and ask him, just lay it right out there and see what he said.

"Callie, what's going on?"

And she did it. She asked him straight-out. "It's you, isn't it, Nate? *You* are Brighter Horizons."

Chapter 10

Nate stared down into her beautiful, flushed face. She was waiting, looking at him so hopefully, *willing* him to admit it.

How in the hell had she put it together, read him so easily? Nobody else had. Everyone was talking about Brighter Horizons, trying to figure out who could be behind the trust. Not a soul in town had guessed it was him—not his parents or his brothers or the ranchers he'd known all his life, not one of the town council members he'd worked side by side with for years.

And he *had* been careful with her, hadn't he?

But apparently, not careful enough.

He didn't want her to know. Didn't want anyone to know. That was the point, for him to do what needed doing just for the sake of the doing alone. He needed to fix this situation and fix it fast.

So he opened his mouth to give her a bald-faced but sincere-sounding lie.

And before he could get a word out, she reached up, cradled his face between her cool, soft hands and said, "Don't. Please, Nate. Don't lie to me. Ever."

He thought of Zoe then. Zoe, who was nothing like Callie, at least not in looks or in her personality. Zoe, with her red hair and pale skin that couldn't take the sun. Zoe, who was shy and a little insecure.

The truth had always been Zoe's bottom line. *Just don't tell me any lies, Nathan Crawford,* she used to say. *Stick to the truth and I'm yours forever.*

And he had. He'd always told the truth to her.

He realized he wanted that with Callie now. He wanted honesty between them.

Nate lowered his head to her, kissed that sweet, soft mouth of hers. And then he breathed the truth against her lips. "Yeah. All right. Brighter Horizons is a trust I had set up. The money in the trust is mine."

She hitched in a tiny gasp. "I knew it. I just…knew it."

He kissed her again. "I don't want anyone to know. But you figured it out and I don't want to lie to you. Will you keep my secret for me?"

"Of course," she said without hesitation, her eyes huge and serious. "And…thank you, Nate. I think this whole town thanks you, even if no one but me knows that it's actually you we're so grateful to." She combed her fingers through the hair at his temple, and a chuckle escaped her. "You look embarrassed."

"I guess I am. A little." He rubbed his nose against hers, breathed in the sweet, tempting scent of her hair. "Come on. I promised to feed you. Let's get going on that."

* * *

They pulled on their clothes. Still a little stunned at what he'd revealed to her, Callie followed him down to the kitchen, detouring in the front hall to grab the bottle of wine he'd left on the table there.

He fired up the grill in back. The meal was the kind men usually cook: steak, baked potatoes and corn on the cob. She volunteered to cut up the salad.

"You grill a mean steak," she told him after the first bite of tender, juicy T-bone.

"All Crawford men know their way around a good steak." He plopped a big spoonful of sour cream onto his potato. "It's a matter of family pride."

He offered a beautiful Boston cream pie for dessert and confessed that his housekeeper, who came in twice a week to keep things tidy, had baked it at his request. Callie couldn't resist having a generous slice. It was as good as it looked.

She helped him clear off and load the dishwasher, and then they took second glasses of wine out onto the deck, where night was slowly falling. He had a wooden bench out there with a carved back and a nice, thick cushion, a long, low table in front of it.

"Sit with me." He pulled her down onto the cushion beside him and wrapped his arm around her shoulders. "Put your feet up."

She hoisted her feet up beside his on the low table and watched the shadows deepen, the stars appearing.

He told her that Laura had come by that morning. She wasn't surprised. Laura Crawford was a determined sort of person, just like her oldest son. "She wanted the details of my meeting with the Traubs—and also to gloat about you and me getting together."

Callie leaned her head on his shoulder. "And then she brought up Zoe..."

Callie popped up straight again. "Wait a minute. I thought you said she never talked about your wife."

"She hasn't. Not for years. But I guess making amends is catching. She told me she was sorry, that she should have made more of an effort to get close to Zoe, to get to know her, to make her feel welcome in the family."

"Did you...accept her apology?"

"Yeah. I did." He seemed easy about it, relaxed.

"Well." She clicked her wineglass against his. "Good for you. Good for *both* of you."

"I had a feeling you'd see it that way."

A minute or two passed. It was quiet. She heard a car go by out on the street, and a dog barked a block or two away.

She sipped her wine and broke the silence hesitantly. "About Brighter Horizons..."

He made a low sound, which she hoped was meant to be encouraging. And he still had his arm around her; he hadn't pulled away or tensed up.

So she went for it. "People want to show their gratitude."

"What are you getting at?" He narrowed his eyes at her.

"Hey." She gave him a nudge in the side. "It's okay. I said I won't tell anyone, and I won't. But have you thought that it would be better for the people you're helping if they knew who to thank?"

He grunted. "Better how? I've known most of them all my life and they are proud people. If some faceless, do-gooding foundation gives them a break, they'll take it and say a prayer of thanks. If it's me giving it to them, they owe me, no matter how hard I try to tell them that they don't. Obligation wears on a man. I don't need that from my neighbors. I'm in a position where I can give where the money's needed and let it go at that."

"But—"

He squeezed her shoulder. "You won't change my mind. Might as well stop trying."

She realized she believed him. "All right. You don't want anyone to know. I'll let that one go."

"There's more?"

"Well, I do have more questions."

"Why am I not surprised?" At least he said it in a good-natured tone. And then he leaned in closer and nuzzled her ear, catching her earlobe between his teeth, toying with it a little, making her breath tangle in her throat, sending a thrill zipping through her.

"You're distracting me."

"I like distracting you…." He whispered in the ear he'd been teasing, "What else?"

She hitched in a slow breath and pressed on. "I just… I mean, I kind of figured you must be doing okay, but I had no idea you were rich enough to donate hundreds of thousands to needy causes."

He withdrew from her then, just a little. He still had his arm around her, but he'd turned his head and now he stared out at the darkening sky. "It's a long story…."

She should probably leave it alone. But she didn't. She clasped his hand, where it rested on her shoulder. "I've got all night."

He was quiet. She let go of his hand and wondered if she'd pushed him too far. He'd clearly made up his mind about how he wanted to give his money away and he didn't seem eager to talk much about it. But then he said, "I won four hundred eighty million in the North Dakota Lottery, but I took a lump-sum payout, so I ended up with about half that."

A laugh burst out of her. "Oh, come on. You're kidding me. Back in January, you mean?"

"Uh-huh. That same day I picked you up with your gas can outside Kalispell."

"No...."

"Yeah. I bought the winning Powerball ticket at a Dickinson, North Dakota truck stop about twelve hours after you put the gas in your SUV and drove away."

She turned beneath his arm so she was facing him. Setting her wineglass on the table, she kicked off her sandals and brought her legs up to the side. "So you collected your winnings anonymously?"

"That's right. I hired a lawyer. He set up Brighter Horizons to collect the money."

She stared at him and shook her head. "Amazing."

He set his glass beside hers. "Callie, I'm no man's fool."

"I don't... What does that mean?"

"I've read about what happens to people who win the lottery, the way they kind of go crazy, the way they become the center of a media circus with everybody after them for a piece of what they've got. A lot of them get completely messed up and messed over. They end up practically throwing their winnings away."

"Well, but you..." She stopped herself.

He caught her chin. His eyes were dark, deep as oceans. "Go ahead. You can say it."

"You seem to be doing that, giving a lot of your money away."

"Believe me, what I've given away so far has hardly made a dent in what I've got." He let go of her chin and trailed the back of a finger along the side of her throat, slowly, with great care, as though he couldn't get enough of touching her. She understood the feeling. She couldn't get enough of *being* touched by *him*. "I plan to give a lot more away, as time goes on. And giving it away through the trust is not the same thing as having everyone know I've got money to burn. This way, I'm not being pressured by anybody. I can sit back and see where help is needed and give where and when *I* want to give."

"I can see how that would be wise," she had to admit.

"I've had some rough breaks in my life. And I've also lost track for a while of what really matters. I didn't want to screw up again. I didn't want all the crazy stuff that comes with winning the lottery to happen to me, you know?" At her nod, he continued, "So when I won, I did a little research and figured out what to do—hire a lawyer who could set up a trust for me and keep my name out of it. I got lucky because North Dakota is one of the six states where winners are allowed to be anonymous. Brighter Horizons claimed the money, so my name isn't even on confidential record with the state of North Dakota."

"I can't believe you could be so coolheaded about it all."

"I'm a coolheaded kind of guy."

She leaned close to him, close enough she could feel his warm breath across her cheek. "Not with me, you're not."

He didn't even bother to try and deny it. "I know.

It kind of scares me, how I am with you, if you want to know the truth."

"Don't be scared. I'm not." That wasn't completely true, so she qualified, "At least, not right at the moment, anyway."

He whispered, "Stay the night."

She kissed him. "I thought you'd never ask."

They sat out there on the deck until the sky was awash in stars and the half-moon glowed bright above, like a silver lamp lighting their way.

Later in his darkened bedroom, after making slow, delicious love again, they whispered together, coming to certain agreements: not to spend *every* night together, to take this lovely thing between them more slowly, to proceed with care.

And then in the morning, he made her breakfast again before he sent her off to work. That night, they stayed at her house. And the next night, at his.

Friday night, Faith and Owen Harper had them over for barbecue. It was fun. They ate out in the Harper's backyard. The men drank beer and tended Owen's smoker barbecue. The women talked about Tansy and how Faith was getting along with all the stress of having a new baby. They also discussed the famous Montana psychic, Winona Cobbs. Lissa Roarke had invited the Cobbs woman to town to give a lecture at the new community center next month. The story went that the psychic, who lived down in Whitehorn, Montana, had contacted Lissa at the urgings of her psychic guides. Winona even had her own syndicated newspaper column, Wisdom by Winona.

When they sat down to dinner, they all joked about what psychic messages Winona Cobbs might be planning to deliver. And then Owen brought up the town's mysterious benefactor. He'd run into Emmet at the Ace a couple of days ago and heard that the clinic had received a big check from Brighter Horizons. Callie said how thrilled they were to have the extra funding and was careful not to look in Nate's direction lest she give him away.

They left Faith and Owen's at a little past ten and went to Callie's house. Later, after making love twice, they discussed again how they were going to give each other some space. They didn't need to rush this thing between them. Nate still hadn't decided whether or not he was leaving town. And Callie didn't think she was ready for anything permanent with a man, anyway. They were going to take it slow.

And then the next morning, he made them breakfast as usual, and they spent the day out at the Shooting Star Ranch. Jesse picked out a sweet-natured, patient mare for Callie to ride. Nate chose his favorite gray gelding. They rode for hours, just Callie and Nate, stopping for a picnic way out at the edge of the property in a field of wildflowers beneath the skimpy shadows of some box-elder trees. While the horses munched the summer grass nearby, Nate and Callie canoodled like a couple of teenagers. Later, as they rode back to town, they decided they needed to get busy on the whole giving-each-other-some-space thing.

So when they arrived at home, he went to his house and she went to hers. After all, they were going to be together again the next day for Sunday dinner at his mom's house. They were certainly due a night apart.

Callie made herself a light meal and then tried not to wonder what Nate might be doing. She hadn't called either of her best girlfriends back in Chicago in a while, so she picked up the phone. One of the two, Janie Potter, was at home. They talked for half an hour. Janie asked Callie's advice on some problems she was having at work and Callie tried not to talk too much about Nate.

But Janie wasn't fooled. "You're gone on this cowboy, huh? Good for you."

"Well, I'm trying not to be *too* gone, you know?"

"Why? You like him. He likes you. Enjoy yourselves."

"He might not even be staying in town."

"So? All the more reason to spend every minute you can with him."

"He was married before. His wife died. He hasn't been serious about anyone in the ten years since he lost her."

"Which proves the guy is truehearted, a keeper."

"You think?"

"Callie. Come on. Life is too short. If you like the guy, *be* with him."

They talked a little longer and when they said goodbye, Callie couldn't stop thinking about what Janie had said.

Who knew how long she and Nate might have together? And why *should* they waste a single moment?

Before she could talk herself out of it, she was out the front door, down the walk and on her way up the steps to Nate's house. She couldn't see any lights on inside, but she rang the bell, anyway.

And then she tried not to be too disappointed when he didn't answer. Evidently, he'd gone out.

Which was great. Wonderful. The guy deserved a

little time to himself, for crying out loud. She was not going to be disappointed about it. She was not going to wonder what Nate might be doing now....

In Rust Creek Falls, if you wanted a little Saturday-night fun, the Ace was the place.

Nate stood at the bar, facing out, nursing a beer, not having any fun at all. Mostly, he was just trying not to think about Callie, not to wish for her there beside him—or better yet—for the two of them to be at home together. Maybe sitting out on the deck, watching the stars come out, or in her cozy kitchen, raiding the fridge.

Or in bed.

In bed with Callie. His bed or hers, he couldn't think of any better place to be.

But the space thing was important. He supposed. She deserved a little time to herself now and then. So he was giving it to her, trying to be a sensitive and understanding kind of guy.

He gave the crowded room a slow scan, nodding whenever he made eye contact with someone he knew. A pretty, black-haired girl down at the end of the bar shot him a big smile. He tipped his hat in her direction to be polite, then looked away. Leaning his elbows on the bar, he stared into the middle distance and wondered what Callie was doing about now.

"Hey, cowboy," said a soft voice at his elbow.

He looked over. Sure enough, the black-haired girl. She put her hand on his arm and he glanced down at it and back into her big baby blues.

"Whoa," she said. "Taken, huh?"

Taken? Was he? "Sorry." He left it at that.

She shrugged and tried the guy on her other side.

He finished his beer, turned around to put his money on the bar and was just about to get the hell out of there when Collin Traub appeared on one side of him and Sutter on the other. The hairs on the back of his neck stood up.

But then he remembered that he had made peace with them, more or less. Which made it unlikely that they'd surrounded him in order to start a fight.

"Hey, boys." He tipped his hat at them.

"We were just talking about you," said Sutter.

"Should I be worried?"

Collin laughed. "Maybe."

"I don't know if I like the sound of that."

Sutter clapped him on the back. "Let's see if our favorite booth is available—three longnecks, Larry," he added over his shoulder to the bartender.

Nate wasn't sure why he followed them into the back room. It didn't seem like a very good idea, but he was trying to be cordial with them. What good did it do for a guy to humble himself apologizing and then act like a jerk the next time he ran into the men he had wronged?

Wouldn't you know, even with the Ace full of customers, that booth stood empty.

As before, Nate took one side and the Traub brothers the other. A waitress appeared and plunked down three beers. They tapped bottles and drank.

Sutter said, "Heard you been seeing Callie Kennedy."

"I am, yes."

"Everyone likes Callie," said Collin, as if that was news. Then he warned, "You treat her right." Which was kind of ironic if you thought about it, coming from a man who'd spent his first twenty-five years or so breaking every heart in sight.

"I'll do that," Nate replied, after reminding himself that he was trying to be a better man and being a better man meant making an effort not to take offense at the insulting things other men might say.

"Willa's over at our place with Paige," Sutter explained. "They're working on some summer-school project or other. Paige isn't teaching summer school this year, with the baby coming so soon and all, but she loves to help out when she can."

"They told us to go get a beer," Collin added. "They don't like us in their hair when they're doing crafty stuff."

Nate wasn't following. "Uh, crafty?"

Sutter clarified, "You know, craft projects. Things with colored paper and glue and glitter and rickrack."

"Ah," replied Nate, as if it all made sense to him now, though it really didn't.

Collin said, "So, we came to get a beer and we were talking about the resort project—and here you are, the main guy."

"Er, the main guy for…?"

"The resort project," Sutter said, as though it was completely self-evident.

It didn't seem self-evident to Nate. "Ahem. I'm not the main guy. I said I would be happy to put some money in, but—"

"Well, see, Nate, this is the deal," Collin cut in. "We need someone to spearhead this thing, get it off the ground, you know? And who better than you? I mean, you know people. You got the education and the background and the connections to get something like this moving."

"Oh, come on. I don't know anyone you don't know. And I've never been in the hospitality industry. I told you I know nothing about building or running a resort."

Sutter shrugged. "You can learn."

"We'll get you hooked up with an expert, Grant Clifton," added Collin. "Grant is the genius behind the Thunder Canyon Resort. He can fill you in on anything you need to know."

"But I may not stay in town and—"

Sutter didn't let him finish. "It shouldn't take that long. We're thinking we start out kind of modest, some kind of really nice vacation lodge but on some prime, scenic acreage with the potential for a ski run and great riding trails, with a river or a creek running through it, for rafting and fishing. Then you can build onto the lodge later, add condos, whatever. Eventually it could be a year-round destination. The thing is to get the right property and get the whole thing moving, get the first stage done this year."

"This year?" Nate narrowed his eyes at the other two. "Wait. This is a joke, right? You're yanking my chain."

Collin frowned. "The hell we are." His eyes got that look, the one he always got prior to throwing the first punch. "You think it's funny, that we want to get this project moving?"

For the second time that night, Nate felt certain a brawl was in the offing. And he didn't want that. He wanted peace with the Traubs. He wished he'd never come to the Ace that night. And he *shouldn't* have come, *wouldn't* have come. If not for the damn space issue, he would be home in Callie's arms.

He put up both hands and got to work backpedaling. "I didn't say I thought it was funny. I just think it's impossible and I thought you were joking with me."

"Oh." Collin thought that over. When he spoke again, his tone had turned mild. "Well, no. Not joking." Then he added with enthusiasm, "And *anything* is possible."

"I'm not arguing with you, I'm only—"

"Yeah," Sutter cut in. "You're arguing with us."

Nate insisted, "But it would be impossible to get this…this lodge opened by Christmas."

"Nothing's impossible," Collin decreed. "You just need the right attitude. And yeah, okay. It's kind of shooting for the moon, but why not?"

"That's right," put in Sutter. "Why not aim for the stars? And right now, you're not running the ranch anymore. It's great that you help out at the family store, but your folks and Nina do most of the work there. You're not in town government. You got your investments to live off of and plenty of time on your hands. It's perfect. You're in a position to take this project on and give it your all."

"But I don't want to take this project on."

"I think you do," Collin piped right up.

"I don't."

"Nate." Collin shook his head. "Come on now. Think about it. Rust Creek Falls needs this. You and me, we've had our differences, but we both love our town. We both want the best for the folks who live here. You spearhead this project. Even if you end up leaving, you know you want to leave your town better and stronger than you found it. This resort project is a way for you to do just that."

Nate gaped at the man he'd hated for so much of his life. "How do you do that?"

"Do what?"

"Tell me all the reasons I want to build a resort when I've told you repeatedly that I don't."

Sutter elbowed Collin in the ribs and proudly announced, "He's a born politician."

Nate had to hand it to him. "He is, indeed."

Collin beamed. "So, then. Say you'll do it."

No way was he saying that. But he did want to be on good terms with them—and that meant a flat-out no right now wouldn't fly. He decided his best option was to stall them until he could figure out a way to let them down easy. "I need some time to think this over."

Collin winced. "Not a great idea, being as how time's the thing we're short on."

"I still have to think about it."

"For how long?" Sutter asked grudgingly.

Maybe he could find someone to step in and get the project off the ground. And he was willing to put in some serious cash. He had to find a way to back out of actually running things—but do it gracefully so he could preserve the goodwill he'd humbled himself to achieve. "Until the end of the month. On August first, I'll tell you exactly what I'm willing to do."

"That's three weeks!" Collin blustered. "We don't *have* three weeks."

"Sorry. Best I can do."

Sutter frowned. "You don't look very sorry."

"Oh, come on. Remember, anything is possible.

What's three extra weeks when you're shooting for the stars?"

Collin grunted. "Now you're yankin' *our* chain. But, hey. All right. Three weeks, and then you tell us yes and get to work."

"I don't think that's exactly what I said."

Sutter chuckled. "Yeah, but see, the thing you don't realize yet is that you *are* going to do this."

"No, I didn't say that I would."

Collin grinned. Slowly. "Last Monday, we got you to agree to invest. Today, you're considering spearheading the project. We are moving in the right direction here. Because we keep a positive attitude."

About ten minutes later, the Traubs got up to go. Nate walked out with them. They shook hands in the parking lot. And Nate got in his quad cab and headed for home.

As he pulled into his driveway, he just happened to notice that the porch light was on at Callie's. He didn't see any other lights on, though, and it was full dark by then.

Maybe she was back in the kitchen. Or in the master bathroom, also in the back of the house, next to the kitchen. She might be having a bath.

Now, there was an image to torture a man. Callie in the bathtub, enjoying her space, her hair all pinned up on her head, but bits of it tumbling loose to curl along her flushed, wet cheeks. She'd have fat candles burning, making her smooth skin glow. And bubbles, wouldn't she? Little bath bubbles clinging and dripping between her breasts, down her thigh and along the perfect curve of her calf when she raised her leg out of the water to give it a nice going-over with one of those loofah things women liked to use.

He parked the quad cab and pointed the door opener over his shoulder to bring the garage door rumbling down. And then he just sat there, staring blankly through the windshield, wondering if Callie was even home.

Probably not. She could be anywhere. She had a lot of friends. Maybe she'd gone into Kalispell to catch a movie.

Not that it was any of his damn business where she'd got off to. He had no chains on her. They were giving each other space tonight, and the woman had a right to enjoy her space any damn way she chose.

And why was he sitting here in the garage staring at the wall?

He seriously needed to get a grip.

Muttering bad words under his breath, he got out of the pickup and went inside. And then, when he got there, he somehow couldn't stop himself from going right on through the laundry room into the kitchen and out the back door.

No lights on in her kitchen. There might be a light on in the bathroom, but it was on the other side of the kitchen and he couldn't really tell.

So maybe she was in there, with the bubbles and the loofah.

Or maybe not.

And either way, it was none of his business.

So, then, why was he turning, yanking open the back door, striding fast through the kitchen and the central hall? Because he was an idiot, that's why.

An idiot who just kept going, out the front door,

down the steps, over to her house and right up to her front door. An idiot who rang the doorbell and then waited, hoping against hope that she might be there, not really believing that she was.

Nothing happened. She wasn't there. He needed to turn around and get back to his house, where he belonged.

But then he only lifted his hand again and punched the doorbell a second time.

Nothing.

She wasn't there and he was hopeless. He needed to leave it alone. He turned for the steps again.

And right then, the door swung inward.

Chapter 11

"Nate." She said it softly, with a glowing, pleased smile.

He took in the short, silky robe and the bare feet and the hair piled up just the way he'd pictured it, her skin all flushed and moist. "Tell me to go," he commanded in a growl. "Tell me to get lost and give you your space, like I promised I would."

She just went on smiling, shaking her head—and then stepping back and gesturing him inside. He couldn't clear that threshold fast enough. She shut the door. She smelled of flowers and oranges and all manner of sweet, wonderful things. And steamy, too.

He fisted his hands at his sides in order not to reach for her. "I don't know what's wrong with me."

She went on tiptoe and kissed him—a sweet, quick brush of a kiss. He had to fist his hands harder because he really, really wanted to haul her tight against him.

"It's okay." She smoothed the collar of his shirt. "I missed you, too. I went to your house but you weren't there."

"I went for a beer at the Ace. I was trying to stop thinking about how I wanted to be with you. Sutter and Collin cornered me. Now they've decided I should not only invest in their crazy resort project, I should run it."

She laughed then. And then, with a soft sigh, she rested her head against his shoulder. "What did you tell them?"

He dared to wrap his arms around her, slowly. With care. It felt so good to hold her. "I put them off, said I'd have to think about it."

She tipped her head back and looked up at him, dark eyes bright as stars. "You don't want to do it?"

"What do I know about building a resort? And they want it done by Christmas. It's completely insane."

"You might enjoy it. It would be a challenge for you."

He groaned. "I might enjoy piloting a spaceship. Or performing open-heart surgery. That doesn't mean I'm an astronaut or a surgeon."

"It's not the same. You wouldn't be building the thing yourself. You could get advice from experts, hire an architect and a builder. And I know you've got the vision and the brains to make it happen."

He kissed the tip of her nose. "You're worse than the Traubs. I can't afford to be pinned down with something like that."

Those bright eyes dimmed just a little. "Oh. Right. Because you need to be free to leave town any day now...."

He thought about that, about leaving her, and doubted

he could do it. But something within him still couldn't quite admit that. "I'm a jerk, huh? And you're mad at me now."

She gave him the sweetest, saddest little smile. "Why should I beat you up? You're doing such a fine job of it all on your own."

He pulled her closer, breathed her in and whispered, "Since Monday…"

"What about it?"

"Monday was our first night together."

"Right." She gave a little nod.

He confessed, "Five days of you and me. And already I can't see myself ever leaving you."

She tucked her head beneath his chin, fitting herself against him as though she was born to be there. "Hold that thought." And then she reached around behind her and captured his hand. "Come on. Let's go to bed."

He pressed his lips into the fragrant silk of her hair. "I get to stay?"

"Of course."

"I really like the way you say that." It came out gruff and ragged, freighted with emotions he'd never thought to feel again.

She turned, unwrapping herself from his arms but keeping a firm hold of his hand. "This way…."

The door to her bedroom was right there, off the entry. He followed her in.

She led him to the bed, which was turned back to reveal soft sheets printed with flowers. "Sit down." He did. She knelt and pulled off his boots and his socks. "Stand up again." He rose. And she unbuttoned and unzipped and took the rest of his clothes away. "There."

She stood back to admire her handiwork. Her eyes were dark velvet. "Oh, Nate…"

He just wanted her naked. Naked in his arms. "Take off the robe." He said it much too roughly.

But she didn't argue or even seem to mind that his tone wasn't as gentle as it should have been. She simply untied the belt, slipped it off and stuck it into the pocket. Then she peeled back the sides of the robe and eased it down her shoulders. It floated to the floor.

And there she was, all womanly curves, velvet skin, with that long, softly curling silky hair he loved to wrap around his hand.

"Callie…" It felt so good it hurt, just to say her name.

"Yes, Nate?"

"Come here."

It was only one step and she took it. He pulled her close and then he guided her down to the bed.

The rest was all he wanted and more than he'd ever hoped for. Her hair, her scent, her skin surrounded him. She made all the lonely years fade to nothing. She was all the answers to the questions a man didn't even have the sense to ask.

And later, when she turned off the light and he tucked her in spoon-style, her back to his front, when he wrapped his arm around her to hold her close to his body through the night, he thought that here, with her, was where he wanted to be.

For now.

And forever.

But he didn't say so. Forever was a mighty big word and a man had to choose just the right time to say it.

* * *

The next night was dinner at his parents' house. His brothers and sisters were all there, even Nina, with Dallas and baby Noelle and the boys.

His mom served her famous fried chicken and mashed potatoes, beans with bacon, and apple pie for dessert. She and his dad beamed at each other from either end of the long family table, to have their whole family together for a Sunday-night meal.

Callie fit right in, as Nate had known she would. She chatted with Nina and Natalie and spent a lot of time holding baby Noelle. His mom got her alone in the kitchen for a few minutes.

Later, at his house, Nate asked her what his mom had said.

"Just that she thinks we look good together and she hopes I'll come to Sunday dinner again."

"Will you?" He couldn't stop himself from asking.

She put her hand on his chest, right over his heart. "Anytime you ask me to."

"She doesn't make you crazy?"

"Your mother? No way."

The days took on a satisfying rhythm. Weekday mornings, Nate cooked breakfast and saw her off to work. They might sleep at his house or hers—but they always slept together.

They let the whole "space" issue take care of itself. She went out on a Tuesday evening with her newcomer girlfriends. And the following Saturday afternoon, she went to a baby shower for Paige.

He had his own independent routines. He helped out at the store, had weekly meetings with Saul in Kalispell, trying to decide which business investments to put money in. And when his brothers needed him, he pitched in at the Shooting Star. He and Callie might be apart all day and all evening. But from bedtime on, it was always the two of them. And she seemed to like it that way as much as he did.

They didn't speak of the future. But he thought about it a lot, thought about how well they got on together, how he never wanted what they had together to end.

He thought about the things he'd never planned to think about again: wedding rings and the two of them standing up before a preacher. About which house they would live in if they made it official.

About the good years ahead of them, building a life.

About children.

After what had happened to Zoe and the baby, thinking about children scared the crap out of him. He'd never planned to get married again. He'd told himself he couldn't do that after what had happened. He would never marry, never have a kid. His wife and son had died. End of story.

Except that now there was Callie. And she was so very much alive. And he was thinking on forever, thinking of the ways to give her everything she wanted.

And if a baby was what she wanted, well, maybe he could even do that. For her sake. Maybe…

On the last Saturday in July, the Traub family was planning a big barbecue out at the Traub ranch, the Triple T. On the Tuesday before the barbecue, Nina asked him to come to it. Then on Wednesday, Paige invited Callie. And then on Thursday, he got a call from Collin of all people.

"Grant Clifton's coming up from Thunder Canyon for the barbecue on Saturday," Collin said. "You'll have all your questions answered."

Grant Clifton. The name was vaguely familiar. Nate asked, "All my questions about…?"

Collin laughed. "You don't remember? Grant Clifton runs the Thunder Canyon Resort."

He remembered then. Unfortunately. "Ah."

"August first is right around the corner." Collin sounded way too pleased about that. "See you Saturday."

Nate hung up and felt guilty, which thoroughly pissed him off. He'd never wanted anything to do with the resort project. Yet somehow the Traub brothers had messed with his mind until he'd started to feel responsible for it. How in hell had they managed that?

He drove over to Kalispell for a quick meeting with Saul. Saul thought the resort was a fine idea—or could be, if Nate got the right team together. Nate was in a good position to get into something like that, Saul said, because he had access to plenty of capital. He wouldn't go under if it took a while for the project to pay off—and hospitality businesses were notorious for taking a long time to turn a profit. Nate drove back to Rust Creek Falls no closer to knowing what to do about the resort project than he'd ever been and muttering bad things about the Traub brothers under his breath.

Saturday, he and Callie headed for the Triple T at two in the afternoon. The barbecue was set up in a pretty spot not far from the barns and the houses owned by various members of the family. They'd put up several canopies for shade and five long picnic tables to accommodate the crowd. There were kids running everywhere, grills and smokers going, beer and soft drinks in coolers and plenty of folding chairs, so you could sit down and visit whenever the mood struck.

Nate got a beer and stuck close to Callie. She wore tight jeans and a little red T-shirt, those red boots and her red hat. What man wouldn't want to stand at her side?

But then Paige and Willa, Collin's wife, grabbed her and took her away with them to do whatever women did at gatherings like this one. He went looking for Dallas and Nina, thinking he'd visit with them for a while, kid around with Dallas's three boys and spend a little quality time with baby Noelle.

He'd just spotted them under one of the canopies when Collin appeared at his side. "Nate. There you are."

"Nice day for a barbecue." That was Sutter. On his other side.

"Come on," said Collin. "We'll introduce you to Grant."

Nate surrendered to the inevitable. The brothers took him over to a shady spot under a maple tree where a tall, blue-eyed man in his late thirties stood with a pretty green-eyed blonde.

Collin made the introductions. "Nate Crawford, Stephanie and Grant Clifton."

Nate shook hands with Grant and told Stephanie how pleased he was to meet her. Sutter went off and came back with folding chairs, so they all sat in a ring under the tree. There was chitchat about life in Thunder Canyon, about how much Grant was enjoying his first visit to Rust Creek Falls.

Eventually, Collin guided the conversation around

to Grant's work at the Thunder Canyon Resort. Grant talked easily, comfortably. About everything from startup costs and property acquisition, to staff hiring and training, marketing and advertising, operations, growth projections and ongoing management. Nate found the conversation fascinating and had to remind himself more than once that he was supposed to be coming up with a way to get *out* of this crazy project—not allow himself to be drawn in deeper and deeper.

When Collin mentioned that they wanted to get the resort up and running by the holidays, Grant did a double take that had Nate biting his lip to keep from laughing. "Now, there's a real challenge for you," Clifton said at last. "Best of luck, boys."

"No law says we can't try," Sutter put in.

Clifton agreed that there was nothing wrong with setting a challenging goal. He promised to make himself available for future consultation as the project moved forward.

About then, Bob Traub, Collin and Sutter's dad, rang the bell to get everyone to start moving toward the tables.

Collin said, "Let's eat." He took over, herding them toward a table under a canopy where Willa, Paige and Callie were already seated.

Callie looked up and grinned at him as he took the chair beside her—and right then, at that exact moment, as her shining eyes locked with his, it happened.

Everything changed. Right then, as he started to sit down beside her under that canopy at the Traub family barbecue, Nate Crawford knew the whole truth at last.

He knew it from the crown of his hat to the toes of his tooled dress boots, in his stubborn head, as well as his yearning heart. There were no more maybes. No more hesitations. No more need to keep thinking things over.

The simple, perfect, undeniable truth was that he loved her. He loved her and he wanted a life with her.

And he was a jackass, and a fool one at that, to keep holding on to the idea that he might leave town. He was never leaving Rust Creek Falls. He wasn't going anywhere that she didn't want to be.

A breeze lifted the long waves of her hair beneath that red hat. She tipped her head sideways and gave him a look both tender and questioning.

He opened his mouth to say it, right then and there, in front of God and the Traubs and everyone.

But before he got the words out, Paige Traub let out a cry and shot to her feet. "Something's…" She let out another shocked, guttural sound. Her body curved over her giant belly. Her face was so red it looked purple, eyes bulging, the veins in her neck standing out in sharp relief. She clutched for Sutter, who had jumped to his feet beside her. "Sutter, oh, no…." Kicking her chair away, she staggered back, groaning some more, her hand, fingers splayed, supporting the heavy weight of her belly. Fluid thick with green streaks ran down between her legs below the hem of the denim maternity dress she wore.

Sutter barely managed to catch her as she crumpled toward the ground.

Chapter 12

Sutter scooped Paige up and headed for the nearest house.

"Callie!" Paige cried. "I need Callie…."

"I'm here," Callie promised. She gave Nate's hand a squeeze and followed.

The house was Dallas and Nina's place. Nate watched as Nina rose from the table several yards away. She gave Noelle to Dallas and raced for the house, too, probably to see if there was anything she could do to help.

Nate stayed with the others. Nobody ate. They all just sat there, waiting, praying, whispering quietly to each other. Even the children were subdued.

Nate didn't talk to anyone. He just waited. Collin said something to him at one point, something meant to reassure—Nate knew that by the gentle tone of Collin's voice. Nate turned to him and stared at him blankly. Had Collin heard about Zoe and how he'd lost her? Nate had no idea. And he certainly wasn't about to discuss it now. He couldn't even make his mouth form words.

He only kept seeing Paige, crumpling to the ground, clutching her big belly, that green-streaked water running down her legs. He only kept remembering Zoe. His lost Zoe. And the little boy they named Logan, who never drew a single breath.

Meconium. That was the green stuff, they told Nate later. Logan had experienced fetal distress. He'd aspirated meconium, breathed it in, gasping for air that wasn't there, trying to be born and not making it.

Never making it…

Nate closed his eyes. As if that could help him blot out the memories, blot out his failure all those years ago. Blot out his wrong choices, that had led to the worst conceivable outcome.

Blot out the horrible possibility that what had happened to Zoe and Logan might be happening in Nina's house to Paige and her baby, too.

He didn't know how long he sat there. It couldn't have been all that long before he heard the siren. The ambulance came speeding down the long road from the highway, kicking up a high trail of dust in its wake. It stopped in front of Nina's house and the EMTs went in with a stretcher.

They emerged a few minutes later, carrying Paige, who had Sutter on one side and Callie on the other, Nina trailing behind. Even from way over at the table where he sat, Nate could see the way Paige clung to

Sutter, could hear her cry out that she wanted her nurse practitioner and her husband with her in the ambulance.

They put her in the back. Sutter spoke to Callie briefly. She nodded, patted his arm. And then he went around and got in with the driver.

Callie and Nina turned and came toward the silent people clustered at the tables. Nate stood up then, without even realizing he was doing it. One second, he was sitting there staring, and the next, he was on his feet. Callie came to him. She wrapped her arms around him.

He looked down numbly at her bare head. She must have left the red hat in the house.

And then she looked up at him. Her eyes were so dark, full of worry. "Come on. I need you to take me to the hospital."

Some of them, including Nina, stayed behind to look after the children. But everyone else formed a caravan and headed for the hospital in Kalispell.

The short drive seemed to take forever. Callie didn't say much. That was fine with him. He didn't know what to say, anyway. Everything seemed way too clear to him now.

Clear in the most final kind of way.

At the hospital, there were so many of them, they overran the waiting room. There weren't enough chairs for all of them, so they stood around, silent as they'd been back at the ranch. Waiting for word.

Callie stayed with Nate. They stood near a wall with a framed picture of a mother holding a laughing, healthy baby. Nate looked at that picture once.

And never again.

Some Daltons showed up—one of Paige's sisters and her mom and dad, Mary and Ben.

Eventually, Sutter came out looking a decade older than he had just an hour before. Everyone stood to attention.

Sutter went to Paige's mom and whispered something. Mary Dalton nodded. Then he looked toward where Callie and Nate stood by the wall. "Callie," he said. "She's asking for you. They said it's okay if you come."

So Callie went with him.

When the two of them had disappeared down the long hallway and through the double doors at the end, Paige's mom told them all that the baby and Paige were hanging in there and there would be a cesarean.

Hanging in there, Nate thought. What did that *mean,* really? It was one of those things people said when it would be too big of a lie to say everything was all right.

They waited some more.

After a while, Nate went and got some awful coffee from a vending machine and drank it—not because he wanted it, but because it was something to do to help pass the time that seemed to crawl by at the speed of a dying snail.

Finally, a woman in green scrubs with a surgery mask hanging around her neck came out of the double doors. She asked for Mary and Ben Dalton. When they stood up, she said she was Dr. Lovell. She said the surgery had been a success and that the baby and Paige were going to be all right.

She led Paige's parents away to see their daughter and have a look at their new grandson.

After that, everyone started talking excitedly, shaking hands and clapping each other on the back. They hugged each other; they cried happy tears.

Nate sank slowly onto a chair. Through the numbness that seemed to enclose him, he was vaguely aware of a feeling of relief.

They made it, he thought. *Paige and the baby will be all right.*

He was glad for them. So glad. Glad for Sutter and all the Traubs. And the Daltons, as well.

Collin, grinning widely, said something to him and clapped a hand on his shoulder. He looked up and replied, nodding, forcing a smile, hardly knowing what words he said.

Now that the danger was passed, people started leaving. Nate stayed in the chair, waiting for Callie, who would need him to take her home.

Eventually, she emerged from the long hallway. She stopped and spoke to the people who were left, telling Collin and Willa that Paige was a trouper, that the baby, little Carter Benjamin, was breathing on his own and doing well.

Nate stood when she finally came to him. He thought that she was so very fine, beautiful inside and out. Everything he could have wanted.

She took his hand. "Let's go home."

He got up and they got out of there.

She didn't say much on the way back to town. That was fine with him. He didn't know what to say, anyway. He kept remembering that moment at the table before everything went wrong, that moment when he knew that his heart was hers and there was no going back.

That moment seemed a million years ago now. He

couldn't find that moment again, couldn't be the man who knew the way to make a life with her.

He didn't love her any less.

He only knew that he couldn't.

Just couldn't.

And that was all.

Something was very wrong with Nate. Callie knew it in her bones.

She understood that what had happened to Paige had affected him deeply, and she understood why. Because he'd told her. In detail. The night that Faith Harper had given birth to little Tansy.

What she didn't know was what to do about it, how to reach him—or even when she ought to try. Sometimes the wisest thing in a situation like this was to leave it alone for a while.

She decided to do that. To give Nate a chance to work through his reaction to the events of the day for himself.

They were halfway home when it started raining, fat drops splattering against the windshield, the wind rising, lightning forking twice across the sky, followed by two long, deep rolls of thunder.

When they got to South Pine Street, she half expected him to say he wanted some time alone. But he surprised her and went to her house with her. The rain drummed on the windows as they threw together some sandwiches, watched TV for a little while, sitting on her sofa, not saying a word. She took his hand twice. Both times he accepted her touch and let his hand rest in hers. But then, within a few minutes, he gently withdrew.

At a little after ten, his cell rang. He got it out of his pocket and checked the display. "It's my mom. She'll want to know about Paige. Would you…deal with her?"

So Callie took the phone and told Laura what had happened. At the end, Laura asked, "Nate?"

"He's right here." She tried a smile for him. But he only jumped up from the sofa and backed away, shaking his head at her. So she told Laura he was busy and would give her a call later.

Laura said, "Is he okay?"

Callie hardly knew how to answer that. "He's… Well, it's been a rough day."

"Take care of him, honey," his mother said softly.

"I will. I promise." She said goodbye.

Nate stood in front of the dark fireplace and stared at her. She watched him, not knowing what to say, until he demanded, "What?"

And she couldn't just go on pretending that nothing was wrong. "Your mother asked if you were all right."

"So?"

"You heard what I told her. We both know it was an evasion. You are not all right."

He waved a hand. "Look. Don't get on me."

"Nate, I'm not getting on you. I just think it would be better, you know, if you talked about it. If you told me what's eating at you."

He put up both hands then, as if she held a gun to him. "Look."

She waited for him to say something more. He stared at her through haunted eyes, slowly lowering his hands until they hung at his sides.

Finally, he spoke again. "Callie." Her name seemed dredged up from somewhere way down deep inside of him. "I… I've really screwed up and I'm so damn sorry. I can't do this, you know? I can't go on and do this anymore."

She gaped at him, her throat clutching, her stomach sinking. "I don't… What do you mean, Nate? What are you telling me?"

He raised his arms again, raked both hands back through his hair. "I thought that I…that we could…" Again he let his hands drop. And this time he drew his broad shoulders back and faced her squarely. "I have to go. I have to let *you* go. This isn't right. You are so fine, so good. So true. You deserve everything, all the best from a good, solid man. I'm not the one for you. You saw what happened to Paige today."

Slowly, she rose. "Nate. Come on. Paige came through okay. The baby is going to be all right. This isn't ten years ago. What happened to Zoe *does* happen. But not very often if there's medical help available." She went to him.

He watched her, warily. "Fine. Right. I know that. But I can't… What if it *did* happen to you? What if we had a baby and it happened to you?"

"It's not going to happen to me." She reached up, brushed her hand along his beard-rough cheek.

He caught her wrist and carefully put it away from him. "You don't know that. You can never know that. Not for sure. You just can't."

She didn't know what else to do, how to get through to him, so she just went ahead and told him what she'd been holding back while she waited for him to admit to her that he loved this town and he loved her, that all his talk about moving away was just that: talk and nothing more. "I love you, Nate. I love you with all my heart."

He winced as if she'd struck him. "Don't love me. Don't."

"Too late. I love you. That's how it is." She let out a sad little laugh. "I used to be afraid that Zoe would always stand between us. But I'm not afraid of that anymore. I know that you loved her, and I'm glad that you did. I know she would want, above all, for you to be happy. And you *can* be happy. I promise you can, if you'll only allow yourself to be."

"Don't."

"I know what's in your heart, Nate. I know that you love me, too." She took his hand, laid it above her breast. "Here. I know it here."

Something flared in those shadowed eyes. For a moment, she dared to hope he would grab her close and tight, that he would confess that she was absolutely right, he loved her, too.

And then he did reach for her. She let out a cry of pure joy as his arms closed hard around her. She felt his lips against her throat, heard the rough groan he couldn't suppress. She knew that it would be all right.

Until he muttered, harsh and low, "I'm sorry, Callie. So damn sorry for what a complete jerk I am, for the way I'm letting you down. But it's over."

She shoved back from him and gripped his shoulders, gave him a shake to bring him back to his senses. "No. No, that's not true."

"It is. And I have to go." He lifted his hands, took hold of hers and, gently, tenderly, pushed her away.

"Go?" She stared at him as he circled around her and headed for the front door. "Go where?"

He took his hat off the peg. "Hell if I know." Then he opened the door and stepped out into the storm.

* * *

Nate was wet to the skin by the time he mounted his front porch steps.

He didn't care. He just knew it was time.

Time to go. As he'd gone from Zoe and Logan's funeral ten years back—driving and driving until he had to stop. Getting away, staying on the move, from one state to another. Trying to forget. Trying to put his love and his hope behind him, trying to outrun a loss so deep it hollowed him out right down to the core of him.

He let himself in the house and went straight up the stairs to his bedroom. He got his big suitcase from the closet and piled some clothes in it. Then he moved on to the bathroom, where he grabbed his shaving gear and stuck it into the zippered leather case he kept under the sink. That went in the suitcase, too. He zipped the damn thing closed, grabbed it by the handle and went out of the bedroom, down the stairs, to the kitchen and out into the garage through the laundry room. He tossed the suitcase into the back of the quad cab and climbed in behind the wheel.

No, he had no clue where he was going. He only knew it was time—past time—to leave. To get away from home, from Callie, from everything and everyone who mattered to him.

He backed out of the driveway, sent the garage door rumbling down, turned the wipers on high and got out of there.

It was a hell of a rainstorm, almost as bad as the one the night Faith Harper had her baby. Lightning fired up the sky and thunder boomed. The wipers could hardly keep up with the sheer volume of water pouring down.

He was careful. He watched the road and kept his

speed under control—not so much because he gave a damn what might happen to him, but because he didn't want to endanger anyone else who might be out in the storm.

Almost to Kalispell, he saw a flash of movement at the side of the road.

A deer. It kept coming, bolting across the highway, directly in front of him. He swerved to miss it—and must have hit a slick spot. The truck started spinning like those whirlybird firecrackers on the Fourth of July. Nate worked the wheel, trying to give it play and steer into the slide as he spun across the center line all the way over to the opposite shoulder of the road.

A big tree loomed in the windshield. There was no steering free of that. He squinted at the sudden wash of hard brightness, the reflection of his headlights on the tree trunk right before impact. A tire exploded. Metal screamed and screeched.

And then nothing.

When he came to himself again, he had a face full of air bag. It hurt, as though someone had whacked him in the mouth with a dead fish. For a moment, he just sat there, listening to the sighs of twisted metal and the wheezing of the wrecked engine.

Then he pushed the air bag aside, unhooked his seat belt and tried the door.

Wonder of wonders, it opened with only a loud creaking sound of complaint.

He got out. And then he bent at the knees and took a moment to wait for his breath to come even, his heart to stop trying to beat its way out of his chest.

The rain was still coming down, not as hard as before but damn hard enough. He'd lost his hat. It was probably in the backseat with his suitcase somewhere. Water ran down his forehead and into his mouth.

When he finally stood straight, he saw pretty much what he'd expected to see. The good news? The deer had gotten away. His pickup? Totaled. The front of it was wrapped nice and cozy around the tree, one headlight still beaming, its light canted crazily toward the sky.

It took him a minute longer to register where he was.

The rain came down, and a shiver worked its way up the back of his neck, a shiver that had nothing at all to do with cold. Beyond the tree that had eaten his pickup, he saw the fence with the For Sale sign on it. Beyond the fence, that thicket of new-growth ponderosa pines. And farther out, in the distance, on a high point looming into the dark sky: *Bledsoe's Folly.*

Nate had crashed his truck in the exact same spot where he'd picked up Callie on the fifteenth of January.

Callie.

He knew then. He saw it all. She'd come into his life and changed everything.

What in hell was he thinking, to leave her? He could never leave her. She was everything to him.

The rain ran down the sides of his neck and under his collar. It plastered his hair to his head, and he had to be careful with every breath not to suck it up his nose. But he hardly noticed all that.

The fog of fear and panic had lifted somehow, leaving him seeing it all so clearly now—what to do, how it would work out.

He stared at the dark shape of Bledsoe's Folly and thought about all those beautiful acres surrounding it, about the mountains farther out where there would surely be just the right spot to put up a ski run. And there was more than one pretty little creek on that property, lots of access to national forest and plenty of horse trails.

The house itself? He could see it now—not as it was, but as it would be. They would put a talented architect to work on it, and it would become the main lodge of the resort. The plumbing and electric was already in place. With a little bit of luck, it might even be possible to have a grand opening sometime during the holidays, just as Collin and Sutter had insisted would happen....

Headlights cut the night, coming from home. He stood there, with the rain running down his face, as the silver-gray SUV pulled in next to the smoking ruin of his truck.

His heart seemed to fill up his whole chest when Callie got out. She'd had the sense to put on a rain slicker. She came and stood at his side, the yellow hood of the slicker hiding her face from him.

Finally, she turned and looked at him. God, there was no woman on earth like her. He could see she was torn between laughing and crying.

"There was a deer," he offered lamely. "It got away."

She stared at him for a moment more, then faced the pickup again. "Did you call for a tow truck?"

"The wreck's well off the road. It can wait till morning."

"You should maybe call Sheriff Christensen, at least, to let him know what happened."

"I'll do that. Yeah." But he didn't reach for his phone.

Silence from her. The rain poured down. All the

things he needed to say to her were tumbling around in his head.

And then she asked, "Need a ride home?"

It was more than he could take. "Callie…" He grabbed her hand and hauled her close.

She let out a cry, and her slicker made silly squeaky sounds as she wrapped her arms around him. "You're soaking wet," she scolded.

"I'm a damn hopeless fool." He pushed the hood away from her neck so that he could bury his nose there and breathe in the scent of her. "I love you. Callie. I love you more than I know how to say."

"Yeah," she said on a soft, little sob. "I know that."

"I completely freaked out."

"Know that, too."

"But damned if I could ever really leave you. There is no way. You are everything I thought was gone, and more. You are the hope I hardly dared to have. And I want us to get married and somehow, I want to find a way to be the husband you need. The, um…" He had to swallow hard before he could say it. "The father of your children."

"Nate." She stroked his streaming hair, cradled his wet cheek. "Oh, Nate, you think *you* got scared? You scared *me.* I heard you drive away. And I stood at my front window and didn't know what to do. Finally, I just got in my car and came after you."

"I'm sorry. So sorry…"

She caught his face between both hands. "I think you maybe need to talk to someone, you know? Work out this fear you can't seem to shake."

He let out a disbelieving snort. "A shrink. You want me to see a shrink?"

"Yeah. Yeah, I do. Someone to help you work this thing through, someone to make it so you can finally, truly move on."

He didn't even argue. Because it was what she needed from him. And because, well, he knew she was right. "I will. Yes. I'll get a little counseling."

She sniffed and palmed water off her streaming brow. "All right, then. Wonderful."

"Callie..." He couldn't get enough of just holding her, of looking at her dripping face. "Callie. If I work it out, if I get past this crap, will you maybe marry me?"

"Of course I'll marry you," she said without a second's hesitation. "And there are no 'ifs' about it. I love you, Nate Crawford. You're the guy for me."

He kissed her then, standing there in the rain by the wreck of his pickup, a kiss that was his promise to move on from the past, his vow to be with her now and forever, for as long as they both drew breath.

Then they got in her SUV. He was about to call Gage Christensen when a highway patrolman pulled up. The patrolman turned in an accident report and agreed that morning would be soon enough to have the wreck towed away.

On the way home, Nate told Callie about his idea for Bledsoe's Folly, how he couldn't wait to tell Collin and Sutter all about it. She laughed and said it was going to be fabulous.

And up ahead, the sky was clearing. He could see the stars. Tomorrow would be a beautiful day.

* * * * *

Christyne Butler is a *USA TODAY* bestselling author who fell in love with romance novels while serving in the US Navy and started writing her own stories in 2002. She writes contemporary romances that are full of life, love and a hint of laughter. She lives with her family in central Massachusetts and loves to hear from her readers at christynebutler.com.

Books by Christyne Butler

Harlequin Special Edition

Welcome to Destiny

Destiny's Last Bachelor?
Flirting with Destiny
Having Adam's Baby
Welcome Home, Bobby Winslow
A Daddy for Jacoby

Montana Mavericks: 20 Years in the Saddle!

The Last-Chance Maverick

Montana Mavericks: Rust Creek Cowboys

The Maverick's Summer Love

Montana Mavericks: Back in the Saddle

Puppy Love in Thunder Canyon

Visit the Author Profile page at Harlequin.com for more titles.

THE LAST-CHANCE MAVERICK

Christyne Butler

To my husband, Len,
for believing in one last chance

Prologue

Carrollton Cancer Center, Philadelphia, PA
Eleven months ago

"Okay, read it to me..." Adele's voice faded for a moment as she struggled to speak against the plastic mask covering her nose and mouth that supplied her with fresh oxygen. "...again. We need to finish our list."

Vanessa Brent swallowed hard against the lump in her throat that refused to go away. Every time she walked into this room—as plush and beautiful and unlike a hospital room as a sun-filled space could be—she had the same physical reaction and it stayed with her until she'd left again.

One would think after three months of being here on a daily basis she'd be used to the sight of her best friend fighting a battle they'd recently accepted she wasn't going to win. That she'd be able to sit here, hold Adele's hand and do as she asked.

"All of it?" Glad her words managed to find their way around the obstacle in her throat, Vanessa glanced at the aged piece of paper she held in her hand. Titled "Adele and Vanessa's Bucket List, created July 4, 2001, Secret Clubhouse, Vanessa's Attic, Chestnut Hill, PA," the well-creased, lined sheet of notebook paper was covered with two distinct styles of handwriting, one belonging to her twelve-year-old self and the other a more mature scrawl. "Or just the things we've added?"

They'd discovered the childhood list one day while going through some forgotten boxes in Vanessa's loft apartment. Back when they'd thought Adele had once again beaten the childhood cancer that returned at the tender age of twenty-five, but then went into remission after treatment.

That had been just before Easter. By early June Adele was back in the hospital, but during those few precious weeks they'd managed to check off some of the items on their list.

"Start at the beginning." Adele turned to look at her, the bright red silk scarf protecting her sensitive scalp brushing against the pillow. "Let's review...what we've done...so far."

Taking a deep breath, she started reading. "Number one—dance beneath the Eiffel Tower. I did that back in college the year I studied abroad," Vanessa said, thankful she had a photograph to honor the event as she technically didn't remember doing so thanks to generous amounts of wine that night. "Number two—swim in the Pacific Ocean. You did that when you were in college."

Adele smiled, but remained silent.

"Number three—get a tattoo." Letting go, she flipped her hand and laid it side by side next her friend's, their matching interlocking heart tattoos visible on their inner wrists. "Number four—see a Broadway show. By ourselves."

They'd done both on a last-minute road trip to New York City that Adele had insisted on in May not long after they'd found their long forgotten list.

"Shouldn't have taken us…until age twenty-five to accomplish—" her friend rasped "—either of those."

"Considering how unhappy your mother was with us for taking off without telling her, not to mention our permanent souvenirs, we're lucky she didn't ground us when we got home like she used to do when we were kids."

"I think my mom was more worried because of me being in remission. Your father never said a word."

Vanessa wasn't even sure her father had even realized she'd left the city, much less inked her body. "Okay, let's see. We did go to Disney World on our senior class trip so that counted for number five. I was lucky enough to visit the White House and shake hands with the president during an art exhibit a few years back. Number six. I attempted to learn to scuba dive while visiting Australia the summer before my mother—well, before she got sick, so that covers numbers seven and eight."

"That's right. So you swam in the Pacific Ocean, too."

"Well, technically, it was the Tasman Sea. It doesn't count. So, other than the first eight, we haven't managed to accomplish the rest of the 2001 list." While

Vanessa was sure that flying among the clouds (and not in an airplane!) was a childish wish that would never come true, she guessed moving out west, learning to ride a horse and the last goal, kissing a cowboy, were still possible. At least for her.

She swallowed hard again, but the unfairness of it all kept the lump firmly in place. "You know, judging from the last few items, I think we watched too many old Westerns back when we were twelve."

"I always liked John Wayne. The strong, silent type," Adele said. "So how many…do we have so far now? With the new ones included?"

"The original twelve and the eight we added while in New York." Vanessa read through the rest of the list. When her friend had insisted on updating it with new goals that weekend, they'd truly believed both of them would have time to accomplish things like going skinny-dipping, being part of a flash mob or dancing in the rain. Knowing now that her friend was never going to be able to accomplish any of them… "I think twenty is a good number."

"No. Need four more. Twelve old and twelve new."

"Well, number twenty is to see an active volcano. I don't know how we're—" Vanessa's voice caught again, but she pushed on. "How we're going to top that."

"Number twenty-one—take a bubble bath…with a man."

She couldn't help but smile at her friend's words as she propped her sketchbook on the edge of Adele's bed, using it as a base to write on. "How do you know I haven't done that already?"

"Because you would've told me. Best friends tell each other everything."

Vanessa nodded. "You're right. And I think that might top the volcano experience."

"Number twenty-two—kiss… Prince Charming and number twenty-three…" Adele's voice fell to a whisper, barely heard over the steady beeping from the row of machines on the far side of her bed. "…have a baby. Or two. Or three."

Vanessa blinked rapidly against the sting of tears, struggling to see clearly enough to add them to the list. Adele's words brought back the memory of how each of them, being only children, had always wished for younger siblings. That shared secret, revealed on the day they first met when Adele's mother had come to work for Vanessa's as a social secretary, had sealed their lifelong friendship. She still remembered the afternoon she'd returned from a ballet lesson and found a scrawny girl, her flaming red hair in braids and wearing a hand-me-down dress with dirt on her knees, sitting on the silk tufted bench in the grand foyer of Vanessa's home reading *Little Women*.

"And number twenty-four…fall in love forever."

Vanessa's fingers tightened on the pen until she was sure it would break. She tried to write the last goal, but the page was too blurry.

Then Adele's fingers brushed against the back of her hand. She latched onto her friend's cool touch and pressed Adele's hand to her heated cheek. "That's… that's quite a list."

"It's not a list. It's a life. Your life." Adele's voice became strong and clear, more than it has been in days. "It's time for you to get back to it."

"Adele—"

"You've been with me constantly over the last year. I'm surprised you've found time to get any painting done, not that I want you to jump back into your crazy work schedule." She paused for another breath. "And I know it's you I have to thank for being as comfortable with this outrageously expensive hospital room. My mom and I are so grateful—"

"Oh, shut up," Vanessa admonished her friend gently, her gaze still on the blurred list. "You know I would pay anything—*do anything*—to have you well again."

Adele jiggled on Vanessa's hand, signaling she wanted her attention. Vanessa brushed away the tears before looking at her friend who'd tugged the plastic mask from her face.

"What's that saying? We only have one shot at life, but if we do it right once is enough? You know better than most—especially now—how quickly life can be taken away," Adele said, her voice low and strained. "Don't get so lost in your art after I'm gone that you forget about all the wonderful things waiting out there for you."

"I still have three pieces to finish," Vanessa said, the familiar argument returning once again. One that had started years ago between them when she'd spent her thirteenth birthday working on a painting instead of attending a school dance. "You know how I get before a show. This is an important one, too. People are coming from Europe, the Far East—"

"You've been painting since you were a kid," Adele cut her off. "You were a star in the art world at seventeen and we both know that's because you buried yourself in your art after your mom died. Please don't do that again. Thanks to your gift and your trust fund, you're set for…life. It's time to live it."

"You make me sound like a nun or something."

"You're not too far off. What happened to that fun-loving girl you were a few years ago?"

Vanessa's memory flashed back to her time in Paris. "That was college, Adele. Being foolish and wild was part of the curriculum back then. Now, it's about my work."

"There's more to life…than work. Than art."

Vanessa had heard all of this before. Adele had always been supportive of her career, especially during the darkest moment in her life after her mother died when Vanessa was only sixteen, but she also constantly reminded her there was more to the world than her beloved brushes and paints.

"Art *is* my life, Adele. It's what got me through the pain and the heartache last time." She pulled in a deep breath, but her eyes filled again. "I'm counting on it to help me again…. Oh, how am I going to…"

Adele tightened her hold. "Please, don't be sad…for too long. We've talked about this. That's why I insisted we finish our list. I want you to go out there and experience all the things we've dreamed about. I want you to put check marks by every single one of those items."

The fact that her friend was spending her last days thinking of her made the constant ache inside Vanessa fracture a bit more, sending icy tentacles deeper and further, their frozen tips scraping at her heart. The feeling was a familiar one, felt for the first time since almost a decade ago.

The time from her mother's diagnosis to her death had been less than eight months, barely any time for them—her or her parents—to come to terms with the illness that would take her life. While her father had thrown himself into his work after the funeral, Vanessa had done the same, her art allowing her a way to express her pain and grief.

Back then she'd poured all her fears onto the canvas in the back of her mind, she too worried that she might die young. Though genetic testing reassured her she was unlikely to develop the same disease, and her time in her studio produced magnificent pieces of abstract art that made her famous, for years, Vanessa had been unable to shake the feeling that something bad was about to happen to her.

She'd never dreamed it would be the loss of her best friend.

It was Adele who'd helped her pick out a prom dress, who came to visit her at art school, who got her to laugh again when the someone she'd thought was her true love had broken her heart. Even more than her father, Adele and her mother, Susan, had become Vanessa's lifeline. They'd been there for every birthday, every holiday and now…

"Come on…promise me."

Adele started to cough and quickly shoved the oxygen mask back into place. Vanessa shot to her feet and bracing herself on the bed, gently laid her hand over her friend's, making sure the device was working properly. "Hey, take it easy."

Adele held up her hand, fingers curled in a fist except for the last, her pinky finger extended into a hook. She looked up, her deep green eyes locking with Vanessa's. "A solemn vow between best friends."

Vanessa saw a lifetime bond that went beyond

friendship in her friend's gaze. Adele was the sister she'd never had. They knew each other's secrets, fears and dreams. They'd shared late night whispers, dried each other's tears and laughed together more times than she could count. "You make it sound like this is my last chance to have a life."

"No, but maybe it's a second chance. How many do you think we get? Just promise you'll work hard to be happy…to fulfill our list."

Vanessa wrapped her pinky finger around her friend's and dropped her forehead to rest against Adele's as both squeezed tight and held on. "I promise."

Chapter 1

Present Day
Rust Creek Falls, Montana

Vanessa wasn't sure she'd heard Nate Crawford correctly.

A rushing noise that reminded her of the crazy bumper-to-bumper traffic on Philadelphia's Schuylkill Expressway filled her ears, except it was the beautiful mountain scenery around her that went a bit hazy as she choked down a mouthful of hot tea. Blinking hard, she focused on the disposable cup in her hand, noticing for the first time she'd grabbed two different flavored tea bags which explained the chocolatey-orange taste burning her tongue.

Even though she'd *remembered* arriving early enough for this morning's meeting to grab some refreshment at the canteen here on the job site—not to mention watching the breathtaking Montana sunrise through the two-story, floor-to-ceiling windows that filled the back wall—maybe it had all been a figment of her imagination.

Maybe she was still tucked beneath her goose-down comforter in that amazingly oversize Davy Crockett–style bed in her cabin, dreaming…

"Are you all right?" Nate asked, getting her attention. She looked up in time to see him rock back on his heels, a slight frown on his handsome face. He then glanced at his fiancée, Callie Kennedy, a nurse who helped run the local clinic, who'd placed a hand on his arm.

"Yes," she gasped, "yes, I'm fine."

No, that was a lie. Vanessa was definitely *not* fine despite the fact she stood in the cavernous lobby and main entertaining space of a log mansion that Nate, a local businessman and member of one of the town's founding families, was converting into a year-round resort.

The gorgeous view of the Montana wilderness was at her back while a stone fireplace big enough to stand in filled the opposite wall. And then there were the rest of the walls. All empty. Her gaze honed in on one of them—freshly painted if the scent tickling her nose meant anything, above the oversize, hand-hewed, carved desk where guests would check in once the resort officially opened.

"You want to hire me—" Vanessa asked, knowing she had to hear the words again. "—to do what?"

"Paint a mural," Nate repeated, gesturing at the large blank space. "I thought it would be a great tribute to the people and places that mean so much to this town, to Montana. Rust Creek Falls has a connected history with both Thunder Canyon and Whitehorn and I'd like see all three towns honored here at the resort."

Her gaze followed, trying to see the vision the man's words created, but nothing came to her artist eye. Zero. Zilch. Her stomach cramped at the now conditioned sensation. How many times had she experienced that same feeling over the past year?

"I think he surprised you, didn't he?" Callie asked.

"Ah, yes." Vanessa glanced down at her cup again. "Maybe I should've gotten something a bit stronger to ensure I was fully awake for this."

"And maybe we shouldn't have asked you to meet us here so early, but we both have to be down in Kalispell for most of the day. Nate didn't want to wait, and you did say—"

"Ah, no, early is fine. I'm usually up before the sun, anyway." Looking up at her friend, she waved off Callie's concern. "But I'm still a bit confused. You're asking me to do this because..."

"Because I was quite amazed." Nate paused and took a step closer, his head bent low even though the three of them were the only ones around, "and pleased when I found out the Vanessa Brent who's running an afterschool art program at the community center and V. E. Brent, world-famous abstract expressionism artist, were one and the same."

Nate's soft-spoken words took her completely by surprise.

Not that she went out of her way to hide who she was or what she did with her life before moving to Rust Creek Falls back in July. When asked, she'd only said she'd worked in the creative arts, but was currently on a time-out, rethinking her career plans. She'd then change the topic of conversation because deep down, the explanation had more than a ring of truth to it.

Or more simply put, she hadn't painted anything in almost a year.

Oh, she'd thought about her craft often, obsessed about it, really. At least until she'd moved out here. Lately, she'd begun to dream about it again, like she'd done as a child. But even though she'd brought along all of her supplies, the white canvases that lined one wall of the cabin she'd rented a few weeks after arriving in town were still blank. Her paints and brushes lay untouched, her heart and her mind as vacant as the walls that surrounded them now.

"Ah, yeah, we're the same person," she finally responded to the expectant looks on Nate's and Callie's faces. "I mean, yes, I'm V. E. Brent, but I haven't… been involved with the art world for quite some time."

Even now, Vanessa was still surprised at the deep depression she'd sunk into after Adele's death last year. Or the fact that she hadn't been able to fill the void with her art.

Adele had hung on until just before Thanksgiving and the day of her memorial service had been the start of an arctic winter that had settled in Philadelphia, and most of the country. Vanessa, too, had become locked in her own personal deep freeze. For months she'd mourned, but unlike when her mother died, she failed to find the same solace and comfort in her work. No matter how hard she'd tried, no matter the techniques or tools she employed, her gift had faded into a vast wasteland where nothing flourished.

Even after she'd finally broken out of her self-imposed grieving this past spring, thanks to an intervention led by Adele's mother, the ability to create was still dormant and she'd decided something drastic was needed to shake her back into the world of the living.

Number ten: move out west.

Vanessa had been reading a weekly blog by a big-city volunteer coordinator who'd moved to Rust Creek Falls to help the town recover from a devastating flood the year before and ended up falling in love and marrying the local sheriff. Soon the idea to move to this little slice of cowboy heaven planted itself in her head and wouldn't let go. So she'd sublet her loft apartment, refused to listen to her father's halfhearted attempts to change her mind and bought a one-way plane ticket to Big Sky Country, placing the first check mark on her and Adele's bucket list in months by arriving just before the July Fourth holiday.

"But you are involved in art," Callie said, breaking into Vanessa's thoughts. "You're great with the kids at the community center."

Vanessa smiled, remembering how she'd gotten roped into helping with a summer day camp that'd showed up at the center looking to entertain a group of kids on a rainy day. "That's pretty much finger painting, playing with clay or simple watercolors. Other than that I'm not…"

Her voice cracked and she looked away, that familiar lump back in her throat. Damn! She walked across the vast space, her gaze centered on the empty fireplace. "I'm not…well, let's just say that side of me—V. E. Brent—she isn't painting. At all."

"Oh, please don't think we've invaded your privacy."

Callie hurried to her side. "We haven't told anyone else who you really are. Nate came up with this idea before we even knew thanks to your beautiful sketches."

She looked back at them. "My sketches?"

"Yes, the ones you've been doing of the locals around town. They're amazing. I love the portrait you did of me when I was tending to a scraped knee at the playground. I never even realized what you were up to until you gave it to me. I've got it hanging in my office at the clinic."

A few weeks after her kids program took off, Vanessa had started to once again carry a sketch pad and colored pencils in her oversize bag.

Something she hadn't done in months.

At first, the blank pages seemed to mock her whenever she opened the pad, but then she'd forced herself to do quick exercises, simple pen-and-ink sketches of whatever might catch her eye.

Surprisingly, it had been people.

The citizens of Rust Creek Falls had become her test subjects, either in the park, the community center or while sitting tucked away in a corner of a local business. Sometimes she asked for permission, but usually the sketches were done so quick the focus of her practice exercise didn't even realize what Vanessa was doing until she'd rip out the page from her sketchbook afterward and offer it to them.

So far, no one had been upset with her. She'd figured most had just been tossed away, but she had spotted a few, like Callie's, posted around town. Evidence that her creativity was trickling back little by little.

"The drawing you did of my mother working the counter at Crawford's Store is now matted, framed and holds a place of honor in my father's study," Nate said. "Callie and I were there for Sunday dinner and that drawing got me thinking about the mural, the resort and you."

Surprised at that, Vanessa's gaze was drawn back to the empty space over the desk, looking very much like the oversize blank canvases in her cabin. Nate's request caused her fingers to itch, a familiar sign they wanted to be wrapped around a paintbrush again. But Vanessa knew what would happen. As soon as she'd pull out her paints…nothing. Sketching a few random subjects was vastly different than taking on a commissioned work, where the nuances she'd have to capture in oils required planning and a delicate touch.

Things that were still beyond her reach.

Moving far away from home and memories of Adele had been her way to start her life again, and deep down, hopefully restore her spark, her inspiration for her craft. Except for those rare moments when she tried to paint and still failed, Vanessa was enjoying her time in Rust Creek Falls. She'd been lucky enough to find a great place to live, joined the Newcomers Club—a social group of women new to Rust Creek Falls—made some great friends and explored the area. The art program at the center kept her busy, she'd gone on a few dates with some of the local cowboys and made a point to appreciate each day of her new life.

Number thirteen: stop and enjoy sunrises and sunsets.

Another check mark on her list, made the first morning she woke up in Montana. Adele had been right. Concentrating on her life, and using their list as a guide, had helped her to find joy again.

Which made this idea of Nate's downright scary. What if she said yes and her creative block kept her from putting anything on the wall? And her work was abstract in the truest sense of the word. Powerful color compositions with no reference of any kind to anything recognizable. What Nate was describing was much more detailed, and in a way, more personal.

Still, she found herself wanting desperately to take on the challenge.

Maybe this mural was a chance—her last chance—to find her talent again.

Jonah Dalton breathed in the cool morning air, holding it for a moment in his nose and mouth, like he used to do as kid. The air had a bite to it—like the fresh tartness of a Granny Smith apple the moment you first sink your teeth into it—that couldn't be matched anywhere but here in the wilds of Montana.

He'd missed that taste more than he'd been willing to admit.

The air in Denver, his home for the past eight years, had a flavor that was a mix of excitement and culture, but that was to be expected in a sophisticated city of over 600,000 people, he guessed.

He released his breath, watching the white puffs disappear. He stood on the large circular drive outside of Bledsoe's Folly, soon to be known as...well, whatever Nate Crawford decided to name his as-yet-unopened resort. All Jonah knew was that when the chance came to restore and revitalize this twenty-year-old log mansion into a state-of-the-art, and hopefully popular destination for year-round vacations, his architect's heart wouldn't let him turn down the project. Not when the initial construction of the castle-like mansion had fueled his love of architecture and design all those years ago.

So he'd taken a leave of absence from his job with one of the top firms in the country and worked pretty much nonstop on the plans and blueprints for the necessary renovations.

And now he was here.

Even though he'd been less than thrilled about Nate's condition that he be onsite for the last three months of the project in case any problems arose, Jonah had always enjoyed seeing his designs come to life. At work, he forgot everything else. And that's just how he liked it.

He figured he could do the same thing here, even if it meant coming home. And he had to admit he was looking forward to the quiet and slow pace of his home town, especially after all the craziness—professional and personal—he'd left behind in Denver. He'd arrived late last night after driving fifteen hours straight and hadn't made it past the living room couch at his parents' place.

Yet, here he was at the job site first thing the next morning, anxious to see his dream turned into reality.

His shiny Cadillac Escalade looked a bit out of place in the parking lot crowded with older-model cars and trucks, but Jonah took the number of vehicles present as a good sign that the crew was already hard at work. He grabbed his white hard hat and turned to head inside, surprised when his older brother Eli pulled up the long winding paved road in a battered pickup.

"What are you doing here?" he asked.

"Good morning to you, too, little brother." Eli waved

a piece of paper at him. "Hey, I found your note on the kitchen counter as I was heading out. Decided to stop by and—"

"What are you doing with that?" Jonah cut him off. "I left that for Mom, warning her I plan to stay out at the cabin and not to worry about getting my old room ready."

"I know, I read it. Here, take this." Eli handed over a travel mug stamped with the brand of the family's ranch, The Circle D. "Jeez, you're just like the rest of the family, a bear without your morning cup of joe. Nice to know some things haven't changed. Oh, and welcome home."

The enticing aroma filled Jonah's nose and his blood cried out for caffeinated bliss. Not wanting to wake his family, he'd only grabbed a quick shower and dressed, figuring he'd see everyone tonight at dinner. He'd guessed there'd be a canteen set up inside for the crew, but this was better.

Jonah took the cup. After Eli shut off the truck and climbed out to join him, he grabbed his brother's outstretched hand and allowed Eli to pull him into a quick hug that ended with a strong slap to his back. "Thanks, it's…ah, it's good to be back, but I still don't get why you took my note."

"You can't stay at the cabin." Eli stepped back and righted the dark Stetson he wore so much Jonah had often wondered if his brother slept with the darn thing. "It's been rented."

Surprised filled him. "You rented out my cabin?"

"Technically, it wasn't me. It was Mom. And it's not your cabin."

"I designed it. I built it. It's on the acreage Grandpa

and Dad set aside for me." Jonah held tight to the mug as the memories that went along with the one bedroom cabin he'd forged with his own hands came crashing back to him. After eight years one would think he'd be over it by now. "Why would Mom rent my cabin to a stranger?"

"I guess because nobody knew when you planned to show your face in town again." Eli turned and headed for the main house. "This place must still have working bathrooms, right?"

Jonah sighed and followed his brother toward the oversize double front doors. Yes, he'd missed both Thanksgiving and Christmas, the two times he made a point of returning home over the past few years.

"I couldn't be here because I was out of the country most of last year working on a major project," he said as he and Eli stepped through the rustic mahogany-and-iron entryway that was original to the building.

"And when you got back to the U.S. you still didn't visit."

"But I did call. I do have a life, and a job in Denver, you know."

"I know that and you know that. Mom? Not so much. She and Dad were really excited to find out you were the lead architect behind the redesign of this place. The fact they had to hear about it from your boss didn't go over so well."

Jonah had planned to tell his folks about working with Nate Crawford, but his life had been going nonstop since he'd agreed to take on the project. "Well, I'm home now and since I'm going to stick around until at least Christmas I'd like to stay at my cabin."

"Why? You never stayed there before."

Because he hadn't actually finished the darn thing until a couple of years ago, working on it whenever he was home. Besides, it was time to get rid of some old ghosts, but Jonah wasn't going to share that.

"There must be plenty of available housing from those who left town after the flood last year." Including his ex-wife, he thought, taking a long sip of the strong brew despite the steamy vapors. "Mom can tell the renter they have to move. Or I'll tell them. It's my place so technically I'm the landlord."

"Great. Here's your chance."

His brother pointed out Jonah's boss across the room.

Nate Crawford stood near one of the room's best features, the original stone fireplace, with two women. One was his fiancée, whom Jonah had met when she'd come with Nate to Denver for one of their many meetings and the other was a stunningly beautiful brunette.

A powerful jolt raced through his veins and Jonah immediately blamed the mouthful of java he managed to choke down. He took in her dark brown hair, a mass of curls that just touched the wide neckline of a bright purple sweater that hung down far past her hips, but still managed to display feminine curves in all the right places.

Or maybe it was her black skintight, sorry excuse for pants that did that.

He couldn't make out what she was holding in her arms, but then she reached up and pushed a handful of those curls off her face, releasing a jangle from the stack of bracelets that slid from her wrist to her elbow as she turned in a slow circle, her gaze seemingly locked on the empty walls of the room as her ankle-high boots clicked on the newly finished reclaimed barn wood floor. Then Nate's fiancée touched her arm and the two started to talk.

Staring was rude, gawking like a teenager was worse, but for whatever reason Jonah was helpless to look away.

"Yeah, that's the typical reaction." Eli reached around and waved his hand in front of Jonah's face. "Not hard to tell Vanessa isn't from around here, huh? Which is why she needed a place to stay. Like *your* cabin."

As if she heard them, or maybe because Callie was now pointing in his direction, the beauty looked over and caught him watching her. Jonah snapped out of his dazed state and pushed his brother's hand away, realizing at that moment the woman he'd been transfixed by was the one sleeping in his bed.

Whoa! Nope, not going there!

Yeah, he'd also built the king-size log bed that took up most of the one bedroom in the cabin, but still…

"She's the renter?" he finally asked, turning his back on her, and his boss, to face his brother again.

"That's her," Eli said, then chuckled. "Can I stick around and watch you go all Scrooge-like?"

"Don't you have someplace to be? Like the men's room? Or the ranch?"

"I'm going, I'm going." Eli grinned and backed away. "Gee, all the Daltons under one roof again. Not sure how Derek is going to feel about that, but the twins and the folks are going to be in heaven."

Jonah scowled, watching his brother stop and chat with a few workers before disappearing around a corner. He should go over and let Nate know he'd arrived, but his unexpected reaction to— What had Eli said was her name?

And why did he care?

The cool touch to her arm jolted Vanessa out of her self-imposed trance. She dropped her hand to her side, noticing for the first time that the interior of the resort had gotten busy as members of the construction crew moved from room to room, the noise of their chatter and work tools filled the air while she'd been trying to conjure up something—anything—for the mural.

At some point during her daydreaming she'd handed off her cup of hot chocolate and pulled a sketch pad from her oversize leather bag, but other than grabbing a trio of pens and holding them one-handed in a familiar pretzel twist of fingers, she had…

Nothing.

"I hope your silence is a sign that you're already brimming with ideas for the mural," Callie said. "I think Nate's suggestion is wonderful."

Despite the panic ricocheting inside of her, Vanessa's smile came easy. One of the first people she'd met after moving to Rust Creek Falls had been Callie, who was also considered a newcomer in town after she left Chicago back in January. "You think Nate is wonderful."

Callie's eyes were bright as she glanced at the tall man next to her talking with a member of the construction crew. "Yes, I do. It's funny, but from the moment I saw him—oh, look, there's Jonah."

Vanessa's gaze followed Callie's pointed finger and amazingly the panic over her creative block quieted, replaced with a warm glow that surprised her as much as the way the handsome man stared at them.

At her.

Did she know him? He looked vaguely familiar, but Vanessa was sure they hadn't been introduced before. No, she'd have remembered if she'd met this man.

Unlike the majority of the men here at the resort and in Rust Creek Falls with their broken-in jeans, T-shirts and flannel button-downs in every plaid pattern and color combination imaginable, he was dressed in black business slacks and a dress shirt.

He was tall, over six feet she guessed, and his slightly mussed brown hair showed hints of gold when the sunlight caught it as he turned away. Her gaze lingered over the way his shoulders filled the expensive cut of his dark gray suit jacket that she'd bet her last pair of Manolos was cashmere. The only thing that made him fit in was the hard hat he held in one hand.

"Who is that?"

Callie smiled and Vanessa realized she'd spoken the question aloud. "I mean, I haven't seen him around town." She paused, catching the capped end of one of her pens between her teeth. "At least I don't think I have."

"Well, you've certainly dated enough of the single men in town to know."

Vanessa flipped her wrist and pointed her pen at Callie. "Hey! Six dates in three months isn't that many."

"Six dates with six different guys."

"Five." Vanessa had made the mistake of going out twice with the same cowboy. There wouldn't be a third time. "But who's counting? Besides, not everyone believes in love at first sight. I'm more of the 'you only live once, so enjoy yourself' kind of girl."

Unlike half of the women in the town's Newcomers Club, it seems.

Besides Callie, two other members—Mallory Franklin and Cecelia Clifton—had also found happily-ever-after in the past few months and were sporting pretty engagement rings, even though Mallory claimed she hadn't specifically moved to Rust Creek Falls for the great "Gal Rush" as many of the locals called the arrival of females over the past year or so. She'd initially come to town to raise her orphaned niece, the little girl her sister and brother-in-law had adopted from China. Then she fell in love with former playboy rancher, Caleb Dalton.

"Hey, Jonah!" Nate called out, "Come over and join us."

The man hesitated, but then spun back around and headed across the room toward them, the hard hat now perched on his head with a rakish tilt. Callie backed up a few steps toward her fiancé and sent Vanessa a quick wink. She grinned in response and followed, happier now that the conversation had shifted away from the mural she still hadn't officially agreed to do.

"Welcome home." Nate held out his hand. "When did you get in?"

"Late last night." He switched his travel mug from one hand to the other and shook Nate's. "Very late. Hence, the need for coffee."

"There's always a need for coffee." Nate released him and turned to her and Callie. "You remember Callie?"

He nodded. "It's good to see you again."

"You, too, Jonah. I bet you're glad to be home."

A shuttered look filled his gaze for a moment bringing Vanessa's attention to his green-gold hazel eyes. Tired eyes. The man looked like he could use a good night's sleep and it was barely eight in the morning.

"Yes, it is," he said, then turned back to Nate. "Sorry I'm a day late. I know I said October first, but I got stuck on business—"

"Hey, one day doesn't matter. Did you read my latest email?"

"I meant to, but yesterday was all about tying up loose ends and a long drive. Did I miss something important?"

"Yes, but I think this is better, anyway. Remember when I said I had a great idea for the lobby?" Nate waved his hand toward Vanessa. "Well, here she is."

The stranger turned his gaze to her, the expression on his face as blank as the walls—as her imagination. Well, blank when it came to the mural. Suddenly she was coming up with some great ideas for her and this handsome guy.

Vanessa forced out a quick laugh, thankful it sounded so relaxed and stuck out her hand. "Gee, you make me sound like a pole dancer or something. Hi, I'm Vanessa Brent."

"Jonah Dalton."

He took her hand in his and heat engulfed her fingers. Where had the tingling come from that turned the heat up to volcanic level?

The widening of his eyes told her he felt it, too, and he quickly released her, tipped his mug again and took a long gulp. It was then she noticed the logo on the side. "Dalton…are you related to either of the Daltons here in town?"

He nodded, tugging the brim of his hard hat a bit lower. "Charles and Rita Dalton are my folks."

"Oh, my goodness! What a small world!" Vanessa hugged her sketch pad to her chest. "Your parents are the sweetest people. I mean, your whole family is so nice. I'm renting a cabin on the Circle D Ranch."

"You don't say."

"Do you know the place? When I was looking to move out of the boardinghouse in town, you mom insisted she had the perfect cabin and she was right! The living room has this one wall that's a huge single pane of glass—" she waved a hand at the windows that filled the other side of the room "—nothing like that, of course, but the views of the ranch and the mountains are amazing. I'm still learning how to work the woodstoves, the nights have been getting chilly, but the best thing is the claw-footed tub in the bathroom." Vanessa closed her eyes for a moment a sighed. "Oh, fill that baby with foamy bubbles, give me a good book and I'm soaking for hours up to my—"

The sound of choking had her eyes flying open in time to see Jonah thumping at his chest with his fist. "Are you okay?"

"Yeah." One more thump and then he cleared his throat. "Last mouthful of coffee went down the wrong way. Yes, I know the cabin. I grew up on the Circle D Ranch."

"So, are you a cowboy like your brothers?" It wasn't hard to picture him in a classic Stetson instead of the hard hat he wore. "Although, I'm guessing from your current chapeau you're working here on the renovation?"

Both Nate and Callie laughed, reminding Vanessa she wasn't standing here alone with this long lost Dalton son she'd now recognized from the numerous family photos in the main house on the Dalton's ranch.

"Yes, Jonah is working on the resort. He's the lead architect on this project," Nate explained. "All the innovative building techniques we're putting into this place to turn it into a premier resort are his. He's also the lead on all of the interior design so you'll be working for him. In a way."

"She will?" Jonah asked, clearly confused. "As what?"

"An artist," Nate said. "I've commissioned Vanessa to paint a mural over the registration desk in the front lobby."

"You have?" The confusion on his face gave way to something closer to annoyance. "When?"

"Just today," Vanessa chimed in. "But I haven't agreed to anything yet."

"Well, that's good."

Hmmm, interesting response. One arched eyebrow from her told him he was free to continue.

"No, that came out—what I meant was we've already got the designs for the interior furnishings in place." Jonah's gaze darted from Vanessa to Callie and back to Nate. "I mentioned earlier this week that Rothschild—the firm in Denver we hired—is sending a representative in a few weeks to give the team a final presentation on everything from furniture to curtains to...well, artwork."

An emotion that hovered between resentment and

relief filled Vanessa's chest. It seemed Nate and his architect weren't on the same page when it came to this so-called mural. Good. While the idea of taking on the commission scared her more than anything had in years, she'd admit she had been leaning toward saying yes, confident her talent hadn't deserted her completely.

Now it didn't seem to matter.

Chapter 2

"Are you telling me you honestly didn't know Nate had hired Vanessa to paint a mural in the resort?" Eli asked.

They'd managed to find an empty table with a couple of tall stools—one with a trio of half-finished drinks still sitting there—in the back corner of the Ace in the Hole, the local bar that catered to everyone from cowboys to bikers. Between the cracking of the pool balls against each other to the country music blaring from the jukebox for the dancers on the crowded parquet floor, the place was loud and noisy and Jonah had to lean forward to hear his brother. "No, I honestly didn't know."

Eli looked at him with one eyebrow raised.

"I didn't." Jonah dropped his gaze and fixed it on

the icy longneck beer he turned in slow circles against the table top. "Not that it matters now."

"Why's that?"

Because Vanessa had walked out this morning with Callie following close behind, leaving Nate to make it clear the mural was going to happen and since the man owned fifty-one percent of the resort, he was going to get his way.

"I missed the email explaining Nate's vision," Jonah said. "Add the fact the rest of the investors had already approved the idea and it's a done deal."

"So your vote wouldn't have made any difference?"

"No, but that doesn't mean—" Jonah looked at his brother again. "Wait, what makes you think I had a vote on the subject?"

Eli's mouth rose into a half grin. "You're one of the investors, aren't you?"

Jonah glanced around. No one seemed interested in their conversation, but he kept his voice low. "Why would you think I'd be—"

"Give me some credit, little brother. You've been in love with that old place from the moment it was built back when we were kids. You used to ride all the way from the ranch just to watch it being constructed. Even when it sat empty for years, you'd sneak in and hang out there. Remember that night with the football players from Kalispell?"

It took him a moment, but then Jonah smiled. "Yeah, we just about had them out of there, convinced the place was haunted, until Derek tried to steal their beer. That was a heck of a fight."

"Only because that one guy had a can of spray paint

aimed at one of the walls. You took him out with a flying karate leap and the fists started flying."

It'd been him, his two brothers and three cousins—the Dalton gang as they'd been known back then—against the entire offensive line from the nearby high school, but they'd won. At least until word got back to the town sheriff and their folks. "I never shoveled so much horse manure in my life as we did that fall."

"Anyway, I figured a rich and famous architect would have plenty—"

"I'm not famous." Jonah cut off his brother and sat back in the tall stool, the heel of his steel-toed cowboy boot caught on the bottom rung. "Or rich."

Eli toasted him with his now empty bottle. "You better be tonight. You're buying and I could use another beer."

Jonah watched his brother turn away and attempt to flag down a waitress. He never confirmed Eli's suspicions, but the man was right. When Nate had contacted him about his plans for the forgotten log mansion and he'd found out about the investor team Nate was putting together, Jonah had insisted on buying in, easily parting with a healthy chunk of his savings.

Still, would he have voted along with the majority for the mural?

Probably, since after talking with Nate and finally reading the email, he liked the idea and what the painting would represent, even though it meant added work for the interior-design team when it came to including the painting in the overall plan. It seemed this Vanessa Brent was a pretty famous artist from back east. He hadn't had a chance to do any research on her yet, but obviously she, and her work, had made an impression on Nate.

Just the sight of her had done something to Jonah that hadn't happened in a long time.

Made him curious.

What was she was doing in Rust Creek Falls? Was she here as part of the influx of females influenced by an online blog about life in the Wild West his mother and sisters had talked about at dinner? According to his dad and brothers there'd also been a fair amount of single men and families who'd come to town as well over the past year, thanks to jobs created by both the recovery work from last summer's flooding and more recently, the resort. They'd even hired on a few new hands at the ranch, putting the bunkhouse to use again for the first time in a long time.

Along with his cabin.

He couldn't help but wonder what Vanessa might have done to the empty slate he'd left behind after she'd moved in. Were the few pieces of furniture he'd put in still there? Including the bed he'd handcrafted and now refused to picture her sleeping in?

And that flash of anger in her golden-brown eyes when he'd shot down the idea of a mural… Why had it changed to relief just before she'd walked out?

Stifling a yawn, Jonah drained his beer and chalked up his interest in Nate's artist to his being dead tired.

Coming to the bar his first full day back in town hadn't been part of his plan for tonight. A quick meal and then crashing headfirst into a soft bed had been more of what he had in mind, but the talk at dinner had quickly turned from the town's population boom to him. His job, his travels and after one too many questions from his mother about his personal life, Jonah had willingly agreed to Eli's idea they'd grab a beer or two to celebrate his homecoming.

Two more beers arrived and Jonah swore this would be his last as he twisted off the cap. It was then he heard a familiar laugh from a nearby table. He turned and looked at the group of men playing a lively game of poker, recognizing one of them right away. "Didn't Derek rush through dinner because he had a big project to do in the barn?"

"Yeah, so?"

Gesturing toward the table, Jonah saw Eli's gaze shift until it landed on their younger brother who sat with his back to them.

"Guess he finished early," Eli said. "Or else he got tired of listening to mom's excited chatter about your many accomplishments."

Jonah's face heated. "I was getting tired of that, too."

"Hey, she's proud of you. Dad, too. You're the first one of us kids to make it big with your fancy Denver penthouse, traveling the world designing everything from skyscrapers to celebrities' homes, not to mention dating a famous ballerina."

"How did you know about that?"

"Mom cut out a picture of you two attending a charity event—nice tux, by the way—from some magazine. She had it hanging on the refrigerator for months until we all got so sick of seeing it she finally moved it to her sewing room."

He groaned. "Please tell me you're screwing with me."

Eli grinned. "She was hoping you'd bring the lady home for a visit."

Not likely. He'd returned from a business trip and walked in on her entertaining a fellow dancer—a ballerina—in her apartment. Hey, he was all for a person being true to themselves, but he wasn't going to be her stand-in. Especially after the way she'd hinted about the two of them getting married. "I haven't dated Nadia in a year. That was over before I left for Brazil."

"Whatever happened to that sexy architect from your office I met when I visited a few years back? Before Nadia?"

Yeah, getting involved with a coworker he'd collaborated with on a couple of projects, moving their relationship from the office to the bedroom had been a mistake, too. He didn't realize that until she decided to move up in the world and left him to marry a partner in a rival company, when he made it clear that he and marriage were not a good fit. Not anymore. "I wasn't rich *or* famous enough for her."

"Well, I guess mom's just getting antsy for one of us to finally settle down," Eli said. "Again. You're the only one who's tried the marriage bit. As much as she and dad were against you becoming a husband while still in your teens, I think she's ready now for some grandchildren to spoil."

This time the memory flashed in Jonah's head before he could brace himself.

The pregnancy test found in the trash. His joy at becoming a father after what he'd thought had been four years of wedded bliss. Lisette's stunned silence. His mistake in thinking her reaction was because he'd ruined the surprise.

Yeah, she surprised him all right—

"Hey, you okay?" Eli clicked the bottom edge of

his bottle against Jonah's, pulling him from the past. "You grip that beer any tighter and it's going to shatter in your hand."

"Yeah, I'm fine. Just tired." He must be. He hadn't thought about that night in a long time. It was almost like it'd all happened to someone else. Someone he used to be. He forced his fingers to relax. "It's been a long few days. Months, actually."

"Well, you'll get a good night's sleep tonight. Back in your childhood bedroom."

Same room, but thankfully the furniture had been updated. There was no way he'd be comfortable in a twin-size bed. "Very funny."

"So, I'm guessing you decided not to kick Vanessa out?"

After the way her eyes lit up and hearing the excitement in her voice as she described the cabin, Jonah knew he couldn't ask her to leave. It wasn't her fault he'd come back assuming the place would still be empty. "The subject never came up, but no, I don't plan to ask her to move."

"She got to you, huh?"

"What's her story?" Jonah avoided his brother's question with one of his own. "What do you know about her?"

"Not much." Eli shrugged. "I hadn't met her until Mom had her over for dinner one night back in August and announced she was renting your cabin. I didn't even know she was an artist until you mentioned it. She's nice, always with a smile on her face and rarely at a loss for company, from what I've heard. But hey, my days usually run twelve to fourteen hours taking care of the ranch. I don't have time for much else, which should show my brotherly love in saving your butt tonight by coming here. Why are you asking?"

"No reason. Just curious about who's living in my place and who I'll be working with for…well, for however long it takes her to paint a mural." Jonah tipped back his beer for a long swallow.

"Maybe you should ask Derek. Seeing how he promised to teach her to ride a horse. Convenient, huh?"

The cold liquid caught in the sudden tightening of his throat. Jonah tried not to cough, but failed and did his best to hide it as he wiped at his mouth. "Derek's chasing after her?"

"You know our brother."

Yes, he did. Derek had been popular with the ladies ever since he'd figured out the difference between boys and girls somewhere back in elementary school. Derek did his share of chasing, but usually it was the ladies who went after him, most winding up with nothing to show for their trouble but good times and a broken heart when they got too serious.

A fire burned in his gut at the idea of Derek messing with Vanessa that way and damned if he knew why. He'd only met the woman today. Just because she'd stirred his curiosity, among other things, didn't mean anything.

Neither did the sparks that crackled between them the moment he'd taken her hand this morning. Maybe he'd just been alone for too long. There hadn't been a woman in his life—or his bed—in a long time. Hell, there hadn't really been anyone since his ex-wife destroyed their marriage eight years ago and just about destroyed him along with it.

"Boy, you really must be tired."

Jonah blinked, realizing he'd been so lost in his own thoughts he'd missed whatever his brother had said. "Yeah, I am. You must be, too. Maybe we should head home."

"Oh, don't leave now." A soft feminine voice spoke. "The party's just getting started."

Jonah and his brother turned in unison and found three ladies standing there. His gaze immediately went to the brunette with bouncy curls who stood head and shoulders taller than the two petite blondes flanking her.

Vanessa.

She reached for the glasses on the table, handing one each to her friends. Keeping the wineglass for herself, she sent him a wink over the rim when their eyes clashed. A quick glance at all three ladies' slightly disheveled appearances and apparent thirst at how they finished off their drinks, made him realize he and Eli had taken their table while they'd been on the dance floor.

"Sorry, didn't mean to steal your seats." His brother quickly came to the same conclusion and slid off his stool, but instead of stepping away—as in heading for the exit—he just moved to make room. "It's pretty crowded tonight. Do you mind if we share?"

"Only if you're buying the next round." One of the blondes spoke while the other giggled.

Yeah, actually giggled.

Vanessa smiled, remembering what it felt like to be barely legal enough be in a bar. Not that at twenty-six she was that much older than her new friends, but there were many times she felt much older than her actual age.

And woefully out of shape.

Grabbing at the front of her sweater, she yanked it back and forth, enjoying the slight breeze against her heated skin. Thursday nights were busy here at the Ace and the dance floor was crowded. She was finally getting the hang of the steps, dips and sways that went along with country line dancing, but boy, she wished she'd thought to change her outfit before coming tonight.

She had, in fact, almost stayed home, but then she'd seen the reminder on her calendar and once again thought about the list.

Number sixteen: learn how to line dance.

She'd arrived early but the bar had filled up quickly, so she'd offered to share her table with the two girls she'd just met tonight who managed somehow not to look the least bit sweaty or have a lock of their flowing golden manes out of place.

"Of course, I'm buying." Eli readily agreed and offered to escort the ladies to the bar. He started to walk away, but then stopped and pointed back at Jonah and her. "No need for introductions, right? You two remember each other?"

She sidled a look in Jonah's direction. Oh, yes, she remembered him.

In fact, Vanessa hadn't been able to think about much else but Jonah Dalton all day, even when she should've been concentrating on the design for the mural that after much more prodding from Nate and Callie was back on.

"Yep, I think we'll be fine." Ignoring the stool he'd vacated the same time as his brother, Vanessa moved closer to the table and set her empty glass down. "Hello again, Mr. Dalton."

"Please, call me Jonah."

There they were again. She'd thought she'd imagined the tingling that felt like a thousand tiny pinpricks dancing along her skin at the smooth tone of his voice the few minutes they had talked this morning, but now he'd only spoken four words and they were back. Like gangbusters.

Maybe she should just peel off this darn sweater. It's not like she didn't have anything on beneath it. In fact, she wore a double-layer tank top—

"What can I get for you at the bar, Vanessa?" Eli asked. "Another glass of wine? Maybe a bucket of ice water?"

His question caused her to stop her frantic moves, her hand now still against her chest. "Oh, an ice water would be great. Just a glass."

Eli smiled, then looked at his brother. "Jonah? Another beer?"

"Yeah, sure. Why not?"

Hmmm, four more words but with an edge to them this time. Eli and the girls disappeared into the crowd. Vanessa leaned against the table, elbows propped along the edge and her beloved bracelets jangling as they landed on the smooth surface. "So, are you having fun… Jonah?"

"I'd rather be in bed."

Five words this time and boy, the heat level rose again. That's it. She straightened and eased behind Jonah, as he stood between the table and the back wall, one hand already under the bottom edge of her sweater. "Do you mind?"

"Mind what?"

He started to look back over one impossibly wide shoulder, but she nudged him forward with her elbow. "Just give me a minute, I need to…"

A quick tug and one arm came free. After a tussle with both her bracelets and oversize hoop earrings, she deftly pulled the garment over her head. The cool air lapping at her damp skin felt wonderful. "Ah, so much better."

Running her fingers through her hair would be a lost cause, the wayward curls did whatever they pleased, but she did it anyway and then adjusted her bra straps to make sure they didn't show.

"Are you finished back there?"

The confusion laced in Jonah's question made her smile. That and the fact he was still using five-word sentences.

"Thanks for being my screen." She stepped back around to the table, laying her sweater over the closest stool. "I don't think anyone noticed."

Ha! Now *she'd* done it. Twice!

"Noticed what?" Jonah asked, looking at her. His gaze stilled, locked somewhere around her mouth before it slowly traveled the length of her body.

The slow appraisal caused those pinpricks to rise into goose bumps along her bare arms. She quickly blamed it on the bar's air-conditioning, but her girly parts enjoyed his perusal so much her toes curled inside her favorite suede ankle boots.

"You—ah, you changed." Jonah's words came out in a low whisper. He lifted his beer to his mouth, ready to tip it back, but then noticed the bottle was empty and set it back down.

"Actually, I just took off a layer." She tugged the edges of the tank top down over her hips, but it barely covered the pockets on her leggings where her phone, driver's license and cash were safely tucked away. "All that dancing made me hot."

"Yeah, I can see that."

Vanessa smiled and leaned against the table again. "Hmmm, I'm not sure if I should take that as a compliment."

Jonah started to reply, but before he could, Vanessa's gaze caught on something—or should she say someone—on the other side of the room.

Without stopping to think about what she was doing, she laid a hand over Jonah's and said the first thing that popped into her head. "Hey, architect, want to be a hero?"

His gaze dropped to their hands for a moment, and then he looked at her again. "Excuse me?"

"There's a cowboy—tall, big shoulders, plaid shirt—heading this way."

Jonah quickly looked around the bar. "You do realize you've just described about every man in here?"

"This one's wearing a hat like your brother's… I know, a lot of men are, but he's standing on the other side of the third pool table and stealing glances at me with a determined look on his face."

This time Jonah glanced to his left and Vanessa watched as the two men made eye contact. Oh, boy, she hoped this was a good idea.

"Is that bothering you?" He turned back to her.

"Well, ever since I told him I don't kiss on the first date, he's been angling to get me to go out with him again."

Jonah's hazel eyes darkened. "For a second date?"

"Third, actually. I didn't kiss him the last time, either," she hurried to explain, wanting him to understand. "I just wanted to get to know him a bit better, but no sparks, ya know? I told him it would be better if we were just friends, but the guy won't take no for an answer."

At that moment Eli returned, setting two beers and her glass of ice water down with a noisy clank before pushing their drinks across the table. "Your friends decided to stop by the ladies' room—drinks in hand—so who knows if we'll see them again. Hey, look at you. Getting more comfortable?"

"Much." Vanessa reached for her glass, enjoying a long sip of the cool liquid. She didn't know if her throat was so dry because of the dancing or this crazy idea of hers. "Oh, I so needed that."

Jonah took a long swallow from his beer. "Yeah, me, too."

"So, what do you say?" She set the glass back down, and gave him a gentle squeeze. "Help a girl out?"

Eli's gaze bounced back and forth between them, before it landed on her hand on Jonah's wrist. "Ah, did I miss something?"

"I just need a favor from your brother."

"Jeez, I'm the one who bought the lady a drink."

Jonah shot his brother a dark look, then turned to her again. "What do you want me to do?"

Now that he was agreeable, Vanessa realized she was at a loss for ideas. Boy, what else was new?

Was it enough they were standing here, practically holding hands? Maybe she should slide a bit closer? Press up against his shoulder?

Biting down on her bottom lip, she tried to come up with something when the jukebox switched songs and a classic country music ballad came on.

"Dance with me," she said.

This time Eli laughed. "Oh, you've picked yourself the wrong rescuer, Vanessa. If there's one thing Jonah doesn't like to do, it's dance."

Okay, maybe it would be enough if she just stood next to him. Surely, her admirer wouldn't cause any trouble if it was clear she was here with someone else, and now that Eli was back…

"How presumptuous of me. I'm sorry." She released her hold, her fingers lightly sliding back across his skin. "I guess I've got to learn that I can't assume every man in town is a cowboy or likes to two-step. Never even thought—"

Jonah surprised her by capturing her hand in his. "Come on, let's dance."

Chapter 3

Jonah ignored the shock on his brother's face, especially when it morphed into a smirk. He instead concentrated on the surprise—turned delight—on Vanessa's. Her asking him to dance was just another way she'd surprised him since she'd walked up to their table tonight. Her table. Hell, since he'd walked into his resort and found her standing there.

"Are you sure?" she asked.

He shot a glance at Vanessa's admirer, who looked vaguely familiar and was heading their way. Releasing her hand, he gestured toward the already crowded dance floor. "After you."

She rewarded him with a bright smile and then turned on one heel of those sexy boots. Moving in close behind her as they maneuvered around the tables, he placed a hand at the small of her back. Her top felt slightly damp and the heat of her skin easily melted through the soft cotton material to warm his fingertips.

Damn, there went those sparks again, just like the glowing spatter from a welder's torch to steel, these figurative sparks would burn just as easily of he got too close.

Maybe this wasn't such a good idea.

His brother was right. Jonah had never been a big fan of dancing and he couldn't remember the last time he'd done any two-stepping, slow speed or otherwise. And since she'd stripped off that sweater and wore nothing but a flimsy tank top that showed off toned arms and sexy cleavage, how was he going to hold her in his arms and not—

They reached the parquet floor and instead of waiting for an opening crowded outer circle of couples, Vanessa moved into the fray, spun around and assumed the position.

He moved in, placing one hand just beneath her left shoulder blade and lightly took her right hand in his. Two quick steps, one slow and—

"Oh!" Her booted foot knocked right into his. "Sorry about that."

"That's okay. It's takes a few minutes to get into the swing—" She did it again and ending up bumping into the couple behind her when she tried to back away and find her rhythm at the same time.

"Sorry about that, folks," he said to the man when he turned and glared at him over his shoulder, then focused again on his dance partner. "Vanessa, do you know how to two-step?"

Her nose scrunched up. "Not really. I've been watching the couples when I'm here at the bar and I want to learn, even though it's not on my—" She stopped and bit down on her bottom lip for a moment. "I've been concentrating on line dancing."

Jonah glanced to his left and found the center of the dance floor filled with couples, but moving much slower. He stepped out of the ring of couples and pulled Vanessa in closer.

"Hey, what are you doing?"

"Dancing." He turned to face her again, this time sliding his hand to the small of her back, holding her in place—much closer this time—as he started to move in an unhurried circle. "Isn't that what this is called?"

"Ah, yes." Her stiff posture relaxed as she smiled, moving her hand up to circle his neck while aligning her body with his from his chest to his knees. "I believe it is. You know, I always wondered why couples would gather out here in the center of the floor and slow dance."

The press of her soft curves reminded Jonah again of how long it'd been since he'd held a woman in his arms. "Maybe because one of them doesn't know how to two-step."

"Or maybe they want to be able to talk and get to know each other a little better."

"They can't do that while sitting at a table?"

She laughed softly, her puffs of breath enticingly warm against his throat. "Probably wouldn't be as much fun."

He couldn't argue with that.

"When was the last time you did any dancing?" she asked. "Country or any other style?"

It took him a minute as he thought back. The charity event in Denver where that photograph of him and Nadia had been taken. "It's been over a year."

"Don't get out much?"

"I've been working quite a bit. Got back from a year in Brazil in the spring and started working on the resort project in August."

"Well, you know what they say about all work and no play, architect."

Yeah, many probably considered him a dull guy, but dedication to his work was what got him through the hardest time of his life.

Not wanting to go down that path, Jonah figured he and Vanessa probably should get to know one another better since they were going to be working together, but first things first.

He tightened his grip on her hand before bringing it in to rest against his chest. "I owe you an apology for my rudeness this morning."

She leaned back and looked up at him. "I take it finding out about me and the mural was a surprise?"

Boy that seemed to be the word for the evening. "Yes." He waited a moment and then added, "But a nice one."

A tilt of her head told him she wasn't sure if she believed him. "Why do I get the feeling a certain architect doesn't like surprises."

That had been more of a statement than a question, so Jonah remained silent. The truth was he hated them. Always had. Even as a kid, he liked knowing what was happening, what was coming down the road and when.

Birthdays and Christmas mornings were only made better once his folks took his detailed lists of gift ideas seriously. His brothers had messed with him a time or two over the years, but once he got into high school his life revolved around his studies and the girl he'd started dating his freshman year.

The only girl for him until everything changed eight years ago.

"No apology is necessary," Vanessa continued, cutting into his thoughts. "I'm happy you're on board with the idea now."

Glad she wasn't upset with his behavior, Jonah wove his way back to his original intent. "Very much on board. I'll need to get our interior-design team in the loop on this, sharing any preliminary drawings and color choices you have for the mural with them."

Vanessa dropped her gaze from his. "Yes, of course, you will."

"I'll admit I don't know much about your work or even how a mural is painted. Do you have any ideas or sketches yet?"

"I just found out about Nate's idea this morning, as well." Her shoulders stiffened and her feet once again became tangled with his. "Oops! Sorry about that. Ah, it's going to take me some time to come up with…a plan, a design."

Jonah wondered how much time, the analytical side of his brain already making plans as he mentally reviewed the upcoming schedule.

"The main hall where you'll be working is pretty much finished except for the furnishings and such, so you won't have to worry about any construction mess getting in the way," he said. "Of course, we'll have to build you scaffolding depending on the size and scope of the mural."

"Yes, I know, but—"

"And find a way to give you as much privacy as you need, but then again, it is a construction site so I hope you can work with noise and people. Do artists tend to prefer quiet?"

"Yes, s-some do. I usually work alone, but I'm sure I'll be able to manage."

Jonah picked up on the hesitation in her words. "Did Nate tell you the grand opening of the resort is planned for the Christmas holidays? That's less than twelve weeks away. Does that time frame work for you? I hate to have the project half finished—"

"Wow, has anyone ever told you that you talk too much?"

Vanessa's question cut into his sentence, silencing him for a moment as he gave it serious thought. "Yes, actually, it has been mentioned a time or two. Especially when it comes to work."

"So, let's not talk about work. Or talk at all." She trailed her fingertips across the back of his neck, just along the edge of his shirt collar. "Just enjoy the music, the dancing…the moment."

She was right. They had plenty of time to talk about the mural and resort later. It'd been a long day and while dancing was the last thing he'd ever thought he'd be doing tonight, he had to admit it felt pretty damn good to hold her in his arms.

Pressing his cheek to her hair, he pulled in a deep breath and a fresh, flowery scent filled his head. He relaxed for the first time since he'd come home.

As the song ended and another began, Vanessa didn't make any move to step away. In fact, she seemed to cling tighter. Her lush curves felt great, especially since the last woman he danced with was so thin and delicate he'd often wondered if she'd break if he held her too tight.

"Not going anywhere," he whispered.

The tension eased from her body and they danced through that song and a third one before the music selection changed and things got lively again.

"Let me guess," Vanessa stepped back when he stopped moving. "You're not interested in doing any line dancing."

"You've guessed right."

She smiled, moved out of his embrace and headed off the dance floor. Jonah fell into step behind her as they made their way through the crowd, almost bumping into her when she suddenly stopped.

"Ah, hello, Tommy."

Jonah looked over her shoulder and found the cowboy she'd been trying to dodge standing right in front of them. Taking a step closer and to one side, he again placed a hand at the small of her back, and moved in next to her.

"Jonah." She turned, a look of relief on her face. "This is my friend, Tommy Wheeler. Tommy, this is Jonah Dalton, my…um, my…"

"Date." The word popped out of his mouth before he could think about it, but the dazzling smile of Vanessa's was worth the white lie. "Nice to meet you, Tommy."

The cowboy pushed up the brim of his hat and offered Jonah a long look before finally taking his outstretched hand. "Dalton," he said. "You related to Anderson Dalton?"

"My cousin, why?"

"Just curious." Tommy finished the handshake. "I've worked on the Daltons ranch for the last ten years or so."

Okay, so maybe that's why he looked familiar. "They're a good outfit. Right up there with The Circle D."

"You don't work for your family's ranch."

It wasn't a question. "No, I'm back in town to work on the renovation of the new resort."

Tommy only responded with a nod of his head, and then turned his attention back to Vanessa. "So, how about a dance?"

"No, thanks. It's getting a bit late."

He glanced at his watch. "At ten o'clock? You and I have been out later than this, darling."

Was it his imagination or did Vanessa just lean in a bit closer to him?

"Yes, but that's all in the past now," she said, her fingers playing with the numerous bracelets on her wrist. "And I think it's time I head home."

"We." Jonah corrected her, again surprised when the word came out of his mouth. Not bothering to think as to why, or maybe he was just too tired, he drew her against his side and slid his hand around to cup her hip. "We're heading home."

They were?

Vanessa felt like a tennis ball, bouncing back and forth between Tommy and Jonah, but she never expected him to say that.

Heck, hearing him call himself her date had weakened her knees. Or was the sensation from how amazing it'd been to be in his arms as they danced? Or the way he held her right now?

"We are?" Her gaze collided with his for a second and she read understanding in Jonah's dark hazel eyes.

She turned back to Tommy and smiled. "Ah, yes, we are. So, I'll—ah, we'll see you later."

With Jonah's hand pressing against her back—oh boy, that felt good, too—she walked past Tommy and headed back to their table. Eli Dalton still sat there alone, but the bottles and glasses had multiplied, indicating he had company at some point while they were gone.

Jonah dropped his hand from her hip, putting some distance between them just before Eli looked their way. On purpose? Probably. A few dances and a few fibs to an ardent admirer didn't make them a couple.

Far from it.

They were...coworkers, she guessed, for lack of a better description, from the many questions he had about the mural. Questions she didn't have any answers to.

Yet.

But she would, she hoped.

She also hoped to get better acquainted with Jonah because she liked him. More so than any of the first dates (or seconds!) she'd gone on since coming to Rust Creek Falls. She'd been waiting for the right cowboy to come along. Could Jonah Dalton be the one?

"Hey, congratulations, Vanessa." Eli said, toasting her with a raised beer. "You not only got my little brother on the dance floor, you managed to keep him out there. What's your secret?"

She glanced at Jonah, already deciding she wasn't going to share that he'd actually been the one who offered to stay for more than one song.

"I'm not sure." She grabbed her glass, which was now just water as the ice had long melted. "Once he figured out I'm still a newbie at two-stepping I'm lucky he didn't go off and leave me standing there."

"I wouldn't do that."

Jonah's soft words caused her to look at him again. "I know that."

He dropped her gaze, focusing on the table for a moment before looking up at his brother. "I guess all of this means you aren't ready to head home? Or are you having a party of one?"

"The blondes returned. They're on the dance floor now and no, I'm not ready to leave." Eli tipped his head toward the poker table. "Besides, Derek's still playing. I thought I'd stick around. You know, just in case."

She wasn't sure what he meant, but Jonah seemed to understand the message. "Any chance you can get a ride home from your new friends? I'm ready to get out of here."

"I'll take you." Vanessa spoke before Eli could open his mouth. "I mean, that's what we said…" Her voice trailed off for a moment. "We're both heading back to the same place. You to the ranch house, me to the cabin. You are staying with your folks, right?"

"Oh, yeah, he's staying at the big house." Eli grinned.

"You okay to drive?" Jonah asked his brother.

Eli nodded. "This is my last one. I'll be fine."

"Okay, then." Jonah turned to her, picking up her sweater and holding it out in her direction. "I'm ready if you are."

They said their goodbyes, but when Jonah started for the front entrance of the bar, she grabbed his hand and motioned toward the back. He followed and soon they were outside in the cool evening air. Cool enough that

Vanessa stopped and tugged on her sweater, wishing she'd remembered her jacket, once again fighting with her jewelry after she managed to get it over her head.

"You must really like those." Jonah said, pointing at her captured wrist.

"Yes, I do." She freed her hand, shaking her wrist to enjoy the noise her precious collection made. She then tugged the ends of the sweater down over her hips. "Some are made of beads or crystals, but my favorites are the individual metal circles that expand when you press on them. Each holds an individual charm."

Her favorite one, purchased during her and Adele's last trip to New York City, caught her eye. She looked down at it, gently rubbing her thumb across the raised heart engraved there.

"Gifts from friends and family?"

"Some." Vanessa blinked hard so the tears would be gone when she looked up at him. "A few I purchased myself. When I couldn't resist one that caught my eye, especially while trolling the internet in the wee hours of the morning."

Jonah seemed to be studying her and she was glad for the dark shadows in the parking lot. Digging out her keys from her pocket, Vanessa pointed toward the first row of vehicles. "I'm parked down in front. A perk of getting here early."

She started across the gravel lot and Jonah fell into step next to her. The music and noise from the bar filtered out through the open windows reminding her again of the huge favor he'd done for her tonight.

"Thank you. For dancing with me…and everything else back there," she said as they walked. "Hopefully

Tommy was smart enough to pick up on the pretending we were doing."

"I think he got the message."

"Let's hope no one else noticed or else we'll be the topic of the local gossip mill come morning."

Jonah halted at her words. She turned, watching as he heaved a deep sigh and closed his eyes.

"Did I say something wrong?"

"No." He opened his eyes again, shook his head and started walking. "I'd just forgotten what a small town this is. Of course, knowing my brother, I'll be getting grief from my family before my morning coffee over the dancing."

She couldn't help but smile at that. "Should I apologize as well as say thank you?"

"No, neither is necessary. I had a good time, was glad to help and I appreciate the lift home." He stopped when she walked to the driver's-side door. "In this? This is your car?"

"Actually, it's a pickup. I'd think a cowboy would know the difference."

Jonah looked over her vehicle with a speculative eye. "I haven't been a cowboy in a long time and this thing has got to be at least twenty years old."

She liked that she had once again surprised him. "Not what you were expecting, huh? And be nice to Big Bertha, she's just celebrated her thirty-first birthday."

"The guy who runs the gas station used to have a truck he called Big Bertha."

"One and the same." She unlocked her door. "I had a rental for the first month I was here, but then I figured I needed something more permanent to get me through my first Montana winter. She's reliable, decent on gas and has never given me a lick of trouble. Head on around. I'll let you in."

Only after she jiggled with the passenger-side door for a few minutes while Jonah waited outside did Vanessa give up and get back out. She hurried to his side of the truck, unlocked the door and it opened right away.

"I think maybe you hurt her feelings," she said, offering a quick smile.

"Then I'm sorry."

Not sure if he was apologizing to her or her truck, Vanessa decided it was best not to ask as she headed back to the driver's side while Jonah climbed in.

"Did you know your inside light's not working?"

She looked up before closing her door. "Yep, you're right. The bulb must've just gone out."

Hooking her seat belt, she waited for a moment while Jonah did the same, once he moved the hardback book away from the locking mechanism. "What's this?" He peered at the cover. *"Harry Potter and the Goblet of Fire?"*

She nodded, starting the engine and heading out the parking lot. "Great book."

"Exactly how old are you?"

She glanced at him, happy to see a smile when they passed under a street light. "Very funny. I'm twenty-six, but that doesn't matter. Harry Potter is for everyone. Besides, I never read the series when it first came out back when I was a teenager. Now, I'm up to book four."

"What made you decide to read them now?"

Number fifteen: read all the Harry Potter books.

Adele had devoured each of the books as they were released, often standing in line at bookstores at midnight to get the first copy. She couldn't understand why Vanessa had never taken time away from her art to do the same. She'd insisted the item be added to their list when they had revived their list.

"Vanessa?"

"Oh, sorry. I got lost in thought there." It only took a few minutes to clear the town limits and soon they were on the back roads heading toward the ranch. She found she liked the darkness of the rural countryside that surrounded them. "One day I saw a display of the books and assorted merchandise in a bookstore and decided it was time. Let me guess? You've read them all."

Jonah nodded. "My twin sisters loved the books from the very beginning. I used to read to them until… well, until I moved out."

"When was that?"

"When I was eighteen."

Jonah stayed quiet after that and she wondered for a moment if she should turn on the radio, but the silence was nice after the mayhem back at the bar. Soon they reached the turn off for the ranch, but still had a few miles to go before getting to the main house.

An idea suddenly came to her and before she could chicken out, she said, "Hey, do you have any plans for tomorrow?"

"Tomorrow's Friday," Jonah said. "I'll be working. Everyone works on Fridays."

She had to admit she was a bit disappointed by his oh-so-practical tone. "Hmmm, you're one of those, huh? Okay."

Silence filled the interior of the truck again as they bounced over the dirt road until he finally asked, "Why?"

"Ever been to BearTrap Mountain?"

"The ski resort?"

Vanessa nodded. "It's about an hour from here, right?"

"Yeah, but if you're looking to ski it's still a bit early. Don't let that snow on the mountaintops fool you. Barring an early storm, it'll be another month before the ski trails get enough cover."

"Oh, I wasn't looking to ski." There was no way she was going to tell him the real reason she wanted to go. She had a hunch Jonah might be a bit too straitlaced for what she had in mind. "Just wanted to check it out."

The headlights of her truck cut across the land that had belonged to the Dalton family for over a hundred years. She loved listening to Rita Dalton, Jonah's mother, talk about the family history whenever she'd go to Sunday dinners at the house. So unlike the quiet dinners when she was growing up when it was usually just her and her parents.

After her mother died, her father often ate in his office or was out on business so she'd either had the housekeeper or more often than not, Adele and her mother to keep her company.

"You can drop me around the corner, back by the kitchen door."

Jonah's words were soft as she turned into the drive and continued on past the front door and the porch that ran the length of the house. Pulling around the side, she eased to a stop just outside the glow coming from the kitchen window.

"Nice to know Mom still leaves the light on for us wayward kids." He released his seat belt. "Thanks again, Vanessa. For the company tonight and the ride home."

"You're welcome. I had a good time, too. Glad you ended up at my table."

Jonah returned her stare for a long moment and just when Vanessa wondered if he was going to lean in closer, a nonverbal request for her to do the same, he turned and reached for the door handle.

"Oh, it's hard to open from the inside. You need to jiggle it to the left three times, up twice and then down while pulling on it."

Jonah followed her directions, but the door wouldn't budge.

"No, three times to the left."

"I did go left."

She sighed and released her belt. Moving her book out of the way, she scooted closer. Propped on one hip, she leaned across his lap. "Here, let me. You just need the magic touch."

"Is that right?"

His words were soft against her hair, his lips right at her ear taking her back to when they'd danced and he'd reassured her he wasn't ready to leave the floor yet. That dizzying feeling came back again and needing to brace herself, she put one hand on the closest surface, which turned out to be his muscular thigh.

Well, it was either that or between his legs, so this was probably best.

"Yes, that's right. Just give me a second..." She continued to play with the handle, reciting the steps silently to keep her mind occupied and away from the fact she was practically in his lap.

The door finally popped open. "There!" Pleased,

she moved back, turning her head toward Jonah at the same time. “All it took was the right…”

Her words disappeared as their mouths brushed, lips clinging until someone, and for the life of her she didn’t know who, moved. Soft and tender, the pressure barely felt until their breaths combined.

She backed away, realizing she now had both hands on his legs, but it wasn’t enough. Her elbows gave way, but he reached for her shoulders, keeping her in place.

“Why did you do that?”

He looked at her. “Do what?”

Was he serious? “Kiss me.”

“I didn’t kiss you.” His gaze left hers and settled on her mouth. Even in the dark she could see banked desire there. “You kissed me.”

A shiver of indignation skirted down her backbone. “I already told you I don’t kiss on the first date.”

“This isn’t a date.”

Vanessa started to protest, but he was right, despite how he’d labeled himself back at the bar. “Point taken.”

His mouth hitched up one corner. “So, that makes it okay that you kissed me?”

“I didn’t! Believe me, architect, if I’d kissed you, you’d have known—”

The rest of her words disappeared once again as his mouth came down on hers.

Chapter 4

Boy, this cowboy can kiss.

A silly thought to be sure. Jonah had made it clear he hadn't been a cowboy in years, but it was the first thing that raced through Vanessa's mind when he interrupted their "who went first" argument by kissing her.

And he kept on doing so.

His mouth was firm when it first crashed down on hers, but it softened when she made it clear she was fully on board with what he was doing by opening her mouth, her tongue darting out to sneak a taste of him.

Heavenly.

A low groan escaped from him as he angled his head, pulled her closer and settled his mouth against hers again. Deepening the kiss, his tongue glided against hers, stealing her breath and when it returned it was a soft moan to let him know how much she was enjoying this.

She hadn't been kissed in a long time and the way he explored her mouth, teasing and tasting, along with a hint of urgency that overrode any hesitation she should be feeling, told her just how much she'd been missing.

Instead, she wanted to test that resolve, wanted to see just where he would take this if she released the tight grip she had on the solid muscles of his thighs and simply crawled into his lap and wrapped her arms around his neck.

The thought of doing just that seemed to melt her every bone, or maybe that was the heat from his body as he held her close, just like when they were dancing.

But then he broke free and drawing in a ragged breath, he slowly set her back on the seat before releasing her. "Ah, that was..."

His husky whisper trailed off and even though he was looking at her, shadows covered most of his face.

Except for his mouth.

The perfection of his still-wet full lips was only inches away, open as if he had more to say, but he stayed silent.

She fought back the temptation to be the one to initiate round two of surprise kisses that came out of nowhere—or would that be round three?—and instead said, "Yeah, I didn't..."

Whatever else she'd planned to say vanished from her head like bubbles popping in midair. Hmmm, guess he wasn't the only one at a loss for words.

She swiped her tongue across her parched lips and he dropped his head a fraction of an inch. Her breath caught, certain he was going to kiss her again. But then he moved and seconds later stood outside, the open door allowing the night's cool breeze to displace the warm sultry air that had filled her truck.

"Thanks again…for the ride home. Good night."

She expected him to shut the door and walk away, but he remained standing there.

Waiting for her to respond? What was she supposed to say?

"Good night."

Yes, that was a clever comeback, but before she could say another word he stepped back and gently closed the door, double-checking that it was shut. He then turned and headed up the stairs until all she could see of him was his legs from the knees down as he stood on the porch.

It took her a moment to realize he was waiting for her to leave. The idea raced through her head of crawling out from the driver's side and joining him, just to see how he'd react, but this was his family's home and heck, he'd been the one to end their impromptu make-out session.

She slid back behind the wheel, put the truck into Drive and slowly pulled away. Not looking in the rear-view mirror was impossible as her gaze automatically went there. Jonah remained on the back porch until she could no longer see him as the road twisted away from the main house.

It only took a few minutes and she was parking next to the cabin. The lights she'd left on, both inside and the porch lamp, welcomed her home. She slipped inside, thinking about Jonah doing the same thing back at his place. Despite the distinct warmth that still flooded her insides thanks to those amazing kisses, she noticed the chill in the air as she locked the door behind her.

Shutting off lights as she headed to the bedroom in the back of the cabin, she went to the small woodstove in the corner. Rita Dalton had been the one who'd shown her how to start a fire and keep it going, but even with written instructions it sometimes took her a few tries. Things went perfectly this time and as she watched the kindling ignite, her thoughts drifted back to the night's events.

It'd been clear that Jonah hadn't expected to see her at the bar, much less for her to ask him to dance. Yes, she should've told him that her two-stepping skills were sorely lacking, but he'd been so sweet in taking her out to the middle of the dance floor instead of heading back to the table. So understanding about her need to avoid an overamorous cowboy.

She liked talking to him, getting to know him better.

At least until he mentioned the mural.

The minute he'd gone all businesslike and started asking detailed questions, she'd felt the dread surge to life deep in her stomach.

"Maybe agreeing to do that mural wasn't your best idea," she said aloud as she placed a couple of larger logs inside the stove. "Not that your block is anyone's fault but yours. Still..."

Her voice trailed off as she stared at the flames, fingers outstretched for the warmth. She studied her hands and thought about how they'd never let her down before. Not once in all the years she'd been painting.

"You've done it before, you can do it again."

Closing up the stove, she then grabbed her pajamas and headed for the bathroom. A hot shower was just what she needed before going to bed. Standing beneath the steamy spray she relived the moments in the truck, still not sure who'd kissed who first.

But she knew for sure that second kiss was all Jonah and for someone who claimed not to like surprises, he'd certainly pulled a rabbit out of the hat the moment his lips touched hers.

She washed away the night's sweat and smells from the bar, but also the rich, spicy scent of Jonah's cologne that filled her head, clung to her skin and made her weak in the knees every time she got close to him.

A few minutes later, she was tucked beneath the covers in the coolest bed ever after making sure the woodstove had enough fuel to keep the room toasty until the morning. She clicked on the radio that only seemed to pick up two stations, country music and a national news show. Soft strains of an old Patsy Cline ballad played as she reached for the sketch pad and the leather case that held her pens and pencils, her gaze catching on the folded piece of paper on her nightstand.

She gently opened it, smoothing it out with her hands. Grabbing one of her pens, she trailed a finger down the list, remembering the moments last year with Adele when they added to their childhood agenda for a happy life.

Number twelve: kiss a cowboy.

When she told Jonah she didn't kiss on the first date, she meant it. A personal rule since she was a teenager. Despite dating quite a few cowboys since coming to town, she hadn't kissed a single one.

In fact, the last time she'd been kissed was well over two years ago after her last relationship ended, thanks to a cheating boyfriend who'd managed to keep both her and a girl in Boston in the dark about each other for over a year.

Heck, she hadn't even dated since then, throwing herself into her art. Just like Adele had said. So when she'd moved here she'd been determined to meet new people. Do new things. Find the joy and happiness missing from her life.

Find someone new to kiss. Find her lost talent.

And she liked to think she had at least started on those goals, even if her gift was only coming through in practice sketches.

She'd made friends, and yes, being as small of a town as Rust Creek Falls was, people tended to know each other's business and felt compelled to offer unsolicited advice at times, but they cared about each other. Cared about their town.

And when it came to kissing…

Well, she knew now why none of the men she'd dated had tempted her to break her rule.

They weren't Jonah.

Technically he was more city boy than cowboy now, but she'd bet her custom-made sable paintbrushes the man could still saddle a horse and ride off into the sunset.

Kissed Jonah Dalton!

She scrawled the words next to number twelve and placed a checkmark there, as well. Another mission accomplished. One she wouldn't mind repeating.

Out of the sixteen remaining goals on their list, she'd completed five so far. Well, she was still working on the Harry Potter books, but she was halfway through them so that goal got a checkmark, as well.

She looked over the list again, her heart giving a

little jolt when she read one of the goals they'd written down when they were twelve.

Number nine: Fly among the clouds (and not in an airplane!)

Impossible? Maybe not.

She'd come up with an idea and in a spur-of-the-moment flash, probably still in the clouds from being held in the man's arms, she'd thought maybe Jonah would—

"Nope, don't go there." Vanessa folded up the list and tucked it back between the lamp and a framed collage of pictures of her and Adele through the years.

"Don't ruin how great tonight ended." She then turned back to her sketch pad. "Okay, let's make some magic for this mural."

She opened to a blank page, switched out her pen for a pencil and held it over the stark whiteness in front of her. Waving the pencil back and forth, the tip hovering over the paper just enough not to leave a mark, she waited for…

Something.

Anything to come to mind that would represent a mural honoring the special place and people that meant so much to this town and its residents.

And yet again, there was nothing.

Her head was as blank as the paper before her.

Sighing, she closed her eyes, shut out the unadorned sheet and focused on the Tim McGraw ballad that filled the air, one of the songs she and Jonah had danced to tonight.

Forcing the pencil to make contact, to glide across the page, stroke after stroke, she allowed the music to guide her, already knowing what she was sketching. When the song ended, she looked and the rough outline of dark eyes, slightly mussed hair and a strong jaw looked back at her.

Jonah.

She tossed the sketchbook and pencil to the empty side of the bed, turned off the light and snuggled deep beneath the covers, determined not to think about the man she'd only met this morning—and kissed tonight!—and get some sleep.

Sleep. Who was she kidding?

Jonah pulled into the parking lot of the Grace Traub Community Center, the town's newest building, built just this past spring.

He checked his watch. Just after four o'clock.

Usually he'd still be putting in at least three more hours of work before calling it a day, but the foreman had pointed out construction was ahead of schedule and recommended starting the weekend a bit early. Jonah had agreed and when the last worker pulled out of the parking lot, he wasn't far behind.

Because of Vanessa.

When she mentioned last night how the town's gossip mill would probably make them dancing together a hot new topic, Jonah had figured it would start this morning at breakfast, but he'd been wrong. Only because both Derek and Eli made the walk of shame as they showed up still wearing the same clothes they'd had on the night before, so all three Dalton boys were on the hot seat.

Their mother had stayed quiet when the two of them walked in the back door at the same time, and all Dad had wanted was for them to shower and eat so they could get started on the workday. Even though she was well aware that all of her children were adults now, it still amazed Jonah how their mother had the ability to express her emotions without saying a word—and she wasn't happy.

That is, until Eli had pulled out the often used diversionary tactic from their youth and asked Jonah about his ride home.

Once Jonah had cleared up the confusion by admitting he'd gotten a lift from Vanessa, his mom had talked nonstop about their tenant. When he'd mentioned Nate had commissioned her to paint a mural for the resort, she'd shown him a pencil sketch Vanessa had done of his father while sitting in the barn one afternoon, drawing as he worked without the old man realizing she'd been there.

The piece was stunning.

She'd captured his father's weathered, yet still handsome features. The deep grooves around his eyes from years of working outdoors, laugh lines he called them, saying they came from being happily married to their mother all these years. The cowboy hat perched back on his head as he concentrated on whatever job he'd been tackling.

Jonah was impressed with her talent and wanted to see more of her previous work, especially since he hadn't done an internet search on her last night when he'd gotten home like he planned.

Not after the way she'd kissed him.

He kissed her.

They'd kissed each other.

The first time had been purely by accident. Although the way she'd leaned across his lap to mess with the door handle—her hand on his leg, her hair in his face, knowing that she only had to turn his way—so yeah, the thought had crossed his sleep-deprived mind.

But the cute way she'd insisted it hadn't been her fault, not to mention the dare she'd practically thrown down made him cut off her protest with a searing kiss.

It was only when he'd pulled her even closer and thought about dragging her onto his lap so they'd both be more comfortable, that he'd put a stop to the craziness, got out of her truck and said good-night.

Before it was too late.

His brothers had used their mother's focus on Vanessa and her artwork to slip out of the kitchen, so thankfully they hadn't seen his mental stroll down memory lane, but his mother had picked up on his quietness. When she pushed, he claimed he was still tired from the long drive from Denver the day before, but agreed that the sketch was terrific.

That was how he'd found out Vanessa been doing similar sketches of many of the locals and about the afternoon program she ran here at the community center on Mondays, Wednesdays and Friday afternoons.

He knew they had to talk about what happened last night and he'd waited all day for her to show up at the resort, but she hadn't. Some of the crew had given him some good-natured ribbing about being in the bar last night with Vanessa, so maybe that's what she was trying to avoid?

Glancing at his watch again, he rubbed at his jaw feeling the day's growth of his beard and wondered if he should've gone home first to shower and shave.

Then he wondered if he was too early, maybe the class lasted longer than what his mother had said, but the front doors of the center opened and a stream of kids and adults came out.

He waited until most had either driven or walked away before getting out of his truck. He headed up the front steps, his architectural eye appreciating how the building fit in so well with the rest of the businesses here on North Main Street. A few of them, like Crawford's General Store on the opposite corner, had been around almost since Rust Creek Falls was first founded back in the late 1800s.

There was an office off the lobby, but it was empty. Straight ahead was the main room, a large space with a stage that could be used for any community event, which was the purpose of the building he guessed, but no Vanessa.

"Excuse me." He spotted a teenage girl in the corner of the room, doing something with a large bulletin board. "Can you tell me where I can find Vanessa Brent?"

"Sure." She pointed with one hand, never taking her eyes off her project. "Go back out to the main hall, head for the right side of the building and follow the music."

"Okay, thanks." He turned, but then thought about what she'd said. "Wait, did you say music? I thought she taught an art class."

"She does. Trust me, listen for the tunes and you'll find her."

Following her directions, Jonah started down a long sun-filled hallway, passing a number of closed doors before the strains of a Frank Sinatra song caught his attention.

He came up to the large windows that allowed visitors to see inside the room, spotting Vanessa right away. With her back to him, she rocked her hips back and forth in time with the swing tune as she moved around a bunch of pint-size tables, picking up art supplies and pushing in miniature chairs.

She was again wearing those same stretchy leggings that had captured his attention yesterday, this time a bright blue color. The same ankle boots were on her feet while an oversize man's dress shirt splattered with every color of the rainbow covered her past her backside, but the sleeves were rolled back showing off her jewelry. Her hair was a wild array of curls, but held back off her face with a hair band the same color as her pants.

The same kick in the gut he'd felt when he'd first saw her—hell, every time he'd run into her yesterday—nearly knocked him over again. When he reached the open doorway, he paused and leaned against it, using the time to get his breathing under control and enjoy the show.

She moved around the room with ease, singing along with Old Blue Eyes questioning what really was a lost last love, as she stacked papers, tossed garbage and filled a nearby sink with dirty paintbrushes.

When she dropped something, she didn't just bend over and pick it up, but twisted to the floor, her hips never stopping as her boots easily moved across the tiled flooring. She rose and spun around in one motion, coming to a complete stop when she finally spotted him.

"Jonah!"

He smiled, liking that this time he was the one doing the surprising. "Sorry, didn't mean to startle you, but I didn't want to interrupt your duet with Frank."

"Jeez, you heard me?" She placed the stuff in her hands on the counter and turned down the portable electronic device sitting between a set of miniature speakers. "Please tell me you just showed up."

"No, and I think the whole building heard you."

Instead of being embarrassed, she only laughed. "Boy, I need to remember to close the door and drop the blinds once the kids head out."

"You play swing music while the kids are here?"

"Sure do. And anything else that comes up on the playlist. We've got everyone from Bon Jovi to Katy Perry to The Muppets. All preselected and screened for young ears."

He straightened and entered, noticing the area in the back of the room was floor to ceiling bookcases, some with doors and others open shelving, filled with every kind of art supply imaginable. Another wall was an oversize corkboard where the prized artwork of her students was on display. "Wow, this is quite a setup you've got here."

"Thanks, I'm pretty proud of it." She looked around, her expressive face reflecting her words as she moved to the sink and turned on the water. "They let me totally redo the room once I explained what I needed for the class. Hard to believe this used to be a stuffy conference room with wall-to-wall carpeting and a kitchenette."

"It's good they had room in the budget."

"What?" She squirted liquid soap, filling the sink with bubbles. "Oh, no, I paid for it."

He looked around the room again, easily adding up the cost of the work needed, never mind the kid-size furniture. "You paid for the entire renovation? What about the ongoing supplies needed?"

She shrugged. "It was my idea for the class in the first place." She smiled and waved a soapy finger at him. "Be careful what you volunteer for."

Here she was surprising him again. He stared at her, his gaze taking in all of her from her curls to her boots, the few feet separating them suddenly made her seem far away. "That's very generous."

She returned his appraisal, then abruptly turned and faced the sink. "I've got connections for great discounts on the art stuff. So, what brings you to the community center this afternoon?"

He crossed the room, joining her at the counter. "You. I was hoping— I thought I'd see you at the resort today."

She kept her gaze on the items she'd washed, rinsed and set to dry on a nearby rack. "Why? I told you last night I haven't even started on the design for the mural yet."

"And you said you had plans for today." He remembered her asking about the nearby ski resort. "Did you make it over to BearTrap Mountain?"

"No, I didn't even get out of bed until almost noon." She shook back her curls and finally looked at him. "I had a tough time getting to sleep last night."

Pulling in a deep breath, he took in the tangy odors of clay, paint, wet paper towels and the same flowery scent of hers he'd discovered while they danced. While they kissed. "Yeah, me, too."

"Really?"

He nodded. "I wanted to see you today so I could apologi—"

"Don't say that." His words disappeared when she slapped a soapy hand over his mouth. " Don't you dare apologize for any part of last night."

He pulled her hand away and wiped at his mouth, the taste on his lips made him cringe, reminding him of a few times in his childhood when the threat of washing out his mouth with a bar of soap truly came to pass.

Vanessa's eyes grew wide. She snatched her hand back to her chest. "Oh! I'm so sorry! There's a water fountain in the back."

He found it quickly, having to bend almost in half to reach it, but rinsed away the residue with the cool liquid. Rising back to his full height he found Vanessa standing there, fresh paper towels in her hand. "Thanks."

"I really am sorry. I didn't think…"

He grinned after wiping at his mouth. "Yeah, I figured that out pretty quickly."

"So now I'm the one apologizing to you, but only for my soapy mishap." She took a step closer, and laid a hand on his chest. "Not last night. I'm glad you showed up at the bar, glad you danced with me, let me take you home and—"

This time he silenced her, but with just one finger pressed to her lips. She could've stepped away and continued talking, but she went still beneath his touch.

"Even though you don't kiss on the first date?" he asked.

"It wasn't a date."

He dropped his hand, the apology he'd practiced in his truck on the way here listing all the reasons why the kiss they'd shared had been wrong—how tired he'd been, they were working together, he wasn't looking to get involved—vanished from his thoughts.

"Are you busy tomorrow?" he asked instead.

She shook her head.

"Would you like to check out that resort? We could head over in the afternoon—"

"How about ten a.m.?"

He smiled. "Okay, ten o'clock. I'll drive."

A mock look of hurt crossed her pretty face. "Are you saying you don't like my truck?"

"I'm saying I want to make sure we get there in one piece. And why so early?"

She beamed a bright smile at him. "Oh, there's an… exhibition there I want to check out."

"Anything I might be interested in?" he asked.

She offered a casual shrug as she stepped back, but he caught a mischievous sparkle in those big brown eyes. "Maybe. How do you feel about flying?"

Chapter 5

She had to be kidding. Zip-lining? That's what Vanessa had been talking about yesterday when she quizzed him on flying?

They had arrived at BearTrap Mountain, a no-frills ski resort an hour's drive north of Kalispell, fifteen minutes ago. Wandering through the main lodge, a simple structure of glass and concrete that was surprisingly busy for an early October Saturday, they found the ski lifts were operating, taking leaf peepers up to the summit to view the beautiful fall foliage. There were also plenty of signs pointing to hiking and mountain biking trails.

When they reached the large open area of the lodge that would be swamped with skiers in another month or so, Jonah had been busy comparing the space to what the resort in Rust Creek Falls would need, not noticing Vanessa had wandered off until she returned with a piece of paper, claiming she needed his signature.

"I have to sign a waiver in order to do this?" he asked.

"Of course. They take safety very seriously, but still..."

"Are you sure you want to try this?" He pushed when Vanessa's voice trailed off.

"Are you kidding? To feel like you're flying among the clouds? Look at the video and the pictures." She pointed at a desk area that showed the adventure that awaited them in full color. "Doesn't it look like fun?"

Jonah sighed, still not believing he'd allowed her to rope him—literally—into this. "Okay, let's go."

Giving a little squeal of delight, Vanessa lifted on her tiptoes and planted a quick kiss on his cheek before she headed for the sign-up desk. Jonah followed her, wondering if that was considered a real kiss, especially since she'd made it clear that was something she didn't do on first dates.

After sitting through a discussion on safety and equipment procedures, they were given helmets and got fitted in a harness with straps that made certain parts of his anatomy a bit uncomfortable. Thank goodness he'd worn jeans and boots today.

They were put in a group with a family with three young boys, a duo of teenagers and a honeymooning couple around about the same age as him and Vanessa.

"How long have you two been together?" the recent bride asked as they sat in the back of a tram that would transport them up to the mountain for the start of the tour.

"Oh, we're not—"

"This is our first date." Jonah leaned forward, cutting off Vanessa as he grabbed her hand. "Her idea."

The couple grinned at them. "First time zip-lining, as well?" the husband asked.

When the two of them nodded, he said, "Well, if you can make it through this, anything after will be a breeze."

"Thanks a lot." Vanessa turned to look at Jonah, concern on her face for the first time.

"Hey, you wanted to do this." Jonah reminded her with a grin. "I was just about to suggest a nice, smooth ride up on the ski lift."

They reached their starting point and headed off into the woods, their guide pointing out the local flora and fauna as they hiked. Soon they reached the first sky bridge, where Vanessa surprised him by agreeing to be the first one in line after the lead guide. Jonah moved into place behind her as they walked across, tethered to a safety cable. He had to admit the scenery was beautiful.

As long as one kept their eyes on the trees and not the ground below. The platform was sixty feet up in the treetops.

"Oh, wasn't that the most amazing thing ever?" Vanessa said as they waited for the rest of their group to join them.

"I think I'll save amazing for what's next. The first zip line." Jonah pointed at the metal cable to their left. "You going first again?"

"Unless you want to," Vanessa said, her eyes bright with laughter.

"Oh, no. Ladies first."

"Chicken," she said, teasing him.

"No, I'd rather you not be here to see me lose my man card when I have to shut my eyes before taking the initial step off into nothingness."

"Don't worry." She leaned in close, her hand giving his biceps a quick squeeze. "Your manhood status is guaranteed with me."

And right then he wanted to kiss her—personal rules be damned—but the platform was crowded as everyone had made it across the bridge.

The boys wanted to be first down the zip line, so he and Vanessa went after the family, with Vanessa again going ahead of him. She stepped right off and let out a "yee-haw" all the way down. Jonah was so impressed with her spirit, he did the same, enjoying the rush as his body zoomed through the trees.

The rest of their two-hour tour went quickly, with everyone taking turns at being the first ones to go at each new station. The last zip line was a dual line, and it was Jonah and Vanessa's turn to go last. The newlyweds went just before them, with the bride declaring it a race just before she stepped off ahead of her husband.

"If winning makes her happy, then I'm happy," he said, waiting a second more before heading down.

Jonah watched as Vanessa stepped up to the platform next to his, both of them clipping on their harnesses at the same time.

"So, are we going to race, too?" he asked.

"I don't know. What does the winner get?"

Jonah had quite a few ideas, but he just shrugged and said, "Whatever they want."

Her answering smile could only be called sassy. "Oh, game on."

* * *

Damn, his body ached from his eyebrows to his feet.

Dropping his tools, Jonah stood and stretched, raising his arms high over his head, feeling the aching protest of muscles he hadn't worked in years.

Whoever said weekends were for kicking back and relaxing hadn't been from his hometown. He'd been on the go since yesterday morning. First, a day on a mountain with Vanessa, and today he was working alongside his brothers mending a fence line until…

Well, until later.

During the past three hours of backbreaking work, which included replacing damaged posts, untangling and stretching yards of barbed wire and replacing missing staples, Jonah and his brothers had fallen into a familiar rhythm. They stayed focused on their work, talking only when it was related to the task at hand. But he could tell both of them had been chomping at the bit to get at him.

About Vanessa.

"You know, I bet spending the afternoon doing ranch work is nothing compared to daily trips to some fancy, expensive gym."

And there was the first volley.

Derek's voice came from behind him. Jonah lowered his arms, turned around and found his brothers had stopped working and were at the truck, taking a break. He yanked off his gloves and rubbed at the red spots on his hands where new calluses were sure to form.

"You're right." Shoving the gloves into a back pocket, he walked over to them. "Eight miles a day on a treadmill and lifting weights is fun, but this is real work. And you two are as good—no, better—at it than I remember."

His younger brother seemed amazed by Jonah's praise. He meant every word. His ass was dragging and they still had at least two more hours to go. Still, he was glad to see the two of them were as sweaty and dirty as him.

"You've got a right to be tired." Eli filled a plastic tumbler with water from the cooler sitting on the tailgate and handed it to him. "You hit the ground running the moment you got home three days ago. Even working on Saturdays? I noticed your truck was gone most of the day."

Jonah froze, the refreshing liquid halfway to his mouth. He had gone over to the resort yesterday afternoon for an hour or so after his adventurous day with Vanessa. Did that mean his brothers thought he'd been there all day?

"Don't let him fool you, man. His truck headed east past the barn yesterday morning before he eventually left the ranch. There's nothing down that way except cattle, horses, the creek." Derek paused, as if deep in thought. "Oh, yeah and his cabin. Or should I say Vanessa's cabin."

"Really?" Eli grinned and winked at him. "So, does your artist know she's sleeping in your custom-made bed yet?"

"If she didn't before, she probably does now," Derek deadpanned, grabbing one of the sandwiches their mother had packed for them.

Jonah lowered his drink, still having not taken a sip. "Is my spending time with Vanessa a problem for you?"

"Why would it be?" Derek said. "If I was interested

in her I would've made that clear when the two of you were getting cozy at the Ace the other night."

His brother looked him straight in the eye when he spoke and Jonah believed him. But it bothered him that he'd never given what Eli had said about Derek offering Vanessa riding lessons—and if that meant anything—a second thought.

Not when they danced.

Not when he kissed her, and not for one moment yesterday.

"So what did you two end up doing all day?" Eli tossed him a sandwich. "Please tell me you really weren't working."

Jonah took his time finishing off the water, enjoying the coldness on his dry throat. He wondered if his brothers were baiting him, already knowing but trying to get him to say the words aloud.

Not sure, he purposely took his time setting the empty tumbler down and then opened his sandwich, waiting until his brothers had both their mouths full before he spoke.

"We went zip-lining on BearTrap Mountain."

In unison, both men choked, but at least Eli managed to keep his mouth shut. Derek ended up spitting out the water he'd chugged a second ago all over his boots.

Jonah laughed at their stunned expressions, which probably matched his yesterday when he and Vanessa got to the ski resort and she finally explained what her cryptic comment about flying had meant.

"Are you kidding me?" Eli finally asked, after swallowing his food and pounding a coughing Derek on the back so hard, the kid hopped off the truck to get away from him. "You? Zip lining?"

"Yes, me." Jonah grinned, giving a casual shrug. "It was something Vanessa has wanted to do for a while, not that I was aware of her plan until we got there.

"Sounds like you had a good time," Derek said.

Jonah nodded. "Zip lining has become really popular over the last few years. Not to mention it's a great way for a ski resort to earn money in the off season. The place was packed yesterday, and not just because it was the last weekend for the activity. The guides said they'd been swamped all summer long."

It was then his brain had gone into high gear. "I'm planning to talk to Nate Crawford about including something similar at the resort once we get started on the outdoor recreation portion—"

"No, that's not—" Derek cut him off, shaking his head. "Jeez, you're a moron."

Confused, Jonah stared at his brother. "Come again?"

"I'm not talking about business. It was gorgeous outside yesterday. What was it like on the mountain with the sun on your face and the wind in your hair?" Derek moved closer, invading Jonah's personal space. "Did you step right off like those kids with a loud 'hell, yeah' coming out of your mouth all the way down the first time? Or were you so scared you could've wet your pants, but hey, there was no turning back?"

Silence filled the air for a long moment as Jonah stared at his brother.

"I think what he's asking is if you, and Vanessa, had fun yesterday," Eli added drily, as he started cleaning up their mess. "But I'm just guessing."

"Yes," Jonah said. "It was fun. *We* had fun."

"I'd say from that smile of yours, you had a lot of fun," Derek said. "Good to know you still have it in you."

Still had it in him? Jonah stared at his brother. "What's that supposed to mean?"

"It means this is the first time you've been out on a date with someone who lives in this town. It means it's nice to see you being social. You know, instead pulling that hermit act like you usually do whenever you come home."

"I have a social life in Denver."

Derek remained silent, returning his stare for a long moment. He then shook his head before pulling on his gloves and heading back for the fence line.

"You've got to admit, he's got a point." Eli jumped down from the back of the truck. "Yeah, we know you've dated some since your divorce, but like you said, that's in Denver. We don't expect you to find true love here again, but whenever you come back for a visit you'd either be at the cabin or sticking close to the ranch working on whatever architect stuff you'd brought with you."

"Finishing that cabin was important to me," Jonah said. At least it had been over the almost six years it took him to complete it. "For a lot of reasons, and I can't just walk away from my work obligations while on vacation."

"Either way, you were never interested in having any fun. Hell, you hardly cracked a smile most times." Eli shrugged and continued to clean up. "It's like you shut down as soon as you crossed the town line. I was surprised when you agreed to get a beer with me the other night."

His brothers were right.

He'd always kept to himself whenever he'd come home.

His mom had often tried to talk to him about it over the past few years, to get him to open up about the end of his marriage and how much he'd changed. Jonah had only reassured her he was doing okay, and proved it by working even harder on the cabin, only accepting help from his family when he had to tackle a job that required more than one person.

But the cabin was done now. It had been for almost two years, sitting empty before Vanessa rented it.

Now that his brothers had pointed out his changed behavior, Jonah had no answer as to why things were so different this time around.

Was it because of a certain brunette who'd captured his attention his first day back?

That same vivacious and gorgeous woman he had a second date with tonight after accepting an invitation for dinner.

At the cabin she still didn't know belonged to him.

This was his place.

Vanessa stood in the small, but efficient kitchen, having just put the chicken breasts into the oven while keeping an eye on the two pots simmering on the stove top, still unable to believe what she'd learned earlier today.

This was his place and he'd never said a word during their adventure yesterday.

Excited that Jonah had accepted her invitation to come for dinner tonight, she'd made a quick trip to Crawford's General Store earlier today.

She'd decided to make him a favorite dish of hers,

so she'd hoped to find a few necessary ingredients, or else she'd have to make the drive to nearby Kalispell.

But as surprised as she'd been at finding angel-hair pasta and garlic cloves in the same place that also sold just about everything from flannel shirts to children's toys to enough hardware to build an ark—or a cabin—it paled in comparison to what she'd overheard while debating which bottle of wine to pick up for the evening.

She'd first heard her and Jonah's names spoken by a couple of females in the next aisle, and then how the two of them were not only seen dancing the other night, but also spotted together at nearby BearTrap Mountain.

Grinning over the fact she was now officially a part of the town's gossip mill, Vanessa had started to step around the corner to actually confirm their stories when one of women mentioned how cozy it all was.

Seeing how she was renting *his* cabin.

A cabin Jonah actually built by hand.

It supposedly had taken him years to complete it, according to one of the busybodies. He'd worked on it only when he came home for visits, refusing to allow anyone to help him. Apparently it had stood empty once he completed it.

Until his mother rented it to Vanessa, that is.

She looked around the open space that made up the kitchen, separated from the combined dining and living room by a V-shaped island. A woodstove, the same style as in the bedroom but a bit larger, stood on the other side of the island, providing heat for the entire area.

The walls were filled with windows that opened up to views of the beautiful Montana scenery and the decking that surrounded the cabin on three sides. There were automatic shades that could be lowered after the sun went down, which it was in the process of doing right now.

She found the remote and pressed the button, watching as the shades silently lowered into place. It wasn't cool enough yet for a fire, so she turned on a few lights, including the intriguing antler chandelier that hung over the dining-room table, and lit some of the candles she had sitting out.

The glow of it all reflected off the pale logs and filled the space with a warm radiance.

It was beautiful.

She'd fallen in love with the place the first time she'd seen it.

Moving into the dining room, she fussed with the table settings, upset again that she'd left the store without picking out a bottle of wine, the news about Jonah and the cabin ringing in her ears.

As soon as she'd arrived home, she'd gone on a cleaning frenzy, wanting it to look perfect when he saw it again, remembering how he seemed transfixed by the place when he'd picked her up yesterday morning.

Now she knew why.

She'd been waiting outside for him, so excited about their day, so he hadn't actually been inside yet. The only thing he'd commented on had been the twin country-red rocking chairs she'd put on the front deck. She'd told him about finding them in Crawford's and how it just didn't seem right to split up the pair.

Looking around the interior, she wondered what he would think of what she'd done to it.

There'd only been a few pieces here when she moved in. The dining-room table with two chairs and that fabulous light fixture overhead, an oversize leather couch that had seen better days, but was oh so comfortable to stretch out on, and the king-size bed made from hand-hewn logs in the bedroom.

Jonah's mother had offered to look around the main ranch house for some stuff and despite Vanessa's assurance that it wasn't necessary, she'd come by the next day with a set of dishes and cookware for the kitchen.

From there, Vanessa had enjoyed filling the place with whatever necessities she needed or any impulse buys that reflected her personal style. She shopped for everything from furniture to artwork to sheets for that glorious bed—

A knock came at the door and Vanessa jumped.

Then she laughed.

"Oh, girl, you are being so silly." She fluffed her wavy hair, tugged her sweater down over her hips and headed for the front door. "Coming!"

That must be Jonah.

He probably didn't care two figs about this place. If he had, he would've said something to her before now. Maybe building it had been part of his job. The man was an architect, after all. He obviously had his own apartment or house in Denver where he lived full-time.

"You're obsessing about this because you're nervous," she whispered to her reflection in the small, ornately framed mirror that hung next to the entrance. "It's just dinner. A second date. Nothing special."

She smiled, checked her teeth as she'd been sampling her cooking, and opened the door.

Jonah stood on the other side, looking impossibly handsome dressed in jeans, a Western-cut shirt and boots. In one hand he held an oversize bouquet of gerbera daisies, a riot of neon yellows, oranges, pinks and greens. In the other hand a bottle of pinot grigio wine.

"Hey there." He held out the wine first. "I didn't know what you're cooking for us, but I remembered your wine at the Ace had been white. I hope this is okay."

He remembered that? She'd downed the remains of her wine within the first minute of finding him at her table.

"And the flowers?" she asked, her words coming out much softer than she planned. "What's their story?"

"Ah, I hope they're not too corny," he said with a sheepish grin as he offered them to her, as well. "As soon as I saw these beauties I knew there was only one woman who'd appreciate them."

She smiled and reached for the flowers, their fingers brushing when he released them to her. "Nothing wrong with corny, which these are not. They're lovely. Thank you."

"So, does that mean I can come in?" He leaned to one side, his gaze darting around the room. "Something smells great."

"Of course. Yes, please." She stepped back, allowing him to enter. "Welcome home."

His footstep faltered for a moment, but then he moved inside and closed the door behind him, his gaze never leaving hers.

"You know, don't you?"

She nodded. "That the cabin belongs to you? Yep. What I don't know is why you didn't tell me."

Chapter 6

"How did you find out?"

"The old-fashioned way." She headed into the kitchen, turning the pots on the stove down to the lowest possible setting before grabbing a vase for the flowers. "I overheard a couple of gossipy old ladies in Crawford's today. I think you and I are the latest hot topic."

"No surprise there."

His tone was sarcastic, but she heard humor there, too.

Turning from the sink so she could put the flowers on the dining-room table, she found him still standing near the front door.

He was looking around, as if he were seeing the place for the first time. Rita had said it'd been finished almost two years ago, but she was the first person to live here.

Was this his first time back since completing the cabin? He seemed to be studying the place. Did he like what she'd done to it?

"There's a corkscrew in the top drawer next to the sink," she said, thinking maybe he needed something to do. "Glasses are in the cabinet above if you want to open the wine."

He nodded and walked behind the leather sofa, his free hand trailing along the back of it for a moment. "Good idea. I could use a drink."

That makes two of us.

Surprised at how nervous she truly was, Vanessa busied herself with rearranging the table to fit the flowers in the center. She then noticed Jonah holding back the blind that covered the large window over the sink. He stood transfixed, staring, the corkscrew forgotten in his other hand.

Unable to stop herself, she joined him, curious as to what caught his eye. Standing close, she could feel the heat from his body as his familiar spicy cologne filled her head. It took some effort, but she managed to tear her gaze from his profile and look outside.

She smiled. Another amazing Montana sunset.

The last rays of daylight washed over the breathtaking scenery while a scattering of clouds seemed to slowly swallow the last remnants of color, the darkness spreading across the copper-colored sky.

How could she have forgotten to take a moment to enjoy this? "Beautiful, isn't it?"

He dropped the blind back in place and turned to her. She waited a moment, her heart pounding in her chest as she felt his gaze on her, but then she looked at him.

"Yes, very beautiful." He studied her for a moment longer, and then turned his attention back to the wine bottle. "You know, I'm surprised my mother didn't mention this place was mine when she rented it to you."

"Maybe she did, but I don't remember. I just know I fell in love with the cabin the moment I saw it." She took the half-filled glass he held out to her. "As soon as I walked in, the first thing I noticed was how it felt so..." She paused, searching for the right word.

"Empty?" He offered.

"Lonely," she said instead, leaning against the counter. "A beautiful house, obviously crafted by someone with a great attention to detail—"

"Thank you."

She looked at him, smiling at his interruption. "But it was like she was waiting for someone to give her a chance to be a home. You know, make her pretty, make her useful. Give her some style."

"Well, you've certainly done that. This place is nothing like it was the last time I was here."

She liked that once again a gentle wit laced in his tone. "You know, those ladies also said it took you a long time to build this place, and that you did it alone." She took a sip of her wine. "How old were you when you started?"

"I got the land from my grandfather when I was eighteen, and played around with the design for a few years." He suddenly seemed very interested in the contents of his glass. "But I didn't start the building process until I was twenty-one."

"Was it a school project? I'm guessing being an architect requires a college degree."

"Yes, the drawings had been part of my schooling,

but it was a place I'd wanted to build for a long time. It wasn't easy to find the time, between my school and work schedule—I was working full-time down at the local lumber mill back then. Of course, I guess it should've bothered me that my ex-wife didn't seem to care about the amount of time I was spending out here."

Shock raced through Vanessa at his words, her stomach dropping to her feet. "You were married?"

Jonah nodded, taking a healthy swig from his glass. "Yep."

"You were so young."

"Graduated high school and got married in the same weekend. We were both eighteen and had been together for four years."

Wow, thanks to her devotion to her art she hadn't gone on a date until she was seventeen. "How long were you married? If you don't mind me asking."

"Four years, almost to the day. Got my college degree and signed the divorce papers in the same week. Poetic justice, huh?"

Vanessa was desperately curious as to what happened, who was at fault, but when he remained silent, so did she.

Then she had another thought. Had he built this cabin for his ex-wife? Obviously they'd been divorced long before he completed it, but it could've started out as something—

"This might be none of my business," she blurted out, "but were you building this place for her? For the two of you?"

Jonah smiled, shaking his head. "No. We had a tiny, two-bedroom house in town that her folks owned. Lisette refused to live on the ranch. In fact, she never saw this place even when it was nothing more than a foundation and framing. She actually dreamed of getting out of Montana altogether. Said she was sick of the winters."

"I'm guessing she doesn't still live in town?"

"She did up until a year ago, moving after the massive flooding last year. I was the one who left town when I got a job offer from a firm in Denver not long after the divorce." Jonah took another swallow as he moved back into the main room, making his way to the tall built-in bookcases in the far corner.

"I would work on this place whenever I came home to visit. Never wanted any help." He shook his head, as if he couldn't believe what he was saying. "How crazy was it that I was determined to finish it on my own? But my dad and brothers pitched in when more than one set of hands was needed. Took me six years but I finally got it done."

"It really is beautiful." She followed him, watching as he looked over her vast array of books. Scattered among them were the half dozen Chinese bamboo plants she managed to keep alive and her collection of crystal miniature turtles, started when her mother gave her one as a birthday gift when she turned ten. "Why didn't you tell me any of this before?"

He turned to face her. "Probably because before I even met you I had plans to kick you out."

"Kick me out?" She started to ask why, but then it hit her. "Because you wanted to stay here."

He shrugged. "That was the plan, but then you started gushing about the cabin when we met at the resort—"

"I wasn't gushing!"

He grinned. "Yeah, you were. Besides, I'm only going to be in town until the resort opens in December. I figured it was unfair to ask you to move, seeing how neither you or my mother knew about my plan. And now that I've seen what you've done to the place, I can't imagine anyone else living here."

Yes, Jonah was only here for a few short months, wasn't he?

Well, that fit perfectly in her new "live for the moment" lifestyle. Her move to Rust Creek Falls was about finding joy and happiness, two things she felt a lot of whenever this guy was around.

"Well, thank you. Would you like a tour of the rest of the place? We've got time before I need to finish dinner."

"Sure."

She spun around, gesturing with one hand toward the open space. "Well, as you can see, I kept the few pieces of furniture that came with the cabin. Did you know about those?"

Jonah nodded. "The leather couch was a castoff from my uncle's law office when my aunt Mary was redecorating it, but I like the pillows and that blanket you've got laying over it."

"Hey, that's a cashmere throw."

"Oh, excuse me." He grinned, and walked to the only other place to sit, a Bergère armchair that had been reupholstered in a faded patchwork quilt. "And where did you get this beauty?"

"At an antique store in Kalispell."

When she saw his gaze sweep the room again, she waited, wondering if he would say anything about the stuff in the far corner. Deciding she didn't want to talk about that, she took a few steps back toward the kitchen. "And the dining-room table?"

"A hand-me-down from my folks," he said, walking with her. "I'm pretty sure it was a hand-me-down to them first."

"You're mom gave me some dishes and stuff, the rest I picked up here and there. Oh, and I love the antlers over the dining-room table."

"Have you told my father that?" Jonah asked with a smile, reaching up to tap one of the lower antlers. "He bought it for the main house, but my mom refused to hang it. The poor thing languished in the attic for years. I asked about it one time and the next time I came back I found it installed."

"Ah, so that's why your dad was so happy." Vanessa winked. "The first time I had Sunday dinner with your family I couldn't stop talking about it." She started walking backward into the tiny hallway that separated the back of the cabin from the front.

Jonah followed, peeking into the closet near the back door. "Nice to see the folks put in a washer and dryer."

"I'm sure I'll appreciate them even more come winter." One more step and she'd be in the bedroom. With Jonah. Not that it meant anything. She was the one who'd offered the tour, but still it was a rather intimate place to be with a man she'd kissed after knowing him less than a day.

And didn't kiss at all yesterday during their zip-lining adventure.

The thought had crossed her mind a few times—okay, more than a few times—but then she'd decided to enjoy the day and just see what happened.

Same plan for tonight.

But that didn't mean she wouldn't mind being in his arms again and having his mouth on hers.

"And last but not least, the master suite."

Ignoring that glorious bed, she clicked on a small lamp and then headed for her second favorite feature of the cabin. Okay, third after the claw-footed bathtub. "I think I mentioned my love for this tub, right?"

Jonah followed her into the bathroom. He gestured toward a pale green bottle. "Yeah, and bubbles and Harry Potter. I remember."

She smiled, recalling that moment back at the resort, as well. She then pointed overhead. "But *that* is hands down the coolest thing I've ever seen."

Jonah's gaze followed, a big grin on his face. "You like that?"

Like it? She loved it.

The only window in the room was high overhead, cut into both the roof and the side wall of the cabin. Half of the glass was horizontal across the ceiling and the other half came down about two feet, allowing a bird's-eye view of the world outside.

"The sunlight that fills the room during the day is amazing," Vanessa sighed. "But at night, with just some candles lit, I lie back in this tub and watch the stars."

Jonah dropped his gaze from overhead, his eyes locked with hers. "Just what I was picturing when I designed it."

Was he now picturing her just as she described? Naked, hair pinned up haphazardly, covered in bubbles up to her neck?

Number twenty-one: take a bubble bath...with a man.

One of the last items she and Adele had added to the list raced through her mind.

Instantly she saw not only herself lying in the tub, but this incredibly sexy man right there with her, holding her as she leaned back into his chest while hot, soapy water splashed around them—

Jonah pulled in a sharp breath, then looked away before closing his eyes.

Oh, no. Did I just say that out loud? Vanessa bit back a groan. Jeez, no pressure for a second date, huh? "Ah, are you okay?"

"Yeah, it's just that..." His voice trailed off as he waved his glass in the air. "Ah, the scent in here...it's very—"

"Strong? Yeah, I'm sorry about that." Vanessa sniffed, but it smelled the same as always to her. Like her. "My shampoo, body wash and lotion all come from the same line. It's a mix of gardenia and white flowers with hint of coconut oil and lime. I think it's very fresh and summery and—"

"Sexy." Jonah opened his eyes, his gaze on her again as he closed the distance between them with one step. He took one of her curls and gently pulled it through his fingers. "That's the word I was going for. It's very sexy."

Hmmm, she liked that. Almost as much as she liked being this close to him, and the way he tugged on her hair made her think about closing the space between them, but there was food cooking...

"Thanks. I think maybe we should get back out into the kitchen. Dinner is blackened chicken, but we don't want to do that literally."

Jonah laughed and took a step back. "After you."

She walked out of the bathroom, her eyes once again going right to that bed. It was probably tempting fate, but she had to ask. "The bed was the only other piece in the cabin when I moved in. It's beautiful. Where did you get it?"

"I made it."

His simple statement had her spinning around. "You *made* it?"

Jonah nodded, the pride evident on his face as he looked it over. "Handmade by yours truly from felled trees found right here on the ranch."

"Oh, Jonah. It's beautiful."

"Thanks."

"No, I mean it." She laid a hand on his arm, waiting until she had his full attention. "Really. It's a work of art."

"That's high praise coming from an artist like you." He clicked his wineglass to hers. "By the way, I noticed you don't have any Vanessa Brent originals hanging in the cabin."

She tried to swallow the lump that filled her throat, but it wasn't budging. A healthy sip of wine did nothing to help. "Ah, that's right. I don't."

Vanessa muttered something about getting the pasta ready, and headed back for the kitchen.

Jonah followed her signature scent that filled the bathroom and now filled his head, not to mention the images his vivid imagination was creating after her words about that damn tub and the innovative skylight he'd put in the room.

Yeah, those images were going to haunt his dreams tonight.

He watched her work at the stove for a moment and he had to admit the smells coming from the kitchen were good.

Almost as good as the one in the bathroom which had made him want to pull her into his arms and start off this second date with a second kiss.

"Hey, how about I get a fire started?" he asked, wanting to do something—anything—to keep busy and take his mind off of…other things.

She looked at him, the gleam in her eye telling him they'd already done that.

"In the woodstove," he added. "It's supposed to get chilly tonight."

"Sure, that would be great." Refilling her wineglass, she held out the bottle with a silent question. He put his glass on the island and pushed it toward her and headed for the wood stacked on the bottom shelf of the bookcase.

Walking up to the front door earlier tonight, he'd been planning to tell her about the cabin belonging to him. But it only took a simple phrase from her for him to figure out she knew that already.

Then again, talking about his ex-wife hadn't been part of his plan.

It wasn't as if he was hiding the fact he'd been married, back when he'd been young and dumb enough to believe in forever, but it seemed once a woman knew he'd been hitched before she became a firm believer that was what he wanted again.

No, thank you.

He was glad Vanessa hadn't asked a lot of questions about his past, but instead went back to the safer topic of the cabin, which he had to admit looked better than he'd even thought it could.

Not surprising, considering she was an artist.

There was color and texture and life in here now. All things he probably never would've thought to add if he'd moved in as planned. To him, it had been just a place to crash until he got the resort finished and went back to Denver. Vanessa had made it her home.

Except for her art.

He glanced around the room again, his gaze catching hold of the easel, standing alongside what appeared to be stacks of blank canvases in the far corner of the room.

Interesting. No slash of paint on any of them.

"I'm going to use the bathroom," Vanessa said, heading toward the back of the cabin again. "I'll be right back."

"Okay. I'll just wash up in the kitchen sink once I get this going."

Turning his attention back to the task at hand, it only took a moment for the flames to catch. He had these same style woodstoves in his penthouse in Denver and used them quite often.

Standing, Jonah held back a groan as his muscles protested. He'd spent an hour under the hot spray getting ready for tonight, but after a long day working alongside his brothers, he was going to be hurting tomorrow.

He walked to the kitchen, washed his hands and then reached for his wineglass just as a painting he hadn't noticed earlier got his attention.

It wasn't large, but it was colorful with splashes of purples, reds and blues and a big drop of yellow in one corner. Unframed, the stretched canvas seemed to hang suspended on the corner wall in the dining area.

Was it one of hers?

He'd moved closer, studying it, remembering what he'd found on the internet about her earlier tonight.

Yes, it seemed Vanessa Brent—the adventurous volunteer art teacher and country dancing wannabe—was a big deal in the art world. Her works fetched hundreds of thousands of dollars and were coveted by collectors all over the world.

And it'd been that way ever since she was a teenager.

"No, that's not one of mine."

Jonah turned and found she'd returned and was once again busy with pots and pans that contained something that looked as good as it smelled. "At first I thought it might be," he said, "but it looks a little…primitive, compared to your work."

She went still for a moment, then went back to preparing two dinner plates.

"A friend of mine did that many years ago."

"I like it."

"Yeah, what do you like about it?"

Jonah turned back and studied the painting again. "It's uncomplicated, as if the artist didn't care what anyone thought. There's a hint of anger in there, but the pop of yellow says all is forgiven."

He looked back over his shoulder and found Vanessa standing at the table, two dinner plates in her hands, staring at him. "What? What'd I say?"

She blinked and shook her head, setting the plates down. "Nothing. That was very…insightful."

Maybe too much so?

Jonah turned away from the painting and headed for the table. "Can I do anything to help?"

Vanessa shook her head again and went back to the kitchen counter for her wineglass and a basket of rolls. She returned and gestured for him to sit, but he waited until she did so first.

"This looks amazing." He looked down at the meal. "What did you say it was again?"

"Blackened chicken with creamy angel-hair pasta."

The food was terrific, but Jonah couldn't get the painting behind him—and Vanessa's reaction to his words—out of his head.

"Can you tell me more about your friend's painting?"

She looked at the art over his shoulder, her face taking on a very faraway expression. "It was our senior year of high school. I had passed on going to my prom because I was up to my eyeballs getting ready for a show. My friend wasn't happy about that, but she came by the next day—still dressed in her prom finery—and found me a bit loopy as I'd pulled an all-nighter."

Vanessa paused and took a sip from her wineglass. "I wasn't happy with anything I had worked on all night, so sure that no one would want to even look at my pieces much less buy one."

"And nothing your friend said could convince you otherwise?"

This time she looked at him. "That's right. So, she grabbed a blank canvas, some paint and a brush and whipped up that beauty. She then handed it to me with a great flourish and told me I was now the proud owner of a rare, one-of-a-kind piece and if I ever found myself destitute I could sell it."

She smiled, light coming back into her eyes as she grabbed her fork again. "We both burst out laughing and I felt a hundred percent better. So I make sure I keep it somewhere where I can see it...and remember."

"So, if that's true, why, then, are your own canvases blank?"

Chapter 7

Could he have said what was on his mind in a worse possible way? Yeah, probably. He could've just come right out and accused her of being a fraud.

Of course, they both knew that wasn't true.

Jonah had found out more about her, and her career, just by looking around her space, than during a twenty-minute internet search and the images of her work he'd seen online were impressive.

Bold and colorful and full of life. Just like her.

But none of that passion was reflected in the empty canvases sitting on the other side of the room.

Vanessa slowly lowered her fork back to her plate. "What did you say?"

The hurt in her voice caused his insides to twist. He should backtrack, apologize for saying something stupid. Then again, he had a feeling Vanessa wouldn't let it go that simply and for reasons he couldn't explain, he didn't want to let it go, either.

"I couldn't help but notice your artist's corner seems a bit too neat and clean," he said. "No soiled brushes, no paint-covered rags, no..."

Spine straight and shoulders pushed back, she appeared almost regal, uncomfortably so as she looked at her plate, jabbing at the food. "No paintings."

He let his silence tell her she'd correctly finished his sentence.

"Maybe I don't like living in a mess." Her focus remained on the pasta and bits of chicken she nudged with jerky movements. "Maybe I cleaned up before you came over."

Both explanations could be true, but Jonah knew they weren't.

Yes, the cabin was neat and beautifully decorated, but it was lived in.

Magazines were scattered on a turquoise colored side table next to the chair, her boots laid forgotten by the front door and the couch pillows were messy, almost as if she'd been lying there, waiting for him.

"Maybe," he finally said. "But I don't think so."

She jerked her head up to look at him, indignant fire in her eyes. "And maybe it's none of your business."

The fight in her wasn't a surprise. He was glad to see it. "True, but when I asked you said there weren't any of your paintings here in the cabin."

"That's right."

"Which I took to mean you didn't bring any of your completed works with you when you moved from Philadelphia—yes, the internet told me where you're from, but does that mean you haven't done any painting since you moved to Rust Creek Falls?"

She held his gaze for a long moment. Jonah had a feeling he already knew what her answer would be, but he waited, wondering if she would answer him.

Or maybe she'd just toss him out of here on his ass.

"No."

The simple reply seemed to take the life out of her.

Vanessa sank deeper into her chair, her shoulders slumped and her chin almost to her chest, her body free of the bravado from a moment ago.

He wanted to go to her, pull her into his arms and tell her everything would be all right. The strength of that wanting surprised him, kept him glued to his chair.

"When did you last paint something?" he finally asked.

"It's been…a while."

She gave up playing with her meal. Resting her elbows on the edge of the table, the numerous bracelets slid down her arm, her fingers so tightly laced together the tips were turning white. She stared across the room at her art supplies, a painful longing evident on her face.

"A long while," she continued, her voice barely above a whisper. "Almost a year."

Jonah didn't know much about art, but for any person to be away from their work for that long…

There must be a reason, which didn't explain why she'd accepted Nate's commission. "Why did you agree to paint a mural at the resort, then?"

The longing disappeared as she turned to face him again, a bit of that rebel still flickering in her gaze. "Are you asking as my boss?"

"I'm not your boss." His tone left no room for argument. Still, he softened it when he said, "I'm asking as a friend."

She sighed, and relaxed her grip, wiggling her fingers for a moment before untangling them to tuck a few wayward curls behind one ear.

"I took the job for a couple of reasons," she said. "One, because Nate was so persuasive in what he was looking for and why he wanted a mural that I really wanted to be a part of his vision for the resort. And two, I thought doing a commissioned piece—with a deadline—might be just what I need to get over this…"

"Block." Jonah finished her sentence when her voice trailed off. "Is that how you've overcome a situation like this in the past?"

"I've never experienced anything like this before. Never been cut off from my gift before. I used to be able to get lost in my work, paint for hours on end. Almost in a subconscious way, but now…" Vanessa's voice trailed off, as if she was lost in her own thoughts.

Then she offered a small smile while righting herself in her chair, her posture back in place. "Boy, that's the first time I've actually admitted that aloud. Not sure how I feel about that."

Relief swept through Jonah at the curve of her lips, even if the gesture didn't quite reach her eyes.

Perhaps asking about her work—or lack thereof—had been a good thing after all. "It happens to everyone, you know."

She dug back into her meal. "Even you?"

"Well, no, not exactly." Jonah admitted, taking a forkful of meat and pasta, as well. "I've been pushing hard, working pretty much nonstop for last eight years.

Starting at the bottom, but with no plans to stay there, I had to pay my dues in my chosen field. Work my way up. I didn't have time to be blocked."

"Sounds like you had something to prove."

Considering what he'd already shared tonight about his failed marriage, she was right on target. "I did. To myself and a few others who thought my dream of being an architect was just the wishful thinking of a kid who preferred Legos and Erector Sets to horses."

He shrugged. "Maybe a part of me still feels that way. I've succeeded in what I set out to do careerwise, enough so that I could take a leave of absence to work on the resort."

"Whereas I just fell into my success before I was even a teenager."

Jonah wasn't sure he liked where this was heading. "Hey, I didn't say that. From what I read you've worked very hard for your achievements."

"I know you didn't mean it that way." She waved off his words, then stilled, her gaze focused on both of her outstretched hands. "Yes, I have worked hard since finding out I could paint, continuing to study and practice my craft. So to have it just up and disappear after fourteen years…is a bit scary."

She dropped her hands, grabbed the basket of rolls and held it out to him. "And how is it you've never been stuck creatively? There's got to be more to your line of work than planning, designing and constructing."

"There is, namely, the customer." Jonah took one of the soft and still warm buns. "Very rarely am I given total free rein to design whatever I want. In fact, the last thing I did that was purely my own from start to finish was this cabin. There are a whole lot of discussions about what the customer wants and needs—be it a private home, factory or a twenty-story high-rise, not to mention all the rules, regulations and red tape that go along with any project, before creativity comes into play."

"So tell me more about how creative you got to be with the resort." She gave him a quick wink. "From what little I've seen so far the place is going to be magnificent."

He knew what she was doing.

Getting him to talk about his work would keep him from asking her any more questions. Okay, fair enough. He'd spoken out of turn. Even if that ended up being a good thing, if she wanted to lead the discussion in another direction, he'd let her.

They resumed eating while he shared his plans and ideas for renovating the old log mansion. He talked about the environmentally friendly steps they were taking to bring the structures into the twenty-first century while maintaining the rustic charm that would be the resort's biggest selling feature. It was a favorite topic of his.

She ooh'd and ahh'd in all the right places, even giving him a big smile when he mentioned adding zip lining to the resort's summertime activities.

Still, that didn't stop Jonah from thinking about what she'd revealed to him a few minutes ago.

He wanted to ask her what—if anything specific—had caused her to be unable to paint. She'd said it'd been almost a year. Had something happened back in Philadelphia? Was moving to Rust Creek Falls this past summer a way of reviving her creative juices?

If so, that had been three months ago. Why hadn't it worked?

They finished their meal, and the bottle of wine, and when they took their dishes into the kitchen, Jonah decided a peace offering was in order.

After all, she was right. Her painting was her business, not his.

"How about I do the dishes?" he asked. "You can consider it payment for sticking my nose in where it didn't belong."

She filled the sink with dish soap, reminding Jonah of her doing the same thing just a couple of days ago at the community center.

"How about we let them soak for a while?" she said, taking his plate and utensils from him to add with hers. "But if you really think restitution is in order, I've got an idea."

Jonah took a step back when she aimed the water spray at the sink, never quite sure what crazy idea she'd come up with next. "What did you have in mind?"

She turned off the water, grabbed a dish towel and dried her hands as she headed for the bookcases. Seconds later a classic Garth Brooks song filled the air.

"Teach me to dance." Vanessa walked back to where he stood. "Country-style two-stepping, to be precise."

Jonah grinned, moving out of the kitchen into the dining room. There might be enough room if they pushed back the leather sofa and the antique chair. "Right here?"

"Nope."

She brushed past him and headed for the oversize, floor-to-ceiling windows behind him. Running her hand down the left side of the middle glass, she found the hidden latch and the window—which was actually a door—opened, pivoting toward the deck outside.

"Can you believe I lived here for almost three weeks before I figured this out?" She turned to him, a light breeze coming in through the opening and ruffling her curls. "Your mom was so impressed when I showed her."

"I'll bet." He glanced down at her bare feet, having done his best not to stare at the bright-blue-polished toes until this moment. "If we're going to do this, maybe you should get your shoes on."

Vanessa looked down. She was barefoot.

How in the world had she'd spent the past hour and a half with this man and not realized that?

"That's probably a good idea. Be right back."

She hurried to the bedroom, grabbing a pair of socks and her favorite ankle boots. Sitting on the edge of the bed, she pulled them on, and then took a moment to check her hair. Pushing a few curls into place, her hand stilled when she saw her and Adele's picture on the nightstand in the mirror's reflection.

He'd noticed Adele's artwork, the evidence that she wasn't painting and how she tried to change the topic of their dinner conversation.

She got the feeling not much got past Jonah.

Not when he came right out and asked about the blank canvases.

For a moment during dinner, she'd toyed with brushing off his questions, and even though he hadn't come right out and asked her why she wasn't painting, he'd been the first person other than her agent to talk about it.

No one among her family and friends had dared to

question her lack of producing anything new. Granted, they'd been worried about the deep depression she'd gotten herself into the past year. But even when she'd finally come out of that there were no inquiries about a new collection.

She'd only told the firm who represented her work that she was taking a break for the unforeseeable future, which ironically had driven up the value of her older pieces in the past few months.

Deep inside, she often wondered if maybe what she'd created in the past fourteen years was all there was.

Nope, not going there.

Giving herself a mental shake, Vanessa backed away from the mirror. "You've got a sexy architect out there waiting to hold you in his arms. That's more than enough to keep you occupied tonight."

She hurried back out to the main room and saw Jonah had stepped out on the deck. Flipping on the outside lamps to give them a bit more light, she joined him. The night was cool, but that didn't seem to bother Jonah as he folded back his shirtsleeves until the cuffed material stopped just below his elbows.

"Gearing up for battle?"

He turned around, a smile on his face. "Good thing I wore my steel-toed cowboy boots."

She faked a pout. "Oh, I'm not that bad."

He offered one raised eyebrow in response.

"Okay, but it's because of lack of practice." She clapped her hands together. "So, what's first?"

Jonah stepped forward, reaching for her and she easily moved into his arms. "You seemed to get the necessity of the framework—the placement of our hands—and the need to keep some distance between us, especially when you're first learning."

Yeah, not as much fun as the intimate way he'd held her when they danced at the bar.

That night their bodies had been touching completely, her soft curves against his muscles as they moved in slow circles—

"Vanessa?"

The huskiness of Jonah's voice made her leave the memory to look up at him. The light from the open door spilled out on the deck, but only on one side, leaving the rest of his face in shadow.

Not enough that she couldn't see the heat in his gaze as his fingers closed around hers while the muscles in his shoulder constricted where she'd placed her right hand.

Was he remembering, too?

"Did you hear me?" he asked.

She blinked, then nodded. "Frame and distance. Got it. It's more of the 'quick, quick, slow, slow' and remembering to start off with my right foot that throws me."

"Just remember what women have been saying since time began," he said. "You're right. About everything, including which foot to start off with."

She smiled. "Very funny. True, but still funny."

"Try to remember to put your weight on your left foot when you get into the ready position so you're all set to step off with the other foot."

Hmmm, that made sense. "Okay, I'll try."

"Oh, and even though the female might be 'right' in this situation," Jonah dipped his head closer, his voice now a whisper, "there is a leader and a follower when it comes to two-stepping. The man is the leader."

Oh, she'd follow his lead anywhere.

One corner of his mouth rose into a grin and she wondered again if she'd spoken aloud something that definitely needed to stay inside her head.

"You're in charge." She schooled her features into an expression of innocence, tossing in a few battered eyelashes at him for good measure. "I'm here to do your bidding, sir."

Jonah straightened, clearing his throat. "And look at me." He locked his gaze with hers when she did. "At your partner. No need to see what your feet are doing. That's only asking for trouble."

They got into position and with Jonah counting off the steps in a low tone, they began. Easily shuffling to the end of the deck near the back of the cabin, where it was much darker even with the outside lighting.

Then came the dreaded turn and she tumbled right into his arms. And onto his feet.

Jonah laughed, but quickly showed her the correct steps for a smooth turn and they were off again, making their way around the entire perimeter twice without a mistake.

"You see, you're doing fine."

"Shhh, don't talk unless you're chanting." She shot back, afraid she'd lose count. "You'll throw me off."

Jonah's laugh was a low chuckle, but he went back to reciting his instructions. When they were on their fourth circuit, dancing to Billy Currington's song about a woman who's got a way with him, Vanessa realized Jonah had gone silent and they continued to move in a natural rhythm.

Even she had stopped saying the words in her head and simply enjoyed dancing and being in Jonah's arms. "I think I've finally got the hang of it."

Jonah nodded. "It's a bit harder in a club or bar where you're surrounded by other couples, all moving in the same direction, but as long as you focus on what you and your partner are doing, you'll be fine."

"This is so great. Wait until the next time I go dancing at the Ace. I'll be fighting off the men who'll want to partner with me."

Jonah stumbled and almost fell backward, but kept the two of them upright by pulling her close. Her hand automatically moved higher up on his neck as he wrapped his arm around her waist, his hand spread wide against her back, anchoring her against him.

Just like Thursday night at the bar.

"Ah, sorry about that." Jonah spoke into her curls. "The deck must be getting slippery."

The warmth of his words against her forehead felt wonderful. So wonderful she'd missed what he'd just said. "What?"

"Vanessa, it's raining. Hadn't you noticed?"

She tipped back her head. A light mist appeared in the glow from the lamps and landed on her skin. She'd been so involved with the lesson she hadn't realized she and Jonah were dancing in the rain.

Oh!

Number nineteen: dance in the rain.

Without any planning or intention, she'd checked off another item on her list. Closing her eyes, Vanessa sent a silent thank you to the heavens and a shiver raced through her in response.

"Are you cold?"

Jonah's hand was warm against her neck, and she opened her eyes to look at him. She shook her head, and when his thumb gently moved back and forth across her lips, she couldn't stop herself from tasting him.

"Vanessa."

He whispered her name, his thumb still against her lips, before his mouth covered hers. His hand tunneled into her hair, pulling her closer.

A hot flush exploded over her as she welcomed his kisses. Wrapping her arms around his shoulders, she held on as a yearning, passionate and deep, raced to every part of her before it returned to settle deep inside her heart.

She'd wondered if her reaction—both physical and emotional—to the kisses they'd shared a few nights ago was due to time and distance, but she'd never felt this sweet pull before.

She'd never been seduced by just a man's kiss before. Wanting it to go on forever, but desperate to see what might happen next. He tasted sweet and spicy as his mouth continued to move against hers, causing another tremor to attack, the intensity of it making her shake in his arms.

He lifted his lips from hers then, but before she could say a word he picked her up in his arms and carried her back inside the cabin. Pausing for a moment, he gently kicked at the door and it swung closed. Walking farther inside, she wondered for a moment if he was going to take her back to the bedroom, but he crossed to the leather sofa and sat, still cradling her in his embrace.

His mouth was back on hers as he pressed her back into the softness of the pillows. She grabbed his shoulders, and tugged, making it clear she wanted him to join her.

He hesitated, breaking free, his eyes dark and questioning.

"Please, Jonah."

He stretched out over her, levering himself up on one elbow as he placed soft, wet kisses the length of her neck from ear to her shoulder where her sweater had slipped off.

His one arm was caught beneath her, but with his free hand he caressed her, his fingertips brushing over the swell of her breasts.

Wanting desperately to touch him, too, she tugged at his shirt, finally freeing it and working her hands to the heated skin beneath the damp cotton material.

He groaned when her fingers met bare skin, a sound that went even deeper when she arched her body, pressing her center to the hard ridge of his erection that told of his need for her.

"Vanessa… I want…" His words disappeared as he claimed her mouth again in a way that spoke of the pleasures to come, but then they changed.

Softened. Slowed. Stopped.

He was pulling away from her, cooling the fire that burned between them even if their bodies refused to comply. Confusion filled her and she wondered if she'd done something to make him think she didn't want—

Wasn't ready—

To make love with a man she'd known less than a week.

A man she'd spent time with every day for the past four days. A good man. An honest man. She knew that about him with every fiber of her being, but did that mean she was ready to be intimate with him?

Yes.

The certainty surprised her, but since so much of her life had been unreliable and crazy over the past year, it felt good to know for sure what she wanted.

"Your brain is racing as fast as your pulse." Jonah placed a kiss at the base of her throat, his tongue tracing over her collar bone for a moment before he pulled away and got to his feet.

"So is yours."

He stood with his back to her, his hands braced on his hips. "Yeah? How can you tell?"

"Because you stopped."

Her words caused Jonah to pull in a deep breath, his shoulders expanding as he did. He remained silent, except for his rushed exhale that she was happy to hear carried a bit of frustration with it.

She got to her feet, one hand hovering at the center of his back for a moment before she touched him. "Are you okay?"

A rough laugh came out of his mouth as he turned to face her, grabbing her hand in his. "Yeah, I'm great."

"Hmmm, why don't I believe that?"

He rubbed his thumb across her knuckles, much like he'd done with her mouth, and the desire fanned to life again. "Look, I should try to explain. I haven't been with…haven't been involved with anyone in a long time."

She nodded, but stayed silent.

"I didn't want to assume…" he continued, but stopped again. "I'm only in town until the holidays, then I'm headed back to my life in Denver. Getting involved with someone while I was home was never part of my plan."

"Hey, if I've learned anything over the last—" Vanessa stopped her words by biting down on her bottom lip. She then took a step closer to Jonah, looked up at him and laid a hand against his cheek. "*Involved* is a complicated word. As long as what's happening between us is right for us—right now—that's okay by me. No demands, no labels, no expectations. I like you, Jonah Dalton, and I'm pretty sure you like me, too."

He smiled, his gaze dropping to the front of his jeans. "Yeah, that's pretty evident, I think."

She laughed, glad to see his playful side had returned. She dropped her hand from his face. "Well, I've enjoyed every moment I've spent with you and I'd love to do more of the same. If you're okay with that."

He cradled her head with the palm of his hand, placing a quick kiss on her lips. "Very okay."

Ignoring the faint twitch in her heart, she smiled. "Good."

"It's getting late and I need to be at the site early tomorrow, but how about I tag along as your date for dancing at the Ace on Tuesday?"

Now, there was a silly question. "I'd love it."

He nodded, dropped his hands from her and started to head backward toward the door. "And maybe you could come by the resort tomorrow or Tuesday. I'll give you a grand tour of the place."

Unable to stand there while he got farther away from her, she joined him at the front entrance. "I'd like that, too."

"Maybe it'll knock some chinks in that wall you've got built around your talent." He leaned in again, and pressed his mouth to hers one more time. A chaste kiss, but neither of them seemed interested in ending it.

"Your work is terrific, Vanessa," he whispered. "The resort would be lucky to have your talent on display for years to come."

She nodded her thanks for the compliment as he slipped out the door and disappeared into the darkness toward his truck. Not wanting to watch him drive away, she closed the door and leaned up against it.

Well, it seemed the one place both she and Jonah would be involved with was the new resort.

That is if she ever found a way to either climb over, around or blast through that damned wall that she suddenly suspected didn't just surround her talent, but was also firmly entrenched around her heart.

Chapter 8

"You want me to do…what?"

Vanessa eyed the dark blue bandanna Jonah held out to her with a dubious expression on her beautiful face.

She'd been waiting for him on the front deck of the cabin, sketchbook on her lap, when he'd pulled up. He hoped that was a good sign, especially considering his plans for them this evening.

Tucking the pad into her oversize tote, she'd climbed into his truck and had given him a quick kiss hello. He'd waited until she clicked her seat belt into place before he'd made his request.

"Come on," he cajoled, adding a grin to sweeten his request. "Turn around and let me put this on you."

"Over my eyes?"

He sighed, dropping his hand. "Yes, over your eyes."

She tried for a suspicious expression, but failed. Or

maybe it the small giggle that escaped that sweet mouth of hers that gave her away. "Why?"

"Because I have a surprise for you. One I don't want you to know about." He paused and smiled again, thinking about all the hard work he'd done this afternoon. "Until I'm ready for the big reveal."

Her own smile came easy as she studied him. Just the sight of her looking so relaxed on this beautiful yet cool Sunday afternoon did wonders for his time-worn attitude.

As did the kiss she'd given him.

A simple one, but laced with ever present hunger just below the surface, too. A hunger he shared, but still wasn't sure he should act on.

Especially now as he was worried he might be over-stepping when it came to his big surprise for today.

They'd seen each other a few times since last Sunday, but things like delayed equipment deliveries, a failed inspection on three of the resort's fireplaces and an onsite injury that thankfully wasn't serious, had added up to a crazy week with him putting in twelve- to fourteen-hour days at the job site.

It'd started on Monday when he'd tried to give her an extended tour of the resort, happy when she'd shown up after he suggested it the night before.

But they'd been interrupted numerous times with issues that needed his attention. He'd finally had to forgo the tour and go back to work after getting a promise from her that she'd let him show her the rest of the place another time.

Then again, if he was being honest, his own personal craziness had started Sunday night when he'd allowed his good sense to override a burning need to make love to this woman.

Even after she'd said she was okay with the fact he wasn't interested in anything long-term, he'd still walked out and returned home to an empty bed.

And he continued to do so every time they were together.

Which made no sense at all. She wanted him, he wanted her. What the hell was wrong with him?

"Okay, go ahead." Vanessa turned away, giving him her back as she brushed her curls away from her face. "I put myself in your hands."

He scooted closer, the cool October air clung to the denim jacket she wore, but his head was filled with that sexy, summery fragrance of hers.

"Hmmm, I like the sound of that." He whispered against at her ear, enjoying the shiver that raced through her.

He quickly folded the material into a long rectangle and placed it over her eyes, tying the ends snugly at the back of her head. "How does that feel? Not too tight?"

"Nope, feels fine."

"And you can't see anything?"

She turned back to face him, her chin tilted upward. "I've got my eyes closed beneath this, I promise."

He fought against the temptation that was her mouth. It would be so easy to take their relationship to the next step. It wasn't as if he'd lived the life of a monk since his divorce.

What was it about Vanessa that made him hold back when he wanted her in a way he hadn't felt in years? Maybe ever. He'd been a teenager when he first married, had loved and desired his ex with the mindset of a kid. Now, as a man, he was experiencing a need for this woman that was brand-new to him.

"Jonah?"

He shook off his thoughts and slid back behind the steering wheel. "Okay, let's go."

"I hope this surprise includes a meal. I'm starving."

Sure enough, Vanessa's stomach rumbled as if to confirm her words.

She laughed and pressed a hand to her middle. "See what I mean?"

"Don't worry, I'll feed you." He headed down the road that led off the ranch. "And I'm sorry about being late. Again."

"That's okay. I'm sort of getting used to it."

Jonah heard the teasing in her words, but she was right.

When she'd mentioned during their private dance lesson how popular she'd be at the Ace in the Hole, there was no way he wanted anyone else being her partner. So he'd joined her twice this past week for dancing at the bar, but he'd run late both times, driving directly from the job site to meet her there.

They'd had a good time, but when she'd invited him back to the cabin that first night after sharing a few sweet kisses in the parking lot, he'd begged off claiming exhaustion, even though it'd barely been nine o'clock.

Two nights later, he'd been tempted to invite himself back to her place, especially when their parking lot goodbye had turned into an old-fashioned make-out session in his truck—something he hadn't done since high school.

Thankfully he'd parked in the far back, dark corner

of the parking lot, but he'd once again been the one to slow things down.

Right before he'd asked her out for dinner and a movie.

All the while trying to do up the snaps on his shirt she'd tugged open, with gusto, minutes before.

They'd had a great time Friday night, and when he'd taken her home he'd accepted her invite to come inside. Passionate kisses and heated touches on the living-room couch soon followed until she'd excused herself to slip into something more comfortable.

And he'd passed out cold before she'd returned.

He'd awakened from a sound sleep around dawn, at first having no idea where he was. When it all came back to him, he'd gotten up and gone to where she was asleep in the bedroom.

But instead of crawling into bed next to her, he'd just stood there and watched her sleep for a few minutes. He'd left her a note apologizing for last night and told her he had to get to the job site, but would call her later.

He had, asking her for tonight's date after the idea for a way to help her overcome her artistic block came to him while running errands.

"I could've sworn we were heading toward town, but you've made so many turns I'm truly lost."

Vanessa's comment pulled him from his thoughts as he made another turn, this one very familiar. He eased into a space in the empty parking lot and shut off the engine.

"We're here?" she asked, reaching for the blindfold.

"Yes, but the bandanna stays put for the moment." Jonah grabbed her hand, stopping her. "As do you. I'll come around and help you out of the truck."

When he got around to the passenger side, she'd released the seat belt and had grabbed her tote. Placing his hands at her waist, he helped her down, making sure she had her balance before closing the truck door behind her.

"You know, I was going to lead you," Jonah said, placing her hand at his shoulder before bending to lift her into his arms. "But I think this way is much safer."

Vanessa squealed in surprise, grabbing at his shoulders. "Hey! Put me down."

"Nope, this is easier." He started to walk. "Even if your bag adds another ten pounds for me to carry."

"It's not that heavy. Besides, I've got something I want to show you," Vanessa said. "Once I'm allowed sight again."

"Yeah, what's that?"

"I..." She paused, tightening her hold on him for a moment, causing him to glance at her in time to see her pull in a deep breath. "I think I've had a breakthrough in the mural design."

Her news caused a hitch in his step. "Really?"

"I was sitting on the deck, enjoying the beautiful scenery when I closed my eyes and grabbed three colored pencils. Blue, brown and green." Vanessa's words spilled out in a rush. "The next thing I knew I was shading the three colors on the page, one right below the other. A few drops of water on my fingertips washed the edges of the colors into each other and I realized I'd matched the sky, mountains and land right in front of me. I added some definition, putting the falls that the town is named after, right in the center. I think it'll be the perfect backdrop for the mural, a reflection of the beauty of Montana with a cobalt-blue sky, the rugged darks of the mountains and the earthy tones of the land."

He managed to get them inside without putting her down while she chatted away, doubting she noticed they'd moved indoors.

Walking past one part of his surprise, he continued into the large space, glad they'd arrived while there was still plenty of light coming in through the windows.

"Of course, I went completely blank when it came to the next step, but at least I've got something to work from. I hope I do, anyway." Vanessa sighed. "So, what do you think?"

"I think it sounds great." He stopped and eased her back to her feet. "I can't wait to see your sketch, but first things first. Stay here and don't move."

"Hey, are we inside somewhere?"

"Yes." He backed away from her, careful of where he stepped. "Now, wait for just a few more minutes."

"Jonah, this is driving me crazy. What are you— Is that—" She sniffed the air. "Okay, I smell something spicy and delicious, but also a hint of— Did you just light a match? And why are our voices echoing?"

Jonah smiled as he hurried to get everything into place. He should've known once he took away her sight, her other senses would be on high alert. "Patience isn't really your thing, is it?"

She smiled. "What are you up to?"

Giving the area one last look and satisfied with what he saw, Jonah went to her and slipped her bag from her shoulder. He then cupped her face in his hands, tipping her head back and lowered his mouth to hers.

She sighed again, opening to his kiss. Her hands went to his waist, holding tight as he groaned beneath his breath. He worked hard to keep the kisses light and easy, but a few slipped along the edge of desperate.

A desperation he felt down to his bones, along with a thirst he hoped soon to quench.

Easing back, he gently pushed the bandanna up and away from her eyes, smiling when she kept her eyelids closed.

"You can look now."

She opened her eyes, blinked a few times and then looked around. "Hey, we're at the resort, but why..."

He liked how her words disappeared as she caught sight of the picnic he'd set up in front of the grand fireplace, where the first official fire was catching hold of the kindling and logs he'd placed there.

Using a couple of old quilts, a handful of small pillows he'd taken from the main house and a couple of lanterns standing by for when it got dark, he'd set up their dinner.

Nothing fancy, just a meal package from the local wings place in town, but he'd brought real china and silverware, and a bottle of chilled wine.

"Oh, Jonah, this is wonderful." Delight shined in her eyes as she looked at him again. "What made you think of this?"

"I'll explain in a minute, but first—" He reached for her tote again. "How about showing me your artwork?"

She took the bag and held it close to her chest. "It's not that big of a deal, just a watercolor sketch."

"I'd still like to see it."

Nodding, she pulled her drawing pad out and flipped past some pages until she found what she was looking for. She tucked the other pages behind the drawing and then turned it to him. "It's not much."

He studied it for a moment.

"Yes, it is. It's beautiful," he said, easily seeing the influence of the view outside of the cabin in the drawing. "It's perfect."

Vanessa looked down at her drawing and shrugged. "Well, the background, anyway. Nate said he wanted to honor the people and places that mean so much to this town, to Montana. I'm still drawing a blank on what to do next."

"I have an idea." Jonah's gaze flickered to the wall behind her. "If you're interested."

"Sure, but can you tell me while we eat?"

He shook his head. "No, I think showing you would be best."

Taking her by the shoulders, Jonah turned Vanessa around just as the setting sun came in through the oversize windows lighting up the wall over what would be the resort's registration desk.

Vanessa gasped, swaying a bit when she saw what he'd done.

Jonah gave her arms a gentle squeeze, one part reassurance and one part to hold her upright. He looked at the blank space, seeing it with the background Vanessa envisioned, and much more.

"What—what have you done?"

He guessed she wasn't talking about the scaffolding he'd had a crew put into place that ran the length of the wall and would allow her access all the way to the ceiling.

No, she was referring to the more than two dozen pen-and-ink sketches—her sketches—that he'd spent most of the day collecting from people in town, and tacked them to the wall. Including the one she'd done of his father.

"There is your inspiration, Vanessa." He pulled her back against his chest, wrapping one arm around her waist when she leaned into him. "You've already captured what makes Rust Creek Falls so special. The people. The people who live here and call this place home."

"But those are just practice sketches. They're not real art."

"They are real because the people are. I know your previous works are abstract contemporaries with intense, broad strokes of color, but the details in those simple portraits up there are just as powerful."

She remained silent, shaking her head as if she couldn't—or wouldn't—believe him.

"Okay, maybe the mural won't include Charlie, who owns the gas station or Daisy from the donut place, or Gage, the town sheriff. Maybe Nate is looking for more historical figures, not to mention places, but that's just research." Jonah pushed, hoping she understood what he was trying to show her. "You *can* commemorate those special people and places because you've already done it. On a very basic level, maybe, but it's an important one. At least to the people who've kept and displayed your work."

When she still didn't say anything, he decided to go all in. Spinning her around, Jonah gently pressed against her chin until she looked up at him, the distress and anxiety in her gaze breaking his heart.

"Maybe your talent isn't blocked, per se. Maybe it's changing, at least for this project. You talked last week about how you'd get lost in your art. You can't do that this time. You're going to have to get up close and personal with every person, every place you include in the mural. You're going to have to be all in, one hundred percent involved."

Doubt filled her beautiful eyes. "I don't know if I can."

He motioned to all the drawings on the wall. You already have. Believe in yourself, Vanessa. In your gift." He pulled her into his arms. "I know you can do this."

She looked over her shoulder again at the wall. "They do look pretty good up there, don't they?"

Jonah grinned. "You bet they do."

A long moment passed as she studied her work. He waited silently, not wanting to push her any more than he already had.

"I'm just about there," she finally said, turning back to face him again. "But I think I know what will convince me one hundred percent…"

"Yeah? What's that?"

She smiled. "At least a half dozen of those tangy, spicy wings sitting on that blanket over there."

Jonah laughed. "I love a woman who's not afraid to eat. Okay, Ms. Brent, let's have some dinner while you let my reasoning percolate inside that pretty head of yours."

They moved to the blankets. Vanessa sat and started serving up the food while Jonah lit the lanterns as the sun was already starting to set. He joined her and poured them each a glass of wine. They ate, and he waited until Vanessa was halfway through her stack of wings before he approached a subject that had him curious.

"When did you first start painting? I mean, I read about you coming onto the art scene when you were just a teenager. Had you been painting for a while by then?"

"I took my first art lesson when I was in the second grade. It was either that, ballet or swimming. I wasn't crazy about being up on my toes or putting my face in the water, so I picked art." She licked at her fingers, a natural side effect of eating wings, and then wiped her hands on a napkin. "I think my mother wanted me to be a dancer."

"Are either of your parents artistic?"

She shook her head, a shadow falling over her eyes. "No, they are—were—very smart, analytical people. They were both financial wizards, met and fell in love while working for the same brokerage firm before opening their own. My mother became a stay-at-home mom after I was born to concentrate on her charity work and me, especially after I was discovered. She died ten years ago, when I was sixteen."

Jonah's heart ached for the pain he heard in Vanessa's voice. "I'm sorry. I shouldn't have asked."

"No, it's okay."

"Was she ill?"

Vanessa nodded, her gaze focused on the plate in her lap. "Yes. Breast cancer. It was less than eight months from her diagnosis to her death. My father, who'd always been a distant presence in my life, chose to handle his grief by throwing himself into his work, while I found solace in my painting. It was a way for me to express my pain and my grief."

"That must've been a tough time for you." He reached out and took her hand, not surprised when she held tight to him.

"It was, but I had good friends and people who were

there to take care of me. And my art. The pieces I produced after I lost her were the ones that really put me on the map as an artist."

"All while still being a teenager?"

She nodded and took another sip of her wine.

"Is your father still living in Philadelphia?"

"Yes. He wasn't crazy about my idea of moving out here, but I think he's finally accepted that I'm happy with my new life."

Jonah wondered how the man could be distant from such a wonderful woman as his daughter. "Not the life he pictured for his little girl?"

"Well, when I dumped my cheating ex-boyfriend a couple of years ago, who just happened to be one of his star executives—and yes, my father set us up—he thought I was making too much of a fuss. As proud as he claims to be of my art, I think he would prefer if I lived a different lifestyle."

Pushing aside his anger at the man who'd hurt her, Jonah found it hard to believe Vanessa was as casual about her estranged relationship with her father as she seemed. Maybe because his relationship with his parents was so tight. Still, if her life, and his, had taken different paths, who knows if they ever would've met.

"Hey, do you hear that?" Vanessa released her hold on him to turn and gaze out the floor-to-ceiling windows on the far side of the room. "It's raining. I love that sound."

Jonah listened as the tiny clicks against the glass told him Vanessa was right. "Very soothing. My favorite is the hiss and crackle of a fire. Hey, I've got an idea."

He pushed aside their dinner and stretched out on

the quilt, piling the pillows beneath his head. Holding on his hand, he beckoned her to join him. “Come on, let’s lie here and just listen to the rain come down and the fire burn.”

She smiled and his heart gave a little lurch, almost as if it was trying to tell him something. She crawled across blanket to him.

Resting her head on his chest, she put an arm across his stomach and cuddled up next to him. “This is nice. Thank you, Jonah…for everything.”

He found he had more he wanted to ask her, more he wanted to know. About her hopes, dreams and plans. But there was time for that later.

Right now, being with her like this was enough.

Chapter 9

"And then Jonah turned me around and there on the wall were my sketches."

Vanessa sat in one of the folding chairs scattered around the meeting room in the community center. It was Wednesday night and she was here for the Newcomers Club meeting.

Most of the members were female and the club was a way to make friends and help the recent transplants adjust to their new lives in the rural town.

"I'll admit I was really worried about being unable to paint for the last—well, for a long time, before I even moved to town," she continued, stirring her coffee.

She hadn't planned on sharing that side to her story, but once she'd started talking, everything came out. "But now, thanks to Jonah, I've been sketching like a crazy woman for the past few days, even though

I'm not sure who or even what will be included in the mural. It just feels so good to have the creative juices finally flowing again."

"Hold up, I'm still back at Jonah blindfolding you. That's something Nick hasn't done to me." Cecelia Clifton, who was originally from Thunder Canyon, had moved to town a year ago to help in the flood recovery, following in the footsteps of her then best friend, now-fiancé Nick Pritchett. She took the seat next to Vanessa, a saucy grin on her face. "At least not yet."

"Not to mention Jonah whisking you away for a romantic picnic at the resort, complete with a roaring fire and listening to the rain," Callie added, joining them. "Now, that's creative."

"And after seeing the way the two of them get all wrapped up in each other while dancing at the Ace, I'd say he's already got her juices flowing," Cecelia added.

Vanessa laughed along with her friends. It felt good to be surrounded by smart and funny women who looked out for each other. A tiny pang centered in her chest, and she quickly rubbed it away, accepting it for what it was, a reminder that while the sisterhood-like bond she'd shared with Adele could never be repeated, she was lucky to have found new friendships since moving to town.

"Ladies, I'm talking about the mural," Vanessa insisted, "and the fantastic resort being built outside of town. Is all you want to talk about is my love life?"

"Yes!"

Her friends answered in unison, joined by Mallory Franklin, who was now engaged to one-time local playboy Caleb Dalton. Another newcomer, Mallory worked for Caleb's father, the town's only lawyer.

"Boy, this doesn't sound like the Jonah Dalton I've heard about," Mallory added. "Caleb described his cousin so differently over the last few months."

Vanessa turned to her. "That's right. Your husband and Jonah are family, aren't they?"

Mallory nodded. "Caleb said he and Jonah were more than cousins growing up, they were best friends. He was even Jonah's best man at this—oh, you do know he was once married, right?"

Taking a quick sip of the still-too-hot coffee, Vanessa hoped the cup's rim hid her mouth when her smile slipped. "Yes, I know."

Not that Jonah had shared any more details about his ex-wife—or the reason for their divorce—with her. She thought they might talk about it during their picnic, especially after the way she'd opened up to him, but that hadn't happened.

She was curious, but he'd made it clear his stay in town was only temporary and he wasn't looking to get involved, so Vanessa worked hard to keep their times together fun, easygoing and firmly entrenched in the present.

Even if doing so was a bit harder on her than she'd thought it would be.

She loved spending time with him, be it dancing or movies or the horseback-riding lessons he promised her.

But after he'd surprised her with his take on the new direction her talent was heading and how much he believed in her, she'd finally accepted a tiny corner of her heart would always belong to him.

Even if he continued to hold himself just a little bit apart from her.

"Caleb made it sound like Jonah hadn't been seriously involved with anyone since his divorce," Mallory continued. "At least, not anyone in town."

That made sense considering what Jonah had told her about sticking close to the ranch and concentrating on working on the cabin during his previous visits home.

Was it wrong that she was secretly thrilled no one else had caught his attention before? Or maybe that was because he had someone back in Denver?

No, he'd told her he hadn't been involved with anyone in a long time. How long was long? Weeks? Months?

"Well, he doesn't live in Rust Creek Falls full time," Vanessa said, realizing her friends were staring at her as if waiting for a reply. "He's only in town through Christmas, just until the renovations on the resort are complete and it opens for business."

"Oh, that's too bad," Cecelia said. "You two make such a cute couple."

"We're having fun and enjoying each other's company." *Living for the moment,* she added silently, because as she'd learned all too well, sometimes that's all we have. "Nothing more."

Nothing but wonderfully fervent kisses, generous touches and a simmering sexual hunger that she'd been sure they would've satisfied Friday night if the man hadn't fallen asleep on her.

"Hmmm, now why don't I believe you," Cecelia said with a grin. "That's quite a devilish gleam you've got in your eyes, Vanessa."

"Do I?" She feigned innocence, wanting to keep her

and Jonah's private affairs just that. Private. "I have no idea what you mean."

Callie laughed. "Oh, I feel sorry for the hordes of lonely cowboys bemoaning their lost chances with you. You're definitely off the market. At least for the next few months."

Yes, Vanessa considered herself taken, for as long as Jonah was in town. When she found herself wishing things might last longer, she stopped, reminding herself that being with him now was better than not at all. "Well, there are plenty of ladies to go around for them to concentrate on."

"Could we talk about something else, please?"

Vanessa and her friends turned around and found another member of their club, Julie Smith, standing there.

As close as the rest of the women were, Julie always seemed to be a bit aloof. Not in a snobbish sort of way, but more as if she wasn't sure she belonged in the group although everyone had been friendly to her.

"Is something bothering you, Julie?" Vanessa rose from her seat and went to the girl, who barely looked old enough to be out of college, especially because she always wore her long blond hair pulled back into a high ponytail. "Have we upset you?"

"No, it's just..." Julie's voice trailed off and she sighed, looking down at the plate of cookies in her hands. "It's silly, but all this talk of men and dating and the invasion of females looking for love... I wish— I mean, no one's even asked me to..."

Vanessa understood, sharing quick glances with the others when Julie's voice faded away.

Yes, her friends liked to tease her about her numerous first dates since coming to town, but it seemed Julie was having the opposite problem.

"You know, I'm sure between all of us ladies we can do a bit of matchmaking," Vanessa said. "Find you a nice guy."

"Oh, no, I'm not—I mean, I don't want—" Julie shook her head, sending her ponytail flying. "Don't worry about me. I'm fine."

Vanessa wasn't so sure, but their conversation was over for the moment as Lissa Christensen, the columnist whose blog put Rust Creek Falls on the map after the Great Flood, had arrived to talk about the big holiday party in the works to celebrate the grand opening of the new resort, to be held on Christmas Eve, of course. Everyone hurried to take a seat as the ideas began to fly.

After the meeting wrapped up, Vanessa had stuck around to help clean up. She had to admit, the idea of her art being such a big part of the resort was still a bit scary.

She loved what Jonah had done to convince her to see her talent in a new light, but what she really needed was to do some research. Perhaps someone at the mayor's office could assist with getting her some history on Rust Creek Falls and the other towns Nate had mentioned.

"Yes, seek and you shall find the answers you need."

Vanessa whirled around, the voice startling her.

There stood an elderly woman dressed in bright colors, a couple of mismatched shawls wrapped around her shoulders. Her weathered face and gray hair, worn in a braid wrapped around her head, spoke to her age, but Winona Cobbs had kind eyes and a warm smile.

Originally from Whitehorn, Montana, Winona had come to town a couple of months ago to give a talk here at the community center about trusting your inner psychic. As a nationally syndicated advice columnist, she was also well known for her special gift.

"How do you know I'm searching for something?" Vanessa asked.

"We are all searching, in our own way, our own time." Winona then offered a smile as she moved slowly toward a seating area outside the center's main office. "The heart knows what it wants."

Vanessa grabbed her tote and followed the old woman. "What I'm looking for is information. It has nothing to do with my heart."

"Of course it does. Your gift comes from your heart, your soul and your brain." Winona sat, her hands folded in her lap. "All must be in harmony so you can share that gift in your painting."

Oh, this could be just the person she'd been looking to find!

Taking the other empty chair, Vanessa leaned forward. "I'm guessing you're quite knowledgeable about some of the prominent families and their histories of Montana's past?"

"The things I know of…things connected to the past," she answered slowly, "and to the future are great indeed."

"I would love to sit and talk with you, to get some ideas for the mural. Would that be okay?"

Winona nodded. Vanessa opened her tote and pulled out her sketchbook. Opening to an empty page, she grabbed a pen and waited.

"Jeremiah Kincaid, of the Kincaid Ranch in Whitehorn, was a rancher. His granddaddy was one of the first settlers of that town, but it was Jeremiah who made Whitehorn his town."

Vanessa hurried to take notes. "Who else might I include?"

"Have you ever heard of the 'Shady Lady' of Thunder Canyon?" Winona asked. "Miss Lily Divine ran a respectable saloon, but, of course, there were those who were sure the bar was just a front for its true business—a house of ill-repute. Miss Divine covered it well, but there were always rumors. Like with most things."

Vanessa jumped once again when this time the old woman reached out and laid her hand on her arm. Winona's fingers were cool, her grip strong. "The trick, my dear, is in knowing where to look for your answers… and to be sure you're ready for what you find."

"Are we still talking about the mural?"

Winona smiled. "Unless there is something…or someone else you wish to discuss?"

Jonah walked out of his uncle's law office and headed across the small parking lot, debating whether he should head back to the job site or not.

It was still early, not even seven o'clock. Vanessa had said something about a meeting tonight so she was busy.

Which was probably a good thing.

Ever since their picnic on Sunday evening Vanessa had been talking nonstop about the mural. It was as if a fire had been lit inside of her. She glowed with excitement and energy and Jonah found himself wanting to be near her, to be with her, in every way possible.

Vanessa wanted to be with him, too. He was smart

enough to know that. He just wished he knew what it was that kept him from making that happen.

Maybe he wanted more than—

A shuffling noise—feet being dragged against the pavement—caught his attention, interrupting his thoughts.

Jonah looked around, spotting a man walking toward him. Shoulders stooped with a headful of scraggly gray hair that shot off in every direction, his gaze fixed on the ground before him.

Jonah moved out of the man's way, otherwise the old-timer would've walked right into him. He wasn't someone he recognized, but so many new people had moved to town in the past year he wasn't surprised.

"You okay, fella?" Jonah asked when the stranger suddenly stopped, head jerking up and his wide blue eyes darting around even though there was no one around but the two of them.

"Homer Gilmore," the man said, his voice scratchy.

"Is that your name?" Jonah asked. "Homer?"

The elderly man nodded, his head bobbing quickly.

"Is there something I can help you with?"

"The past is the present," he rasped. "The present is the past."

"I'm sorry?"

The old man repeated the same cryptic phrase as he slowly backed away.

Jonah stepped forward, wondering if he should direct the old-timer to the sheriff's office at the end of the block. He looked as if he could use a hot meal and decent night's sleep.

A quick glance at a patrol vehicle parked out front

told him someone was in the office, but when he turned back the old man was gone.

Okay, that was weird.

Jonah looked around again, but the man had vanished. He shrugged off the odd encounter and dug his keys from his pocket.

"Hey, stranger. It's about time I saw your ugly face."

Grinning this time at the familiar masculine voice, Jonah looked up. "Careful, boy, we're related. That makes you as ugly as me."

"Naw, my side of the Dalton clan got the beauty and the brains." Caleb Dalton stood next to Jonah's truck. "But I'll admit you've got a sweet ride here."

Jonah laughed and when his cousin grabbed him and yanked him into a quick embrace, complete with a hearty slap to the back. He did the same. "Damn, it's good to see you."

"Tell me about it." Caleb took a step back. "You've been back in town—what? Two weeks now and this is the first time we've seen each other?"

Guilt filled Jonah. Out of everyone in town, he'd always made a point of meeting up with his cousin whenever he returned home. "Yeah, sorry about that. I've been really busy."

"I know. I heard."

"Things have been a bit rough at the job site, but that's to be expected with a project this big," Jonah said. "Especially since we're in the final stages, but I planned to give you a call once—"

"I'm not talking about the resort," his cousin said, a big grin on his face. "I'm taking about your busy social life. Dancing, zip lining, a good old-fashioned dinner-and-movie date night."

"What the hell? Is this published somewhere?" Jonah shook his head. "Jeez, small towns."

"You free to grab a beer down at the Ace and catch up?" Caleb asked. "I've got some time before I need to pick up Lily at a friend's house."

Jonah frowned. "I thought your fiancée's name was Mallory."

"It is. Lily is her daughter." Caleb's shoulders squared up proud. "And as soon as we get married and I put through the necessary paperwork, she'll be my daughter, too."

Jonah offered his friend congratulations and the men parted, each getting into their own trucks. Minutes later, they'd were seated in a corner booth at the Ace in the Hole. Thankfully the place wasn't busy yet, with the jukebox off while the Colorado Avalanche battled against the Boston Bruins, already down two goals, on the televisions hanging over the bar.

Jonah waited until the waitress dropped off their beers before he spoke, knowing he had something to say to his friend.

"I'm sorry, man."

Caleb stared at him. "What for? You bought the first round."

"I'm talking about back in August when you called looking for some advice." Jonah leaned forward, cradling his beer in one hand. "You were trying to figure things out between you and Mallory, and me telling you to cut and run was pretty useless."

"Yeah, you weren't exactly helpful that night." Caleb took a swig from his beer.

"I was under a lot of pressure playing catch-up with work, having just returned the previous month from being out of the country for the last year," Jonah explained, even though his friend already knew that. "Then Nate and his resort fell into my lap and my life was all about the renovations, twenty-four seven. Giving relationship advice was the last thing on my mind. Not to mention, just about the least thing I'm qualified to do."

"You know, I was stupid enough to follow what you'd said for a few days." Caleb's smile was easy, but Jonah could see the painful memories behind it from the man's eyes. "Good thing I got some better insight from another source on what it means to be in love."

His parents, maybe? Jonah's aunt and uncle had been happily married for over thirty-five years. Much like his own folks. "Some fatherly wisdom?"

"Nope. Kid wisdom. Lily was the one who set me straight on how I was acting and how much I was hurting Mallory."

Jonah grinned—although his mouth had to stretch tight to do it—and held out his beer. "And they all lived happily-ever-after."

"Amen to that." Caleb lightly clinked the long neck of his beer bottle against Jonah's. "And speaking of happy, you seemed to be in a far better mood than you were a couple of months ago."

"I am."

"So, is it just from working your dream job on that resort?" Caleb pushed. "I know you've loved that old log mansion ever since we were kids."

"Yeah, having free rein on the renovations and turning that place into what will be a world-class vacation spot is one of the best things I've ever done in my career."

"And dating Vanessa Brent?"

Jonah paused for a moment, but then said, "Yeah, dating Vanessa is part of it, too."

"I got to admit, I didn't believe it at first when I heard you were spotted dancing right here in the Ace with her," Caleb said. "The last time we talked you weren't too gung ho on the female species."

"Vanessa is one of a kind."

"She must be. The last girl you spent any time with in town was Lisette."

His ex-wife was the last person Jonah wanted to talk about. "That's been over for a long time."

"I know, but she worked you over pretty good. After what you went through, most guys would be a bit hesitant about getting involved again."

"We're not involved."

Caleb only offered a raised eyebrow at that statement.

"Okay, we're dating, but one of the reasons it's easy to be with Vanessa is because she hasn't made any emotional demands," Jonah explained. "She knows I'm divorced, but she didn't pry into what went wrong."

"And you haven't told her."

"The past is in the past, it's got nothing to do with what's happening now. Besides, I made it clear I'm only in town temporarily and left the ball in her court. She was very up-front about not wanting to put any expectations or labels on what we're doing. She's a free spirit who lives for the moment."

"And that's exactly what you're looking for?"

It was, but that didn't explain why Jonah still hadn't taken their relationship to a more intimate level. Every cell in his body wanted her, wanted to make love to her.

So what was he waiting for?

* * *

Vanessa was getting tired of waiting.

She paced back and forth along the scaffolding, looking at the background she'd finished up just this morning.

The colors matched perfectly with the smaller sketch she'd done. Using a grid format, she easily transferred her vision to the large wall. Both the mountains and the land needed more details added, as did the waterfall, but the essence of her vision was there.

It took her a few false starts to loosen up, but once she did the work flowed. What a great way to end the work week.

Now, if she could just get Jonah Dalton to loosen up on the chivalrous attitude.

Climbing down, she grabbed her sketch pad before backing up a few steps so she could see the entire wall.

Busy with writing down notes about which areas of the mural needed work before the next phase started—talking with Winona Cobbs had given her a great place to start and she now had a list of people and places that were going to be included—she didn't notice anyone had approached her until a hand landed on her arm, making her jump.

"Hey, it's just me."

Nate Crawford stood in front of her, and a handsome man with enough of the same features—tall, dark brown hair, but serious deep blue eyes—as Nate's that he must be his brother, at his side. "I wanted to stop by and tell you how impressed I am with what you've done so far."

"Well, it's not much, but it's a start." Vanessa smiled

at the men. "Things are going to get interesting soon. The devil is in the details, as they say."

"You'll do fine."

Vanessa kept smiling, hoping it hid her nerves. "You have to say that. The paint is already up on the wall."

The man with Nate had turned and studied the wall for a long moment before he looked back at her. "I agree with my brother. Very impressive." He held out one hand. "Hi, I'm Jesse Crawford."

"Vanessa Brent." She put her hand in his and right away she felt at ease with this man. "And thank you. Do you know anything about art?"

He shook his head. "Nope, and even less about people. I prefer the company of horses than most humans I know."

She couldn't give a reason why, but Vanessa felt like Jesse had spoken those words with just a hint of quiet resignation.

After Jesse and Nate said their goodbyes, Vanessa went back to working on her notes, once again getting lost in her thoughts.

Especially when those thoughts turned to Jonah.

Which happened quite often.

As happy as she'd been since moving to this small town, Vanessa now truly felt more alive than she had in a long time. Thanks to Jonah. Yes, he reignited her passion for art, but just being with him made her feel good. Special. Wanted. And it was the simple things that did it. Eating lunch together, except when he had a meeting scheduled or was off site, like today. Dancing and being with friends at the bar, enjoying cozy nights in front of the woodstove watching either action movies he prefered or the chick flicks she liked.

Her feelings for the man were growing deeper by the day and she wanted to share that with him in every way possible—

"Wow, you're kicking butt on this mural."

Another interruption, but when Vanessa looked up, she found Cecelia, who worked on the site as a construction assistant, standing there. "Thanks."

"I don't know where you get the energy." Her friend sent her a wink. "Must be all those pleasurable hours spent after work with Jonah, huh?"

Vanessa sighed. Her friend's innocent question reminded her again at how much she missed Adele. She so wished she could talk to her best friend about Jonah and where things were—and weren't—going between them.

"Is everything okay?" Cecelia asked.

"I could use some advice."

"Hey, what are girlfriends for? Ask away."

Before she did, Vanessa grabbed her friend's wrist and dragged her to a corner of the room. Despite the fact hardly anyone worked in this section of the resort, and if they did they'd be at lunch at the moment, Vanessa wanted as much privacy as she could get.

"Actually, Jonah and I haven't…well, we haven't taken things to the next level," she confessed in a low whisper before she could think about if she should. "Yet."

"Oh." Confusion filled Cecelia's face for a moment, but then understanding dawned. "Oohh! But why?"

Vanessa blew out a frustrated breath, sending the curls dangling over her forehead flying. She'd been asking herself the same question over the past few days.

It wasn't like Jonah was a virgin, for heaven's sake.

Their make-out sessions had been toe curling, heart pounding and downright wonderful, but he always seemed to pull back before things went too far.

Was he doing it for her? Did he think she wasn't ready to take the next step? Physically, she was. Emotionally? Well, that was something else entirely. Jonah was quickly finding a way into her heart. Would making love to him cause her to fall for him all the way?

"Maybe his former marriage has something to do with him holding back. Maybe he's trying to protect my feelings." Vanessa spoke her thoughts aloud. "Perhaps a little extra push in the right direction is what he—what *we*—need."

"Well, if anyone can do the pushing, my money's on you," her friend said.

"You know, I could surprise him with a few candles, a great bottle of wine, me wearing something sexy..." Vanessa's voice trailed off as she warmed to the idea. Yes, she needed to show Jonah just how much she wanted him, wanted the time they spent together to be even more special.

Even if it meant putting her heart on the line.

Chapter 10

Jonah Dalton Designs. J. Dalton Designs. Maybe simply JD Designs?

Yeah, he liked the sound of that.

Over the years—heck, ever since he was a kid—he'd dreamed of what he'd name his own architectural design firm one day.

Today he'd been asked three times about his business. *His* business, his firm. Not the place where he was still employed despite his current three-month leave-of-absence.

His calendar had included an onsite meeting with Nate and a businessman who had a property north of Seattle along the coast. He wanted to redo the place into a getaway resort and had heard about the work being done in Rust Creek Falls.

There were also two unplanned phone calls from

former clients. Both were interested in what he and Nate's team had accomplished in renovating the old Bledsoe place and in Jonah's environmentally friendly design plans.

Nate had joked that Jonah should grab one of the resort's offices and hang out his shingle. He'd brushed off the comment, but since his ride home took him into town to pick up a bottle of wine for tonight, Jonah couldn't stop the thought from returning.

A thought that blew up into a crazy idea as he'd passed an old Victorian house on the corner of Falls and Commercial Street that caught his eye every time he drove by. Now, tonight, as he headed back to the ranch to meet Vanessa for dinner, he couldn't resist swinging by that house again, just for a fast look, he promised himself.

From the outside, the empty home looked a little worn, but a coat of fresh paint and a clearing of the yard would make her shine again.

The front porch took a sharp turn and continued down the side. The large windows were numerous, including two that projected out from the front of the house bow-style, one right over the other. He guessed they were for a dining room with a bedroom overhead on the second floor. Either would make a perfect sun-filled office—

Whoa! Getting a little ahead of yourself, aren't you?

Jonah stopped halfway to the door of the cabin, wine bottle in hand. Yeah, it'd been flattering this afternoon to find so much attention centered on his work, but he'd had accolades and compliments for previous projects.

Why was he suddenly considering now was the right time to be heading out on his own?

And here in Rust Creek Falls?

The idea of moving back had never crossed his mind in the past eight years.

As much as he loved his family and the stark beauty in this part of his home state, there'd always been too many bad memories here. Memories that had kept his visits short and solitary.

Not this time, though.

He'd dreaded the idea of being home for three months from the moment Nate had said it was a required part of the job offer.

Now, just a couple of weeks into his stay—two weeks after meeting Vanessa—he was feeling more relaxed and at the same time more…alive than he'd felt in years.

Because of Vanessa?

His fingers tightening on the wine bottle, he pushed that thought firmly from his head, and continued walking. The outside light came on automatically as the sun had gone down almost an hour ago and dusk had fallen over the distant hills.

Determined to think only about the evening ahead, he reminded himself the good thing about a Halloween party two weeks before the actual holiday was that costumes weren't necessary. At least not according to Vanessa, who'd tracked him down this afternoon between meetings to ask if he was interested in going to a party with her tonight.

Still, she'd had a mischievous gleam in her eyes when she talked about their plans that he found very sexy.

Hell, everything about Vanessa was sexy.

Eager to see her, even though it'd only been just a

few hours since they'd been together at the resort, he knocked on the door.

"Come in."

The words came faintly from the other side and stepped inside, quickly closing the door behind him to shut out the cool night air.

"What the..."

His voice faded as his senses were attacked from every angle.

First was the pale purple radiance that filled the room. Mixed with the firelight from the woodstove and flicking candles perched on every surface imaginable, the inside of the cabin glowed.

The scent of sandalwood and vanilla surrounded him, but the familiar flowery essence that was all Vanessa was there, too. He inhaled deeply, enjoying the mixture while soft jazz music played in the background.

His gaze then took in the spider webs, jack-o'-lanterns, miniature ghosts and skeletons scattered around the room before being drawn to the colorful silk floor cushions that rested on top of a plush, faux, white bearskin rug. All the elements combined to give the room the appearance of a haunted gypsy encampment or harem.

"'Step into my parlor,' said the spider to the fly."

Her soft words shifted his focus to the bewitching creature that stood on the other side of the room.

Vanessa.

Leaning against the doorway that led to the back of the cabin, she was in the shadows. There was enough light to see she wore something lacy and silky and looked so damn beautiful his breath caught in his throat.

She smiled and turned a bit to one side allowing the flowing material to sensually slide open, revealing a bare leg from her toes to her hip.

Any plans for breathing vanished.

Of course, other parts of his body were working just fine and responded instantly to the sight before him, including his brain, which quickly put two and two together and came up with an amazing night ahead.

He'd been thinking about being with her like this for a while. Hell, from the moment they'd met. It finally hit him today that he'd been using his past relationships, including marriage—and how poorly they'd ended—as a barrier between himself and Vanessa. Which wasn't fair to either of them. He cared about this woman, enjoyed being with her. Vanessa felt the same. Tonight was proof of that. He should've known that when he balked at making the first move, Vanessa would take matters into her own hands.

In spectacular fashion.

"Please tell me the party is here tonight," he said, grateful for the ability to speak. "And that it's just the two of us."

"You don't mind?"

One corner of his mouth rose into a grin. "No, I don't mind."

"Why don't you put that in the kitchen and then join me back here." She stepped farther into the room, gestured at the forgotten wine in his grip. "I've already got dessert waiting."

He was looking at dessert. The sweetest concoction known to man.

Jonah had forgotten all about the bottle, surprised he'd managed to hold on to it all this time. He did what she asked, unable to tear his gaze from her while walking into the kitchen.

When she moved into the light from the woodstove, the lace on the top half of her slinky outfit turned into intricate tattoo-like images on her skin. She then sat on the rug and the material pooled around her legs.

His blood turned to fire. Anticipation filled him and he found himself glad he dressed casually, leaving his shirt untucked as his ability to hide his body's response to her was gone.

He left the wine on the counter and headed back into the living room. Stepping in front of the quilted chair, he noticed for the first time a tray resting on the couch that held a plate of fresh cut fruit and bowl of whipped topping.

This was getting better and better.

"Why don't you take those off before you sit down?" Vanessa gently tapped one toe of his cowboy boots with the end of an empty wineglass. "You'll probably be more comfortable."

Sitting in the chair, he did as she requested, again unable to take his eyes off her as she filled two glasses from a chilled bottle of wine on the floor next to her.

He joined her on the rug, his back to the woodstove and one hand braced just past her hip, his knee almost touching hers.

She twisted back to face him and held out a glass, the liquid sloshing around inside gave away the slight trembling of her fingers.

Glad he wasn't the only one feeling some nerves here.

Instead of taking the drink, he leaned forward and

rested his fingertips against her neck, feeling her pulse jump at the base of her neck.

"Aren't you thirsty?" Vanessa asked.

Her question had his gaze locked on her mouth.

"Parched." His thumb moved to her lower lip, lightly brushing back and forth.

A low moan slipped past and he gave into temptation. Capturing her mouth with a gentleness he labored for when all he wanted was to consume her, body and soul, the way she'd done to him, he kissed her.

When she met the pressure of his lips by opening hers and slanting her head to one side, he slipped his hand farther into her hair, fisting her curls. Groaning as their tongues slid against each other, he tasted the softness, heat and unspoken promise of an unforgettable night for the both of them.

He held his desire in check and enjoyed her taste, warm and minty. Finally, he pulled back, reluctant to part from her as he pressed lingering kisses to her mouth, chin and lastly the tip of her nose.

Vanessa remained perfectly still, wineglasses in her hands, eyes closed. "Hmmm, that was nice." Her voice was slightly breathless.

Jonah relieved her of one of the glasses while he took the time to study her attire up close. The pale pink of her negligée looked almost translucent against her skin, except for where the dark shadows of her nipples pressed against the fabric.

He took a sip of wine to soothe his very dry throat. "I agree."

She opened her eyes. "You hungry?"

A light blush filled her cheeks as she read his answer in his gaze. "I mean for dessert," she added.

He nodded.

Vanessa turned back and grabbed a strawberry, dipped it into a bowl of whipped cream and then held it out to him.

Jonah opened his mouth and she placed it inside. The cool, tart juiciness of the fruit mixing with the topping reminded him of the beautiful woman in front of him.

He swallowed the tasty morsel and said, “My turn.” Reaching past her, he brushed her bare shoulder, his hand lingering against her warm skin for a moment as he studied the plate. “Have a favorite?”

“Surprise me.”

He grinned and picked up one of the green slices and followed her example.

“Ah, kiwi.” She spied the offering when he held it in front of her. “Why’s that?”

“Because it’s the most unique. Just like you.”

Vanessa smiled, and then opened her mouth. He placed the fruit on her tongue. She closed her lips, capturing his thumb and lightly sucking away the dollop of cream there.

Every muscle in his body tightened as she lightly nipped at the end of the digit before letting him go. He thought about leaning in for another kiss, but the rumble from her stomach stopped him.

“Is someone hungry?” he asked when Vanessa slapped a hand to her middle. “Maybe we should bring the food over here before you waste away to nothing.”

“No chance of that, but yes, I skipped dinner.”

Jonah put down his wine and then moved the fruit plate and the bowl of whipped cream, setting both between them on the rug. “Dig in, darling. You’re going to need your strength.”

“Am I?”

He read a hint of uncertainty in her eyes. His past behavior when they’d been this close, this intimate, the cause. “Oh, yeah. No one’s leaving early or falling asleep tonight. Unless that’s what you want.”

Vanessa grinned, the playfulness returning. She grabbed a hunk of watermelon. “Then perhaps you should build up your energy, as well.”

He liked the sound of that.

They ate, feeding each other and themselves, until most of the dessert was gone and they were each on a second glass of wine. There were lots of kisses and laughter and Jonah found he liked the slow pace of the evening.

Both of them knew where this evening was heading. The slow build of anticipation only whetted their appetite for each other. He was so aware of her, the delicious heat that hummed in his veins made him tight and hot every time he caught her looking at him.

When she lifted a hand to his chest, her fingers playing with the snaps on his shirt, he remembered how she’d tugged them open in his truck, before pulling him down over her as she laid back against the seat….

The sound of the first snap coming undone sent an arrow of pure desire straight to his groin. Her featherlight caress and the scrape of her nails against his skin as she opened a few more rocked him to his core. By the time she reached the last one, the back of her hand was tantalizingly chafing the hard ridge pressing against the button fly of his jeans.

Unable to resist any longer, he brushed his fingertips

along the tiny strap holding the lacy material against her breasts. Following their path downward, he palmed her fullness, his thumb rubbing lightly over one rigid nipple, causing her to shiver and ease from his touch.

He dropped his hand. "You cold?"

She shook her head, drawing her hand away from him, as well. "No, although I am slightly less clothed than you."

Yes, she was and even with his shirt now fully open, he was burning from the inside out.

Still, he asked, "Should I add another log to the fire?"

She bit down on her bottom lip for a moment. "If you want."

Jonah rose and tended to the woodstove, thinking maybe Vanessa was looking for a moment or two alone.

To rethink her decision?

Stopping now would just about kill him, but he meant what he said earlier. She was calling all the shots tonight. It wasn't like this was the last chance they'd have to make love.

There was plenty of time to take things to the next level. They had until the holidays before the project was finished and he left again.

Ignoring the sudden tightening in his chest, Jonah returned to where Vanessa sat and saw she'd moved the dishes and wineglasses back to the tray on the couch and was reaching toward the lamp on the end table.

Still standing, he leaned over her, snapped off the light, extinguishing the purple glow that he guessed came from a special lightbulb. Their hands bumped, knocking over a wicked-looking witch, complete with a tiny broom and a pair of what looked like monkeys with wings.

"Oh, jeez, could I be any more a klutz?"

"Nope, my fault," he said, straightening her things before joining her on the floor again. "I'm guessing decorating this place took up most of your afternoon."

"I think I bought out the craft store in Kalispell." She looked around the room. "Halloween has always been my favorite holiday. Do you like it?"

He again let his gaze slowly travel the length of her body, taking in every lace-and silk-covered curve laid out before him.

He half growled, half laughed. "Oh, yeah, I like it."

Her laugh was sexy and sweet at the same time as she returned her focus to him. "I was talking about the decorations."

Reaching out, he wrapped a finger around the silk cord that held together the sheer lace panels that met at the dip in her cleavage. One gentle tug and the loop would disappear.

He managed not to test that theory. Yet. "So was I."

"I want you, Jonah." A dark heat filled her eyes. "I guess that's pretty evident, from everything that's happened so far, but did I go overboard? You know, with planning all of this? Did I push too much?"

Jonah's need for her slammed into his chest the moment she said aloud she wanted him. He'd been a fool not to take everything she'd offered before this night. The fact that she was worried she'd overstepped somewhere along the way made him determined to make everything from this moment on, perfect for her.

"How about you let me take over the pushing from here?"

* * *

Oh, that sounded good to her.

Vanessa had been second-guessing herself from the moment she started placing each pumpkin, spiderweb and candle. Not to mention the sexy nightie she'd been so sure was perfect after buying it in a mad rush of shopping this afternoon.

The room did look great, exactly as she pictured it in her head when she'd come up with this crazy idea. When Jonah had finally arrived, she'd stood quietly, watching his reaction.

As hard as she'd worked toward this new "be bold, be happy" lifestyle, there was a part of her that was still the introverted artist who found comfort in being alone.

His surprise at the cabin's decor had turned to sensual awareness the moment he'd spotted her. The naked longing in his gaze gave her a boost of confidence that had lasted through dessert. It allowed her to be brave enough to get him a bit closer to being as undressed as she was when she easily unsnapped his shirt, revealing his chest, lightly dusted with fine curls and an impressive six-pack of abs.

But then she'd given into the nagging doubt that maybe she'd gone a bit too far with her plan. Did she seem desperate? That maybe, despite his obvious arousal, he was only here because…

Of what?

The man had come right out and said he wanted to be with her and he'd been the one to kiss her first—

"Boy, you've got a lot of thinking going on up here." Jonah pushed back her curls, his fingers lightly massaging her temple. "Want to share?"

She smiled, hoping it concealed her confusion. "Are

you kidding? I can't even make sense of the craziness in my head. I wouldn't want to put you through that."

"Maybe we should leave the thinking for another time, then." He whispered the words against her lips.

When she nodded in agreement, he kissed her.

This time he devoured her mouth in a way that was wet and deep, powerful and seductive. He leaned into her, his hand moving to the back of her neck, offering support as he pushed her gently backward.

She grabbed onto his shirt, fisting the two sides as she returned his kisses, arching her body until her lace-covered breasts met the heat of his skin.

He groaned, his mouth breaking free to move along her jaw to her neck, nibbling and kisses here and there as he gently lowered her to the softness of the rug.

Wanting nothing between them, she reached for the knot between her breasts that would allow the material covering her to fall away, but Jonah's hand was already there.

He pulled and tugged and then cool air flowed over her skin before it was replaced with the heat of his mouth closing over her nipple.

She hissed, dragging in the outdoorsy scent that clung to him deep inside her, tunneling her fingers into his hair to hold him in place as his lips and tongue moved over her.

A deep pang of longing filled her, a sharp edge of pleasure that drove straight to her core making her wet and ready for him. She moved against his jean-clad leg where it laid between hers.

"Jonah."

Yanking his shirt down over his wide shoulders, she was impatient to have it gone completely, but he ignored her, moving from one breast to the other, licking and sucking and teasing, his fingers stroking the dampness left behind.

His hand then moved, slowly trailing over her belly until he cupped her, brushing back and forth across the lace that covered her, but couldn't conceal the damp evidence of what he was doing to her. His fingers slipped inside her panties, touching her while his mouth never left her breast.

"Jonah, please."

She felt him smile against her skin as he slowly moved both his hand and his mouth away, but only for a moment as he pushed the silky material of her nightie to either side, baring her completely to him. Then his mouth returned, his tongue leaving a wet trail behind, pausing when he reached the edge of her matching panties.

Vanessa waited, wondering if he would see, ready to show him how easy it would be, but then she felt his mouth against her hip. The bow on the side releasing as he tugged the string holding it in place with his teeth. The material fell away and then he was at the center of her, nudging her to open wider to him as he dipped his head. He kissed, stroked and teased as one finger, then two, dipped inside her.

She gasped, already feeling the tightening deep within as her passion rose, right on the edge. He loved her in ways she'd never experienced before, ways that told her just how much he meant to her, in her heart where it truly mattered.

A part of her wanted to push him away, wanted them to be together when each of them reached that moment. Then, as if he read her thoughts, Jonah pulled back, rising to his knees. She watched as he yanked off his shirt. He then got to his feet, making quick work of his jeans and briefs and socks, his eyes never leaving hers.

But hers did move away. She wanted to see all of him, his wide shoulders, lean hips, the proof of his desire for her. He stood in the glow from the fire, the hard planes of his body as strong and sure as the mountains right outside. Then she returned to meet his stare, so powerful when he gazed down at her it caused a sting to bite at the edges of her eyes.

Naked, he retrieved a condom from his wallet, and quickly rolled it down his sex before he joined her again, stretching out over her.

She rose to meet him, eyes closed to hide her tears as she cradled his face in her hands while they kissed. He thrust into her, filling her completely and she welcomed him home. Clinging to him, she chanted his name again and again as he buried his face in her neck.

"Vanessa," he whispered against her skin, as he kissed her there.

He rocked his hips, moving back and forth, pressing deep and holding before retreating and then doing it all over again. He lifted one hip, angling her to give her more. Giving and taking back all she offered as she matched his desire.

"Yes. Oh, please...yes."

Vanessa pulled him closer, the perfection of this moment washing over her as she pressed her heart to his. The truth deep inside spilling free as she spiraled upward and then exploded into a million pieces as Jonah went rigid, straining with his own release as he groaned her name.

She loved him. She loved Jonah Dalton.

In that moment both the deepest joy and powerful heartbreak filled her soul, knowing she'd never experienced emotions this devastatingly profound in her life.

And after tonight, she never would again.

Chapter 11

The morning sun filled the cabin with a warm glow, but thankfully the still-pulled shades kept out any piercing shafts of light.

Vanessa stirred on the plush rug in the living room, stretching, feeling the soreness of muscles that hadn't been used in a long time. The softness of the aged quilt moved against her skin while the scent of freshly brewed coffee filled her head. The aroma awakened her senses, even though she usually greeted the day with an oversize mug of her favorite chai tea.

"Good morning, sunshine."

She froze. Jonah's greeting came from behind her, the low tenor of his voice sending her heart thumping in her chest.

Memories of their wonderful night together came rushing back.

They'd made love twice more, the final time long after midnight once she'd slipped away to blow out the candles and banked the fire in the woodstove. Thinking he'd fallen asleep, she'd grabbed a quilt from the couch and moved to lie next to him again, unfolding the faded patchwork material over the two of them.

It was then that Jonah grabbed her, pulling her on top of him, silencing her squeal of surprise with a kiss. A kiss that led to many more and they'd made love again. That time she'd straddled him as he held tight to her, allowing her to set the pace until he sat up, pulled her to his chest and claimed her mouth again as they both exploded in a mutual release.

And each time, when their passions cooled and he held her closely tucked to his side, she'd waited.

Waited for the never-before-felt kaleidoscope of joy and ecstasy and love careening around inside her to settle down. To fade away.

It didn't.

If anything, the emotions grew even stronger. And so did the niggle of fear that came along with them.

The night had been wildly romantic. They'd been working their way to this moment since they met. Of course, things would change once their relationship became physical. They were both young, healthy and each had made it clear it'd been a while since they'd been involved with someone.

That's all it was. Compatibility.

Fun. The next step in their…friendship.

Great sex. Great sex with a guy who was smart and funny and caring and creative—

"Hey, are you not awake yet?"

His question cut into her thoughts. Good thing, too.

She refused to allow herself to believe that any of the crazy feelings bouncing around inside of her meant anything more than—what had she called it again?

Yes, compatibility. Not love. She had to have been mistaken last night.

Accepting that, she finally replied, "I'm awake. I'm just not used to talking to anyone before I shower."

Hmmm, that sounded mean.

Surprised that any words managed to make it past the tightening of her throat, Vanessa rolled to her back and opened her eyes to find him standing over her. "Sorry. No offense. I meant to say good morning."

"None taken."

"What time is it?" she asked.

"Almost ten o'clock."

"Ten?" She bolted upright, clutching the blanket to her chest. "Are you serious? Ten? Oh, I missed the sunrise!"

"No, you didn't. Don't you remember? We watched it together."

That's right, they had.

Her internal clock had made sure she was up just before the first light broke over the mountains. She'd slipped from Jonah's embrace, wrapped herself in a blanket and made her way to the oversize glass door, raising just the one shade so as not to disturb his sleep.

Vanessa had watched the world awaken and offered a silent greeting to her friend, thanking her once again for insisting it'd been past time for Vanessa to take a chance and dare to live a different life.

If she hadn't, she never would've met Jonah.

Moments later, she'd jumped when he'd stepped in

behind her, wrapped his arms around her and placed a gentle kiss in the wild mess that was her hair.

He'd then asked if she was all right.

She'd lied and told him yes.

But that hadn't been a lie. Not fully. Being with him had been more than all right. It'd been wonderful.

Then she'd made up some excuse about being an early riser even on the weekends, but not a morning person. When Jonah had suggested she get back beneath the quilts while he got the woodstove going, she'd readily agreed and must've fallen back asleep.

"Here." He sat on the edge of the couch and held out a mug to her. "Maybe this will help welcome you back to the land of the living."

She took his offering, pleased to see he'd remembered her preference for tea, thanks to their morning breaks at the job site. After the first sip, she then noticed that unlike her, he was fully dressed, right down to his boots.

He was leaving?

She had to admit she hadn't thought about the morning after when she'd planned their private party for the previous evening. The truth was she hadn't been completely sure of its success, never mind him staying all night.

"Yeah, I have to go," he said, having picked up on her perusal. "Derek texted me about twenty minutes ago asking if I still planned to help him and Eli today on another section of fence that needs mending."

"Ah, okay."

Jonah took a sip from his own mug, and then grinned at her over the rim. "If I wasn't too tired, that is."

That meant his brothers, if not his entire family,

knew he'd spent the night here. She wondered how long it would be before the entire town knew.

Not that she was ashamed of being with him. Those who knew them probably already assumed they were sleeping together, but Jonah didn't seem to like the gossipy side of living in such a small town.

"But we're still on for lessons this afternoon," he added. "I'll see you at the barn around four?"

Number eleven: learn to ride a horse.

The item from her list flashed inside her head, as did Jonah's offer last night to again teach her when he'd shared stories about growing up on the ranch.

She'd mentioned Derek's offer for lessons and how he hadn't been able to find the time other than the first afternoon. Then the lesson had been cut short when he'd been called away, before she'd even gotten in the saddle.

Jonah had insisted if she was still interested in learning, *he'd* be the one to teach her. She'd liked that his tone had held just a hint of jealousy, even though she'd never thought twice about his brother in that way.

She'd never thought—or felt—about anyone the way she did toward the man in front of her.

And that scared the bejeebers out of her.

"Oh, I don't want to take you away from anything important." She pulled her knees to her chest, keeping the blanket firmly in place as she drank a bit more of her tea. "We can do the lesson another time. After all, you're not going anywhere for another couple of months. Right?"

Wow, where had *that* come from?

Jonah's brows dipped into a sharp V over his forehead. "You won't be taking me away. I want to do it."

"Okay, I'll be there."

He got to his feet, walked into the kitchen and poured the contents of his mug in the sink. "What are your plans for today?"

"I don't know." She shrugged. "Working on sketches for the mural. Cleaning up this place."

Jonah joined her again, dropping to one knee so they were eye level. "Don't clean too much." He placed a finger beneath her chin and tipped her face up to look at him. "I think Halloween is turning into my favorite holiday, too."

And just like that, her heart was gone again.

Something was wrong.

Jonah couldn't say exactly what, but Vanessa had been acting strangely for the past week. Ever since their first night together, in fact.

Which had been incredible. As was every moment he'd spent time with her since, both in and out of bed.

Being with her had made him feel like a new man. She was passionate and fun in her lovemaking, just as she was in life.

But his gut was telling him she was bothered by something.

She'd cut their horseback-riding lessons short the following afternoon claiming she had to get back to work on her sketches, but considering his sisters and his mother had tagged along for the trail ride, he couldn't really blame her.

Not that they'd said anything to her about him spending the night. At least she'd claimed they hadn't. His brothers had been quick to inform him when he'd finally joined them that the entire family was aware his truck had been spotted outside the cabin.

All night.

Still, he'd invited her to dinner with his family for the following day. His mother had pointed out that Vanessa hadn't been to the main house since he'd come home, but when he called to ask, she'd been out at the resort working and hadn't wanted to stop her creative flow.

They'd gotten together later that night and he'd stayed over again on Monday and Tuesday as well, making love to her in the bed he'd built for the cabin after they'd gone to the Ace in the Hole to dance.

She'd been just as spirited and lively as always, surrounded by a crowd of people, and while he'd enjoyed being there with her, all he'd wanted was to get her alone.

To ask her to come to Denver for a few days.

He'd gotten a last-minute phone call from his office Tuesday evening and due to a couple of issues on a job there that needed his attention, he was heading back to the city for a few days the following morning.

At first, he'd been surprised when the idea of inviting Vanessa to go along with him had popped into his head, but the more he thought about it, the more he wanted her with him.

Wanted to show her his penthouse, his office. Take her to his favorite steakhouse for dinner. Squeeze in a visit to the Denver Art Museum if they had time.

She'd turned him down.

Her eyes had lit up when he first brought up the idea on the drive back to the cabin. He'd been so sure she was going to say yes, but then she looked away for a moment before telling him there was no way she could be away from the mural for that long.

He'd tried to convince her, but in the end he'd gone alone. Due to a bad storm, he hadn't gotten back to Rust Creek Falls until late last night. As tempted as he'd been, he hadn't gone to see Vanessa when he got back to the ranch.

And today, they'd only exchanged a few text messages as she was working again on the mural. On a Saturday. Not that he had a right to complain. He'd worked plenty of Saturdays and today was no exception.

"You did good today."

His father's voice cut into Jonah's thoughts, causing the brush he was using to rub down Duke, a buckskin stallion he'd gotten for Christmas his senior year in high school, to tumble out of his hands.

He quickly scooped it off the ground, glad he was done with the animal's grooming as it meant he was due to see Vanessa in a couple of hours. "Thanks, Dad."

"Things went a lot faster with you helping out." His father stood in the open doorway of the stall. "Your brothers might not say it, but they liked having the extra set of hands around. As for me..."

Jonah fed the horse the treat he'd taken from the tack room refrigerator, but his gaze was on his father.

Charles Dalton had been a rancher all his life, like his father before him. The years of hard work showed, but he was still strong and tough and worked his land right alongside his sons and their crew.

Two of his sons, anyway.

"I appreciate you chipping in."

His father was a man of few words and that was as close to a thank you as Jonah was going to get.

He gave his horse one last slap on the rear that sent the animal out into an outside corral before he exited the stall. "I enjoy ranch work. I always have."

"Just not enough to make it your life's work."

Jonah stopped to look his father in the eye. "No, not that much."

The two men walked together toward the front of the barn, Eli and Derek nowhere to be found. Jonah wondered if this was going to turn into another lecture on family legacy. It'd been a while since his father had pulled out his "you're a Dalton and Daltons are ranchers" speech.

Jeez, at least five years or so.

They stepped out into the afternoon sun and headed for the corral with a few horses roaming around, including Duke. Stopping at the railing, they each propped their hands on the highest slat. It'd been a beautiful fall day, but there was a nip in the air now and it was expected to drop below freezing tonight.

A good night for two people to stay in and—

"You know, it meant a lot to me when you asked for your birthright."

His father's words again jolted Jonah and he tucked away any thoughts of Vanessa to concentrate on what the old man had to say about the acreage promised to each of his sons. "Even if I used the land to build one of my designs?" he pointed out.

"I didn't care what you did with it— No, that's not true. I did care, I do care. I was glad to see you building a home there." His father kept his gaze locked on the horizon, the brim of his Stetson pulled low on his forehead. "Glad to have you back on the ranch. Knew it meant you were coming back. Even if it was only for a few hours a week."

"Dad, I was busy with school and work—"

"And your wife, I know." A wave of the old man's hand cut him off. "But it felt like the moment you married and moved to town, you turned your back on your life here."

"I was living my own life."

"And you had someone who supported your dreams, which is more than I did back then."

Despite the fact he had two sons already involved with running of the ranch, Charles Dalton had wanted all of his boys to work the land with him.

"You paid for my college."

"That was your mother's doing. She insisted, no matter what studies you were working toward. Same with your brothers and sisters."

Jonah nodded, but stayed silent not sure where this conversation was heading.

"We had hoped that you and Lisette planned to move out here, once you graduated college and finished that place." This time his father glanced at him. "Thought maybe she'd changed her mind about ranch living."

Jonah shook his head. No, that had never happened and his marriage had ended only four years after it had begun. Of course, that had nothing to do with the ranch and everything to do with the choices Lisette had made.

"Did you know I almost screwed things up with your mother?"

Jonah looked at his dad this time, but the man was once again staring straight ahead. He had no idea what his dad was talking about. His folks had been happily married for well over three decades.

"We met in high school, too, like you and Lisette, but I was a couple of years older. After graduation, I told her—and my folks—that I wanted to rodeo professionally, so off I went."

Jonah and his siblings had heard this before. His father's trophies and awards from his bronc riding days were in his study.

"And she stuck with me. Of course, she was still in school for the first two years. So I'd go off and do my thing, get injured, come back here to heal and work for your grandpa until it was time for me to head out again. Sometimes we were together. Sometimes we weren't."

His father paused, his rough-as-leather hands laced together tight out in front of him. "After about five years of this she told me she was tired of waiting on me to make up my mind. I didn't believe her and we had some real knock-down, drag-out donnybrooks over breaking up or staying together. Until the time I came home and she said I had one last chance to get it right or she was gone."

Jonah knew what the answer was, but he asked, anyway. "What happened?"

"I finally told her the truth. I was scared I'd end up like my dad. A man who couldn't honor his wedding vows no matter how much he tried. Lord knows, with three marriages to his name, the man tried hard. Told her I'd already messed around while we were apart, told her everything. You know what she did? She asked me to marry her."

Jonah smiled. "And you said yes?"

"Hell, yeah, I said yes." He returned Jonah's grin. "I might've been dumb back then, but I wasn't stupid."

No, he wasn't that.

"The point to this story is I may not know all the details, but I do know that girl hurt you bad when she ended your marriage." His father's tone was serious now. "And you've been running from your home, your family and this town ever since. Your work on that resort has finally brought you back and a special lady is making you happier than you've been in a long time. Maybe it's time for *you* to think about what it is you really want out of life."

Jonah remained silent, letting his father's words sink into his head. It was spooky how much they matched his own thoughts over the past few nights as he'd laid alone in his bed in Denver.

Missing Vanessa.

"Are you saying this is my last chance?" he finally asked.

The old man stepped back from the railing. "Last chance, second chance. Who knows? Maybe it's just time for a little honesty."

With that his father gave him a quick clap on the back, turned and headed for the main house. Jonah watched him go.

He made a lot of sense, and not just because Jonah had been doing a bit of self-examination lately, being back here in town.

Exploring the past, thinking about his future.

Especially since the first time he'd made love to Vanessa and felt something deep inside that he'd never felt before with anyone, not even Lisette.

Maybe it was enough that he was finally concentrating on something besides what had consumed his life for the past eight years, his work.

Unable to wait a moment longer, Jonah dug into his pocket for his cell phone.

Chapter 12

Vanessa barely heard the special ringtone she'd given to Jonah's phone number over the sound of rushing water. She hurried to turn off the tub's faucets. Gallons of hot water awaited her with enough bubbles to last for the hour she planned to soak, along with a glass or two of wine.

All to be enjoyed in anticipation of seeing Jonah again for the first time in three days.

And yeah, that was her fault.

She could've gone to Denver with him, but it was harder to keep things simple and casual between them. It had taken daily self-talks and a bit of distance—emotional and physical—even though they had spent the night together three more times in the past week—to keep up the appearance.

Spotting the reminder on her phone's calendar that

her best friend's birthday was fast approaching, and the fact she'd completely forgotten about it in the midst of "living for the moment," helped to remind her that nothing in life was certain.

Catching a glimpse of his life in Denver would've only been a reminder of that uncertainty because Jonah had made it clear he was heading back there when his stay in Rust Creek Falls ended.

Yes, staying behind had been the right decision.

Still, her heart pounded in her chest when she grabbed her phone from the dresser in the bedroom. She swiped her thumb across the screen and forced a lighter tone to her voice when she said, "Hey there, cowboy."

"What are you doing?"

Hmmm, short and to the point. She glanced at her reflection in the mirror, taking the silk bathrobe she wore and her curls, pinned up and out of the way. Should she tell him?

Live for the moment. "I'm about to ease into a steaming hot bubble bath. You?"

His sharp intake of breath could be heard clearly through the phone. She waited, wondering what he'd say now.

"Need someone to wash your back?"

Vanessa smiled. Just what she'd hoped for.

Because she missed him.

Missed seeing him, talking with him, kissing him. She could at least admit that much if to no one else but herself. "Come on down."

"I need to grab a shower first."

She laughed. "Doesn't that negate the hot soapy water available at my place?"

"I've been working on the ranch all day, darling. I smell like dirt, sweat and horse."

Okay, she'd been in Montana too long because all of that sounded wonderful. At least it did on him.

"Okay, do what you need to," she said instead. "I'll leave the front door unlocked, but don't take too long. I could be asleep by the time you get here."

"I'm sure I can come up with some way to wake you."

She was sure he could, too.

They ended the call and she stood there, the phone pressed to her chest, the happiness inside of her warring with the truth.

She loved Jonah. No matter how she'd tried to talk her heart out of it, the truth was there. And that love scared her.

Even more than thinking about how it would feel when he moved on with his life. The real fear came from planning for a future she wasn't sure she should have, deserved to have.

She had no idea what was coming down the road and wasn't that for the best?

Take life as it comes.

If the events of *her* life had taught her anything it was that nothing was certain. It was better not to make any hard and fast plans. Life could change in a heartbeat.

Or end just as quickly.

Putting the phone down, her gaze caught on the folded sheet of paper tucked into the corner of the mirror.

Her and Adele's bucket list. She opened it and read it again, even though she knew it by heart.

Number twenty-one: take a bubble bath...with a man.

She grabbed a pen, placed a check mark next to the item and again wrote Jonah's name on the paper.

Just like she'd done five times before.

So far she'd completed nine of the remaining sixteen goals since her friend's death almost a year ago. Jonah had played a part in six of them.

Was it a good thing or not to see so many of her goals were connected to one man? He'd made it clear from the beginning he was only in town for a short while.

His life wasn't in this place that Vanessa had come to love in the past few months. But hers was, and it was so different from what she'd known in Philadelphia. The only thing that city held for her anymore was a distant father and unhappy memories. Even Adele's mother had moved on, following her husband to Florida before Vanessa had even made the decision to head out west.

She felt at home here, enjoyed her new friends, and the new direction in her art had her excited in ways she hadn't been in years.

Again, thanks to Jonah.

Yes, she'd accomplished a lot in the past few months, but did any of that matter? What right did she have to pursue these dreams when her best friend never had the chance?

"No, not going to think about that now." She shook off the sadness before it could take hold. "Enjoy today."

Minutes later, with music playing and candles lit, Vanessa climbed into the tub, oohing at how delicious the silky, hot water felt on her skin as it rose almost to her shoulders.

Lying back, she tried to picture Jonah in here with her and although the tub was certainly big enough for two people, that would probably mean some of the water had to go.

Did he really plan on stripping down and climbing in?

She wasn't sure—maybe she shouldn't have been so quick to make that check mark—but she adjusted the water level, anyway. Now, there was nothing to do but wait. Less than fifteen minutes went by—she'd been watching the clock—when the faint click of the front door told her he was here. Listening to his boot heels on the hardwood floor, he came toward the bedroom.

"Vanessa?"

Okay, how silly was it his voice caused her to jump, sending bubbles flying?

Where else would she be? Did he not believe her when she'd told him her plans for this afternoon?

"In h-here."

He entered the bathroom and the first thing she saw was his beautiful smile. Then she noticed the single yellow rose he held in his hand.

Darn, her heart just gave itself to this wonderful man all over again. How many times could that happen before it belonged to him forever?

She blinked hard, hoping it would be enough to hold back the tears. Cupping a handful of soapy froth, she blew them in his direction. "Hi."

"Boy, you look good in bubbles."

He walked to the tub, bent down and covered her mouth in a kiss before handing her the rose. He smelled fresh and clean, his familiar cologne tickling her nose. He'd showered after all.

"I've missed you," he whispered.

"Me, too." The words slipped out before she could catch them. She lifted the rose to her face, inhaling its sweet fragrance. "I mean, I missed you, too."

He smiled and straightened, his hands already tugging the ends of his Henley-style shirt from the waistband of his jeans. "Want some company?"

She nodded, unable to speak as he reached back behind his head and easily pulled his shirt off his body. Hmmm, same wide shoulders, lean hips and flat stomach she'd seen many times since their private party last week, but her body still responded in a rush of heat at the sight of him.

Next came balancing on one foot, then the other, as he removed his boots, then his socks. Finally, his hands went to the button on his jeans, but he only undid the top one before his smile turned into a suggestive grin. "Is this where I should start dancing?"

She laughed. "You don't hear me complaining, do you?"

Jonah chuckled, but it faded as he undid the next few buttons. Even with the overhead light dimmed, the half dozen candles gave off plenty of light that played across the perfection of his body.

By the time he got to the last button her fingers had tightened on the stem of the rose so much she almost broke it in half. She tore her gaze away and looked around, wondering what she was going to do with—

"Here, let me take that."

Jonah lifted the rose from her hand and walked out of the bathroom. He returned a few minutes later with the bloom safely tucked into a tall, half-filled drinking glass. Setting it on the bathroom counter, he then proceeded to quickly strip down to nothing.

Vanessa's breath disappeared.

He walked to the tub and she had enough brain power left to scoot forward so he could climb in behind her. The heat from his body as he sat, his legs stretched out on either side of her, enveloped her as the water rose up over her breasts.

For reasons she couldn't explain—probably because her brain had stopped working—she remained sitting forward while cradled between his powerful thighs.

He leaned in close, one large hand coming around to rest against her belly and she jumped again.

"Hey, you okay? It's just me."

His whispered words flowed over one shoulder before he placed a slow kiss on her neck.

She closed her eyes, loving the way his fingers gently spread out over her skin. "I know. It's just that I've… well, I've never…"

Jonah waited as her voice trailed off, a bit surprised at her admission.

Her fresh, citrusy and sexy scent had filled his head from the moment he'd walked into her bedroom. He'd called out, wanting her to know he was close by and the slight hesitation in her voice now made him pause.

Then he reminded himself she'd accepted his offer for help washing her back. He just hoped that meant he'd be doing it while in the tub with her.

The delight in her eyes at his simple gift made him glad he'd snagged one of the roses from the bouquet his sister Kayla had brought home. The way that emotion changed into pure desire as she watched him undress had his body responding before he'd gotten anywhere close to her.

Now that she was in his arms, but still kept her distance from him, despite his kiss and his arm wrapped around her had him finishing her sentence. "You've never taken a bubble bath with anyone."

Vanessa nodded, still not looking back at him.

"Me neither."

"Really?"

He smiled at her amazement. He kissed her again, same spot, but his lips lingered a bit longer. "I'm glad my first is with you."

His admission was enough for her to relax and she eased back against his chest. The length of the tub was no match for his long legs so his knees rose a bit above the water line. A perfect resting spot for her hands.

She followed when he leaned back and he waited until she laid her head at his shoulder before he gently turned her face to his, a soapy hand at her chin, and kissed her.

She welcomed him, twisting in his arms to allow both of them to deepen the connection between them.

"Hmmm, have I mentioned how much I've missed doing that?"

He spoke the words against her lips, even though they weren't needed. She probably guessed that much with the hard evidence of his arousal pressed against her hip.

"No, you haven't," she said, then she turned to face front again and gave a little wiggle as she got comfortable. "Not in so many words."

He groaned. She giggled.

He fell in love.

As simple and as complicated as that, Jonah finally allowed his heart and his mind to accept what had been obvious from the moment he met this amazing woman.

He loved Vanessa.

For the second time in his life and for the first time as a grown man, he was in love. Vanessa's passion for life, and all the wonder and excitement it held, had awakened him from the lifeless existence he'd been staggering around in for the past eight years.

Yeah, he had a kick-ass career that was getting better by the day, but he'd poured so much of himself into his work, there'd been nothing left for anyone or anything else.

Until now.

He wanted to shout it from the rooftops, whisper it against her skin. Was this the right moment to tell her? He hadn't said the words in such a long time.

Dropping his head, he again kissed the back of her neck, making his way up to her ear.

"So, you've never bathed with a woman before?"

Her question surprised him, but it was the perfect lead into what he hoped wasn't going to be a difficult story to tell. She deserved to know about his past before they could talk about the future. "A shower, but not in a bubble bath, and that was after my divorce."

She went still for a moment, then continued to trail her fingers back and forth across the tops of his thighs. "You and your wife never… I mean, not even showered together?"

"We were so young, just kids when we got married. Of course, you couldn't tell us that back then. Eighteen and so sure we were ready."

The memories of that time, both the good and the

bad, came flooding back. He rarely thought about his ex, but he needed to tell Vanessa how his marriage had ended.

"Lisette was such an innocent. So was I, actually. We were each other's first loves, first lovers. We dated over two years before we had sex for the first time."

"Let me guess. Prom night?"

"Cliché, but true. Our junior year. I proposed six months later, to both our parents' dismay. I already told you we were married the day after we graduated from high school."

Vanessa nodded, but remained silent.

"We lived in a house owned by her family and went to college while working. Thankfully both her folks and mine had money set aside that they didn't hold back despite their feelings about our marriage. When Lisette got her degree in paralegal studies, she went to work for a law firm in Kalispell while I worked at the lumber mill and continued my classes. We were happy. At least, I thought we were."

"So what changed?"

"I was a few months from graduating, knowing I needed more schooling in order to be an architect. Seattle or Denver would've worked," he paused, the memories returning as fresh as the day it happened.

"We'd always talked about starting a family after I got my degree, but Lisette had been dismissing the subject whenever I brought it up those last few months. I knew how much she wanted out of this town and I thought if I could just get us away, she'd be happy. Well, I came home early one day, excited about a job opportunity in Denver. Lisette wasn't home and I still can't remember how it happened, but I found a home pregnancy test in the kitchen trash.

"I was so excited, thinking all our plans were coming together. All that changed when she got home. She told me she'd been seeing one of the lawyers at the firm where she worked. She wasn't sure who her baby's father was."

Vanessa gasped. Her hands dug into his knees as she held tight to him. He welcomed the pressure, liking the grounding it gave him, especially for what he still had to share with her.

"As you can probably guess, her announcement didn't go over very well. There was a lot of yelling about getting tested and filing for divorce. Then I did a real mature thing, took off for a camping trip in the mountains with my brothers. They were smart enough to leave me alone, but it gave me a lot of time to think and make some decisions.

"I returned home and told Lisette I wanted to make our marriage work. For the sake of the child. I knew there was a chance the baby wasn't mine, but in the eyes of the law I'd be the child's father."

"Obviously things didn't work out that way."

He shook his head. This part of the story still stung, but not as strong as it had in the past. Maybe the woman listening was the reason?

"She had divorce papers waiting. I signed them and moved back home with the understanding she'd get tested to find out who's child she was carrying. Shortly after that, Lisette lost the baby. I never found out if the child was mine or not."

"But you mourned the loss just the same."

Yeah, he had. Except for confiding in his cousin

and best friend, Jonah had never told anyone the real reason behind his divorce.

Everyone assumed they'd just grown apart. Maybe that was true. His ex had turned into someone he barely recognized the last year of their marriage. Maybe he had, too. He'd been so occupied by school, work and clearing the land for the cabin that they rarely saw each other.

"Thankfully, the job I'd lined up in Denver was still open. I left town and never looked back, and I've only rarely been back, for holidays and such."

"And to work on this amazing place."

Jonah pulled in a deep breath, feeling better than he had in years. Maybe time did heal all wounds. Or maybe, it was just what he'd thought…the beautiful woman in his arms accounted for him being able to share the worst moment of his life with her.

And come out of it realizing he'd done the best he could've back then.

Had he been the perfect husband? No, but who was? He'd done his best by Lisette and it hadn't been enough for her. But all of that was in the past. It was time to start looking toward the future.

His future.

"Thank you," he said, gathering her into his arms, loving how easily she fit there.

"For what?"

"For listening."

"I didn't mind." She traced a soapy pattern on his forearm where he held it over her breasts. "But I'm sorry you had to go through all that."

"Me, too," he agreed, suddenly wanting to talk about something else. Anything else. "But that's in the past.

I think we need to leave it there and concentrate on the more recent past. And the future."

Vanessa's fingers kept moving, but he detected a slight tension in her shoulders.

"What do you mean?"

"Well, I've got to admit being back in Denver, even for a few days, felt really strange. It was too noisy, too crowded." Jonah gave her a gentle squeeze. "I found myself missing the wide-open spaces and peace here in Rust Creek Falls. Missing you."

"Well, maybe you're just a country boy at heart."

"I never used to think so, but lately everything I thought I knew, *believed,* is now upside-down and twisted inside out." Jonah chuckled again. "I'm finally ready to move forward. Damn, after eight years, it feels good to say that."

"I bet it does."

He laid a hand along her cheek and lightly turned her face until she looked at him. "You're a big part of that, too."

Her beautiful brown eyes widened. "Part of what?"

"Of some decisions I need to make." He dropped a kiss to her lips. "Plans for the future."

She pulled away from his touch, twisting in his arms so she could reach forward to flip the switch that held in the water before she stood, the bubbles sliding off her beautiful curves. "Ah, as interesting as that sounds, my only plans for the future are getting warm and rinsing off these bubbles."

Jonah sat there, watching as she got out of the tub and tiptoed across the room to the oversize tiled stall shower. Seconds later, the water inside came on and it only took a moment for the glass door to steam over.

The abruptness of her move floored him and all he could do was sit as the water inside of the tub slowly emptied.

Then the door opened again and Vanessa popped her head out. “Hey, sexy. You going to stay over there or join me?”

He smiled, his body relaxing again, and got to his feet. Okay, now this was more like it.

Chapter 13

Vanessa almost made it past the main ranch house when she spotted Rita Dalton in a pretty burgundy dress, perfect for Sunday-morning services, waving at her from her front porch.

When Jonah had left the cabin this morning, he'd asked about her plans for the day—mentioning again his mother's standing invite for Sunday dinner—but she'd managed to sidestep answering him.

Much like she'd done for most of yesterday.

When he'd shared the reason for his marriage ending during their bath, Vanessa had worked hard to stay composed when all she'd wanted to do was rail against the hurt and injustice his ex-wife had put him through.

But then he started talking about looking forward, about the future. After her own internal battle about being worthy of even being alive an hour before, she'd bolted from the tub using the cooling water as an excuse to change the subject.

And the location. He'd joined her in the shower and after that, she'd kept him too busy to talk.

When his cousin Caleb had called soon afterward and said he and Mallory were looking for company for a late dinner, she'd jumped at the chance to go.

All because she was frightened of what he might say. Or ask.

Which was crazy, of course.

One would think a person would be excited if the man she loved started making plans—especially if those plans included her. But she now knew it wasn't the unknown when it came to her relationship with Jonah that bothered her as much as the fact she wasn't sure she had the right to even think about the future.

A belief confirmed by a voice mail left for her while she and Jonah had been making love in the shower.

She'd listened to it while Jonah had been making plans with his cousin, surprised at first when she heard Adele's mother's voice, but with Adele's birthday coming up soon, she guess she shouldn't have been. What the woman had said left her dumbstruck.

Easing her truck to a stop as Rita hurried down the steps, Vanessa glanced at her own paint-splattered jeans and old sweater. It was obvious she wasn't heading to church this morning.

No, she was hoping to get lost in her painting.

She'd gotten used to working on the mural with an audience around and the interruptions weren't too bad. People were genuinely interested in the images that were slowly coming to life and she'd gotten a few requests to turn her simple pen-and-ink sketches into full-color portraits.

Still, she found she missed the solace and peace in being alone with her art.

Vanessa put the truck into Park, but left it running. It was then she noticed the box Jonah's mother held in her hands as she came down the walkway.

An icy blast roared through Vanessa that had nothing to do with the cool morning air coming from her now open window.

No, not yet. She wasn't ready.

"Good morning, Vanessa. I'm glad I caught you."

Rita's greeting came with a warm smile, but it did nothing to thaw the deep freeze Vanessa was encased in. She tried to speak. Her mouth opened, the words ran through her head, but there was nothing.

"Vanessa?" Jonah's mother reached through the window and placed a hand on her shoulder. "Are you okay, honey?"

She blinked hard and fought though the aching hurt, amazed at the power it still had over her.

Even after all this time.

She'd been so lost for so long in the sorrow that engulfed her when her friend died. To be so easily pulled back into that dark place was frightening.

"Ah, yes, I'm fine." Vanessa forced out. "I'm sorry. I was lost in thought for a moment."

"Well, this is yours." Rita held up the box, the return address from Florida clearly visible. "Marcie dropped it off yesterday afternoon during her postal rounds since she was driving by the ranch."

Vanessa nodded and reached for the package, surprised at how much it weighed. She held it to her chest for a moment, but when her eyes started to burn she quickly set it on the seat next to her. "Ah, thank you."

"You know, we do need to get an official address for the cabin, instead of using ours. Not that I mind collecting your mail for you," Rita quickly added. "But I totally understand a person's need for privacy. Even if we do think of them as family."

"Rita, I'm not—"

"Oh, I don't mean to push, but you should know how happy we are that you and Jonah have found each other." The woman cut off her protest. "He's needed a special someone in his life for a long time. Someone to keep him grounded while supporting his dreams. I think maybe you need that, too, dear."

Not knowing how to reply to that or if she'd be able to and not break down in tears, Vanessa only thanked Rita again, and drove away.

She made it to the main road, before she reached down and rested one hand lightly on the box.

"Hello again, dear friend."

"…and before I knew it, I'd agreed to buy the whole block. Well, not the actual block. Just one section, from street corner to street corner. Can you believe that? Vanessa? Hello?"

Vanessa looked up from the salad she'd been pushing around with her fork instead of eating. The resort's main dining area was currently being used by the contractors and construction crew as both a meeting place and a lunch room. At least, until the fancy furniture arrived.

The kitchen wasn't operational yet, but the oversize

refrigerators worked so many brought their noontime meal with them to work.

Including Vanessa, when she took the time to eat. Her clothing already felt looser.

She'd refused to take a break from the mural the past couple of days, mainly because she was struggling again. And that scared her.

Her vision for the massive painting wasn't quite so strong, the colors not as bright and clear in her head as they had been. She was second-guessing the work she'd already completed, both the faint outlines and the finished portraits, and there was still so much—so many important people and places—that needed to be added before the deadline that was less than two months from now.

When Jonah had found her today sitting on the edge of the scaffolding, staring off into space, he'd insisted she join him for lunch. She'd hardly been able to argue, especially when her empty stomach had loudly rumbled in agreement.

Knowing what she had to do later on today, eating had seemed like a good idea at the time.

"Vanessa?" Jonah repeated her name, a look of concern and frustration on his face.

"I'm sorry," she said. "What did you say?"

"Where are you?" he asked.

Was that a trick question? "I'm right here."

"No, you're not." He dropped the remains of his sandwich to the paper it'd been wrapped it. "You've been lost in your own little world for the last three days. What's going on?"

She looked away, her gaze back to her barely touched food, not wanting to have this conversation.

Again. Jonah had picked up that something wasn't right with her when he'd come by the cabin Sunday evening, but she'd waved off his questions claiming to be tired.

She wasn't ready to talk about it. Not with him, not with anyone.

And not today of all days.

Her stomach clenched, the lettuce and cut vegetables she'd managed to eat now sitting like rocks deep inside. Coming in today had been a mistake. She should've stayed home until she found the strength to complete her task.

"Nothing is going on," she said, filling the silence between them. "I was just thinking…about work."

"So much so that you didn't hear a word I said about buying four houses in town this morning."

Surprise filled her. "You did what?"

"Yeah, I'll admit I even shocked myself." He grinned now. "My meeting with the Realtor was just supposed to be about looking over the properties, getting information. Actually, there was only one house I was really interested in, but the four of them—all on the same side of Falls Street, all empty, built around the same time with good-size yards in between each one—they're perfect."

Okay, now she was really confused. "Perfect for what?"

"Model homes. I told you I've been looking into ways of taking certain design aspects from my work here at the resort and scaling them down to be used in the private sector, especially the environmental elements. Remember?"

Yes, she remembered. Sort of.

Trying to keep her distance from Jonah was harder

than she'd thought. Not physically. That part of their time together was wonderful, but it was the "getting to know you, share your dreams, plans for the future" conversations that were difficult.

Which didn't make any sense.

Most people would want to have those talks, especially with the man you were in love with, but Vanessa just couldn't do it.

She couldn't let herself believe in the future.

"Yes, I remember," she finally answered him. "But you never said you planned to do that work here in Rust Creek Falls."

His smile slipped. "Is that a problem?"

"No, but that's a lot to put on your plate, what with all the work that still needs to be done around here."

Jonah looked around the room, pride in his gaze. "I know we're going to be busy right up to the grand opening at Christmas, and afterward, with the expansion plans for phase two I'm working on. And yeah, buying property in town was impulsive, but it's a good investment for the future. For my future." He took her hand and gave it a squeeze. "Dare I hope to say…our future?"

Suddenly unable to breath, Vanessa yanked her hand free and pushed back her chair. She stood, mindful that people were staring, but needing…needing to get away.

Now.

"Vanessa? What's wrong?"

Ignoring Jonah's question, she hurried from the room. Never breaking her stride, she marched past the scaffolding and kept on going until she was outside with the fresh air hitting her face. Even then, she didn't stop until she reached her truck.

"Hey, hold on."

A strong hand took her arm. Jonah. He'd followed her. Of course, he followed her. Squeezing her eyes shut, she kept her head down as he gently turned her to face him.

"Talk to me, honey," he pleaded. "Please. Tell me what's going on."

She shook her head, her watery gaze focused on the asphalt beneath their feet. "Nothing's going on."

Jonah cupped her cheek, his fingers pressing on her jaw until she had to look at him, her eyes brimming with tears.

"What can I do to help? Just tell me and I'll do it."

Angry at herself for letting it get this far, Vanessa again shook her head and brushed the wetness from her eyes. "It's nothing."

"Don't say that." Jonah put his hands on her upper arms, keeping her in place. "You've been—I don't know, pulling back, pulling away…putting distance between us ever since we slept together that first time."

She should've known he'd pick up on what she'd tried to do. "And here I thought you were having a good time in my bed."

"Being in your bed, or anywhere with you, is great. Wonderful. Perfect. So perfect, I want to be there for a long—"

Vanessa laid her fingers to his mouth, stopping him.

How had she gone from being worried that all he wanted was something causal to being terrified that he wanted more?

"Please. Don't."

He pulled her hand from his face, but held tight to her fingers as he now grasped both her hands. "Every time I've dared to mention the future—for us—other than what we might be doing in the next day or so, you cut me off. Change the subject. Why?"

"You were the one who was worried about getting involved, remember? You were only going to be in town for a short while. I assured you no demands, no labels and you seemed happy with that." She took a step back, but he still wouldn't let go. "We've known each other less than a month, Jonah, and here you are making plans for me…for us."

"Is it too soon?" He finally released her. "Are you saying you're not thinking about us that way? You're not interested in a future—"

"I'm saying it's not a good day for this discussion. I have to— You don't understand."

"I can't understand if you won't explain it."

"It's not that simple." She dug into her pocket for her keys. "I have to go."

"Go where?"

Jamming her key into the lock, she twisted and then yanked the door open and climbed inside. Jonah stepped into the space, crowding her, keeping her from pulling the door shut.

Tunneling his fingers into her curls, he crushed his mouth to hers. She pushed at his chest and he softened the kiss, but it was the slight trembling of his lips against hers that did her in. She fisted his flannel shirt, pulling him closer, deepening the kiss, desperation clogging every pore in her body.

Both of them were now demanding and greedy, giving and taking in a white hot rush of desire that burned deep inside of her. She loved this man, loved him with her entire being—but something was stopping her from taking that next step. From believing, from taking a chance.

The need for air had them finally breaking free, their breathing ragged and hot as he pressed his forehead to hers. "Don't leave, Vanessa."

His words came out a harsh whisper, a plea that involved so much more than this single moment in time. He was asking her not to leave…him. She blocked out the inference, shaking her head. He stepped away without another protest. She closed the door, started the truck and pulled out of the parking space.

Driving away, she refused to let her gaze go to the rearview mirror knowing he stood there, watching her do exactly what he'd asked her not to. Leave.

Chapter 14

Forty-two minutes.

Jonah checked his watch again. Vanessa had been gone almost an hour. He had no idea where she'd gone and she wasn't answering her phone.

Enough. He wasn't sure where she'd gone, but he'd tear this entire town apart until he found her.

After replaying what happened between them earlier over and over in his head, he still didn't have any answers, but one.

It was time for them to be honest with each other.

He should've told her he loved her.

Maybe that would've kept her here. Allowed her to open up to him. To share whatever it was that had her scared.

He thought back to the few times she'd shared bits and pieces about her past.

She'd warned him she held things deep inside. That being an artist went hand in hand with being an introvert and it took a long time for her to let people in. That the loss of her mother while still a teenager, a distant father and being cheated on by her ex-boyfriend had taught her to rely on herself.

She needed to know she could rely on him, as well.

His first stop was the cabin. Jonah's truck rounded the corner, disappointed that hers wasn't here. Where else could she be?

Pulling into the spot where he usually parked, he started to turn around, but something about the front door caught his eye. He put his truck in Park and hopped out, the engine still running.

The door was open.

He went inside, calling for her even though he knew she wasn't there. Had she come here after leaving the resort?

He looked around. Everything seemed okay. Taking out his phone, he called her again, but again he got nothing. Not even her voice mail. Determined to keep looking, he started back for the door when something on the leather couch caught his eye.

A piece of paper. Maybe she left him an explanation. He grabbed it. His name was written over and over, but it wasn't a note. Instead he saw a series of checkmarks some with Jonah's name scrawled next to them.

What the hell was this?

He went back to the top, noting the crease lines that showed how often the paper had been folded and refolded.

A bucket list? Vanessa's? And who was Adele?

There were quite a few things listed, the majority of

them having been checked off, but he focused on the ones where his name was written.

Fly among the clouds (and not in an airplane!).

Learn to ride a horse.

Kiss a cowboy.

Learn how to line dance.

Dance in the rain.

Take a bubble bath...with a man.

All the crazy and wonderful things he and Vanessa had done together over the past few weeks.

What did this mean? Had she been using him? And why was she suddenly checking off each item she could find? What was the big rush? Vanessa was still a young woman.

The questions whirled around inside his head. Then he saw the small notation written at the bottom of the page and his blood ran cold.

List updated September 23, 2013. Carrollton Cancer Medical Center, Philadelphia, PA.

No. That couldn't be. Vanessa wasn't—

Jonah shoved the list into his jacket pocket, refusing to let his mind go there. He went back outside and got in his truck, then spotted Eli coming over the hill on horseback.

He waved his brother down and the two met in the middle of the road.

"If you're looking for your lady love, she's been here and gone."

Was that good news or bad? "You saw Vanessa? Did you talk to her?"

Eli shook his head. "I watched her drive up from the far hill. After she got out of her truck, she paced back and forth on the outside deck for a few minutes, waving her hands around."

"Was she on the phone?"

"I don't know. I was too far away, but like I said, her hands were flying, almost as if she were having an argument with herself." Eli pushed up the brim on his Stetson. "I was just about to head down to see if she was okay when she went inside."

"Did you see her leave again?"

"Yep. She came back out a few minutes later carrying a package or something. Then she took off, tires spinning and gravel flying," Eli said. "What's going on?"

"Hell if I know." Jonah put his truck into gear. "If you see her again, call me. Scratch that. If you see her, stop her and keep her with you while you call me."

His brother started to smile, then stopped when he saw how serious Jonah was. "Is she okay?"

"I don't know," Jonah answered honestly, not wanting to believe the list he'd found meant she would do something crazy. "But I need to find her."

He headed into town, stopping first at the community center but she wasn't there. He drove by the beauty and doughnut shops, and then the wings place. Going up and down each street, he kept an eye out for her truck, even stopped by the clinic to ask Callie if Vanessa had been in to see her.

Nothing.

He didn't see her truck outside of Crawford's General Store, but he went inside, anyway. Trying not to get caught up in too many conversations, he figured by the number of people asking him about Vanessa, no one had seen her in here today.

Back outside, he thought for a moment about getting a hold of the sheriff. Was that really necessary? He didn't have anything to go on except her crazy behavior and a bucket list—

"You look a bit lost, young man."

Jonah spun around. "What did you say?"

"I said you looked lost."

The old woman closed the distance between them, peering up at him with sharp, eagle-like eyes. "No, you're not lost. Not anymore. But someone else is."

"I'm sorry, have we met?"

She placed a wrinkled hand on his arm. "I'm Winona Cobbs."

The psychic. Vanessa had told him about this old woman who'd come to town to give lectures and hand out free advice. She'd approached Vanessa about the mural and shared stories about the history of Montana, which Vanessa had used in her research.

He had no idea what real talents this old woman possessed, if any, but he had to ask. "I'm trying to find Vanessa Brent. The artist you spoke with about the mural she's painting out at the resort. Have you seen her?"

The woman hugged her shawl closer to her chest. "No."

Jonah waited. She didn't say anything more, but her gaze never left his.

"I'm worried about her." He tried again. "Can you help me find her?"

Her eyes narrowed for a moment, then closed. She pulled in a deep breath, slowly let it out and repeated the action two more times. "I see a white owl," she finally said.

His shoulders slumped. This wasn't going to work. Grabbing his keys, he headed for his truck. "Okay, thanks."

"And a waterfall."

That got his attention. He turned back. "A waterfall?"

"A white owl and a waterfall."

If the psychic was right, Jonah knew exactly where Vanessa was.

But could he trust her? "Are you sure?" he asked.

"As sure as I am of you. The question is, are you?"

Jonah had no choice. He thanked the woman, who waved off his words as she continued on her way. Back in his truck, he headed out of town straight to Fall Mountain and the waterfall that gave Rust Creek Falls its name.

It had been years since he'd been out this way. So much had changed. He drove past a picnic area and direction signs to a lower falls viewing area he didn't remember being here the last time.

No sign of Vanessa's truck at either spot.

Continuing farther up the mountain, he reached the turn off to the trail that would lead him to Owl Rock, so named because the large white boulder with twin peaks at the top which resembled the woodland creature. It protruded out over the falls as if keeping watch over them.

Checking his phone as he made his way up the trail, Jonah wasn't surprised to find service spotty at best. It didn't really matter, since Vanessa hadn't answered his previous attempts, but what if something happened and he needed to call for help?

Refusing to allow that thought to form, he was glad

it was a clear and sunny afternoon. As he kept walking, the noise of the falling water led him to a clearing.

Then he saw her, standing by the rock and way too close to the waterfall for his comfort.

A glimmer of fear sprang to life inside him. What should he do? If he yelled to her, she could get startled, slip on the slippery rock and plummet to her death. If he did nothing, and she was up here for some crazy reason…

He did the only thing he could. He headed toward her as softly as he could and said her name.

Hearing Jonah's voice didn't surprise her.

She turned around, not bothering to hide her tears. What was the point? More would follow. "What are doing here, Jonah?"

"Do you really need me to answer that?" He came a few steps closer, his hands held wide at his sides. "You had to know I'd look for you."

Yes, she did know that. And while she appreciated his cautious approach, she wasn't about to do anything stupid.

On the contrary. What she had to do was probably the simplest, and yet the hardest thing that had ever been asked of her.

"You can relax, you know," she said, walking toward him. "I'm okay."

A raised eyebrow translated his skepticism, but he did drop his hands. "Yeah. Don't get mad when I say I don't believe you."

Her lips twitched, as if they wanted to smile, but then Vanessa looked down again at the square, glittery red box she held cradled to her chest.

"Red was her favorite color," she said instead as the tears returned. "Not crimson or burgundy or maroon. Nope, it had to be a candy-apple, fire-engine, the-brighter-the-better red."

"Here."

She blinked, bringing into focus the square cloth Jonah held in his hand. Looking up, she found him right in front of her now and a spurt of laughter somehow made it through the tightness of her throat. "Is that an actual hankie?"

He shrugged. "My mother raised me right."

Vanessa took his offering and pressing the soft material to her face, breathed in Jonah's familiar scent. Turning away, she wiped the wetness from her eyes, so thankful he was there.

That surprised her, although it shouldn't have. She loved him. It seemed right that he should be there.

Why was she just realizing this now?

Maybe she could get through this after all. "Today is Adele's twenty-sixth birthday…would've been. She was my best friend."

It was so hard to talk about her in the past tense. That someone so alive and vibrant should no longer be there.

"Tell me about her," Jonah murmured, the wary tension in his face easing.

"Adele Marguerite Dubront." She pulled in a deep breath, and then released it. The shudder that accompanied it was a sign she was okay to talk now. "A big name, but she so lived up to it. From the moment we met as little girls, she was someone I admired. Wanted to emulate. My best friend, my partner in crime. My sister."

Jonah stayed silent, but he moved closer, one hand warm and solid at her lower back.

"She was fearless, always the first one to try new things, say hello to people and then she'd listen intently to whatever they had to say."

"Sounds a lot like you."

This time her laugh had a harsh edge to it. "Oh, no. Maybe the person I've tried to be in the last few months, but before that…no, I was very much the stereotypical artist. Wrapped up in my own little world. Content with just my paints and canvases for company. But she wouldn't let me stay there. No, she would dare me and entice me and drag me along on another of her crazy schemes.

"All of which made finding out about her childhood battle with cancer so hard to believe. Until it returned with a vengeance last year. She'd beaten it once before. We were so sure she could do it again. And she tried. Gave it her best, but then we had to accept—*I* had to accept that she was going to be taken from me far too soon."

"Those are her ashes."

Vanessa closed her eyes, and nodded, not surprised Jonah had figured out what was in the box she held so tightly. "Her mother left me a voice mail a few days ago. When I called her back she explained about a special request Adele had left in her will. Something she'd asked her mother to keep from me until after…"

Opening her eyes, she focused on the beautiful waterfall directly in front of her. "Well, until I'd had the chance to move on with my life. Until I started working on our list."

"Your bucket list."

She spun around, stumbled over her feet, but Jonah was there to catch her. His arms strong and secure. "How do you know about that?"

"I went to the cabin to find you and I found it—you left it on the couch. I'm sorry, but I couldn't help reading it." His gaze held hers. "Especially once I saw my name. I didn't understand what it was at first and when I read the name of the cancer center—"

"You thought it might've been me who was—"

"You've been acting so strange lately, I was afraid..." He brushed back some of her curls, tucking them behind one ear. "I'm so sorry for your loss. I know what carrying that kind of weight can do to a person. But you've helped me lift my burden. Why won't you let me do the same for you?"

Could she? She wasn't sure.

"I know this is going to sound crazy, but I feel guilty." As hard as it was to do, Vanessa stepped out of his embrace and walked past him, farther into the clearing. "Meeting you...loving you—and yes, I do love you despite my best efforts to keep my distance—my feelings are so strong, Jonah. You make me happy. But why am I entitled to that when Adele never got that chance?"

"Because she would want it for you, Vanessa. You know she would, from what you've told me about her. You deserve to be happy, to be loved." Jonah followed, stepped in front of her and framed her face in his hands. "I love you, Vanessa. I have from the very first time I saw you. There's no excuse as to why it's taken me until now to tell you that. I love you."

Her soul soared at his words even as the fear that had invaded her heart remained.

"But you said… I tried so hard to keep things light and easy between us because I don't think I can handle another goodbye. There've been too many of them in my life."

"I'm not saying goodbye, Vanessa. Count on it."

"And then today you talked about buying property in Rust Creek Falls, which sounds a lot like you're planning to stick around." Vanessa talked over the top of his protest. "But that's scary, too. What if something happens to you this time?"

"Sweetheart, there are no guarantees in life. But there are promises, and I promise I am going to love you for as long as you'll have me." Jonah tightened his hold, his fingers pressing into her hair. "No, I'm going to love you for the rest of *my* life, no matter what comes our way. We'll make Rust Creek Falls our home and keep my place in Denver. Hell, I'm going to take you to Hawaii so you can see a live volcano."

Number twenty on her list.

Tears swarmed again, but this time they were ones of surprise and joy. "You'll do that for me? Help me finish my list?"

"If there is anywhere you want to go—anything on your list you still want to do—count me in."

She shook her head. "All I want, all I need is you. I think you're right. That's what my friend would want for me. For us. I love you, Jonah."

She grabbed at his jacket with her free hand, lifted herself up on her toes and kissed him, pouring all her love and passion into this moment. His hands slid to her shoulder and then circled around to her back, pulling her close until—

"Oh, I..." Vanessa stepped back and held out the box. "I still need to honor Adele's final wish. She wanted me to find the most beautiful, most perfect place..."

Jonah covered her hands with his. "Let me help."

They stood at the edge of the rock and held the box at an angle over the falls, allowing the down breeze to lift the ashes and carry them away.

Vanessa closed her eyes, offered a silent goodbye, thanking Adele for their years of friendship and for insisting she take their list to heart. If she'd never made that promise to take a chance Vanessa never would've found the love and happiness that filled her at this moment.

"You ready to head home now?"

Vanessa nodded, loving how wonderful those six simple words sounded.

She placed her hand in Jonah's and as they walked back down the trail, she noticed a smudge of something dark on his cheek.

Dirt, perhaps?

No, she knew exactly what it was—her friend's stamp of approval. Instead of brushing it away, she peeked back over her shoulder and sent a quick wink to the heavens.

Vanessa studied the costume that hung on the back of the bathroom door.

She was supposed to be Pocahontas for Halloween. An idea she'd come up with to go along with Jonah's cowboy costume (men had it so easy!) when he'd reminded her just this morning they needed to be dressed up for the Halloween party at Callie and Nate's tonight.

Considering how quickly she'd pulled this outfit together, thanks to finding faux-suede fabric and a blue beaded necklace during a quick shopping trip to Kalispell, the costume had come together nicely except for her wayward curls.

She'd planned to straighten her hair now that her makeup was done, including the tribal tattoo wrapped around her right biceps, but putting the dress together had taken up most of the afternoon and Jonah was set to pick her up at any moment.

Thankfully her progress on the mural was moving at a quick pace. She still had quite a few portraits and landmark buildings to paint, but she was sure she'd finish well ahead of the December deadline. Seeing the mural unveiled at the resort's grand opening over the holidays would be very exciting.

A knock came at the door. She tightened the belt on her silk bathrobe and hurried to answer.

Jonah had decided he'd get dressed at his folks' tonight, despite the fact he was slowly moving his stuff to the cabin, something about getting his hands on a special addition for his costume.

She guessed it would be one of his father's rodeo belt buckles that Charles had showed off with such pride after a family dinner last night.

A dinner that turned into a celebration when Jonah shared his plans to make Rust Creek Falls his home again. There were still a lot of details to be ironed out, but everyone was so excited, none more than her.

Being happy and in love was wonderful!

Ready for a night of fun with their friends, Vanessa opened the door. "Hey, you're early! I still need to get dressed—"

Her breath disappeared. Her words were gone, too.

Jonah stood on the deck, looking amazing in dark slacks and a fitted jacket made from a beautiful red brocade material with a high collar and richly decorated epaulets at the shoulders. A collared shirt, complete with a cravat-style tie at the neck, a leather belt and a sweeping cape that just about touched the ground completed the look.

No, the sword he carried at his waist was what truly made him look like a member of a royal family.

"What's this?" she asked, unable to hold back her delight when he bowed deeply from the waist. "Where's my cowboy?"

"Gone for the evening, milady." Jonah straightened, then grinned. "I hope you will allow Prince Charming to escort you to the festivities this evening instead. I do believe meeting him was on your list."

Vanessa gasped, one hand pressed to her lips.

Number twenty-two: kiss Prince Charming!

She couldn't believe Jonah remembered her list and had hunted down a fitting costume for tonight. "Well, actually, the goal is to *kiss* Prince Charming."

Jonah's grin widened. "Oh, I think we can arrange that."

Vanessa stepped back and waved him inside. "Where did you get that outfit?"

"My sisters are involved with a theatre in Kalispell that put on a version of Snow White last year," Jonah said, closing the door behind him. "When I asked if I could borrow it for tonight, they were very happy to help. As long as I agreed to pose for pictures."

"Well, you look wonderful. You're probably plastered all over the internet by now," Vanessa said, then laughed as she started back for the bedroom. "Give me a few minutes to get dressed and we'll be on our way."

"Hey, wait a minute." He took her hand, stopping her. "I've got something else for you."

"Really? What might that—" She turned back and once again found herself speechless when he eased the sword to one side before he slowly knelt before her, one knee on the hardwood floor. "Jonah!"

"I know this is sudden. We've only been a part of each other's lives for a short time, and it's only been two days since I said I love you. But with everything I am and everything in me, I know being with you forever is what I want."

He pulled a small velvet box from a hidden pocket and opened it to reveal a solitaire diamond ring that sparkled brilliantly in the light.

"You don't have to answer me now. Take as much time as you need," he continued. "I won't even say the words yet if you're not ready, but I want you to know—"

"I'm ready."

Her reply came out of her with such certainty Vanessa knew, to the depth of her heart, it was true. She'd been so lucky to find this special man. She didn't want to waste one more moment.

Not when time, and life, was so precious.

"You can ask me." She smiled at the look of pure love that filled Jonah's handsome face. "I mean, since you're already down there."

“Vanessa Brent, will you do me the honor of becoming my wife?”

“Yes!”

* * * * *

Before he testifies in an important case, businessman Michael "Mikey" Fiore hides out in Jacobsville, Texas, and crosses paths with softly beautiful Bernadette, who seems burdened with her own secrets. Their bond grows into passion...until shocking truths surface.

Read on for a sneak peek at
Texas Proud,
the latest book in
#1 New York Times *bestselling author Diana Palmer's Long, Tall Texans series!*

Mikey's fingers contracted. "Suppose I told you that the hotel I own is actually a casino," he said slowly, "and it's in Las Vegas?"

Bernie's eyes widened. "You own a casino in Las Vegas?" she exclaimed. "Wow!"

He laughed, surprised at her easy acceptance. "I run it legit, too," he added. "No fixes, no hidden switches, no cheating. Drives the feds nuts, because they can't find anything to pin on me there."

"The feds?" she asked.

He drew in a breath. "I told you, I'm a bad man." He felt guilty about it, dirty. His fingers caressed hers as they

HSEEXP0920

neared Graylings, the huge mansion where his cousin lived with the heir to the Grayling racehorse stables.

Her fingers curled trustingly around his. "And I told you that the past doesn't matter," she said stubbornly. Her heart was running wild. "Not at all. I don't care how bad you've been."

His own heart stopped and then ran away. His teeth clenched. "I don't even think you're real, Bernie," he whispered. "I think I dreamed you."

She flushed and smiled. "Thanks."

He glanced in the rearview mirror. "What I'd give for just five minutes alone with you right now," he said tautly. "Fat chance," he added as he noticed the sedan tailing casually behind them.

She felt all aglow inside. She wanted that, too. Maybe they could find a quiet place to be alone, even for just a few minutes. She wanted to kiss him until her mouth hurt.

HSEEXP0920

Love Harlequin romance?

DISCOVER.

Be the first to find out about promotions, news and exclusive content!

Facebook.com/HarlequinBooks

Twitter.com/HarlequinBooks

Instagram.com/HarlequinBooks

Pinterest.com/HarlequinBooks

ReaderService.com

EXPLORE.

Sign up for the Harlequin e-newsletter and download a free book from any series at

TryHarlequin.com

CONNECT.

Join our Harlequin community to share your thoughts and connect with other romance readers!

Facebook.com/groups/HarlequinConnection

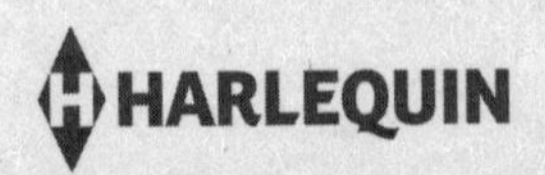

HSOCIAL2020